CRITICAL PRAISE FOR SHIRL HENKE'S HISTORICAL ROMANCES!

"*McCrory's Lady* is a wonderfully tender romance!"
—*Romantic Times*

"*Love A Rebel, Love A Rogue* is a fast-paced story with many subplots that Ms. Henke beautifully ties together."

—*Romantic Times*

"As always, with *A Fire In The Blood*, Shirl Henke pens a realistic, action-packed Western that portrays the good, the bad, and the ugly."

—*Romantic Times*

"*Return to Paradise* is a story you'll remember forever...definitely a book you'll keep to read again and again!"

—*Affaire de Coeur*

"*White Apache's Woman* resounds with the majesty of the early frontier....A not-to-be-missed read for Shirl Henke's fans."

—*Romantic Times*

"Another of Shirl Henke's wonderfully intricate and extremely well-researched tales, *Paradise & More* is a sumptuous novel!"

—*Affaire de Coeur*

BROKEN VOWS — SHIRL HENKE

"Historical romance at its best!" —*Romantic Times*

WORDS OF LOVE

Rebekah's palms rested against Rory's chest, feeling his heart beat erratically, just as her own did. He was so hard and warm, so beloved, yet she felt shy, uncertain of what to do or say. Maybe she should do nothing, remain silent. Yet her uncertainties made her speak out. "I want you to love me, Rory—I don't want to wait—but could we at least exchange vows between ourselves? That's how it was done in olden times, I think, and it was considered true marriage before God."

"Aye, I've heard that, too." In a low, husky voice, he began solemnly, "I, Rory Michael Madigan, take thee, Rebekah"— he hesitated at her middle name and she whispered it, her eyes aglow—"Beatrice Sinclair, to be my wedded wife, to have and to hold from this day forward, for better, for worse, for richer, for poorer, in sickness and in health, to love and to cherish, till death do us part."

Rebekah repeated the words, her voice sweet and clear in their moon-dappled chapel. When she had finished, he kissed her fingers, lingering over the third one of her left hand. "I only wish I had a ring. One day soon I will, I swear it, Rebekah—a gold ring."

"Oh, Rory, I love you so!" She reached up and caressed his cheek as his hands once more moved to her shoulders to slip the nightgown from her body.

Other *Leisure Books* by Shirl Henke:
McCRORY'S LADY
LOVE A REBEL, LOVE A ROGUE
A FIRE IN THE BLOOD
WHITE APACHE'S WOMAN
TERMS OF SURRENDER
TERMS OF LOVE
RETURN TO PARADISE
PARADISE & MORE
NIGHT WIND'S WOMAN

BROKEN VOWS
SHIRL HENKE

LEISURE BOOKS NEW YORK CITY

For Dan Reynard,
who had to eat liver.

A LEISURE BOOK®

October 1995

Published by

Dorchester Publishing Co., Inc.
276 Fifth Avenue
New York, NY 10001

Printed in the United States of America.

Acknowledgment

In telling our tale of a preacher's daughter and an Irish immigrant, my associate Carol J. Reynard and I wish to thank those who helped make Rebekah and Rory's happy ending possible. As always, we relied heavily on the excellent resources of the Maag Library of Youngstown State University as well as the public libraries of Youngstown, Ohio, and Adrian, Michigan. Dedicated reference librarians are worth more than water in the desert to writers.

It was my husband Jim's idea to make Rory a bare-knuckle prizefighter, an interesting departure from cowhands and gunmen. Jim, a former Navy boxer, blocked out all the boxing scenes, including the coaching strategies of January Jones and Blackie Drago. When I attempted to execute his instructions, he chuckled at my gaffes and corrected them.

Carol did the same for the sequences I wrote describing horses and their tack. She also showed me where the story really opened, which happened to be in the middle of the first chapter as I had originally written it. We both wish to thank Dr. Walter Magee and Mr. Mark Hayford for convincing our computer and printer to talk to one another.

As always, for the array of weapons employed by the good guys and the bad, we are in debt to Dr. Carmine V. DelliQuadri, Jr., D.O., our weapons expert.

BROKEN VOWS

PART I

COVENANT

My beloved is mine and I am his . . . until the day break
and the shadows flee away. . . .

Song of Solomon 2:16–17

Chapter One

Rebekah Sinclair heard the solid thump of a fist striking flesh followed by a rapid series of sharper raps before the roar of the crowd drowned out the conflict. Unable to resist, she slipped onto the porch and stood at the railing beside her companion. Below them, the open space in the center of the crowd revealed two men engaged in a brutal bare-knuckle fight. She recognized one of the men at once—Cyrus Wharton, a smithy's apprentice and a hulking brute of a man known in town as a brawler. The other, who had just landed a series of punches, was a stranger to her. Not that she was familiar with denizens on the wrong side of the track, but she would never have forgotten him if she had ever seen him before.

He was stripped to the waist and sweating. A thin trickle of blood trailed from his left eye, and his jaw was set in a grimace of determination, bringing out the fierce predatory beauty of his features in spite of the battering he had taken. His face was angular, with a finely chiseled nose and strongly arched eyebrows. Although bruised, his cheekbones were high and well molded, as was his forehead, but his eyes were what held Rebekah mesmerized. Narrowed in concentration on his foe, they seemed to blaze like frozen flames. Cold. Blue. Ruthless.

She stared in rapt fascination.

Rory Madigan had taken the punch to his midsection with teeth clenched, expecting the low, clumsy blow that opened up his larger and slower opponent to several swift left jabs to the jaw, dazing the brute and staggering him back. Off balance with his arms lowered, he was wide open for Rory's hard right punch that sent him toppling into the dust. He landed flat on the seat of his pants. At once his seconds hauled him up by yanking on his arms, dragged him to his corner, then splashed his face with water from the bucket until he shook his head like an enraged bulldog, sending droplets flying in every direction. His swollen eyes fastened on the tall, slim Irishman with the mocking expression on his pretty face, and Cy Wharton waded back into the fray, fists flying.

Unable to tear her eyes away from the carnage below, Rebekah watched the calm, skillful arrogance with which the smaller man bested his far larger, heavier opponent. The young stranger's body was whipcord lean yet sinewy with sleek muscles that glided like satin beneath his sweat-sheened skin. She could see the pattern of hair on his chest vanish tantalizingly beneath his belt. His complexion was swarthy, and his inky black hair hung shaggily at his nape. Yet he was not Mexican or Indian, but sun-bronzed, probably from being stripped half-naked for numerous such fights.

"Ugh! They're both bloody and sweaty. Let's go, Rebekah," her companion said with disgust, pressing a scented lace handkerchief to her nose. Celia Hunt was regretting her suggestion that they climb onto the porch of the old deserted newspaper office to watch this fighting display. The crowd below was made up largely of rough-looking miners, mule-skinners, and cowhands, along with a sprinkling of women—only the most disreputable sort, with gaudy clothes and painted faces. They were a crude and dangerous lot.

"I think this was a mistake, Rebekah. Let's go," Celia repeated nervously.

"No. I want to see who wins," Rebekah replied quietly, her eyes never leaving the Irishman. She could hear the jibes from the crowd as they cheered for Cy Wharton.

"He's only an ignorant mickey, Cy."

"Pound that paddy into pus, Wharton!"

"You can take thet skinny ferriner. Shit! He ain't much bigger 'n a Chinee."

But in spite of the encouragement, it was increasingly clear even to Rebekah's untutored eye that the Irishman was winning. He dodged, bobbed, and weaved gracefully away from most of Wharton's powerful swings and deflected those that he could not slip completely. His own fists shot out with lightning speed and accuracy, continually jolting the big man off balance. With each blow it seemed as if the power traveled up his whole body from his legs through his torso and into his arm, culminating in the turn of his fist, palm down, connecting squarely with its target.

"There's almost a rhythm to it, like watching a ballet—if you don't look at the blood," Rebekah whispered, more to herself than to Celia, who gasped in shock.

Rory watched the townie go down again and stood by the mark, waiting for the seconds to rally the poor sod. He felt

15

an itch on the back of his neck, as if someone was staring at him. He was used to that after earning his living the past several years traveling across this vast country fighting for prizes. But it wasn't the milling, cursing men in the angry crowd or their cheap, blowsy women. Someone else.

Then his eyes were drawn up to the dilapidated old shanty across the street. He saw the two women, a plump, homely little redhead and a blonde. Mary, Mother of God, what a blonde—slender and delicate with hair the deep gold of a desert sunset. Her thick lashes shaded wide-set eyes of some mysterious color, staring at him in rapt fascination.

Rebekah felt his eyes travel up her body in a frank male appraisal that almost undressed her. She fought the desire to step back from the railing and wrap her arms around herself in protection. Then their eyes met . . . and held. She was unable to look away as a strange heat gathered deep inside her, causing her heart to hammer in her breast and her whole body to thrum with life. She felt a heady warmth that owed nothing to the sun and all to the tall, blood-smeared man staring up at her.

She wanted to reach out and touch his face, brush the lock of black hair back from his forehead. Then the spell was broken as a small bandy-legged black man in the Irishman's corner yelled a warning.

"Rory, 'e's comin' atcha!"

Wharton had lurched to his feet after being doused with another bucket of cool water. He came toward Rory fast and low, raising his right hand like a lumberjack swinging a broadax to fell an oak. When it connected, Rebekah screamed, but her cries were drowned out by the roar of the crowd, now ecstatic that the local champion had reentered the fray.

Rory was felled by the unexpected blow, which opened

up a cut across his left cheek that bled profusely. Instantly, January Jones, his manager and promoter, was at his side, propping him up and sponging him with water. "What th' bleedin' 'ell were ya doin'? Gapin' at th' bloody view?" the little black man squawked in a thick Cockney accent.

Rory muttered something unintelligible as he shook his head and struggled to his feet, pushing January away from him. She had cried out a warning when he was hit—as if she wanted him to win. Well, if she did, she was the only resident of this godforsaken town who did. His speed was giving out. He had to end the contest quickly. The girl could wait till later.

Gritting his teeth, he slipped under a high roundhouse swing, then swiftly countered with a right uppercut to Wharton's exposed solar plexus, followed by a sharp left hook to the blacksmith's right cheek. As soon as Cy stumbled back gasping for breath and dropping his hands, Rory moved in, throwing a hard overhand right with his full weight behind it. The blow connected solidly with Wharton's jaw, sending him to the ground. This time even two buckets of cool water could not revive him.

As the crowd booed and groaned, hurling epithets such as "nigger" and "mick," January held up Rory's bloodied fist in victory. "Not a bad purse, 'specially considerin' 'ow ya near mucked it up."

"The winner is the Kilkenny Kid. I'll settle up, gents." The impresario was Cal Slocum, owner of the Thunder Gulch Saloon.

As the tall Irishman held a wet cloth to his bleeding face, his companion, the wizened little black man, collected their earnings. Rebekah watched the Irishman adjust the compress and studied his battered face. What a pity to mar such a strikingly handsome countenance. But Cy Wharton's beefy features had fared far worse, being beaten almost beyond recognition. Thinking that the same might have happened to the Kilkenny Kid made her shudder. Just then he looked up, and their eyes locked again.

"He is a bold one," Celia whispered, her tone indicating that she was uncertain whether she was more shocked by the Irishman's blatant appraisal or Rebekah's equally blatant return of it. "We have to get out of here before anyone else sees us. That mob could get ugly."

"They already are. They expected Cy to win," Rebekah replied as her friend tried to pull her away from the railing. Just then the Irishman arched one of those expressively elegant eyebrows and winked at her. Rebekah felt the heat fly to her cheeks and gave in to Celia's urging.

Rory watched the women—girls really—turn tail and dash from the porch. A good thing, before any of the drunken louts in this rough crowd got the wrong idea. They were obviously not scarlet poppies from the deadfall side of town. He decided to find out who the blonde was—after a decent interval of celebration and some time for his cuts and bruises to heal a bit. The greatest drawback to boxing was the wear and tear on his face, but he planned to quit someday, when something better came along. January's words brought him back from the reverie inspired by the fetching golden-haired girl.

"These 'ere blokes wants a rematch. Ya feel up ta goin' a few rounds tomorra' night in Virginia City? Th' purse'll be a thousand dollars!"

While Rory and January discussed the next fight, Rebekah and Celia crept down the rickety stairs to the first floor and headed to the side door. The overflowing crowd had dispersed, but a number of men were still milling around it. In a panic, Celia whispered, "How can we get out?"

18

Rebekah scanned the dusty office, then saw a rear window partially obscured by the remains of a wall. "We can climb out of that," she replied, making her way to the window. Just as she reached down to yank the partially open sash higher, a voice coming from the alley froze her.

"I'll drug his drinkin' water before that little limey nigger gets ahold of the bucket. Once he takes a swallow, the mick'll be a goner."

"Yew shore this here stuff'll work quick enough?" his coconspirator asked dubiously.

Shushing Celia, Rebekah crouched down beside the window glass, which fortunately had been rendered opaque by encrusted filth. The girls listened to the plan unfold. The conspirators were Whitey Folson and Cal's brother Bart Slocum, two mean street toughs from the Comstock mining district. She had to warn the Irishman!

After a few heart-stopping minutes, the men shook hands on their shady deal and departed. Weak-kneed, Rebekah cautiously opened the window and checked the deserted alley, then motioned for Celia to follow her and hoisted up her skirts to climb out.

"I'll ruin my gown," Celia said in dismay, holding back.

"Better the gown than you if those men catch us," Rebekah replied tartly.

That moved her friend to hasty action. "Oh well, I shall just have to buy a new one if this gets torn, but how ever shall I explain to Mama about getting so mussed up?"

"You'll think of something. You always do," Rebekah said, her thoughts already racing ahead, thinking up and discarding plans to get a message to the Kilkenny Kid.

In the arid isolation of western Nevada, whiskey cost more than water and only one death in a dozen was from natural

19

causes. But in the river valleys of the Truckee, the Carson, and the Walker, the alkali wilderness bloomed. Amid the pungent tang of sage and spruce, the bawls of fat cattle were heard. Orchards lay heavy with pears and apples while patient farmers tilled the earth, harvesting wheat and corn, peas and potatoes. This verdance of the western valleys owed less to the industry of agriculture than it did to the mining boom that created the demand for its produce, for between the Truckee and the Walker lay the richest cache of gold and silver ever known to man, the Comstock Lode, whose brief yet brilliant magnetism created the state of Nevada.

The glitter of the gold and silver camps was miles removed from the prosperous little cow town of Wellsville, north of the bustling railhead of Reno in the Truckee River Valley. Life moved at a more prosaic pace for a citizenry relatively untouched by the lure of overnight riches. The community had been built on the solid values of frugality and hard work, reinforced with rock-hard religious piety.

Rebekah did not feel the least bit pious as she waited for an assignation with a forbidden man. As she paced nervously across the bandstand in the park, not certain if she was afraid he would not come or that he would. It was nearly noon, the time she had set for the rendezvous in her note to him. She had bribed Zack Springer, a neighbor's boy from her Sunday school class, to deliver the message to the Irish fighter. Word had quickly spread about how the Kilkenny Kid had defeated Cy Wharton, and Zack's eyes had nearly popped from their sockets when she had made her request to the boy.

"You know the Kilkenny Kid? Wow!"

"No! That is, we've never met—been introduced." Her fumbling explanations had gone downhill from there. She had simply thrust the note and a coin in the lad's grubby hand and sent him to the den of iniquity where the Irishman was staying.

Now, as she waited to see if the Kilkenny Kid would answer her summons, she marveled at the impulsive folly that had led her to this pass. Was it only yesterday morning that she and her best friend Celia Hunt had been shopping for hats? Well, Celia had been shopping. As usual, Rebekah had only been along to watch enviously.

"I still think I should take the pink. It would contrast with my hair," Celia had said, smoothing a small, slightly plump hand over her auburn curls as she preened before a large mirror in the millinery shop, admiring the smart straw bonnet perched atop her head.

"It is lovely, but perhaps the yellow would be better," Rebekah had replied, dubious about the combination of pink bonnet and red hair, even though her companion seemed oblivious of the clashing colors.

Shrugging her shoulders, Celia said, "Well, I shall solve the matter quite simply and take them both. Unless you would like the pink? You did seem taken with it."

Rebekah shook her head. "No, really, you take it and the yellow, Celia." She turned away and walked across the small, crowded shop. Honestly, there were times when it seemed her friend was as dense as the pines around Lake Tahoe. Rebekah's father, Ephraim Sinclair, was the local Presbyterian minister, while Celia's father, Tyler Hunt, owned the town's largest mercantile. Celia's wardrobe contained all the latest fashions. Rebekah had to be content with plain, inexpensive clothes, often castoffs from her older sister Leah.

Celia was dressed in a beautiful blue silk suit with a smart bustle and fitted jacket. Rebekah wore an old green sprigged-muslin frock with a childishly rounded neckline and gathered skirt. How nice it would be to have beautiful things. *And how selfish of you to think only of yourself.* It seemed she was constantly upbraiding herself for the sins of covetousness and vanity. Her mother was right. She was indeed an iniquitous sinner.

There were so many less fortunate than she in the mining camps, not to mention right here in Wellsville. Why the poor Chinese who worked in town had only tents to live in and were humiliated and threatened every waking hour. Of course, her mother said that was their own fault for being heathens and rejecting God's word, but she couldn't feel that the Lord wanted anyone to live so meanly or to be treated in such an unchristian manner. Her father—gentle, scholarly Ephraim, impractical and unworldly—was the soul of kindness and was chiefly responsible for his younger daughter's concern for others, much as his wife Dorcas was responsible for Rebekah's overwrought sense of guilt.

Yet Rebekah occasionally had shocked both her parents, for beneath the layers of propriety beat the heart of a free spirit who secretly read her father's Greek mythologies, scandalous stuff to assault the eyes of a proper young lady, or indeed even the eyes of the bold adventuress who had slipped off with Celia when they were in pigtails to swim naked in the pond behind the Hunts' summer house. Her childish pranks and escapades had always met with stern retribution, sometimes in the form of Dorcas's canings and even more devastatingly when her beloved father admonished her with stricken bewilderment in his hazel-green eyes. In all of nearly eighteen years, Rebekah had felt like an outcast and never understood why.

"Oh, fiddle, Rebekah Beatrice Sinclair, you look as hangdog and pious as your sister Leah. Whatever has come over you? It must be the heat. I allow this is one of the hottest

22

summers we've had since that day when we slipped out of old Miss Framinghan's Sunday school class and went skinny dipping.'' Celia's round, cheerful face had split with a fond grin of remembrance as she clasped her friend's arm with genuine affection. ''I suppose we're too old to do that again. . . . ''

Rebekah's mood had lightened at once. Bother the silly old hats she could not afford! A chuckle bubbled up inside her. ''No, I don't think that muddy old pond would be so alluring now as it was when we were nine years old. Why not take a stroll up to Benton Street?''

Celia's big brown eyes had almost popped from their sockets! ''Benton Street! Where all the saloons and fallen women are? Ooh, how absolutely delicious!''

''Well, we wouldn't have to go that far down the street—just sort of walk along the edge of the glitter district where no one would accost us.'' Rebekah could see her mad impulse had taken hold of Celia, who clapped her hands in glee.

The two young women had walked well past the park, up Elm Street to where it intersected with Benton, when they saw the crowd and Celia suggested they view the fight from the balcony of the abandoned newspaper office.

Returning to the present, Rebekah looked around the deserted park and shook her head. Of all her escapades, this was indeed the most dangerous—and exciting! Would he come?

As he headed to the park, Rory reread the note again, wondering if he was a fool to venture out on such a wild goose chase.

''Mr. Kilkenny,'' it had begun. He chuckled at the salutation once more, then continued to scan the page. Someone was going to drug his water bucket during the fight tonight.

If he wanted to know who, he should come to the bandstand in the town park at noon. Even before he rounded the thick copse of cedars at the edge of the park, he knew it was her. His blonde. She was wearing another simple dress, a demure pastel blue with a frilly high lace collar that looked like a recent addition. As the product of an orphanage himself, he recognized made-over clothing when he saw it.

He came up behind her silently as she paced. "Are you my golden guardian angel—or are you trying to make up for nearly getting my head knocked off yesterday?"

Rebekah whirled around with a sharp intake of breath. The bluest eyes she had ever seen stared out of that arrestingly beautiful, albeit a bit battered, face. He wore a blue shirt, open at the collar and unbuttoned indecently low to reveal a tuft of black chest hair. The soft fabric clung to his broad shoulders, and his denims hugged his long legs. He was grinning now and looked much younger than he had during the fight. She judged him to be no more than a year or two older than she. "You startled me, Mr. Kilkenny."

"It's Madigan. Rory Madigan. The Kilkenny Kid is only a ring name," he said, taking the bandstand's six steps in swift, long-legged strides.

When he stood before her, he looked much larger than he had from her vantage point on the porch the day before. He was at least six feet, probably a bit more, compared to her five-foot-five. In high-heeled shoes, Rebekah seldom had to crane her neck to meet a man face-to-face. She fought to regain control of her scattered wits. "I'm Rebekah Sinclair, Mr. Madigan, and I—"

Before she could go any further, he raised her hand and saluted it with a soft kiss. "Charmed, Miss Sinclair," he murmured, delighted by the blush staining her cheeks. "You're the very loveliest fight fan I've ever seen," he said,

24

turning on what Sister Frances Rose O'Hanlon had always called his "gift of the blarney."

She withdrew her hand swiftly. "I detest violence, Mr. Madigan. It's unchristian." Lord, she had been crazy to come here! If her parents ever found out that she'd been seen with a common saloon brawler, the consequences did not even bear thinking on.

"Then you must be my guardian angel. What's this about someone trying to rig the fight so I take a fall?" She was frightened to death, and not just of his overtures.

She licked her lips with the tip of her tongue and swallowed. "I overheard Whitey Folson and Cal Slocum's brother Bart discussing it in the alley behind the *Self-Cocker* office when my friend and I were leaving after the fight."

He crossed his arms over his chest and stroked his chin consideringly. "The Slocums I've met. Describe Folson to me."

"Small and wiry with thinning sandy hair. He has a rather prominent nose that's been broken and a scar here." She made a motion across her left cheek.

"Umm. Think I remember one such. I'm much obliged to you, Miss Sinclair. They didn't see you, did they?" Was she afraid of the bounders?

"Heavens, I hope no one there at that spectacle saw us!" Rebekah's voice nearly broke.

Rory threw back his head and laughed. "Whatever possessed a fine lady such as yourself to come to that part of town, much less to climb up and watch a fight when you purport to be such a foe of violence?"

"It was just a girlish lark—a very foolish mistake that I don't dare repeat."

He looked at her face, now pale. Her green eyes were enormous, swimming with golden flecks. He reached out and

25

touched her arm in reassurance. "I'll see no one hurts you, Miss Sinclair. Don't worry about Folson and Slocum."

"It's not them . . ." She looked nervously around the deserted park.

His expression hardened. "Afraid of being seen with a dirty mickey, is that it?"

She looked up into his face, startled by his swift anger. Anger that masked hurt, she was suddenly certain. "No, no, that isn't it at all. No matter if you were the Prince of Wales, it isn't proper for me to be here unchaperoned. We've not even been properly introduced. My parents are very insistent on such things." She sighed in frustration as his cool blue eyes studied her disbelievingly. "I'm afraid I've always been a grave disappointment to them. Nothing like my sister Leah."

"Leah must be a paragon," he said, a touch of the former amusement returning to his voice. "How old are you, Rebekah?" He liked the sound of her name on his tongue.

"I'll soon be eighteen, and I've not given you leave to use my first name." But she loved the sound of it on his tongue. An unwilling smile curved her lips.

"I'll give you leave to call me Rory. It's only fair to reciprocate. I'll soon be twenty-one," he added, answering her unspoken question.

"Why do you fight? It's so dangerous. And your face . . ." Her fingertips lightly grazed his bruised cheek before she could stop herself. Whatever had come over her? She was bewitched! Rory clasped her hand before she could completely withdraw it. "He wouldn't have landed that punch if I hadn't been looking up at a golden-haired angel."

"I'm hardly an angel," she scoffed. "I do foolish, impetuous things. I'm reckless and selfish, and my mother tells me I'm altogether too forward for a minister's daughter."

"Not like your sister Leah," he said, nodding gravely.

Then he winked. "Thank the saints above."

A small frown marred her forehead. "You're Catholic, aren't you?" It sounded dreadfully accusatory.

"And you're a preacher's daughter."

Somehow his tone didn't sound nearly as serious as hers, the rogue. Rebekah had no experience with beaus other than the young men from church. Staid, proper, in awe of her father and perfectly boring. Rory was neither staid nor proper, and she very much doubted if he would be tongue-tied in front of Ephraim Sinclair. And he most certainly was not boring. But he was Catholic, she reminded herself. "My father is the Presbyterian minister for Wellsville and the whole valley. He even preaches and tends to his flock in the Comstock towns."

"A bold man of faith indeed to venture into the Comstock in search of souls to save."

She felt his hand pressing hers, his surprisingly long, slender fingers laced between her own. "I really must go. We shouldn't see each other again, Rory." She had not meant to use his given name. It tumbled off her tongue altogether too smoothly in spite of its foreign lilt.

"Oh, I think we will see each other again, Rebekah." He raised her fingertips to his lips and kissed them one by one, a trick a scarlet poppy back in New York had taught him when he was sixteen. It seemed an eternity ago, so unreal. But the girl who withdrew her hand and fled like a frightened fawn was all too real.

"She's not for the likes of you, boyo," he muttered to himself as he turned and headed back to the squalid whiskey row where his "likes" were always consigned to live. But he knew that he'd seek her out anyway. How difficult could it be to find the Reverend Sinclair's beautiful blond daughter in a town the size of Wellsville?

Chapter Two

As Rebekah hurried home, she could not stop thinking of Rory Madigan. Her first real beau. Or was he? Then she recalled her conversation with Celia last week. Most likely the Irishman's charm was not to be trusted. Although she and her best friend were both seventeen, Celia possessed a far more jaded view of life. They had been discussing Celia's latest beau, Newt Baker.

"Newt's probably a fortune hunter. His father's blacksmith shop is about out of business and he has no prospects—unless he can marry a rich girl." Celia had sighed disconsolately. "I know you'd like to have my money, but I'd like to have your looks even more. When a man comes to call on you, you know his affection is genuine."

Startled, Rebekah had looked at her friend, amazed at the sudden flash of insight the irrepressible, spoiled, yet plump and plain Celia had given her. "I suppose I never thought about money having anything to do with courting—but you're foolish to think men would only court you because of it. Why, you have a fine figure and beautiful russet hair. I'm just a pale, skinny stick by comparison," she added earnestly.

"Don't start that nonsense about Leah being the family beauty with her silver-blond hair and china-blue eyes, or I swear I shall expire from pure exasperation. Rebekah, she's as plump as I am and will go to fat by the time she's had her first baby. I'll never understand how you feel inferior to that prim and proper, holier-than-thou sister of yours. Why, she settled for Henry Snead, for land's sakes."

"Henry is a fine figure of a man!" Rebekah always defended her brother-in-law. Big, brawny Henry with his waxed handlebar mustache and wavy light brown hair was indeed quite a catch—or at least Rebekah had always thought so. "He's ever so kind and has a very responsible position with a promising future."

"He's full of himself, and if Amos Wells hadn't hired him to run the Flying W, he'd be no more than a common cowhand," Celia said with a sniff.

"You wouldn't be saying that because Henry chose my sister over you—and me," she hastily added.

"That just goes to show what sense he has. He's a nobody. I intend to marry a man with breeding, a man with a real future, who'll take me away from this dusty, boring old town."

"A man like Amos Wells?" The minute she said the words, Rebekah could have bitten her tongue, for Mr. Wells had never expressed the slightest interest in Celia, in spite of her friend's best efforts to attract the eligible widower's attention.

"He's only been out of mourning for his dead wife for a few months. I expect there's time enough," Celia replied huffily.

"Time enough if he doesn't pass on of old age. Honestly, Celia, he's positively ancient."

"He's only forty-three, in the prime of manhood. And he's rich and distinguished, from a fine old New England family. Soon he'll be Nevada's next United States Senator. My father said so. Imagine going to Carson City to have tea with the governor's wife and living in Washington, D.C."

"Well, as much as I would love the opportunity to travel east, I won't ever marry anyone unless I love him—and he loves me."

Could she fall in love with a man like Rory Madigan? The very thought rocked her. As she turned onto Bascomb Street, she forced herself to consider more sensible things. "What will you tell Mama if she asks where you've been?" she scolded herself, praying she would not be late for the midday meal. If questioned, what could she say without lying? She *had* taken a stroll to the park and she *did* forget the time. Rory Madigan probably made all the girls he charmed forget the day of the week, much less the hour! *I can't lie to Papa and Mama.*

Perhaps she would make it in time and her earlier absence would not be noted, although since Leah was married and gone, her mother expected Rebekah to help with all the food preparations. She had pared carrots and turnips, braised the rump of beef, and set it all to boil before she left. Hopefully, her mother would consider that a sufficient contribution. It seemed that no matter what she did, it was never equal to Leah's superior culinary skills, the loss of which their mother continually lamented.

Rebekah was deep in thought over her intense and confusing feelings about the handsome young Irishman when she neared her father's stately white-frame church and the adjacent modest parsonage. She circled around toward the back porch, hoping to slip in unobserved, when she heard a sharp exchange that stopped her in midstride. Inside the sitting room, which her father used as his study, Dorcas Sinclair was dressing down poor Zack Springer.

"You explain yourself, young man, this very instant!"

"Now, Dorcas, you're frightening the lad," Ephraim said in his rich, melodious voice. "What were you doing over in that terrible part of town?"

Leah Snead's voice was smug with accusation as she held Zack by his left ear. "I heard you boasting about delivering a message last night to some despicable saloon brawler."

Rebekah wished for the earth to open up and swallow her as she made her way into the house, knowing the whole horrid escapade must now be confessed. Poor Zack. No doubt Leah had dragged the unfortunate boy to her parents' home because she already knew her scapegrace sister was involved. She had not intended to get him in trouble. If only he had not felt compelled to boast about his errand. Like a convicted felon heading to the gallows, she opened the door of the study and confronted her family.

"Zack was only delivering a note for me. He's not a habitué of saloons and the like. Please excuse him, and I'll explain everything."

Dorcas Sinclair's round, florid face grew even redder as she regarded her younger daughter with furious anger. A heavyset woman with faded gray hair pulled severely back in a tight bun, she had always had plain, homely features and a doughy, shapeless figure. Everyone back in Boston had remarked that it was a marvel she had snared a fine figure of a man like Ephraim. The girls took their blond good looks

31

from their father. "This is a very serious matter, Rebekah. It's not bad enough that you act the hoyden, associating with riffraff, but you've dragged down an innocent child with your irresponsible actions!"

"Zack, perhaps it would be best if you ran along home," Ephraim said, gently disengaging the boy from Leah's grasp. Then he turned his sternest clergyman's demeanor on the lad. "Do confess what you've done to your father when he returns from work this evening. I'll expect to see you Sunday morning."

"Y-yes, sir, Reverend Sinclair. I will," the youth said to the tall, silver-haired man whose stooped shoulders and gaunt frame still commanded immense respect. With a quick look of apology at Rebekah, Zack fled.

"You have some explanation for all of this, I'm sure," Leah said, her pale blue eyes snapping with a self-satisfied pleasure that her calm voice belied. She was shorter than Rebekah but possessed of an hourglass figure of legendary voluptuousness and pale silver-gilt ringlets demurely held back in a pale gray snood that matched her elegant new day dress of extra-fine poplin. Henry had become a very indulgent husband, buying her all sorts of things she could not afford as a poor preacher's daughter. Leah stared at her younger sister, tapping her toe impatiently, still jealous and angry with her sibling in spite of her own rise in fortune the past year. "You wouldn't want to bring disgrace to the family name, surely?" she asked sweetly, enjoying witnessing the glib, clever Rebekah at a loss for words this time.

"Of course not, but I felt it my Christian duty to warn Mr. Madigan about a grave danger that could cost him his life." Rebekah stopped her headlong plunge to glance from Leah's dainty face to her mother's beefy one, then to her father's sad, patient hazel-green eyes.

32

"Mr. Madigan? Would that be the Irish prizefighter who is touring the Comstock?" Ephraim asked worriedly.

Dorcas and Leah both gasped in outrage. "You've become involved with a common brawler—and a foreign papist in the bargain?" Dorcas thundered.

"Perhaps you'd best start at the beginning, Rebekah," her father said, sinking down into the large, battered chair behind his modest desk and motioning for his family to be seated.

Dorcas and Leah took the shabby two-chair-back settee, leaving Rebekah with only a straight-backed chair facing her father's desk. Well, she preferred to tell her tale to his more sympathetic ears anyway. Quickly, lest she lose her nerve and fumble with words, Rebekah outlined the lark, omitting any mention of her friend Celia in her narration about being drawn by the crowd in glitter town and witnessing the boxing contest with its frightening aftermath.

"So, you see, when I overheard them planning to drug Mr. Madigan, I had to warn him," she concluded.

"You should never have been in such a heinous place, witnessing the barbarity of half-clothed men battering each other—you, an unmarried girl," Dorcas said, fanning herself.

"You're never likely to be married if you continue behaving the way you have," Leah interjected snidely.

"Be that as it may, why did you compound the folly by meeting this rascal instead of simply warning him of the plot in your note?" Ephraim asked.

Leave it to her father's Yale-trained intellect to cut to the heart of the matter, Rebekah thought in misery. *I wanted to meet him in person.* Lord, she couldn't say that! "Er, well, I had to explain who the men were and describe them. I didn't think a note sufficient."

"You didn't think at all. You never do, else you'd not be courting the ruin of your reputation this way. Of all your disgraceful escapades, this tops the list. An—an assignation with an Irish saloon ruffian!'' Dorcas wrung her pudgy, reddened hands in agitation.

Ephraim regarded his younger daughter with worried perplexity. She had always been the brighter, more inquisitive child, the free spirit of the family, and she was his favorite, just as Leah was the apple of Dorcas's eye. But perhaps his wife was right and he had allowed Rebekah too much free rein over the years. This jaunt to the wrong side of the tracks could have resulted in real physical harm, not simply scandal. ''Perhaps it would be best if I talked with Rebekah in private.''

When the Reverend Ephraim Sinclair made a suggestion in that tone of voice, even the shrewish Dorcas knew it was advisable to assent. Huffing, she ushered Leah from the study, saying, ''Do help me see to putting dinner on the table. Not that I shall be able to eat a bite, I'm that upset.''

Ephraim waited until they were gone, then unfolded his lanky frame from the overstuffed chair and walked around the desk. Rebekah watched him, feeling the weight of guilt fold around her like a rain-soaked woolen cloak. All her mother's histrionics and her sister's pious meanness did not have half the effect on her as one condemning look from her father—especially when he looked as hurt as he did now.

''I'm sorry, Papa. Sneaking over to glitter town was a very foolish thing to do, and I offer no excuse.'' Her shoulders slumped.

''It was highly dangerous, Rebekah. There are men over there—terrible men—who could harm an innocent like you. This box fighter might well be one such despoiler.''

''Oh, no! Rory isn't at all like that,' Rebekah blurted out before she could stop herself. When would she ever learn to guard her tongue!

"Rory? You seem to have become rather taken with the young man. Is that the real reason for meeting him?" he asked, rubbing his forehead with a pale, veiny hand.

"No—that is, well I—I don't know." Her face flamed as visions of Rory Madigan's lean, sweat-soaked body flashed through her mind. She could still feel the heat of his lips tingling on her fingertips. "He's not what you think—a ruffian. He's well-spoken and polite." *Polite? A lie, Rebekah,* her conscience chastised.

"But he is a prizefighter, drifting from one rough saloon district to another. And an Irish immigrant, also no doubt Catholic. Do you have any idea what these things mean, Rebekah?"

"I'll never see him again, Papa. I only had to warn him about the danger," Rebekah replied miserably.

"That appears to make you unhappy, daughter," he replied gravely. "Think, child. He is not the kind of man with whom you should be keeping company. The Irish mostly are a drunken lot, I fear, and firmly entrenched in Romanish superstitions. You've been raised with a fine religious heritage, Rebekah. Your faith should be everything to you, as it is to me."

She could feel his eyes on her, sad and gentle, yet censuring all the same. Although a tolerant champion of blacks and Chinese, as well as many of the other diverse immigrants to Nevada, Ephraim Sinclair's intense dislike of Irish Catholics had always been steadfast since her earliest childhood memories. She often wondered why, but never dared to ask such a personal thing. "I'm certain Mr. Madigan will be gone in a few days, Papa. There's no danger to my faith."

Ephraim sighed. "Ah, but you're coming of age, and it is natural for you to think of marriage. The important thing is to find a suitable husband—a fine, God-fearing man from my flock. Did I mention, Rebekah, that Amos Wells is coming for dinner on Sunday after church?''

Rebekah's head shot up in amazement. Amos Wells was a deacon at First Presbyterian and the wealthiest contributor in the congregation. But what did he have to do with her reaching a marriageable age? The man was positively ancient. "I'm sure Mama will be thrilled. Mr. Wells is the leading citizen of the town. After all, it was named after him. His mining and banking ventures made Wellsville," she said, testing the waters. Her father was a man who often kept his own council when it suited him. She looked at him expectantly.

Ephraim cleared his throat, more nervous than was his usual wont, uncertain of how to phrase what he needed to say to Rebekah. Perhaps the bald truth would serve best. Rebekah was willful, and if she did not fancy the match he would never force her, no matter what Dorcas wished. "Mr. Wells has been a widower for over a year now. He is a vigorous man in the prime of his life, a wealthy man without heirs since the Lord did not see fit to bless him and the late Mrs. Wells with offspring. He's looking for a wife, Rebekah, and expressed to me an interest in courting you. I said I was pleased, but the final decision, of course, must be your own. He's a fine, upstanding man, Rebekah.''

She felt poleaxed, unable to speak a word for several moments. "Celia Hunt favors him," she finally blurted out.

Ephraim shook his head and sighed. "Celia is a dear, sweet girl, but far too scatterbrained and spoiled for a man like Amos.''

"But—but, why me? I'm scatterbrained, too, and not at all pious and proper like Leah.''

Reverend Sinclair smiled. "You're impulsive and a bit rebellious at times. For example, jumping in the creek to save

36

Laban Parker's little boy at the Sunday school picnic before one of the young men could do it. Or the time you took all the food from your mother's pantry and distributed it to the miners' children. But you have a fine mind, Rebekah. You've read every book in my library, even the Greek mythologies your mother deemed unsuitable for a young lady.'' He made a mock scowl. ''You far outpaced all your teachers over the years.''

''I remember,'' she said with a blush of mortification. She had been caught with the page open to the story of Leda and the Swan, for which crime she had been soundly paddled and sent to bed without supper by her mother. Sometimes she had wondered about the frankly carnal descriptions of mating in Greek myths and what truly went on between men and women to beget children. What would it be like to have a man touch her unclothed body? Rory Madigan's devilish wink and white smile flashed before her once more. Then she thought of Amos Wells's austere countenance and shuddered at the very idea of him coming near her that way. What was wrong with her? Her father was right. Rory was completely wrong for her. But surely Amos could not be right.

''Well, Rebekah? How do you feel about Amos's suit?'' he pressed when she sat rigidly in front of him, not meeting his eyes. He had anticipated that this would not be easy.

''I suppose there's no harm in conversing with him over Sunday dinner,'' she capitulated glumly. Perhaps being nice to Amos Wells for a while would cool Dorcas's wrath over her latest escapade. And most of all, she did not want to hurt her father any more than she already had.

Shirl Henke

Virginia City

A short, voluptuous whore in a gaudy yellow satin dress and black fishnet tights sat on Rory's lap, running her fingers through his hair as he took a swallow of forty rod that burned all the way down. Her rouged cheeks and carmined lips gave color to the otherwise pale complexion of a woman who saw little more sunlight than did her miner patrons. Brittle yellow hair hung in banana curls that fell over her bare shoulders. He touched one, then dropped the dry, frizzy clump.

"Whatzamatter, Irish? You don' like Sadie no more?" She hiccuped drunkenly, planting a wet kiss against his neck. "I brung ya luck at faro."

Rory had won a sizable pot at the rigged table before losing it between there and the bar, which was the establishment's plan. He knew it. Just as he knew in a sudden rush of drunken honesty that he had picked Sadie because she was a blonde like Rebekah Sinclair. But Rebekah's soft, silky skin and hair, her innocent charm and humor, were sadly lacking in the mining camp girl. If Rebekah could see him in the wild and raucous Comstock, she would be appalled.

The Howling Wilderness was typical of the saloons lining C Street, a bustling thoroughfare set between the steep, barren mountains under which men gouged out the biggest fortune in history. They worked in blistering heat in a labyrinth of tunnels containing as much timber as it took to build the city of Chicago. Virginia City was big and sprawling and ugly, a festering sore above and below the ground, where life was cheap and death as easily come by as bad whiskey and worse women.

A typical crowd tromped about on the sawdust-covered saloon floor—garishly dressed Jezebels danced and drank with red-faced Welsh and Cornish miners, while hard-eyed Mexican pistoleros diced. Fancy Eastern lawyers with the stink of larcenous litigation on them played poker. Crude Pikes from the hills of Missouri and Arkansas, their Bowie knives gleaming and ready, spat lobs of brown tobacco in the general direction of gummy, fly-covered cuspidors.

A fight erupted in one corner of the saloon between a Chilean miner and an Italian grocer, but the piano player continued his discordant plinking. No one paid any mind to a scuffle unless shots rang out. Roulette wheels clacked while bluff and hearty Saxon cattle buyers raised their beer steins. A small, swarthy French Canadian sat in one corner paring long, dirt-encrusted nails with a gleaming stiletto, his solemn gray eyes as old as the volcanic mountains in which the mother lode lay.

Rory was in his element, raw and uncivilized, where foreigners outnumbered Americans. How different this desolate hellhole was from the lush verdancy of the Truckee Valley, only a few dozen miles away as the crow flew. Fleetingly, he wished he could be as free as a bird to fly away from the sounds of curses and breaking glass, the cloying smell of Sadie's cheap perfume.

"Dreams, boyo, only dreams," he muttered beneath his breath, ignoring the scarlet poppy who was expecting him to take her upstairs at the end of the night. The thought of a sexual liaison with her was even more repugnant to Rory than bedding the drunken gold-camp denizens was to the whores.

He scooted the blonde from his lap and stood up, deciding on a breath of fresh air to clear his head. Elbowing his way through the press of sweaty, cursing men garbed in flannel and denim, he walked into the darkness of the street via a side door. Leaning against the brick wall, which was still warm from the day's blistering heat, he lit a cigar in the chill night air. Smoking was a rare and expensive extravagance he allowed himself only after winning a big purse.

Taking a long drag on the pungent tobacco, he wondered idly how it might be to always have the best, to sleep on clean sheets every night and wake up with a beautiful, golden-haired lady at his side every morning. To make love to a woman he had not bought for a night.

The rematch last night with Wharton must have addled his brains, even if the clumsy oaf had scarcely landed a glove on him. He chuckled to himself, recalling the surprised look on his opponent's face when January "accidentally" kicked over the water bucket just as the first round ended, then ran to refill it while the two men again toed the mark and continued to box. He had taken the Wellsville Wonder in only sixteen rounds this time.

The purse was the biggest he had ever won, a thousand dollars. And he owed it all to Rebekah Sinclair. Rebekah, who was a minister's daughter, a lady as far above him as the stars. But that did not stop him from dreaming—or squandering his cut of the take on cheap women, whiskey, and cards. Spending money was easy to do at gold-camp prices. Such had become the cycle of his life since he had come west five years ago in search of his brother. Better not to think of that. Better not to think of Rebekah Sinclair either.

But he could not stop himself. Ever since he had kissed her soft fingertips and looked into her green eyes with the gold specks floating in them, her memory had tormented him. With a muttered oath, he flicked away the last of the cigar and returned to the bright lights and noise inside the saloon.

"Rory, mate, wake up. Bloody 'ell, it's gonna take me a bleedin' month ta get you in shape again." January's scarred, strong little fingers dug into the big Irishman's scalp, lifting his face from the pillow. "Wake up, bucko. It's past noon 'n the *lydies*"—he emphasized the word mockingly— "wants us out of 'ere."

Rory mumbled something unintelligible and rolled onto his back with one arm flung across his eyes to hold back the agonizing rays of brilliant sunlight pouring into the dingy little room. Not even the sooty window could sufficiently filter the glare to his bloodshot eyes. Lord, his head pounded worse than the base drum in a Salvation Army marching band.

"I'm up, I'm up." He rolled to the side of the bed and cradled his head in both hands as the wizened little black man scooped up his clothes and shoved them at him.

"You 'ardly got any money left. Blimey, Madigan, ain't you ever gonna learn? Them blacklegs 'n whiskey morts pick you clean every time you win a purse," the Cockney scolded.

"What else is there for a fine Irish bucko like meself to be doin', January?" Rory's brogue returned only when he was drunk or angry. At the moment he hated the world, but most of all, he hated himself.

"You could be puttin' a bit 'o yer stash away, like I'm doin'. Got me enough ta go back 'ome 'n start a fight club outside London, I does."

"Then why don't you be off, you little bugger?" Rory cocked one eyebrow, then winced at the stab of pain that lanced through his skull.

January winked his good right eye. The other was glass. He had lost it in a boxing match against a man twice his size in Liverpool when he was a youth. " 'Ere now. I couldn't be leavin' you, mate. You was gettin' yer brains beat out

41

when we met up in Denver—what little brains a mickey ever 'ad.''

"Some talk from a one-eyed black Sassenach," Rory scoffed fondly. In truth, January had probably saved his life. He took a green boy who was only a clumsy brawler working his way west with his fists and turned him into a highly skilled professional.

After Rory finished dressing, the two men made their way down the back stairs and headed through the bustling streets of Virginia City. Huge ore dumps were scattered like random heaps of excrement from some monolithic dragon. No one seemed to mind the ugly scarring in their quest for silver and gold. Miners, bankers, lawyers and cowmen made their way through the streets, each intent on having his own cut of the mother lode. The unlikely pair walked quickly to a false-fronted frame building a few rows down from the saloon. The sign out front read Chickin' 'n Fixins, Rosie O'Roarke, Prop. It was not as respectable or elegant as the dining room at the International Hotel, but the food was hearty, cheap— by gold camp standards—and plentiful.

As they sat at the end of a long trestle table, their plates cleaned, Rory and January drank more of the scalding inky coffee that was Rosie's specialty.

"You seem a million miles off, Rory. What's chewin' on you? Maybe we should leave the Comstock."

"No. That cave-in that buried Ryan was six years ago. Nothing can bring him back—or Patrick. There's nowhere left to run or hide, January. This is as good as anywhere else I've been since I was fourteen years old."

"Even I'd 'ardly call th' Five Points o' New York as good as 'ere," January said with a mirthless chuckle.

Rory's shoulders shrugged expressively. "It was poorer, yes, but my parents were alive—and Sean and Ryan and

Patrick. We were a family, come to America filled with hopes and dreams.'' His voice turned flat, and he returned to sipping his coffee.

'' 'Ere now, mate. While you was busy with doxies 'n cards, I been takin' th' measure 'o the brawlers 'ere 'bouts. You could best any o' th' stumblebums, once we shape you up.''

Rory looked across the chipped rim of his cup, his dark blue eyes studying the seared, grizzled black face of his friend. ''You serious about going back to England and starting a fight club?''

''Yes, but I thought you said you'd never live by Sassenachs.''

''I won't. Not that it's much better here. 'No Irish need apply' isn't just a slogan in London—it's even more commonplace on the East Coast. I thought coming west would make a difference.'' He set down his mug and stared into the silty grounds at its bottom. ''But that was when I still dreamed of finding my brothers.''

''There's plenty opportunity out 'ere for a bright bloke like yerself—bloody 'ell, even bein' Irish, you ain't black. Look at John Mackay, Jim Fair, Billie O'Brien 'n Jimmy Flood—all of 'em Irishmen 'n all of 'em Comstock millionaires.''

''I'll never set foot in a mine. Not after how Ryan died.''

''Well then, 'ow 'bout startin' trainin' for yer next fight?''

''What if I don't want to fight anymore, January?''

The older man nodded and swallowed his coffee. ''Umm, I been wonderin' 'ow long it'd take you ta figger out you didn't want that pretty face ta end up lookin' like mine. What made up your mind?''

The vision of Rebekah Sinclair flashed before his eyes, her soft cool hand brushing his bruised cheek with concern

43

and tenderness in her emerald eyes. Aloud he said, "I don't know. Maybe I'm just tired of waking up like I did this morning, beat up and hung-over. I train and practice for weeks, win a big purse and then . . ." He gestured with one bruised hand. "I blow it all on a few nights' carousing. There has to be something better, more lasting . . . some way to drown the pain."

January studied his young friend intently, recalling the two young ladies on the roof in Wellsville the other day. One of them had almost gotten Rory's head taken off, she distracted him so much. "Sounds to me like yer talkin' 'bout a woman—not these 'ere gold-camp lightskirts neither."

Rory shrugged dismissively. "Maybe there is. Hell, I don't know, January. Right now it seems impossible. It probably is . . . she wouldn't like a brawler to come calling. I was thinking of trying some safe, regular job." He looked at the dubious expression on January's face. "Doesn't sound like me, I know."

"A bloody female can do most anything to a bloke. Change 'is whole bleedin' life."

As he rode into Wellsville, Rory remembered how different it had looked only a few days ago when he and January had approached the sleepy little cow town from the opposite direction, headed straight to the row of saloons and bordellos. The deadfall side of town looked like a thousand other places he had seen over the past years, filled with cheap shanties and gaudy gin mills, teeming with the roughest and lowest dregs of humanity. The sour smells of beer, sweat, and stale perfume mingled together, as hard-eyed men and even harder-eyed whores welcomed the amusement of a good fight.

This time he headed down the main street. Aspens and shaggy pines shaded businesses which lined the streets; a general mercantile stood two stories high next to a prosperous modiste's shop. Farther down was a newspaper office—this one, unlike the defunct *Self-Cocker,* bore the lofty title *The Wellsville Truth.* Wryly he wondered if truth in Wellsville was somehow different than elsewhere in Nevada. Across the street sat a bank, the local Wells Fargo office, and a livery stable. He could see the steeples of several churches scattered among the prosperous businesses and wondered which one belonged to Rebekah's father.

"Not the side of the tracks where we're usually welcome, is it, Lobsterback?" Rory asked his bay, giving the big red stallion's neck an affectionate pat. He had purchased the dark red horse in Denver, and no matter how much he gambled or drank, he had never given up the splendid beast. The bay was a sharp contrast to the far less flashy brown gelding January had ridden.

He would miss his old friend and mentor. January had found him when he had been down and out, a hungry runaway from an orphanage in New York. He'd given Rory's life the purpose and discipline of the boxing art. Of course, January's discipline and training had seldom curbed his pupil's excesses after they had won a big prize. But that was all behind him now. January was off to start a new life in London, where being a man of color would not prevent his owning a fight club. Rory would make a life here in Nevada, no matter the stigma of being Irish. After all, January was right about there being Irish millionaires aplenty on the Comstock.

As he reined in before Jenson's Livery Stable, Rory had no grandiose schemes in mind to become fabulously rich. The wants of a Presbyterian minister's daughter should be simple enough. But would she want a man like Rory Madigan to come courting? He'd see soon enough, but not until he had a steady job. Dismounting, Rory headed through the

45

wide-open double door of the mammoth livery, leading his bay. The sound of an argument echoed from out back, where another set of doors stood ajar, leading into a large series of corrals.

"I told y'all once, I told y'all a dozen times, Herrick, no tearin' up the mouth on a good piece of horseflesh. You're fired." The angry bass voice belonged to a big, heavyset man with the jowly face of a bulldog. Rory recognized him from the first boxing match across town.

"Yew cain't break wild horses with sugar treats 'n sweet talk. Yer a fool, Jenson," the lanky, hard-faced cowboy said with a distinct Appalachian twang. He threw down the Spanish bit he had been holding and stalked off furiously, leaving the thickset Jenson trying to calm a pinto mare that rolled her eyes and backed away from him.

Rory tied Lobsterback to a stall inside, then approached the livery owner. "I might be able to help," he offered.

Jenson squinted suspiciously at the tall, black-haired man. "Say, ain't you the feller who boxed Cy Wharton's ears the other day? Heard tell y'all beat him again in Virginia City."

Rory reached out and gently touched the pinto's neck, stroking it slowly as he spoke. "Yes, I'm Rory Madigan, formerly the Kilkenny Kid." The horse quieted a bit and Jenson stood back, letting the Irishman continue soothing the mare as he watched. Rory spoke low Gaelic love words in her ear and blew his breath into her muzzle. As she calmed, he very carefully pulled back her lips and examined the bleeding mouth. "Your handler would only break the spirit of a horse treating it this way."

"That's what I figgered, but hell, it's hard to find a good man. All the fellers young enough to work stock is either green tenderfeet that don't know comere from sick-'em 'bout horses, or else they got gold fever and head fer the mines."

He watched Madigan soothing the mare, then asked, ''Y'all quittin' boxin'?''

''Aye. I'm sick of getting beaten bloody, even if I do win the fight—sort of like this girl here. I don't want to end up scarred and mean either.''

''Heard that rematch with Wharton was some fight. Wish I could've seen it. Bet ole Cal Slocum was fit to be tied.''

Rory grinned. ''Let's just say he was surprised at the way the fight ended. Wharton would've been too—if he'd been conscious.''

''Y'all seem to know horses. That big stallion of yourn is a prime piece of horseflesh,'' Jenson said, looking at Rory's horse standing with his ears pricked toward the mare in the corral.

''My father was head stableman for an English earl in Galway. I grew up around fine racehorses. The gypsies moving through the countryside taught me a few tricks, too. That man you just fired was wrong. You can gentle a horse with sweet talk—provided it's Romany or Gaelic,'' Rory added with a grin.

''Y'all want a job, Madigan? I need a man to work the horses I buy. I run a string of racers, too. Could use someone to help with the training and lend a hand at the track. I'll pay ten dollars a week—more if y'all prove yourself. I know it ain't miner's wages—''

''That doesn't matter. I'll never dig in a mine,'' Rory said abruptly. ''Mr Jenson, you just hired yourself a horse handler.''

Chapter Three

Amos Wells sat in his opulently appointed office, which was filled with maroon leather and blue-velvet furniture. Racks of antlers and the stuffed heads of a mountain ram and a snarling puma attested to his skill as a sportsman and hunter. He leaned back in the big swivel chair behind his mahogany desk and considered the gilt-framed photograph in his hand, brooding at the narrow, unsmiling face of the woman in it. Heloise's thin lips pursed and her narrow eyes glared back at him as if she were ready to launch into another of her weeping tirades. Cold, unnatural woman. He was glad she was dead. Now that his year of mourning was over, he could get on with the business at hand and find a more suitable replacement for her. He had been young and foolish when he wed her, and truth be told, greedy. Her father had settled a sizable dowry on him for taking his spinster daughter in marriage.

Amos had used the money to invest in his first banking

and mining ventures. Within a decade he had become a rich man, moving on from California to Colorado to the Comstock. Now he owned controlling interest in three banks, two railroads, and half a dozen mines, and he had built a mansion on his huge ranch, the Flying W. He was putting down roots in Nevada. The political climate suited him. A handful of millionaires, mostly California bankers and Nevada mine owners, controlled the silver state. He had spent years cultivating those who were useful and making his own connections in the state legislature.

Amos Wells planned to be the next United States Senator from Nevada, but there was one complication. He needed a wife, someone beautiful to fire his blood and turn the heads of jaded politicians and cynical silver kings, yet someone young and malleable with an even disposition who would do his bidding without shrewish whining. Heloise had always had a high opinion of herself and her family's blue blood. She had made him feel that he was unworthy of her from the first day of their sham marriage.

Stroking the point of his carefully manicured Vandyke beard, he smiled faintly as he slid the old photo into a bottom desk drawer and closed it, considering how to approach his courtship of Rebekah Sinclair. Dinner last Sunday had gone well. Her parents were both favorably impressed with him, especially since he had volunteered to pay for a new pipe organ for the church, a luxury which heretofore only the Episcopalians of Wellsville could afford. Rebekah herself had been pleasant in a quiet, unassuming way. She was quite young, but that only meant she would stand in awe of him. Indeed, she had said little during the course of the meal, leaving the conversation to the men while she assisted her mother in serving the superb meal.

Rebekah had been raised in genteel poverty, doing without

fancy clothes or servants to cook and clean for her. He knew every young girl's silly head was turned by a bit of silk and lace. Wait until she saw his twenty-room home on the Flying W and the elegant brick city house he was going to purchase in Carson City once his election as a Nevada senator had been voted by the legislators. Never would his wife have to bake her own bread or redden her hands by scrubbing dishes. Nor would he allow her to grow plump and dowdy like her mother.

Just then a light tapping on the door of his office interrupted his ruminations. Henry Snead entered at Wells's command and took a seat across from him. Snead was a big man with the sort of craggy blunt features and wavy light brown hair many women found pleasing. He always had a ready smile, which accentuated his heavy handlebar mustache and straight white teeth.

"Glad you could get away from the Flying W for the day, Henry. You've been working too hard. Surely your bride doesn't like to see you gone so much of the time," Amos said, measuring Snead's reaction.

"There's no problem with Leah," Henry replied with a wave of one meaty hand. "She's tickled to death with that fancy new stove I just bought her—and with the two Chinks I hired to help fetch and carry for her around the place. The spring roundup went really well, and we should get top dollar for those blooded steers when we sell the beef this fall. I figure to invest my share of the profits in your latest mining stock deal."

"You want to branch out, eh?" Amos said, a sly smile hovering on his lips.

"I don't plan on running stock the rest of my life." Henry's smile gleamed like a tooth powder advertisement in a mail-order catalogue. "And I do appreciate the opportunities you've given me, Mr. Wells."

Amos nodded in approval. "You'll go far with me, Henry. Far indeed. Mr. Bascomb was commenting on your acumen just the other day."

Snead's eyes lit up. Hiram Bascomb was the president of the Greater Sacramento Trust Bank and a major stockholder in several of Wells's mining operations.

"Yes, indeed, stick with me, my boy, and soon you'll be buying that pretty blond bride of yours jewels and furs. Tell me, Henry, how well do you know your sister-in-law, Rebekah? Are she and your wife close?"

Henry was not surprised at the sudden shift in the conversation. "Rebekah is a sweet girl," he said noncommittally. He'd heard a rumor that Amos Wells had asked Reverend Sinclair's permission to court the girl. "She's like her pa, I expect, concerned with Christian charity." He was not about to burst Amos's bubble by telling him Leah thought her younger sister a hopeless hoyden without a spark of propriety. "Miss Rebekah is headstrong and high spirited, but she'll make some man a fine wife."

Wells ran his fingers through his dark hair, which was liberally streaked with gray. "As you know, Henry, the year of mourning for my dear departed Heloise is past. I must have another wife, someone suitable as a hostess for the business and political entertaining I must do. Do you think Rebekah Sinclair would serve?"

Snead could feel the dampness of perspiration against his shirt. Damned wool suit was too heavy for Nevada's hellishly hot summers, but a man of property had to look the part. It was expected of him now. "Yes, I do. She's studious and bright. I could see her learning her way around the politicians' wives in Carson City, even those in Washington, given time.'' *If she'll have you.*

''Good. I concur. And I count upon your good offices as a member of the Sinclair family to support my suit.'' Without waiting for Snead's reply, Wells picked up a sheaf of papers from his desk and shoved them toward the younger man. ''These are instructions for the managers at the Silver Star and Glory Gulch mines. Production is down and we need to—er, boost market interest before selling our stock.''

A sharkish grin raised the tips of Snead's mustache. ''Looks as if there's going to be another big bonanza by next week. I'll get right on it.'' He picked up his new bowler hat from the chair and rose to leave, but Wells's parting words stopped him short.

''Do remember me to your sister-in-law when you and Mrs. Snead dine with the reverend and his family tonight. I'd be most interested in your impressions of how Rebekah is receiving my suit.''

Rebekah Sinclair sat staring out the kitchen window, not seeing the pale pink mountains on the distant horizon or the riotous gold sunflowers growing against the picket fence out back. Mechanically she snapped beans for dinner, going through the motion like a sleepwalker as her thoughts tumbled through her brain.

Why couldn't Amos Wells have set his sights on Celia Hunt? Celia would swoon in bliss to have the rich, powerful man for a suitor. But he had fixed his attentions instead on the Reverend Sinclair's second daughter. *Why me?* She was no great beauty—her figure was far too slender, possessing none of the hourglass flair so in vogue. Her hair, unlike Leah's pale silvery blond, was a brassy dark yellow that had always seemed tawdry to Rebekah. Lord knew she was no pious, proper clergyman's daughter, although she had tried to be on her best behavior at dinner last Sunday.

What an ordeal it had been, smiling, trying her best to be shy and modest so as not to embarrass her father in front of his treasured parishioner, yet at the same time trying not to encourage Amos in his courtship. He had made no overt gestures to her that in any way betrayed his prior conversation with Ephraim. But he was a shrewd silver baron, used to keeping his own council, hardly the sort to come with nosegays and candy boxes in hand. If only he were not so aloof and pompous, so old. When Celia heard about his intentions, Rebekah knew her friend would be hurt and jealous.

Why did nothing ever seem to work out the way anyone wanted? Dorcas wanted a rich son-in-law and her father wanted her settled down with a suitable man. Celia wanted Amos, but Amos wanted her. What did Rebekah Beatrice Sinclair want? A pair of laughing blue eyes with a lock of inky hair curling over a high forehead flashed into her mind. Rory.

Don't even think about him, she scolded herself angrily, pulling the end of a bean so hard the whole thing came apart in her hands.

"Mind what you're about, young lady," Dorcas admonished. "It will be a fortunate thing that you'll have servants to cook and clean for you as Mrs. Wells. You're a poor enough help around here."

"I'm not affianced to Mr. Wells yet, Mama," Rebekah replied crossly, pushing a wisp of burnished gold hair from her cheek. The heat was growing worse, and the hour neared noon. A kettle boiled away on the stove, and the big granite coffeepot sat ever ready with steam rising from the spout.

"Mind your manners and you soon will be."

"But I don't love Amos Wells. He's . . . he's more than twice my age. Leah got to choose her own husband, and I shall do the same.'' There, she had said it, even though she knew she would pay for it.

Dorcas's ruddy face grew even redder in the hot kitchen as she yanked the bowl of green beans from Rebekah's hands. "Old indeed. Mr. Wells is in his prime. A fine figure of a man. You should be honored that a man of his importance has even taken note of you. Your sister was always a dutiful girl who chose a man her family approved. Now, you, who have never felt a shred of family responsibility, have the best catch of the valley interested in you, and this is how you respond! If only Leah were single, she would make Mr. Wells a perfect wife." Dorcas sighed in martyrdom and tossed the beans in a pot along with a chunk of salt pork.

Knowing how taken Leah was with Henry, Rebekah had a strong suspicion that even her saintly sister for once would have balked at their mother's wishes. She said nothing, however, just began to set the table with their chipped but serviceable everyday dishes.

A loud banging on the front door, followed by a low, urgent conversation between her father and another man, drew both women to leave the kitchen and investigate. Reverend Sinclair was talking to Emett Watkins from the Pelonis Peak Mine.

The minister's face was grave as he said to his wife, "There's been an accident at the mine—an explosion. A dozen of the miners are trapped below, and nearly twenty more have been brought up."

"Pelonis—isn't that the fellow who hires all sorts of foreign riffraff? Irish and Cornish—even those yellow heathen?" Dorcas asked, her face tight with distaste.

"Most of the injured men are Chinese, yes, but they're not all heathen. You know I've baptized several families down in Alder Gulch. It's my duty to see if I can help, Dorcas.''

His wife gestured in frustration, knowing he would risk life and limb for those worthless foreigners and she could do nothing to stop him. The tribulations of being a minister's wife were a heavy burden at times.

"I'll go with you, Papa. I could help with the injured," Rebekah volunteered.

"You most certainly will not, young lady. No daughter of mine will set foot among those rough men.''

"Your mother is right, Rebekah. A mining camp is no fit place for a young innocent like yourself," Ephraim said firmly. "Please fetch me my Bible." He turned to Dorcas and took her hand. "I would appreciate it if you would have the ladies from the guild gather medicines and blankets."

Rebekah was left behind to tend to the dinner, which would have to be warmed over when her busy parents returned. Dorcas gave her explicit instructions about storing the food, along with a list of other chores to occupy her daughter's idle hands, then bustled off for a nice long visit with her friends. The guild ladies would gossip as they did their Christian duty. Once Rebekah had cleaned up the kitchen, she felt restless and frustrated. Her life seemed so meaningless at times such as this. Only married ladies had the freedom to go out in society and perform useful tasks, not that she relished the prospect of rolling bandages while Lucinda Maybury carried on about the latest scandal in the congregation.

"I want to be free. Maybe I just want to get away from Wellsville. For certain I don't want to be married—at least not to Amos Wells or any of the other eligible men I've met." But she did want to wear silk dresses and travel in elegant sleeping cars on the Central Pacific, drink champagne and dance all night in big eastern cities—all the exciting things she had only read about in books. ''I must stop being so selfish. Just think of all the poor people involved in that mining cave-in. In fact, imagine how poor their lot in life is compared to yours—and you're pining away for frivolous pleasures like Celia talks about.''

Rebekah stared out the kitchen window at the vegetable garden. Heat rose in shimmering waves from the dry alkali soil across the road, but here in her backyard the earth was dark and moist. The parsonage sat beside a deep well that yielded water enough to allow the luxury of gardening—if one considered canning peas and carrots and pickling cabbage and beets a luxury.

Sighing, Rebekah prepared to tackle the weeding. Then a thought danced into her head. Another frivolous one. Mama would not return until supper, and her father would probably be later yet. Who would know if she broke just a few tiny rules, nothing more than foolish social conventions really? She laid aside the ugly sunbonnet and heavy gloves, rolled up the sleeves of her old muslin dress, and unfastened the top buttons. There, much cooler and more comfortable. Who would be there to see her anyway?

Rory had spent the week in back-breaking labor—indeed, potentially bone-breaking labor. Luckily his were all still intact, thanks to his ability to communicate with horses. He had broken a dozen wild mustangs to accept bit and bridle and trained six others to bear his weight and respond to the rein and knee signals. As soon as the wild herd was ready for sale, Beau Jenson had promised to take him out to his track to meet the trainers who worked with his thoroughbreds.

Rory knew he would prove himself even more valuable to

his employer handling fine racers. In any case, Jenson had been so impressed with his new man's breaking methods that he had given the enterprising young Irishman the afternoon off, saying it was too hot to work horses. Ostensibly he was going fishing, a pole slung over his shoulder as he walked his bay down the street, but he planned a small detour past the parsonage of Wellsville's First Presbyterian Church. He had made it a regular part of his nightly trip to the river outside town where he bathed off the smell of horses and dust.

The first thing he had done after unpacking his saddlebags in the small room above the stable was to make some casual inquiries about the Reverend Sinclair and his flock. If any of the men in the Dry Gulch Saloon thought it odd that an Irish Catholic was curious about the local Presbyterians, no one mentioned it. They remembered all too well how wickedly he wielded his fists.

The water buckets were heavy. Rebekah had overfilled them, but laden with her burden it was better to eliminate at least one trip the length of the large yard. She had to soak the hard earth around the cabbages and beets before she could pull weeds, a slow, laborious process involving filling the heavy tin sprinkling can with water from the buckets and plying it across the long, even rows of vegetables. Most of the big plot was neatly wet down and cleaned of weeds.

Rebekah could feel the itch of mud beneath her fingernails and knew her face and arms were smeared with it. No matter, she would soon be finished. A long soak in the big iron tub in the washroom sounded heavenly. She could hardly wait and picked up her pace, letting the water slosh carelessly over the side of the pail. Unfortunately, the garden sat on a slight incline and she was heading downhill with her burden.

The spilled water rolled ahead of her in an ever widening rivulet on her well-beaten path between the rows. Heedlessly, she persevered until one of the pesky pumpkin vines, which twisted in and out between all the other vegetables, caught her ankle and she lurched forward, struggling to regain her balance and kick free of the vine.

One bucket dropped to the ground with a loud clank, followed by a splash. Her left heel slid in the mud. Before Rebekah realized what had happened, both feet flew up in the air and she landed on her backside in a puddle of muddy water. She let out a loud squawk of surprised indignation, then a very unladylike swear word which Dorcas would have caned her soundly for using.

"If I'd known you liked to play in the mud so much, I'd have invited you to ride up around Pyramid Lake to where the sulfur pots bubble up out of the ground," a familiar mocking voice taunted.

Rory Madigan leaned against the side of the shed with one booted foot resting negligently over the other and his arms across that magnificent expanse of lean-muscled chest she had so admired the day of the boxing match. But Rebekah Sinclair was in no mood to admire anything at the moment. She raised one mud-covered brown hand and shoved angrily at the wad of hair that had come loose from its moorings and hung in her eyes.

Succeeding only in snarling it worse than before, she yanked the pins from it and shook it back out of her face. "I hope I've amused you sufficiently, Mr. Madigan."

Her green eyes glared up at him, and the bright afternoon sunlight highlighted the gold flecks swimming in them. Rory fought the urge to kiss away the mud smear across her nose. Instead he reached out chivalrously and offered her his hand. "I thought we'd dispensed with surnames, Rebekah. I'm never amused by a lady in distress.''

She looked up at the devilish smile on his handsome face and gave in to one of the impulsive urges that had made her the bane of Dorcas Sinclair's existence since she was a toddler. She took his hand, then yanked him from his casual stance at the edge of her self-created mud wallow. He tumbled to his knees, then rolled into the trough between rows of cabbages and pumpkins.

''So, it's a dirty fight yer wantin', eh colleen?'' he said, his brogue thickening as he chuckled while pulling her closer to him until he lay on top of her. He could feel her breasts through the wet, muddy fabric of her dress, pressing intimately against his chest. Although tall and slender, Rebekah Sinclair was very soft and very female—preacher's daughter or not. He grinned impudently down at her sputtering face, then gave in to impulse as well, for Rory Madigan had never even tried to curb his baser instincts, especially when they came to lithesome females. He placed his hands on each side of her head and slowly lowered his mouth to hers.

Rebekah knew he was going to kiss her, out in her own backyard, lying on top of her right in the middle of the cabbage patch! Anyone who happened up the side street could see them. If Widow Pruitt next door were home, which thank heavens she was not, she could see them from her kitchen window. Rebekah responded the way any intelligent, gently bred young lady would in like circumstances—she held on to him for dear life and kissed him back.

Rory gave her plenty of time to resort to maidenly modesty and turn aside his kiss, but she startled him by throwing her arms around his neck and pressing her lips firmly to his. It was instantly apparent that she possessed no knowledge of the finer points of the art. Doubtless her previous experiences with kissing were confined to innocent pecks from green boys. Her mouth remained primly closed and she attempted to make up what she lacked in finesse with enthusiasm and enough pressure to crack his teeth.

He took her delicate jaw in one hand and restrained her as his tongue rimmed her lips, then teased at their seam, giving her the idea that he wanted to be inside. When she opened enough to emit a startled little gasp, he took advantage and ran the tip of his tongue along her small white teeth, then darted deeper to tease and twine with her tongue as his mouth moved over hers masterfully. Two young soiled doves at Pearly's Palace in Denver had taught him the finer points of kissing, letting him practice for free until they pronounced him the best ever. He worked on perfecting that skill as assiduously as he did his boxing.

Rebekah felt the blood rushing to her head as his mouth mastered hers, eliciting tingling pleasures that robbed her of breath. Then she followed his clever coaxing and let her tongue dart between his open lips, tasting and teasing as he did. Suddenly the blood seemed to rush lower, leaving her light-headed and spinning out of control as heat pooled in her belly. One of his long legs was slung possessively across hers, and his hips pressed shockingly against her own, moving in a slow lazy roll that was mesmerizing.

His chest brushed across her breasts each time he raised his head to reposition his mouth for another of those soul-robbing kisses. The thin wet cloth separating their upper bodies allowed her to feel the rasp of his chest hair on her delicate skin and the most appallingly delicious thing was happening to her breasts. Her nipples tingled, radiating the most pleasurable ache. She could feel what she had always thought of as her most inadequate feminine endowment swelling as she arched against him like the brazen hussy she surely must be.

Rory was one step from ripping the clothes from her and taking her there in the middle of the garden when her small startled whimpers of surprise and amazement began to penetrate his consciousness. She had never even been properly kissed before in her life—a young sheltered girl, totally innocent. He was taking shameless advantage of a warm, passionate nature that her sanctimonious family had probably spent a lifetime trying to squelch. *Rotten bastard.*

Rebekah felt him break their wild kiss and roll away from her. When she opened her dazed eyes, he sat staring down at her with a troubled expression. Scarlet shame heated her face, and she rolled over in the mud, too humiliated to look at him. Then she felt his gentle hand on her shoulder.

"I'm sorry, Rebekah. I apologize for taking such ungentlemanly advantage of an innocent." He felt her flinch away from his touch.

"I pulled you down beside me. That was hardly ladylike," she whispered, fighting a losing battle with humiliating tears.

He reached into his back pocket and extracted a handkerchief, old and frayed, but luckily not mud-soaked. He began to wipe gently at her face. "You're making trails through the mud," he said, striving for lightness. "Could I borrow some to wash my face?" That did the trick. She looked up at him, and a wobbly smile curved her lips.

"Why is it that I feel I've known you all my life?" The question seemed to ask itself.

He shrugged and gave her a sunny smile to ease her fears, ignoring the persistent ache in his nether regions. "I could say the same thing, although the last time I even associated with a respectable girl was back at St. Vincent's when I was thirteen years old."

"St. Vincent's? Is that your church?" She dabbed at her face with his soft old handkerchief, which was filled with the subtle male aromas of tobacco and horses.

"No. It's an orphanage in New York City. The Sisters of Charity took me in when my parents died in an influenza epidemic. We'd just arrived from Ireland a few months earlier," he added softly.

Her own misery and embarrassment forgotten, Rebekah reached out and laid her grimy hand on top of his. "How tragic to be all alone with no family—especially when you were such a little boy yet."

"I still had family at first. Three older brothers. But Sean died of consumption. He was the eldest. Ryan and Patrick were too old for the orphanage. They had to leave me there, but they promised to come back for me when they'd made their fortunes."

"What happened?" Rory Madigan seemed alone in the world now.

"Ryan died in a Comstock silver mine back in sixty-four—in a cave-in. Patrick's ship was lost off the China coast in a monsoon. That's what happens to Irishmen who dream of striking it rich," he said bitterly.

"I'm so sorry, Rory."

Her sweet, soft voice brought him back from his bitter memories. "I've never told anyone but January Jones about my family."

"Is he the little colored man I saw at the fight?"

"He was my manager as well as a good friend—my only friend until now."

She smiled shyly as he helped her to her feet in the middle of the ruined patch of garden. "I'd like to be your friend, Rory." *And more than your friend,* some inner voice taunted.

He raised her hand in the same elegant salute he had given her that day on the bandstand, ignoring their muddy dishabille as he kissed her fingertips. "I was going fishing, but now I think I'll use the river for a bath instead. Care to join me?'' he dared her.

Rebekah looked down at her ruined clothing and the shambles around her. ''Oh, my goodness! Look at me, and Mama will be home shortly expecting me to have the garden watered and weeded. I have to finish the weeding and then . . . oh dear, how will I ever get clean without ruining the bathtub and washroom!''

He picked up a half-filled pail of water and said, ''You've done a fair job with the watering part of the project. Let me help with the rest. But you're right—we'll have to hurry, not only because of your mother.'' At her puzzled look, he added, ''If we let this mud dry on us, we'll crack and break like sun-dried apples.''

Rebekah smothered a giggle behind one muddy little fist. Soon they were working side by side, sprinkling the remaining dry soil and weeding between the rows of half-grown vegetables. He worked fast with sure, strong hands, pulling out thistles and pepper grass, then smoothing the muddy gouges in the earth until all telltale traces of her accident were erased.

''You're an awfully good gardener,'' she observed.

''My mother kept a garden back in Galway,'' he said with a faraway look.

''That's nice. I never thought of the Irish as farmers.''

''We grow more than potatoes,'' he retorted angrily. ''My father was the head groom for the Earl of Walthem. My brothers and I took our lessons with his own son's tutor.''

''I didn't intend a slur on your family—or on your being Irish, Rory.'' His pride was prickly indeed. How often had her father said the Irish were the stubbornest race on earth?

His hot temper was just as quick to cool when he saw her genuine hurt and bewilderment. ''I'm sorry, Rebekah. I'm

63

so used to being insulted for being Irish that I take offense when none's meant. I suppose if there's one true fault of the Irish, it's a rotten temper.''

"I never thought of that as any nation's special trait. Anyway, you don't seem to hold a grudge. That's the important thing—and you admit when you're wrong. Some folks will never do that.'' She picked up the sprinkling can, her hoe and other small gardening tools, and he took the empty pails and followed her around to the shed.

As she replaced the gardening utensils on the pegs along the wall, he asked, "What about cleaning up in the river? You could at least scrub off the worst of the mud and spare your family washroom.''

Rebekah hesitated until he added, "I've got my horse with me. I can have you back in plenty of time for supper. Promise.''

"Exactly what my already hoydenish reputation would need—to be seen covered head to foot in mud, riding with a stranger to bathe in the river! Thank you, Rory, but I must decline.''

"I do want to see you again, Rebekah, although I suspect your family won't approve of me,'' he added stiffly.

"I'd like to see you again, too.'' She chewed her lip for a moment. "You're right. You're an Irish Catholic. Even my father, who's a very kind and tolerant man, wouldn't approve of my keeping company with someone outside our faith.'' She did not mention her father's unreasoning dislike for the Irish.

"I always go fishing on Sunday afternoons down at the river—out that direction, past where it curves around that big stand of alders. If you could slip away and meet me, no one would know—at least until you wanted to tell them about us.'' His voice was cautious and neutral.

"I'll try if I can this Sunday." Her voice was frightened and breathless.

He whistled and his big bay stallion came trotting obediently around the corner of the shed. "This is Lobsterback," he said as Rebekah admired the horse.

"Lobsterback. What an odd name for such a magnificent animal." She scratched the bay's forehead and grinned at Rory. "Don't tell me *that's* not a real slur against the English."

"Sassenachs," he said, but without rancor as he swung up and returned her grin. "But I like the horse even if he does have a red coat." He kneed the bay forward, calling out to her, "I'll meet you at the river Sunday."

Rebekah stood rooted to the ground as he rode off, his words echoing enticingly. *I'll meet you at the river Sunday.* "That was probably how Satan tempted Eve back in the garden," she chided herself. But she knew she would be there on Sunday, come high water . . . or hell.

Chapter Four

Rebekah dressed for church that Sunday morning with particular care, glad she had been able to finish sewing the new dress length into a pretty summer frock. It was only an inexpensive lavender calico, but at least it was made to fit her, not taken in from her sister's more ample proportions, with the hem let down for her ungainly height. She piled her hair on top of her head and plied the curling iron to create a cluster of soft ringlets, then hid the fancy hairstyle beneath a demure bonnet she could discard after worship.

When she inspected her slender form and sun-kissed face in the mirror, she was pleased in spite of the light dusting of small gold freckles across her nose and cheekbones. Mama had scolded furiously because she had worked outdoors without taking precautions. If only she knew what else her daughter had done that afternoon in the garden! Forcing the disquieting thought aside, Rebekah smoothed the bodice of the simple dress over the soft swell of her breasts. If only she were large-breasted with wide, flared hips instead of being so . . . well, flat! But Rory didn't seem to mind.

She scolded herself. Such a thing could not be dwelt upon during morning worship. Bad enough that she was sneaking out this very afternoon to meet a man. What should she do if he asked to court her openly? It would be one way to discourage Amos Wells. But such a scheme could backfire and cause her parents to force her to wed the older man.

"I'll never marry a man I don't love," she whispered stubbornly to herself. Then, seeing her father's stricken hazel-green eyes, so gentle even in stern reproach, she realized how difficult the choices that lay ahead would be.

Her Sunday school class was pandemonium that morning. Ten-year-old Thad Taylor let loose a garter snake right in the middle of her explanation about Moses and the Ten Commandments. The rest of the boys dived down onto their hands and knees in pursuit while the girls squealed and jumped up on their chairs. Old Miss Haversham, the organist, was practicing when the chaos erupted. Hearing the shrieks of "snake, snake!" she fainted dead away onto the keyboard, resulting in a discordant wail from the organ, which drowned out the children until Deacon Becker pulled the elderly lady back on her bench and revived her.

Rebekah and Celia Hunt, who taught the younger children, chuckled about the fiasco after the snake had been released outdoors. The students calmed down, and the classes were dismissed. The two young women walked down to the shade of the big cedar tree out behind the church to enjoy a few minutes of blessed cool before the regular worship began at eleven o'clock.

Looking resplendent in her new yellow silk dress, Celia strolled carelessly by a juniper bush, paying no heed when it snagged the hem of her skirt. "There is something I wanted to discuss with you, Rebekah."

Rebekah's heart sank. *She's heard about Amos Wells asking Papa if he could court me.* "Celia, you know we've always been friends—"

"And all the more reason I should warn you—acting so recklessly as to let gossipy old Tess Conklin see you with that awful Irish boxer. Was he really kissing you right out in public—on the bandstand in the park?" Celia's brown eyes were alight with a mixture of censure and excitement.

"He only kissed my hand," Rebekah retorted guiltily. *That time.* "Look who's being so prim and proper all of a sudden, Celia Hunt. You weren't exactly hanging back when I suggested that walk over to Benton Street, and *you* were the one who insisted we could see him better from the porch of that old newspaper office."

"I didn't even know who he was!" Celia replied indignantly. "Really, Rebekah, he's a nobody—one of those drunken, brawling Irish. Why, he works in Beau Jenson's stable, for pity's sake."

"You sound like my mother. Being Irish doesn't automatically make a man drunken." Even as Rebekah rushed to Rory's defense, she realized that he had not told her about working for Mr. Jenson. But he had said January Jones *was* his manager. Did that mean he had quit boxing? Was he going to settle down in Wellsville?

Her jumbled thoughts were interrupted by Celia's insistent voice. "Why, you are positively moony-eyed over that fellow. I will admit he's fine looking, but he's impoverished, Rebekah. I always thought you wanted a man who could provide you with security and comforts, even if you don't favor one as distinguished as Amos Wells."

At the mention of Amos Wells, Rebekah's heart froze for

an instant. She had to tell her friend about his suit before Celia learned of it from the town gossips. Swallowing for courage, she said, "There's something I need your help with, Celia . . . about Mr. Wells."

A wary look came into Celia's normally warm brown eyes. "What about Amos Wells?"

"He's asked my father's permission to call on me," Rebekah blurted out, seizing her friend's hands and adding frantically, "It took me completely by surprise. I've certainly never encouraged him, and I won't marry him. I know you think he'd make a splendid catch, and I do so want you to be happy, Celia. Please don't be angry with me," she pleaded.

Celia stood rooted to the ground, a small O forming on her lips, making her face seem even rounder than usual. Then, sensing her friend's obvious distress, she hugged Rebekah. "Don't take on so. I know you never set your cap for Amos—even though why you'd prefer that penniless stablehand to him is beyond me," she added in exasperation.

Ignoring Celia's denigration of Rory, Rebekah replied, "Maybe there is something we can do to help us both get the men we want. Next Sunday is the box lunch social. I'm certain Mr. Wells will expect to bid on my lunch basket. Now, here's what we could do, if you want to. . . ."

Rory sat gazing out at the river glittering beneath the brilliant azure sky. He cast the bobber into the water and watched the cork dance on the lazy, rippling current. Would she come? Did he really want her to come? There would be all sorts of complications if they became involved. Until the reckless incident in her garden, he had never realized how volatile the feelings between a man and a woman could be.

Working his way across the country, he had sampled more

than his share of females—eager young slatterns who wanted him to take them away from the grimness of poverty, jaded older women with shady pasts who merely wanted to use his strong body to relieve their boredom. But never had he known a girl like Rebekah—a lady raised in a sheltered provincial environment, a complete innocent.

He smiled to himself, recalling the fire that burned deeply within her and how startled she had been that he could evoke such wanton responses from her. She was a quick learner, and he was an excellent teacher. But where would this lead them? Her family would scarcely consider him ideal husband material, and involvement with a girl like Rebekah meant marriage, no two ways about that. Well, he had quit boxing and gotten himself a steady job. The money was meager, but it was honest work with an opportunity for advancement. If Rebekah was willing to take a chance on him, they would find some way to appease her family.

The object of his musings approached the river and stood hidden in the dense stand of willows, watching Rory and working up her courage to approach him. He reclined against a willow log, one long leg bent at the knee and his forearm lying casually across it. A cane pole was propped up on the bank between two rocks. He stared at the river, deep in thought.

Taking a steadying breath, she stepped from her hiding place and approached him. "You seem a million miles away. The fish could carry off your pole, hook, line and sinker and you'd never know it."

He rolled up in one lithe motion and let his eyes sweep appreciatively over her, enjoying the blush that stained her cheeks. The lilac-colored dress accented every sweet, subtle curve yet was curiously demure. "The fish don't matter. I was thinking of you. I like what you did with your hair," he said, reaching up to touch the soft cluster of curls piled on top of her head. "I was afraid you weren't coming."

When he took her hand, it seemed the most natural thing on earth to stroll with him over to the log and sit down on it. "I had a hard time getting away from my family. Leah invited us all over to her house for dinner after church, and I had to invent an excuse not to go."

"I'm glad you found one," he said, smiling at her.

She chewed her lip for a moment. "I'm afraid I told a lie—or at least an exaggeration. I said the heat was bothering me so much I couldn't bear the long ride to Leah and Henry's place. I pleaded a headache and said I was going upstairs to rest."

"Henry Snead's the ramrod at the Flying W. That *is* a long, dusty ride. You weren't really lying."

"I'm not at home in my bed with cool rags on my forehead either." When she looked into his merry blue eyes, and he smiled that way at her, the little deception no longer seemed to matter. She smiled back.

"That's better," he said, touching his fingers to her chin, then brushing her nose with a light kiss. "Since you've given up your family dinner for me, the least I can do is share my lunch with you. It's not very fancy, but it's filling." He hoisted up a bag from behind the log and withdrew a half loaf of bread, a wedge of yellow cheese, and several peaches. "The bread and cheese are from Stricker's Restaurant. I filched the peaches from that orchard near your house."

He did not look at all contrite. "Shame on you," she said, dimpling.

"I could go to confession. Such a small thing couldn't cost more than a few Hail Marys," he replied.

Her smile faded. "You go to church, don't you?"

He shrugged uncomfortably. "I haven't been in a long

time. In fact, I fear I've been a poor Catholic since my parents died, although Sister Frances Rose did her best to instill a bit of piety in my benighted soul," he said, chuckling.

"You sound fond of her. Was she kind to you?" To Rebekah, nuns and penance, everything about the Catholic faith, was shrouded in mystery.

"Yes, she was. Not that she wasn't hell on a handcar with a hickory cane for your backside when you broke the rules. But she had the most wonderful sense of humor, and she bluffed better at draw poker than anyone I ever played against."

Rebekah's eyes widened and she drew herself up in shock. "You—you mean she *gambled* with her charges?"

"She played for pennies, and everyone's winnings had to be dropped in the poor box," he added in defense of the beloved old nun who had been good to him. "She's a remarkable woman. With only a handful of nuns, she keeps a roof over the heads of nearly a hundred orphaned children."

"That is a remarkable feat," Rebekah conceded.

"Not half as remarkable as her left jab. She was my first boxing coach."

Now Rebekah's jaw dropped. "B-boxing. A woman—a nun—taught you to box!"

"Aye, that she did. She had a brother who was a London prize ring champion in his day." He offered her a chunk of cheese and a slice of bread, then set to carving up the peaches.

Rebekah was poleaxed by the casualness with which he described such horrendous behavior. Perhaps her parents and Celia had been right. She was mad to be attracted to Rory Madigan. But she was. His religion was too alien and mysterious for her to discuss further, but on the issue of prizefighting she felt safe testing the water. "Boxing is a dangerous way to earn a living. My friend Celia Hunt told me you were working at Jenson's Livery Stable. Have you given up the fighting life?''

''For now,'' he replied obliquely. ''Now that January's gone back to England, I decided to take a steady job. I'm good with horses, and Mr. Jenson seems pleased with my work, although I doubt if breaking mustangs is any safer than the prize ring.''

''Breaking mustangs! Oh, Rory, you mustn't.'' She set her uneaten food on the small cloth he had spread and reached out to clasp his hand.

''I didn't mean to frighten you, Rebekah. I'm finished with the mustangs. Anyway, I don't ride them down like most bronc busters do. I use other methods. Next week I'm going to begin working with his racers. In time I'll get a cut of the gate when the ones I've trained win.'' He looked at her, trying to read her expression.

''I'm glad you're staying in Wellsville, although I'm not certain if my father will approve any sort of gambling—even training racehorses.''

''And your father's approval means a great deal to you, doesn't it?'' His voice was flat. He tried not to care.

''Yes, it does. My father is a wonderful man. Kind and gentle, a real scholar. He graduated third in his class from Yale Divinity School and gave up an offer from a prosperous congregation in Boston to come west and spread the Gospel. My mother always favored Leah, but Papa—well, he's always been there when I needed him. I don't want to disappoint him. But, oh, Rory, heaven help me—I don't want to lose you either! I'm a brazen hussy to say that. I shouldn't even be here, alone with you in this secluded place, and I certainly shouldn't have kissed you and done the other things we did in the garden.'' She could no longer meet his cool

73

blue eyes but fidgeted with her skirt, smoothing the wrinkled calico nervously as she spoke.

"You're no brazen hussy. Take that from a man who's known more than his share." He was pleased with the small flash of feminine jealousy that turned her green eyes cat-gold. He stroked her cheek. "You've never even had a real beau, have you, Rebekah? I know no man ever kissed you before me."

She sighed. "Everyone was always more interested in my sister. She's petite with a perfect figure and silver-gilt hair, and she's a proper lady who never misbehaves or does wild, impulsive things."

"And you? What about you?" Why should a beauty like his Rebekah play second fiddle to anyone?

She sighed. "I'm too tall and practically flat chested." She blushed beet red and hurried on, cataloging her faults. "My hair is brassy and straight. It's so heavy I have to use an iron to get it to curl this way, and as for my behavior—well, most men in Wellsville think I'm a hoyden."

"Most men in Wellsville are fools. You're just the right size, and your hair is glorious—rich as Comstock gold. Didn't anyone ever tell you gold is worth more than silver?" he asked with a teasing smile. "And then, there are your eyes with their thick lashes and changeable color. Did you know they turn from green to gold when you get excited?" He stared deeply into them as his mouth drew nearer to hers, but this time he kept a sensible distance between them, allowing only his lips to brush hers, whisper soft. After a few light, sweet kisses, he broke away, afraid of his own passion and her answering response, which flared to life so quickly.

"When I'm with you, I forget the whole rest of the world," she confessed breathlessly as he drew slowly away from her and offered her a slice from one of the peaches. It was sweet and juicy on her tongue, mixed now with the spicy taste of Rory's kiss.

"So do I. I've never met a girl like you before, Rebekah. I can't believe how lucky I am no man's snatched you away before I found you."

Amos Wells's face flashed into her mind, ruining the tranquillity of the very private moment between them. "You were right that I've never had a beau before, but . . ."

"But what?" he prompted, seeing the shadowed look that had come into her eyes. "Is there someone else, Rebekah? Someone your father approves?" Dread squeezed his heart.

"Yes." A shudder rippled delicately across her shoulders. "Amos Wells has asked permission to court me, and my father thinks he'd make a fine husband."

"Wells—as in the Wellsville Wells? That old man! How could your father want you to marry him?"

"He's only forty-three. Everyone says that's a man's prime. And he's rich and socially prominent. He'll be Nevada's next United States Senator." She sounded just like Celia, but she had to defend her father. "And most important of all, I'm afraid, he's a member of the First Presbyterian Church."

"But in spite of his being such a paragon, you don't want him to come calling, do you?" He studied her, confused by her ambivalence.

"No, but you made it sound as if my father was selling me to some beastly old man. Celia Hunt—you remember, she was with me the day you fought Cy Wharton?"

"The plump little redhead," he supplied, impatient for her to explain.

"Well, she's always been smitten with Mr. Wells. When I told her about his interest in me this morning, I was afraid I'd lose my best friend, but she's loyal and understanding.

In fact, we've concocted a scheme to give her a chance to catch Mr. Wells's eye at the box lunch social next week.''

She quickly outlined the deception that she and Celia had devised. "So you see, Mr. Wells will bid on her basket with the pale pink ribbons because I've told him I'll be using pink. Mine will have rose-red ribbon, and after all the sales are made, he'll have to do the gentlemanly thing and eat with Celia.''

"And who will get your basket?"

She shrugged. "It really doesn't matter, just so Mr. Wells and Celia end up together.''

"So, you're really willing to pass up all his money and political aspirations? You could be a senator's wife and travel back east. Live in mansions and wear furs and jewels. I thought all women wanted those things.''

She flushed beneath his scrutiny, tracing the pattern of the frayed checkered cloth that lay between them. "I'd be lying if I said I wasn't a covetous person. In fact, I suppose if I was a Catholic, I'd have to say a lot of Hail Marys to make up for my sins. I've always been envious of Celia's pretty clothes and the places her family has taken her.''

"But you wouldn't marry just to get them?" he prompted. When she shook her head, his chest, which had been tight with apprehension, eased and he took a deep, cleansing breath. They had problems to overcome, but perhaps money would not be one of them. He leaned over to raise her chin for another kiss, but just then a loud splash interrupted. His pole was bent at a precarious angle, and the cork had vanished beneath the surface. As the rocks holding the pole in place rolled away beneath the pressure, the cane started to slide into the water.

Rory jumped up and grabbed for it, but missed as it glided just out of his grasp. With an oath, he splashed into the water and promptly slipped on the mossy, slick rocks beneath the shallows. As he tumbled face forward into the river, he seized the pole and yanked hard on it while rolling to sit upright, waist deep in the water.

Droplets splashed everywhere, spraying onto Rebekah, who had also jumped up and run to the edge of the river. She squealed with excitement, then tried to suppress her giggles as he rolled around in the water, soaking his clothes to his skin. A long shock of midnight hair lay plastered to his forehead. He gave her a baleful glare, then turned his attention to the fish.

"Laugh at me, will you," he said with mock ferocity as he turned the pole to the shore, dragging a fat, thrashing trout across the top of the water. He flipped the hooked fish neatly at her feet, then rose, pole still in hand, and waded back onto the bank, where he made a courtly bow, using the pole as if it were an overlong gold-handled walking stick.

Rebekah gave a startled squawk and jumped back, then burst into gales of laughter. "You should've seen your face when you tripped on those rocks and fell in headfirst."

"You should've seen yours when that trout tried to jump up your petticoats . . . not that it's such a bad idea. . . . " he said in a husky voice as he threw the pole and his catch aside and reached out for her. All laughter died between them.

She watched the incredible grace with which he moved, unable to turn away or protest—unable even to tear her eyes from his compelling male beauty. His simple white cotton shirt had become almost translucent, revealing the curling mat of black hair on his chest. Every lean, sinuous muscle in his body stood in bold relief beneath the clothes that clung to him so sensuously. The age-softened denims hugged his legs as he stepped up to her and reached out to take her in his arms.

His hands were cold from his dunking and she gasped in surprise, but as soon as he pulled her against him, the heat of his hard body enveloped her. The pounding of his heart was a dull thud, pillowed against the softness of her breasts as he bent his head to kiss her. Her hands came up, soft palms running along the wet, slick contours of his biceps, then curving around his broad shoulders. His mouth was like his hands, cool at first touch, then meltingly hot as he made contact with her flesh.

A low, feral groan tore from him as he felt her respond, opening her mouth for the invasion of his tongue. He held her tight, molding her soft curves against his wet body until he had soaked her, put his mark on her. His lips moved from the sweetness of her mouth across her cheeks, brushing her eyelids, nose, and brows, then moved lower to ravish her slender throat, unfastening the tiny cloth-covered buttons until he could taste the silky skin stretched across her collarbone. His hand cupped her breast, lifting it in his hand as his mouth descended toward it. He was lost, all his good resolutions fled.

Rebekah felt his heat, gloried in the impossible breathless pleasure of his hands and mouth gliding over her body, unbuttoning her dress and taking liberties with her breasts that no other man would ever have dared. Then she felt his hand slide down over the curve of her hip to stroke her buttock and lift her lower body against his. The familiar ache of desire that she had experienced last week in her muddy garden swept over her again, and this time they were in a secluded place, far away from the prying eyes of the town.

''Rebekah,'' he murmured against her hair as he pulled it free of its pins. Long, heavy waves of dark gold cascaded down her back and he wrapped his fingers in it, tugging on her scalp until her head fell backward, exposing her throat and breasts to his voracious kisses.

She was ready to give in, to sink down to the soft, grassy riverbank and let him do with her as he wished. Then the trout, lying forgotten on the ground, made one last desperate series of flops, arching its tale and flipping around their feet. Rory's words flashed into her mind. *That fish tried to jump up your petticoats . . . not that it's such a bad idea.* She could feel his hand lifting up her thin cotton skirt, gliding along her thigh. She pushed against his chest and jumped back, nearly tripping over the floundering fish. One hand covered her mouth, and the other tried to pull together the prim little buttons of her dress. Her eyes had turned so dark green that they looked almost black, like deep pools of shame. The spell was broken.

To allay her fears, he knelt and seized the fish, then freed it from the hook and tossed it back in the river. "I've let it go. And I'm letting you go, too . . . for now. Only for now, Rebekah."

His voice was low and raspy, as intense as his dark blue eyes which bored into her. Rebekah turned and fled. Rory made no attempt to stop her as she scrambled up on her old mare and kicked the poor beast into a trot.

Celia and Rebekah stood among the nervously chattering young girls and a few slightly older women, all clustered together beneath the tall oak trees in the city park. The box lunches prepared by the single females of First Presbyterian and its neighboring church, Wellsville Methodist, were spread before them on a long trestle table situated on the bandstand. The picnic baskets had each been carefully trimmed with ribbons, flowers, and other decorations, indicating to the eager males in the crowd whose prize—and whose company—they were "purchasing."

"Do you think Amos will be angry?" Celia whispered nervously to Rebekah as they scanned the crowd.

"I don't think so. After all, we'll just say it was a mis-understanding—pink and rose ribbons could be mistaken." Rebekah really was not certain if Amos Wells would care, but for Celia's sake, she hoped not. She was still mystified as to why a rich, older man like him had decided to court her in the first place. He hardly knew her. Prior to the Sunday dinner two weeks earlier, he had scarcely spoken more than a few dozen words to her in her life.

But Rebekah was absolutely certain her parents would be angry. In fact, Mama would no doubt be in a towering rage because she had missed the opportunity to flaunt such a pres-tigious suitor in front of the whole community. Papa would be disappointed, too, and that bothered her a good deal more. Thank heavens Mama had come down with one of her head-aches just before the picnic and Papa had decided to stay home with her. The Hunts had picked her up in their fancy new German landau with its top rolled down to accommodate the warm summer weather. She was relieved that Leah and Henry had decided not to attend the social.

"Deacon Wright is about to start the bidding, and I don't see Amos," Celia said, scanning the crowd.

"Oh, he's here. I saw him earlier." *When I assured him that my basket had the pink ribbons,* she thought with a tremor. Well, at least this would probably end his suit.

"Who do you think will bid on your basket, Rebekah?"

Celia's friend shrugged. "I haven't told anyone which one is mine." *Except Rory, and he won't be here.*

"Wouldn't it be awful not to have anyone buy it!" Celia's eyes grew huge as the thought suddenly struck her.

Rebekah laughed. "Celia, in a state where men outnumber women ten to one, do you honestly think there's a chance of that? Look around you.'' She gestured with one hand, then quickly brought it to her throat in shocked dismay.

There, tall as a church steeple, was Rory Madigan, standing in the back of the motley crowd, leaning with casual arrogance against the trunk of a cottonwood. He was dressed in a simple white shirt, black breeches, and a black leather vest.

''Ooh, I don't believe his nerve! A papist like him coming to our church gathering,'' Celia hissed. ''And look at the way he's dressed. Why that shirt collar is open so low, you can actually see his chest.''

She looked at Rebekah with enormous eyes, but Rebekah was staring at Rory in such horror-struck fascination that the words barely registered. She had seen a good deal more of that hairy chest—and felt it! Not to mention even more private parts of his anatomy. Wouldn't Celia be shocked? Wouldn't everybody?

He was heart-stoppingly handsome. A flat-crowned black hat trimmed with silver conchos was shoved carelessly on the back of his head, and that disturbing lock of inky hair hung across his forehead as he regarded her with heavy-lidded eyes.

Among the awkward cowhands in plaid shirts and denims and the pale town clerks sweating in woolen suits, Rory looked dark and dangerous. He was an outsider whose very bearing indicated that he did not give a damn what anyone thought. Not only was his shirt unbuttoned indecently low, but his sleeves were rolled up, revealing those long, sinewy forearms with fine black hair growing on them.

He grinned at her and winked. *I'm letting you go . . . only for now, Rebekah.*

He wouldn't dare. Would he? With a sinking heart, Rebekah realized that he would, and short of betraying Celia

81

and indicating to Amos that the rose-ribboned basket was hers, she could do nothing but wait and pray that someone else outbid him. How much money could a stablehand have, after all?

Rory had enough, since he had held on to the last of his prize money when he returned to Wellsville and began working for Jenson. Two double eagles jingled in his vest pocket, and he was willing to spend every cent, if need be, on that rose-trimmed basket.

He had stayed away from Rebekah all week, working from dawn to dark with Jenson's racers at the track outside Reno, deliberately driving himself to exhaustion. Every night he had fallen onto his narrow cot, too tired to lie awake and think of her. Yesterday, when Jenson had paid him his wages, he had gone into the thriving city of Reno and purchased the fancy new clothes, spending more on the silver concho hat and vest than the rest, but deciding he preferred the way they made him look, like a Westerner, yet different from the cowboys in denims or the townies, sweating in their hot, silly suits.

She's wondering what I'm going to do. Or maybe she isn't. With Rebekah, it was always difficult to tell. She was strikingly beautiful and bright, yet thought herself plain and lacking in the female accomplishments men admired. She had to believe he wanted her. His passion had frightened her, yes, but it had also ignited an answering desire in her. Perhaps that side of her own nature frightened her most of all.

The first few baskets were held up, their contents peeked at and extolled, then bid upon, usually in prearranged order, each courting man having an understanding with his fellows not to encroach when he bid. In a few instances, two or three swains smitten with the same girl would bid up her lunch as high as the princely sum of a half eagle. Although the women were to remain around the bandstand until the auction was complete, many edged away into the shelter of the trees with their suitors once their transactions were satisfactorily completed.

Celia's pink-ribboned basket came up before Rebekah's. Old Will Wright, the auctioneer, started the bidding at the usual half dollar. Rebekah and Celia stood, primly chatting with Maude Priddy, neither giving an indication that they knew whose it was. Amos Wells waited until a yellow-haired cowboy and a gangly young drummer had bid it up to a quarter eagle. He raised his hand and said in the stentorian voice of a practiced politician, "A gold eagle."

A surprised murmuring spread through the crowd; then a buzzing began to hum around the park. No one had expected Amos Wells to participate in the bidding, certainly not to pay the unheard-of sum of ten dollars for some young lady's basket! The older men spat lobs of tobacco and jested about Wells needing a wife to take with him to Washington, and the married women's eyes glittered as they gossiped among themselves about who the lucky girl might be.

"I shall simply die if he's angry, Rebekah." Celia's normally pink complexion had grown pale as she watched the crowd's reaction.

"Would you rather switch baskets and eat with Rory Madigan?" Rebekah was not certain if she made the offer because she feared offending Amos or if spending the afternoon with Rory frightened her more.

"You actually think he'll dare participate in the bidding?"

"I know he will. He wouldn't be here unless he had a reason."

The deacon then held up the rose-ribboned basket and said, "Opening bid is half a dollar, just like the rest, fellers. If'n it goes for half as much as the last one, both churches

83

will have pretty near enough to build on extra steeples!''

Several bids had brought the price up to a quarter eagle when Rory Madigan's clear, deep voice cut through the murmuring of the crowd. ''A double eagle.'' He held up the twenty dollar gold piece, letting the sunlight glint off its brilliantly polished surface.

No one bid against him.

Chapter Five

If a mildly surprised murmur spread through the crowd when Amos Wells made his bid, it was nothing like the reaction Madigan's bid elicited. A stunned silence followed him as he made his way forward to deposit the money with Deacon Wright. The crowd parted in gape-jawed amazement, staring at the stranger.

"Who *is* he?" a clerk from Elkhorn's General Store asked.

"Thet there's thet boxer feller whut beat tarnation out of Cy Wharton—some mickey name or other," a Flying W wrangler replied.

"The Kilkenny Kid. Yeah, I bet on him," another younger cowhand said, then turned beet-red when he realized his mistake, surrounded as he was by Wellsville citizenry who did not take kindly to outsiders, least of all foreigners, coming in to defeat their local sons.

Rory ignored them as he picked up Rebekah's basket. His eyes swept the tittering, whispering crowd of young women until he found her, standing frozen beside an equally pale and uncertain-looking Celia Hunt. He raised the basket in a mock salute to her, then sauntered off as the next box lunch was bid upon.

Ernestine Carpenter, thin and hatchet-faced, the worst gossip in the county, elbowed her way up to Rebekah and whispered in a hiss that could be heard across Lake Tahoe, "He's that Irish fellow who came to town as a box fighter. Works for Beau Jenson now. Yer pa sure won't like him courtin' you."

"If he's Irish, then he must be Catholic," Maude Priddy squeaked, fanning herself with a soggy lace handkerchief.

"Rebekah didn't know he was going to bid on her basket," Celia said in her friend's defense. At least that much was true, strictly speaking. Rebekah stood silent, letting the other girls exchange gossip.

"How'd he know it was hers, Celia? Yer pa carried both yer baskets up to the bandstand," Ernestine said, as logically tenacious as a Philadelphia lawyer.

Celia ignored Ernestine's question. The box lunches were all sold now, and the men holding their trophies approached the women, waiting for them to come forward. Amos Wells was less reticent than the rest, bearing down on Rebekah. Celia felt Rebekah's hands against her back, shoving her forward with a whispered, "Go get him, and don't forget to smile."

"Why, Mr. Wells, you surprised me. I'm really flattered that you paid so much for my basket, but it is for Christian charity, isn't it?" Celia was babbling, something her mother told her she did altogether too often.

Amos looked at Celia's plump, possessive hand on the

pink-ribboned basket he held, then moved his gaze to her companion. Rebekah imagined she saw a flash of furious anger in his cool, slate-colored eyes before he looked away. She shivered, then decided it was just fanciful imaginings because of her own guilty conscience when Amos tipped his hat gallantly to Celia and offered his arm.

Rory took his time approaching Rebekah in the crowd, knowing the townsfolk were dying to know whom he would claim—and if he had known in advance. He waited, giving Rebekah the chance to save face by coming forward to claim her basket as Celia had done. She did so, walking slowly and steadily toward him, looking neither left nor right, ignoring the scandalized whispers surrounding them. She reached for the basket, saying in her husky contralto, "I believe you've overpaid for some fried chicken and devil's food cake."

"Devil's food from the preacher's daughter?" he asked, removing his hat with a flourish.

She fought the urge to kick him in the shins. Bad enough to plan the switch with Celia, but to have Rory show up and purchase her basket, not to mention paying a king's ransom for it! Why had she told him about the scheme? *Maybe you wanted him to come*, an inner voice taunted.

He offered his arm, daring her to refuse it. She gritted her teeth and took it. They walked through the crowd of curious onlookers, all the girls paired off now with the men fortunate enough to have snared a picnic partner. The rest stood around, some wistful, other jealous, all no doubt dying to know what was going on between Rebekah Sinclair and the stranger.

As soon as they were out of earshot of the nearest people, Rebekah whispered, "Everyone will be talking about that outrageous bid. A gold double eagle! What did you do, rob a bank?''

He chuckled. ''It was part of my last fight purse. Honestly won—and it was given for Christian charity, as your friend told Wells. Somehow I don't think it consoled him much,'' he added dryly, guiding her toward a copse of pines at the eastern corner of the large park, well away from the crowd.

''We shouldn't go off alone. People will talk,'' she said, tugging at his arm to slow down his long-legged stride.

Rory held her hand firmly on his arm and continued on his course. ''Don't be silly. All the young couples have gone off to feast in private. Except for Wells and your friend. Seems he's more interested in talking to the voters than he is in talking with his companion.''

Rebekah felt a flash of pity for Celia. ''Surely Amos wouldn't be cruel to her, would he? I really know so little about him. . . .'' Her voice trailed off as she turned and glanced back at the picnic tables where the town's leading citizens were congregated with Amos and Celia in their midst.

''Yet your da wants you to marry him. I bet Amos Wells will do whatever he has to, to get what he wants, and the devil take those who get in his way.''

Recalling that flash of icy fury she thought she had seen in his eyes, Rebekah was afraid Rory might be right about the older man. ''Surely not. My father is a fine judge of character.''

''And Wells is a pillar of his church. Probably a big contributor, too.'' The minute he said it, Rory felt her pull away with a fierce yank of her wrist. She spun, intending to run off, but he caught her hand and pulled her into the concealment of the trees, drawing her resistingly into his arms. ''I'm sorry. That was unkind and ill-spoken of me. I don't even know your father. I'm just jealous because he favors Wells. And I want you for myself.'' He stared down at her, willing her eyes to meet his.

Rebekah could feel his hard, strong body pressed against her softness, his heart pounding fiercely in rhythm with her own. She was compelled to raise her eyes to his, and was lost when she did so. She shook her head, trying to break the spell. ''This is all wrong. We can't—I can't—my parents are going to be furious when they hear what you've done. They won't let you call on me, Rory.''

''Because I'm lowly Irish scum?'' His voice was soft, but his eyes glittered cold, dark blue, just as they had when she first saw him fighting Cy Wharton.

''Don't make it sound so awful. It isn't that you're Irish.'' That was not strictly true. Her mother detested all foreigners, and then there was her father's intense antipathy for the Irish. ''It's your religion.'' She seized on the one thing he should understand. ''You're a Catholic and I'm a Presbyterian, a minister's daughter. Surely you see I couldn't desert my faith and my family.''

''And you think I'd ask that of you?'' Her head flew up and her eyes widened in shocked disbelief as he grazed her cheek with his knuckles. She looked so startled and confused. He bent down and placed a light kiss on her nose. Then he placed the picnic basket down on the grass, sat down, and patted the space beside himself.

Warily she took a seat, arranging her skirts primly, too nervous to meet his gaze. ''You—you mean you wouldn't ask me to—'' *He hasn't proposed to you yet, you ninny!* She had about said, *You mean you wouldn't ask me to be married in your church?*

''I've always been an indifferent Catholic at best—at least since I lost my family.'' He shrugged. ''I don't know, I guess it's always been a part of my identity—a tie to the old country and to my mother and father, my dead brothers. But since I left the orphanage and came west, I haven't seen the inside of a church. If it means that much to you . . . we could talk about it.'' He placed his hand over hers as she fidgeted with the ruffled edge of her blue gingham skirts. ''There's more, isn't there? It's the money. Your family wants a rich man for you, like Wells.''

She looked up then, unable to bear the hurt in his voice. He had been willing to meet her more than halfway. ''If only I wasn't so selfish and insecure,'' she said passionately. ''My family has always been poor, Rory. My mother and father only want something better for Leah and me. We always had to wear cast-off clothes and help Mama cook and clean, while all the other ladies and their daughters had fine new fashions and servants to do the work for them.''

''Then why don't you marry Amos Wells and be done with it? He could give you everything you want,'' he said angrily.

''I could never love Amos Wells.'' Her voice broke, and she bit down on her knuckle until she drew blood, trying to hold the confused, miserable tears at bay.

''Could you love me if I was rich, Rebekah? I could quit my job with Jenson and go back to fighting.''

His voice was detached, flat. Was he mocking her or was he so angry that he dared not let it show? She had hurt him, and suddenly Rebekah realized that hurting Rory Madigan upset her more than hurting anyone else in the world. ''No! I don't ever want you to box again! You could be injured, even killed!'' She threw her arms around his neck and held on to him, burying her head against his shoulder.

''I could make a lot of money boxing. I have before, only I had no reason to hang on to it then.'' He stroked her silken hair and pulled her onto his lap. "After a few big fights, I'd have enough of a stake to come back and ask your da to let me court you properly."

"No, Rory, please." She sat back with her palms pressed against his chest. "I don't want to lose you. Those awful men who tried to drug you—there are others like that, aren't there? You might never come back."

"But if I'm just a stablehand, your family will never accept me. Boxing is all I know—that and horses."

"Surely in time Mr. Jenson will give you a better job. You said he was letting you work with his racers." Her voice was hopeful now.

He scoffed. "Time is right. It could take years—and I'd still be Irish, a foreigner with no social standing, no family."

"I'll wait for you, Rory. I'll wait forever before I marry anyone but—" She stopped abruptly. Her cheeks crimsoned, and her hand flew to her lips in embarrassment.

A crooked grin slashed across his face and he winked at her, his earlier somber mood broken. She loved him, and she would have no other. It would all work out. "You'll not marry anyone but me." He thumped his chest in boyish arrogance and pulled her into his arms. "And I'll not marry anyone but you—somehow I'll figure a way for us to wed, Rebekah."

"But no boxing. Please promise me, Rory?" Her eyes were a fathomless dark green now.

He sighed in capitulation. "No boxing. And now, if you don't want me to ruin what's left of your reputation, we'd best eat this lunch before another hunger wins out, and my baser nature takes over."

Rebekah scrambled off his lap, realizing that anyone could stroll by and catch them in such a compromising position. Opening the basket, she took out a cloth and spread it on the grass, then lifted out a covered dish filled with fried chicken, a jar of her mother's special pickles, and a bowl of Boston baked beans.

He sniffed appreciatively. "Smells divine. Where is that devil's food cake?"

"It's in the basket," she said, nervously thrusting a heavy crockery jug at him. "Please pop the cork. It's lemonade. I hope it's still cool enough to taste good."

He took a bite of the chicken, then tugged the cork out of the jug. "Everything is wonderful. You are some cook! Or did your Mama do all the work—after all, she thought it was for Amos Wells, didn't she?"

"I made everything myself except the pickles, and I didn't do it for Amos Wells—or for you either, so wipe that cocky look off your face, Mr. Madigan," she said like a schoolmarm scolding a particularly devilish and endearing pupil.

"Yes, ma'am," he replied as he attacked a crisp dill pickle with his white teeth.

Rebekah's appetite was not nearly so voracious as Rory's, but she watched him with a warm glow of purely feminine pleasure as he enjoyed her cooking. Yet no matter how much she delighted in being with him, she knew there would be grave repercussions for their time together. Forcing the unpleasant thought aside, she decided to enjoy the afternoon and dug into her chicken and the sweet, savory beans. "Tell me about Ireland, Rory. I've never been farther east than Kansas." She made a face. "That's where I was born. My parents moved to Nevada when Leah and I were little girls."

"And we all know how long ago that was," he said with a chuckle. A faraway look came into his eyes when he leaned back against a tree trunk and laced his fingers behind his neck. "Ireland . . . strange, but I haven't thought of it in years. Green as your eyes, it was, and the air heavy with mist every morning. Nothing like this dusty, wild country.''

"You said your father was head groom to some noble-man.'' Her expression held a hint of awe, for she had never even seen a person with a title, much less known one.

"The Earl of Waltham. He wasn't a bad sort—for a Sas-senach. He let my brothers and me attend classes when his son was tutored. Waltham Hall was a grand place. Built in the sixteenth century, a great drafty fortress it was—more castle than country estate.''

"Do you know that when you speak of your childhood, your accent returns?'' Rebekah asked softly, guessing how lonely and frightened he must have been.

"Aye. When I lose my temper it comes back, too. And I've a terrible swift temper, as you might have guessed,'' he said with a heart-stopping smile.

"So I've noticed. It's a proud and prickly man you are, Rory Madigan,'' she said, mimicking his brogue with a saucy tilt of her head. Then her expression grew serious as she reached out and touched his hand tentatively. "I can't imag-ine what it's like to lose everything—everyone you love. You're braver than anyone I've ever met, Rory.''

"No, I'm not brave, Rebekah. I'm just a survivor, that's all. I've spent years wandering from place to place, living from hand to mouth. I've made a lot of money boxing. Then lost it just as fast gambling, drinking . . . and other things.'' He held her hand, feeling the delicate pulse inside her wrist.

She snatched it away angrily. "Those *other things* wouldn't happen to be women, would they?''

He sat up with a low chuckle and reached for her, pulling her into his arms. "I'm a reformed rake, Rebekah. You have my word on it. No more drifting, no more carousing.''

"And no more women?'' she asked, pouting, yet waiting as his lips drew nearer.

93

"Only one woman," he murmured against her mouth as he drew her into a kiss.

The Hunts brought Rebekah home after she and Rory said a very formal, proper good-day at the park. A decidedly cool Amos Wells had done the same with Celia. Neither girl had been able to confide in the other in the Hunts' presence, but Rebekah knew all had not gone well between her friend and Amos in spite of Agnes Hunt's excited chattering about what an honor it was that her daughter had been lucky enough to attract Mr. Wells.

Rebekah had no more than stepped inside their door before her mother launched her attack, seizing her with red, meaty fingers and dragging her into the parlor for the dressing down of her life. "How could you do such a thing? What were you thinking of, to go off with that—that Irish trash! Rachel Dalton just left. She felt it her Christian duty to tell me what a scandal you created at the park." Dorcas Sinclair was so angry that tears of sheer fury formed beneath her puffy eyelids. She blinked them back as she glared at her younger daughter. If only Ephraim were home, but he had been summoned to the Grants' place, where the elderly grandfather had just passed on.

"Mr. Madigan outbid everyone for my basket. What was I to do? Surely having lunch with him isn't anything I should be ashamed of—and he did contribute twenty dollars to charity for the privilege."

"Twenty dollars indeed—the last money that profligate will see for the year or I miss my guess. Is that the price you place on your reputation?"

"My reputation isn't harmed—"

"Don't you interrupt me, young lady," Dorcas snapped irrationally, ignoring the fact she had asked the question.

"And what about Amos Wells? He expected to get your basket and ended up with Celia Hunt. I know the two of you cooked up the scheme. Don't compound your sins by denying it."

"She wants Mr. Wells's attention. I don't," Rebekah said baldly, knowing it was utter folly, but not caring.

"You selfish, stupid girl," Dorcas hissed. "You're not just throwing away your own chance for a brilliant marriage, but ruining the rest of the family as well." When all else failed, guilt might work to bring a headstrong child like Rebekah to her senses.

"I know Papa will be disappointed, but I've already told him I don't favor Mr. Wells. He said I didn't have to marry any man I didn't love."

"Love!" Dorcas threw up her hands. "Come down from those clouds and face the real world, Rebekah. Amos Wells is not only the largest contributor to your father's church, but Henry Snead's employer as well."

Rebekah blanched as Dorcas's words sank in. "He couldn't be so vindictive as to dismiss Henry if I refuse his suit." Her voice carried no conviction as she recalled that flash of ruthless fury he had quickly masked when he discovered the deception over the lunches. She had not mistaken it. "How could you ask me to marry a man like that?"

"Amos Wells is a fine, upstanding member of the community, but a man doesn't become rich and powerful without using that power. He can make or break any person in Wellsville. Henry could have a brilliant future with him. So could your father's church—and so could you, if that scoundrel hadn't come along and lured you down the path to hell and damnation!"

"Rory Madigan isn't like that! His intentions are just as honorable as Amos Wells's."

Dorcas pounced. "So, he is trying to court you, isn't he?" Her hands rested on her hips, balled into angry fists.

Rebekah's chin came up. What was the use in denying it? "Yes, but he said I didn't have to convert for him. He—"

"He's deceiving you, child," Ephraim's voice interrupted as he stepped dolefully into the parlor, his hat in hand and a somber expression on his face. "I know his kind. There are things I could tell you. . . . " He shook his head and sat down wearily on the sun-faded easy chair by the window.

A look of panic flashed in Dorcas's eyes and she wrung her hands. "Ephraim, don't—" Her voice choked and she turned and walked quickly from the room.

Shaken and confused, Rebekah looked from her mother's retreating figure back to her father. "I—I don't understand, Papa. You've never met Rory. I know he was a boxer, but he has a steady job now and—"

"You're correct, Rebekah. You do not understand. He's Irish, and he's Catholic."

"I do understand about the religion. I won't convert, Papa, but why do you hate the Irish if not for that?"

"He tells you now that you don't have to turn from your faith, but when the time comes to marry—then he'll lure you into his church. That's their way. I grew up in a poor section of Boston adjoining an Irish neighborhood. Believe me, I know them for what they are—drunken brawlers and whore-mongers."

"I've made a lot of money . . . lost it just as fast . . . gambling, drinking . . . other things." Rebekah could hear Rory's rueful confession of sins. Did he well and truly consider them with enough regret to mend his ways? Could she trust him? Trust her heart? Standing there, looking into her father's sad eyes, she was seized by cruel doubts.

"This has all happened so fast. Meeting Rory—and Amos

96

Wells coming courting," she temporized.

"That was a childish trick you played with the box lunches, Rebekah. Several folks stopped me on the way home to tell me what happened at the park. You and Celia Hunt planned it, didn't you?"

"Yes, Papa—but only to give Celia a chance with Mr. Wells. I didn't know Rory would bid on my basket, honestly."

"If Amos wanted to pay court to Celia, he would do so. He chose you instead, and you led him to believe you would share that picnic with him."

She sank onto the chair across from her father, realizing how badly the whole scheme had turned out. "I guess I owe Mr. Wells an apology, don't I, Papa?" she said in a small voice, still cringing at the thought of Amos Wells's veiled anger. Would he retaliate against her family because of her childish actions?

"I'm certain he'd be happy to hear it, Rebekah. Give him a chance. Don't let this young drifter turn your head with empty promises. He'll only break your heart."

What might Amos Wells do, if provoked? Her father saw only good in the man. He would dismiss his wife's threats about reprisals against poor Henry, not to mention Wells withdrawing his support of the church. But Rebekah could not do that. She must tread very carefully around Amos and Rory for the immediate future, at least until the gossip died down. After that, she had no idea at all what she would do.

"I'll write a note to Mr. Wells and ask if he would be so kind as to pay a call this week."

"There's my good girl," Reverend Sinclair said, patting her hand fondly.

* * *

Rebekah sat on her bed with the crumpled note clutched tightly in one hand as she stared, unseeing, at the eastern sky outside her window. She hugged her sheer batiste nightgown against her legs as she hunched over with her knees bent, watching the first gray light touch the dark horizon. Sunrise in Nevada was sudden and breathtaking as the sky changed from the faint glow of silver to the dazzling brilliance of gold.

Smoothing out the note from Amos Wells, Rebekah read it for what seemed the hundredth time. Since Henry had delivered it to her last night, she had practically memorized the lines.

My Dear Rebekah,

I shall call upon you tomorrow evening precisely at seven. We shall put behind us the unpleasant mistake at the park this afternoon and plan for our future happiness. Remember, my dear, happiness and security are purchased only with prudence. Make no mistake, to this fact both your beloved father and brother-in-law will attest.

Until Monday evening,
Amos

The handwriting was a series of bold slashes across the expensive, water-marked stationary. She stared at it numbly, reading the stark ruthlessness in every word, every pen stroke. "Your beloved father and brother-in-law will attest," she whispered to herself with a surge of rising hysteria. Poor Henry Snead was haggard and silent when he handed her the note, telling her parents that Leah was expecting him home for dinner and he had no time to visit. She had read the message, then quietly told her father that Mr. Wells would be calling the next evening.

Rebekah was unable to bear his concern and burden him by revealing the veiled threats Wells had made. Her mother had already said Amos might take reprisals against Henry. She could only imagine what punishment he would mete out for her "unpleasant mistake." After a night spent tossing and turning, Rebekah had risen nearly an hour ago and watched for the dawn like a felon waits for the last walk to the gallows.

"Damn him! He can't do this to me! To my family." She threw the note into the litter basket beside her vanity. But no sooner had she uttered the words, than she realized that Amos Wells could do anything he pleased—at least as far as withdrawing his support from First Presbyterian or dismissing Henry Snead from his post at the Flying W. Rebekah bounded off the bed and began to splash her face with cold water. By the time she had performed a simple morning toilette and dressed in a white shirtwaist and brown cotton riding skirt, the sky was growing light.

She would just have to eat crow and let the vain, mean-spirited silver baron lord it over her. The trick with the box lunches was a childish, irresponsible means of discouraging his suit and obviously did not help Celia's cause either. Embarrassing Wells the way she had had probably lessened Celia's chances, not to mention creating a whole new series of problems to be resolved. No, if she were to extricate her family and herself from Amos's clutches, she would have to do it very carefully, and the last thing she needed was for Rory to show up at another critical point and further exacerbate the situation before she had convinced Wells to change his own mind about courting her.

She needed to talk to Rory—to plead with him if need

be—so that he would stay away until Amos had withdrawn his suit and her family was safe. If there was one thing the stubborn and impetuous Irishman understood, it was family loyalty.

Yesterday, before they parted at the picnic, he had asked her to meet him this morning at the river to discuss his plan to call on her father. There had been no time to dissuade him before Celia and several of the other young women from church had come looking for her, but today she had to make him see reason. They had agreed on eight o'clock, but she could not wait several more hours. Maybe he would arrive earlier.

She prayed he would as she crept through the dim light filtering into the house and slipped silently out the back door. Monday was the nearest thing to a day off her father ever allowed himself in his busy schedule. To accommodate him, her mother did not rise early to wash as most of the local women did, but waited until Tuesday. Rebekah would not be missed until after nine. *Please be early, Rory.*

As she rode her old mare Bettie May to the river, Rebekah began to have second thoughts. Maybe this was a mistake. *Am I using my fear of Amos as an excuse to see Rory again?* Just thinking about him set her pulse to racing. Blood thrummed through her veins, and her heart beat erratically when she replayed the time she had spent alone with Rory Madigan. What spell had he woven over her? She had only seen him a handful of times, yet she shared his laughter and his pain and his passion in such full measure that it robbed her of all reason.

"I'm insane to be here," she whispered to the old horse as she dismounted and tied the reins to a sapling. She walked through the soft dust, rounding the thick trunk of a willow tree and peering through its dense, low-hanging branches.

Even before she saw him, she heard the sounds of splashing accompanied by melodious whistling. She almost called out as she reached to shove away the leafy barrier, but then her eyes fastened on the shallows. Her heart skipped a beat. Her tongue stuck to the roof of her mouth. She struggled to swallow and forgot how.

Rory Madigan was wading into the water for a morning swim—stark naked! She had already seen those broad shoulders and powerful arms bared, but never the rest of him. Breath failed her as her eyes traveled lower, past the tan line at his trim waist, to fasten on the lighter flesh below, untouched by the blazing Nevada sun. Hard, narrow buttocks moved rhythmically as his long, sinewy legs carried him deeper until he suddenly dove forward into the current and vanished cleanly beneath the surface.

Frantically she watched the water. Good heavens, had he drowned? Then his head broke the surface. He shook his shaggy hair from his eyes as he began to slice cleanly across the river, heading toward a large pink rock jutting out into the current about twenty feet away from her. He climbed up onto the rock and sat, with his body turned in profile, watching the sun rise over the southeast side of the river. She was close enough to see the early morning light catch the glimmer of water beading in iridescent droplets on the smooth contours of his hard muscles. He raised one hand and combed his fingers through his hair, shaking it back from his forehead.

Rory leaned lazily backward against the rock and tilted his head toward the sunrise, as if to nap. When he spoke, she almost fell to her knees in panic. "Are you going to hide and peek all morning or come join me? It's warm here, and the water's cool and refreshing before the heat of the day."

Rebekah clutched the willow branches like a lifeline. How

did he know anyone was there? Surely he could not know it was her.

"I know it's you, Rebekah. I can see Bessie May tied up above the rise."

Infuriating man! "I came to talk with you, Rory, not to frolic like Aphrodite in the waves," she shouted breathlessly.

"But first you decided to look your fill." There was laughter in his voice.

A hot denial sprang to her lips, but the truth of his accusation made her choke on it. She swallowed and took a deep breath, knowing her face was glowing as red as a beacon. That was probably what he recognized, not her fat old mare. "I'm going to turn around, close my eyes, and wait until you're decent. Then we need to talk."

"You'll have the devil's own wait, darlin'. I've never been decent. Sister Frances Rose, not to mention my own mother, always assured me of it."

She spun around to wait as he dove into the water and swam back to shore. When she heard the rustling noise of denims scraping over wet skin, all sorts of erotic images flashed into her mind, but she rubbed her temples, attempting to subdue them and concentrate on the problem at hand. Then his hand touched her shoulder lightly and she gasped in surprise. He turned her around and pulled her into his arms. His flesh was still wet, yet surprisingly warm to the touch as her fingers pressed into the black mat of hair on his chest. Gleaming beads of water glistened and dripped from his hair and ran down his shoulders and arms. His scent was clean and tangy as he drew her closer, staring into her face, his lashes spiky with water, his eyes intense.

"Now, what's upset you so much that you're over an hour early for our meeting?"

Her mind went blank. She stammered as he lowered his

mouth to brush against her brow and temples, then nuzzle lower, past her jaw to her throat. "Amos Wells," she finally blurted out.

He tensed, then drew back and looked at her, a troubled expression on his face. "What about Wells?"

"After yesterday . . . well, I knew he might be angry about my switching baskets with Celia, but when you paid so much for mine . . . well, it made him look like a fool and everyone in town started gossiping about it. When I arrived home, my mother had already heard."

"I can just bet half those old biddies from the picnic raced over to tell her," he said grimly. "Rebekah, I know I'm not rich like Wells, but I'll go to your father—"

"No! That is, you're not Amos Wells. He can ruin my father's church and my brother-in-law's new job. I've embarrassed him, and I have to make my apologies—"

"I won't have you abasing yourself before that petty, pompous ass. No man with an ounce of pride in himself would blackmail a woman with her family's security. And no family who loved you would let you sacrifice yourself." He seethed with anger, his fingers digging into her arms until he felt her wince. "I'm sorry, darlin'."

She shook her head as he rubbed her arms tenderly. "You don't understand, Rory. My father and Henry haven't asked me to do anything. In fact, my father doesn't even know about his threats." She explained about the exchange of notes and Amos's carefully veiled threats, knowing Rory's anger had been ignited but desperate to make him realize that she had to handle the situation in her own way.

"I'll break his neck with my bare hands," he said in a low, deadly voice, his eyes blazing with fury.

"You'll ruin any chance we have if you do! If you go after him, you'll only be killed and then he'd take far worse reprisals against me and my family. Please, Rory, please." Her voice broke as she raised her hands and cupped his face. "Don't interfere. Stay away while I soothe his wounded pride. I do owe him an apology for the trick I played, and once the gossip dies down, he'll realize we don't suit and look elsewhere for a wife. But if you come courting, my parents will be angry and Amos will feel cast aside. Everything will be hopelessly complicated." She looked beseechingly up into his face.

"If you feel you have to do it this way . . ." He halted grudgingly, then sighed and said, "I'll stay away—but only if you let me know that everything is all right and only for a reasonable length of time."

She felt the tight knot in her stomach loosen. With a tender smile, she asked, "And how long is a *reasonable length of time?*" Her fingertips skimmed over his cheek and traced the strong, beautifully sculpted planes of his face. She was drowning in his eyes, in the heat of his nearness, in the hypnotic spell cast by his lips as they nipped at her fingers. His teeth seized her thumb and bit softly into the pad of flesh, sending small shivers of delight coursing down to her toes.

"Have you ever been for a morning swim, Rebekah?"

"Rory, you promised you'd wait—not interfere."

He shook his head as his hand captured hers and drew it to his mouth, nibbling on her sensitive fingertips. "I won't barge in on your father's parsonage or accost Wells on the street . . . but now you're here and we're alone." He continued the seduction of her hand and felt her tremble. "Let's go for a swim, Rebekah."

"I can't. I don't know how to swim," she added breathlessly. This was madness!

"I'll teach you," he said, sweeping her into his arms and carrying her from the shelter of the willow into the warm blaze of sunlight.

Chapter Six

"You're mine, Rebekah. I love you and I want to marry you. Say yes," he whispered as he held her against his chest. She had wrung from him that crazy promise to let her get rid of Wells, but he was going to make damn certain she never forgot that she belonged to him. He waited for her reply, holding his breath as he let her slide to her feet, pressing her breasts against his chest so that their hearts beat together. Their breath mingled, and he stood very still.

"Yes," she said softly. "Oh, yes, Rory." It felt so good, so right to be in his arms, surrounded by his scent, to have him touching her, making her feel things she had only dimly imagined before.

There was so much she wanted to learn, and he was the man who would teach her. Then his mouth again claimed hers in another of those soul-robbing kisses that made her feel like soft clay waiting to be molded by him. He held her tightly, with an urgency that she had never felt in him before, almost desperation as his hands moved possessively over her, one hand teasing her breast until the nipple hardened and she ached. He quickly unfastened the buttons of her blouse and reached inside, shoving her camisole aside as his fingers made contact with her soft skin. His other hand cupped her buttock and lifted her against his lower body, which rocked them in a mysterious yet instinctually familiar rhythm.

His fingers on her breast drew a sharp little gasp of surprised pleasure from her, which led him to grow bolder. He pulled her blouse completely open and slid the camisole straps from her shoulders, baring both milky globes to the warm morning sun. She held on to him, hearing his hoarse murmur, ''Beautiful, so beautiful, Rebekah.'' She felt the intimate shock of the breeze touching her bare flesh. Even more intimate was the pressure of his lower body against hers.

Rebekah knew nothing of the ways of men and women. She had read the Greek myths about gods and mortals coupling and puzzled over how the deed was done. She had never dared ask Dorcas, although she had overheard bits and snatches about a woman's marital duties from various older women who always fell silent when young girls approached. Men were made differently than women in that most secret, shameful place, and Rory's body seemed to want to touch hers there. She could feel the hard bulge against her lower belly as his hips moved against hers.

Then his lips trailed soft wet kisses down her throat and caught a breast, closing hotly over it. Frissons of fire shot through her, and she arched involuntarily against him, forgetting in an instant what the mysterious and menacing changes in his lower body meant. As he feasted on her breasts, moving from one to the other, licking, suckling, and teasing with his tongue, they sank to their knees in the soft grass. But when he raised his head, his face ferocious and glazed with passion, the spell was broken. She could feel his hands at her waist, unfastening her belt and beginning to pull her skirt down. He looked like a stranger, some demonic god from mythology. This was not her Rory, who laughed with her and shared his childhood sorrows. This was a stranger.

And she was a stranger to herself as well, shamelessly naked, allowing him to look at and touch her bare flesh as if he had the right when they were not yet wed. She twisted away, reaching down to seize his hands and pull them from their task. "No, Rory, no! Please, it isn't right. I can't."

His hands stilled, but he did not release her. Trembling with all the youthful desire he had supressed since he first met Rebekah Sinclair, Rory gritted his teeth, fighting for calm. "It is right. I love you and you love me—you said you'd marry me." His breath came out in labored gasps, halting his speech.

"Yes," she whispered brokenly, still not daring to look at him. "But we're not married yet."

"We could be. You're the one who's asked me to wait, to stay away from you and your family while you let Amos Wells call on you."

"Amos Wells means nothing to me!" she cried, her head flying up as her tear-blurred eyes met his harsh gaze. "I only want to get rid of him. It's you I love. But this is wrong, too. I'm not . . . I can't, I'm sorry." She struggled to slip her camisole up, once more covering her breasts.

"You're afraid. Don't be. Not of me, Rebekah. Not ever." He sighed roughly, then began gently helping her refasten her badly disheveled clothing, his touch gentle and slow. He had been rough, passion blinded, wanting to place his mark

108

of possession on her, and he had taken advantage of her own repressed sexual desire. "You're a real lady with high morals. I'm the one who owes you an apology. You have nothing to apologize about—not to me and not to Amos Wells either."

She rose shakily with his help. "It always comes back to Amos Wells, doesn't it?"

"Until he's out of your life. You will send him away, won't you, Rebekah?"

She looked at his earnest yet wary expression. He was jealous and afraid. Afraid of losing her to an older, wealthier man from her parents' world. This was her Rory again, her love, the man she had felt such a bond with from the first moment they had met. Her proud, yet frightened Irishman. "Yes, Rory. I will send him away," she echoed, so filled with the awe of his love and his vulnerability that she ignored the monumental difficulties in keeping such a vow.

"I'll be here at the river every evening this week. Try to slip away and meet me."

"It will be difficult with Mama watching me, but I'll try." Her hand reached out tenderly, and he took it in his. Together they walked past the willows and up to where her fat old mare grazed contentedly.

"It's getting late. My parents will be up, and I'll have to explain where I've been if I can't slip in before they notice I'm gone."

He helped her mount the sidesaddle and then took her fingers and planted a soft kiss on them before releasing her. "I'll be waiting for you, darlin'."

His voice echoed as Rebekah rode toward town.

Rebekah adjusted the collar on her dress, surreptitiously slipping her finger inside the neckline to ease the stricture.

109

She was so nervous that she felt as if she would choke, sitting in the family parlor waiting for Amos Wells to arrive. Her mother fussed with a starched lace doily on the pedestal table in front of the window.

The room looks like I do, forlorn and threadbare, Rebekah thought. The chairs and sofa were faded and mismatched, acquired as donations from parishioners. The various tables in the room, although polished painstakingly, were of poor quality, each covered with a doily and cheap knickknacks Dorcas had collected over the years. A small tea table sat in the center of the room with her mother's pride and joy atop it, a sterling tea service that had been a wedding gift from Ephraim's cousin Noah, a prosperous Montana cattleman. Its luster made the frayed blue brocade of the sofa look even more washed out. The lace curtains hanging crisp and white on the windows were thin from repeated launderings, and the lace was mended in many places.

The parlor reeked of genteel poverty, as did the dress she had chosen. Of course, Rebekah's reason for choosing it was not to emphasize her lack of the finery a man like Amos could provide, but to discourage him with her prim, dowdy appearance. The gown was an ivory silk sprigged with tiny green leaves. The leg-of-mutton sleeves and pleated bodice were fashionable, as was the high lace collar, but the overall effect was unflattering. A castoff of Celia's, it had been taken in for Rebekah's slimmer figure. The fit was still too loose, and the color made her gold hair seem dark, her complexion sallow and washed out. And the high collar was as prim as any schoolgirl's father could wish.

Dorcas had wanted her to wear a pale pink dress of Leah's which was newer and fit her better, but could not dispute the fact that this dress was, after all, silk. Rebekah owned mostly castoffs, and both mother and daughter were acutely aware

110

of their poverty. Dorcas had set her face in a stern, disapproving expression and stalked off after admonishing Rebekah to mind her manners with Mr. Wells or the consequences would be dire.

As if she did not already know that! Just then a light rapping sounded at the front door, and Ephraim answered it. Rebekah could hear the two men exchanging pleasantries as they walked down the narrow hall into the parlor. After constrained greetings and a few nervous remarks on the weather, Ephraim and Dorcas excused themselves, leaving Rebekah seated on the edge of her chair, facing Amos across the tea table. His gray eyes were veiled, his expression revealing nothing.

She took a deep breath for courage, then plunged ahead at once. "I owe you an apology, Mr. Wells, for what happened yesterday. It was not my intention to embarrass you, only to give my friend Celia the opportunity to share her basket with you. She is quite smitten with you."

"And you are not." It was not a question, but his voice was surprisingly gentle.

She met his eyes and saw them crinkle in amusement at her discomfiture. Feeling as if she were walking a twisty path through quicksand, she ventured, "I would be less than honest if I used the word smitten. You are a fine-favored man, Mr. Wells, and many of the ladies in town—the single ones, that is—would be honored by your attentions—not that I'm not. Honored, that is." She ground to a halt, realizing that she was sinking deeper into the quagmire with every word. *Please don't let him be angry.*

Wells smiled thinly. "So, you're honored, yet you told me your basket would be trimmed in pink, then switched to rose ribbons."

"It was childish of Celia and me to switch." What else

should she say? Do? Prostrate herself at his knees like some harem slave?

"Yes, Celia is an impulsive young lady. Rather used to getting her own way. Unlike you, who under the Reverend Sinclair's upstanding moral guidance, are used to a more self-sacrificing life."

"You give me too much credit and Celia not enough," she said in her friend's defense. "The switch was at my instigation."

"So that Irish stablehand could purchase your basket?" His eyes were cold now, all traces of good humor suddenly erased.

"No! That is, I didn't know he would even be at the picnic. I certainly had no idea he would bid on my basket." That at least was the truth. If only he did not ask if Rory knew it was hers—and how he had come to learn that fact.

Wells seemed to relax his menacing posture, and his expression softened. "I am relieved to hear that. The attentions of a man of his ilk would greatly distress your family. I will be very honest with you, Rebekah. I know I'm a good deal older than you, but I find you to be most ideally suited to be my wife."

"But why me?" she blurted out in spite of her attempt to be cautious. "I—I mean, we scarcely know each other, and there are so many more attractive, wealthy ladies in all the big cities you visit."

"You underrate yourself greatly. You are highly intelligent and well read—thanks to your father—and you are skilled in the domestic arts because of your mother's fine Christian efforts. You also show promise of great beauty."

One hand flew to her cheek in genuine surprise. "Beauty? Me? My sister Leah is the beauty of the family. Besides," she said, quickly recovering and remembering her father's

112

admonitions, "beauty is of the soul. The body is only an outer shell of far less importance."

"It is nevertheless a decided asset for a politically ambitious man to have such a fine 'outer shell' on his arm, provided she is also bright and ambitious herself. As I'm certain you know, the Nevada legislature will most probably name me to the United States Senate. I need a wife to accompany me to Carson City and then on to Washington."

"You do me a great honor, Mr. Wells, but it is all too sudden and overwhelming." *Just as it was with Rory, yet I fell in love with him at once!*

"Your affections are not otherwise engaged, and you've had no gentleman callers as yet. I fear, as an older man, that if I were to wait another year to press my suit, you would select someone younger. Why not give us the opportunity to get to know each other?"

What could she say without revealing that her heart was engaged? If he even suspected that it was the Irishman she loved, his vanity would suffer a terrible blow. The reprisals against her family could be terrible. But he had not really seemed threatening tonight, just afraid of looking the fool— an older man who needed an ornamental young woman to further his political career. He had been honest with her. And she had—at least by omission—not been as forthcoming with him, nor dared she be. *Make no mistake.* She wet her lips nervously. "As long as you understand that I will never marry a man I do not love."

He nodded, "Yes, at your age love seems all important. I was wed when I was scarcely older than you. The first Mrs. Wells passed on after twenty-one years. She was a dear lady, and I have missed her sorely, but it is the companionship, not some grand passion, that one truly comes to value in a marriage. I expect someone like Celia Hunt would not have

113

the maturity to appreciate that. But you, my dear, I think, could, given time.''

Rebekah nodded mutely. This was not going at all as she had hoped. "Might I offer you some tea, Mr. Wells?'' She gestured to the table laden with her mother's treasures, trying to think of a way to extricate herself from his web.

"That would be charming, my dear. You make a gracious hostess.''

Struggling to hold the heavy pot steady, she poured.

Rory had waited by the river every evening for the past week, hoping Rebekah could slip away. But she had not come. He knew her parents kept a strict watch over her, especially since he had come into her life. Amos Wells's threats and overtures worried him. The man had a fearsome reputation in the Comstock towns as a ruthless mine owner who manipulated men's lives as easily as he did stocks.

Rebekah was being harried, a lamb at the mercy of a wolf, yet she insisted that she had to fight this battle alone. He feared discouraging Wells would not be easy, especially considering how strongly her parents encouraged the match. Wells had all the ammunition he needed—power, wealth, social standing. Everything Rory did not possess.

He had spent the past five days working with some of the finest thoroughbreds he had seen since leaving Ireland. Normally, after a backbreaking week, he would take the pay he had just collected and head to the nearest saloon to celebrate, but no more. He was going to have to change his ways if he expected to win Rebekah, and that meant not only giving up carousing but saving his money as well.

The thought that Rory Madigan would ever become such an industrious and sober man brought the hint of a mocking smile to his lips. It was a wonder what a woman—the right woman—could do. Morosely, he considered his chances as he climbed the stairs to his spartan quarters above Jenson's stable.

"Madigan, some kid delivered this for you while you were gone," old Wilt Blevens said, scratching the half dozen or so greasy gray hairs straggling across his scalp as he hobbled across the livery floor toward the stairs.

Rory turned and reached down to take the piece of paper from Blevens's hand. Who would be sending him messages? Rebekah? Mumbling his thanks, he hurried upstairs as he unfolded the note. It was only two lines, hastily scrawled, unsigned.

Be at the river road south of town around half past seven. You won't like what you see.

A prickly sense of warning raced up his spine, causing the hair at his nape to bristle. What was going to happen, and who was setting him up to see it? Somehow, deep in his gut, he knew it had to do with Rebekah. He crumpled up the message and tossed it into a corner, then sprawled across his bunk and stared at the cobwebs woven through the crude rafters overhead. Should he go?

"Are you ready, Rebekah? It's almost a quarter to the hour," Dorcas called up the stairs, her voice cheerful.

Why shouldn't she be cheerful? Her mother was getting exactly what she wanted. Amos was taking her on a ride around town to show off his fancy new George IV phaeton. He had called twice more at her home the past week, the soul of courtly kindness in front of her parents, seemingly impervious to her attempts to put off his suit. He had made no further veiled threats but rather had turned on his charm, making himself so vulnerable that to refuse this outing would have been tantamount to a churlish insult. As long as he remained polite and made no attempt to kiss or touch her the way Rory had, she would continue to see him. In time he surely would realize that his plan was doomed to failure and become bored with the minister's prim daughter.

She was attempting to enhance that image by dressing as demurely and drably as she could without arousing her mother's suspicions. The yellow muslin dress with its gray jacket and ruffled trim was surely as ugly as anything she owned. She picked up a matching gray bonnet and started to tie it on her head. Ugh! No, it was simply so dreadful that her mother *would* become suspicious. When Elmira Priddy had given it to her, she had told Dorcas she would never wear the monstrosity. Hearing the carriage pull into their driveway, she tossed the hat aside and headed downstairs. The sooner they took the ride, the sooner it would be over.

Once they were out of town on the river road, Amos turned to Rebekah. "You seem distracted, my dear. Is anything wrong? Perhaps I've been so anxious to show off my new rig that my driving is a bit too fast for you." Amos reined in the matched pair of Morgans and leaned back against the rich burgundy velvet upholstery of the phaeton.

"No, the rig gives a smooth and splendid ride," Rebekah admitted truthfully, running her hands across the lush cushions. A breeze from the river loosened a curl from the coil of hair at her nape. The evening was so beautiful and the carriage so grand that she would have loved to pull down her heavy mass of hair, letting it blow in the wind as the rig raced full-out across the open river road. But of course, she could never do that, not with a man like Amos. With Rory, though, she could fly, soar like the wind itself. But Rory would never own anything as expensive and elegant as a George IV phaeton.

"I'm pleased you're enjoying the ride, Rebekah. The carriage was worth every cent. So were the Morgans.''

"You bought them from Mr. Jenson, didn't you? I understand he's becoming one of the leading horse breeders in Nevada.''

"Beau is a partner of mine.'' At her look of surprise, he chuckled indulgently. "Few people know I lent him the money to start his livery and even backed the racetrack. Don't tell your father. I know how he feels about gambling,'' he whispered conspiratorially.

In the soft evening light he looked younger, handsome in an austere, distinguished sort of way. She could not help the small peal of laughter that escaped her lips. "No, I shall not tell him.''

"Would you like to see a race on Sunday afternoon? Quite a few of the ladies from town attend—with proper escorts, of course. There's a special box reserved for the owners and their families, away from the lower sorts in the crowd.''

It sounded like a marvelous adventure, but not with Amos Wells. Besides, what would Rory say? He might be there, since he worked for Mr. Jenson. Then the thought struck her. Amos could have Rory fired just as easily as he could dismiss Henry. "I think perhaps it would be unwise, in light of my father's opinion on gambling,'' she demurred.

"A lady of principle. How admirable.''

His voice was dry and teasing. If he was disappointed or angry with her refusal, he gave no indication of it.

Across the road, hidden by thick clusters of sagebrush, Rory stood watching the slipper-shaped conveyance as it glided slowly past him with its top down, revealing the man and woman seated inside. He could hear Rebekah's laughter float across the warm evening air, see her return Wells's smiles, engrossed in softly murmured conversation.

"No wonder someone wanted me to be here,'' he said to

himself with an oath. So much for her getting rid of Wells!

If he drove her to his fancy mansion on the Flying W and seduced her in a silk-sheeted bed, she would forget her fine religious scruples easily enough. And why not? Amos Wells could offer her all the things he never could—security and wealth, social position, glamorous travel, servants and jewels. But Rebekah, his Rebekah, who had responded with such artless passion in that cabbage patch, would never sell herself. *Or would she?* a nagging voice sneered.

Too agitated to sleep, Rory made his way silently through the empty streets of the respectable neighborhoods. The moon rode low in the starry night sky, full and golden. A dog yipped in the distance, then grew silent as he drew near the tall, white-steepled church. The old frame parsonage was situated beside the church. Dressed all in black, riding his blood bay, he blended into the shadows cast by cottonwood trees along the way.

The churchyard was large. Behind it lay the cemetery, where gravestones were interspersed with thick stands of juniper and peach trees. Rory tied Lobsterback's reins to a low-hanging branch and then made his way to the side of the parsonage. Rebekah had told him she often watched the sunrise from her bed. He calculated that there was only one upstairs window from which that would be possible. He would gamble that he did not awaken the reverend or his wife. Even so, it was unlikely that a preacher would own a gun or would shoot him if he did, he thought sardonically as he picked up a few small pebbles and aimed them at the window, which was half open to catch the night breeze.

Rebekah awakened with a start when the first small pebble landed on her sheet with a light plink. She sat up as another fell to the floor beside her bed. What on earth? Was it hailing in her open window in midsummer? She scooted off the bed, stepped over to the window, and looked down. When she saw Rory standing directly below her, she thanked the lord that her parents' bedroom was across the hall from hers. Dorcas snored so loudly that she had always slept with her door securely closed to drown out the noise.

"What are you doing here?" she whispered as she stuck her head out the window.

"Better question, darlin', is what yerself was doin' laughin' and smilin' with the likes of Amos Wells out on the river road tonight?" His tone was bitter and the brogue was pronounced, a sure sign that he was angry.

"You were spying on me!" she accused him defensively.

"You promised to discourage Wells, but it's an odd way you have of doin' it," he said, taunting her, his glittering eyes piercing through her thin cotton nightgown. When she drew her head back and crossed her arms over her breasts, he felt a swift stab of anger. "I thought you were my woman, Rebekah. Don't hide from me."

"Go away, Rory. If anyone sees you—if my parents wake up—"

"Not until we settle things between us," he said stubbornly, standing with his feet braced apart and his fists curled at his sides. "Come down where we can talk."

"I—I don't dare."

"Then that means you've chosen the easy way out. Wells's money will be your consolation in a cold marriage bed," he said tightly, turning on his heel to stalk away.

"No, Rory, wait—you're wrong. Please."

Her voice carried on the warm night air, pleading with an edge of desperation in it. He stopped with his back still turned and waited.

"I'll slip down to the peach orchard out back."

He was waiting for her, half hidden among the shadows of the low-growing trees. At first she did not see him; then he stepped out from behind his leafy cover. She had quickly thrown on a shapeless old rose-pink chenille robe. Her bare feet peeped out from beneath the hem.

She curled her toes in the grass and said, "I didn't want to make any noise when I came downstairs, so I went barefoot. It feels kind of good," she added, nervous and appalled at her folly. Why didn't he say something instead of standing there, scowling at her?

Rory watched as she stood with the raggedy old robe closed across her bosom like a shield.

She wet her lips and blurted out, "I had to go on that ride with Amos."

"You didn't have to enjoy it so much," he retorted, taking a step closer to her.

"I didn't enjoy his company—only the phaeton." She took a step forward, too, looking defiantly into his eyes. "How did you know I'd be out on the river road with Amos?"

"Someone sent me a note, saying I should go there around seven."

A look of horror came into her eyes, and her hand flew to her lips. "Someone knows about us."

He shrugged stiffly, trying not to let his temper flair. "Would it be the end of the world if people knew?"

"We've been over this before. Of course it would—and not just for my family. Amos Wells owns a share in Jenson's properties, too. He could have your job as well as Henry's. Then where would we be?" She started to tremble. "Oh, Rory, what shall we do? I'm so frightened. Who could know about us?"

He reached out and drew her into his arms, stroking her

long, silky hair, warming her with his body. "Don't cry, Rebekah, darlin'. Whoever it is, he hasn't gone to your parents or Wells. In fact, sending me that note, he seems to be taking my part. We'll get through this if only you love me. When I saw you sitting there so close to Wells, heard your laughter—I nearly went crazy. I could've killed him."

She could feel the barely leashed violence in him. It should have frightened her and yet it did not. Instead, she felt a thrill of excitement and heat from deep inside her. She slid her hands up his chest. The contours of his body were familiar now.

With a curse that was more of a groan, he buried his hand in her hair and cradled her head, tilting her face up to meet his descending lips. "Rebekah, I love you so much. I can't bear to let another man near you." His mouth ground down on hers possessively.

Rebekah knew she should stop him now, before things got out of hand again as they always seemed to do when the two of them touched. They were alone in the dark. It was utterly wrong. Yet when his hands glided up and down her back, caressing her, his arms enfolded her, and his mouth moved with such rough desperation over hers, it felt so right, so good. The warm, spiraling heat swept over her in dizzying waves. She gave in to it and raised herself on tiptoes to return his fierce, sweet kiss. They sank slowly to their knees on the soft grass beneath the peach trees.

Chapter Seven

Lacy patches of moonlight danced in and out through the leaves, dappling their bodies, bathing them in a soft silver glow as they melded together. Rory's lips brushed frantic kisses across her face and throat as his hands pressed her to him. She answered, burying her fingers in the long shaggy mane of straight black hair, pulling his head lower as he murmured against her skin.

"Please, Rebekah. Let me love you. Don't turn away. Tell me that you're mine." His hands reached for the collar of her robe and pulled it open, revealing the sheer nightgown beneath. Then he stopped, letting his arms fall away, waiting for her assent, even though he ached to pull her down to the soft grass and cover her with his body.

She trembled, not from cold or even fear, although she was afraid of what his big male body would do to her delicate female flesh. The mystery of it would at least be over. So would her innocence. And her morality. Doing this violated every tenet by which she had been raised, yet Rebekah knew she would do it anyway. She let the robe fall from her arms and drop to the ground, covering her feet. Then she raised her arms in invitation. "I love you, Rory," she whispered softly.

With a moan, he pulled her back into his arms. "And I love you. I'll go slow, Rebekah. I can make it good for you." He knew he would have to hurt her at first, but he would not frighten her with the stories other women had told him about losing their maidenheads. He would be gentle and careful. In spite of his tender years, he had plenty of experience to guide him, although he had never taken a virgin before. Rebekah was his, and only he would ever have the right to touch her. No woman had ever belonged to him this way before—and he had never belonged to any woman this way either. *We're both virgins—in love.* Just thinking of the enormity of this commitment, a lifetime together, made him tremble.

After spreading her robe like a blanket on the grass, Rory turned back to her and let one hand glide lightly over the sheer cotton nightgown. He could feel the darning threads on the shabby, much mended garment. But when it revealed her lovely young body, it seemed to shimmer in the moonlight, a thing of regal beauty because of the woman who wore it.

Reverently, he curved his hands around her breasts, molding them and teasing the nipples with his thumbs, then moved lower, over the indentation of her slender waist to the soft swell of her hips and down her sleek thighs. "You are so lovely," he breathed as he reached up and untied the drawstring at the neck of her gown, letting the loose, gauzy garment fall open at her shoulders.

Rebekah's palms rested against Rory's chest, feeling his heart beat erratically, just as her own did. He was so hard and warm, so beloved, yet she felt shy, uncertain of what to do or say. Maybe she should do nothing, remain silent. Yet her uncertainties made her speak out. "I want you to love me, Rory—I don't want to wait—but could we at least exchange vows between ourselves? That's how it was done in olden times, I think, and it was considered a true marriage before God." Would he laugh at her missish vapors?

"Aye, I've heard that, too." In a low, husky voice, he began solemnly, "I, Rory Michael Madigan, take thee, Rebekah . . ." He hesitated at her middle name, and she whispered it, her eyes aglow. "Beatrice Sinclair, to my wedded wife, to have and to hold from this day forward, for better, for worse, for richer, for poorer, in sickness and in health, to love and to cherish, till death do us part."

Rebekah repeated the words, her voice sweet and clear in their moon-dappled chapel. When she had finished, he kissed her fingers, lingering over the third one of her left hand. "I only wish I had a ring. One day soon I will, I swear it, Rebekah—a gold ring."

"Oh, Rory, I love you so!" She reached up and caressed his cheek as his hands once more moved to her shoulders to slip the nightgown from her body.

Slowly, reverently he peeled it down, kissing her bared flesh. She grew bold and unbuttoned his shirt, pulling it open and tugging it free of his pants. He helped her, shrugging it off, then watched as her gown floated to the earth, puddling around her knees. Willing himself to go slowly, he laid her back on her robe and then disentangled her gown from her lower legs. Leaning over her, he gazed down at her as she looked up into his eyes, her expression worried and uncertain.

"I'm too thin—"

"You're perfect. Women with too . . . too much go to fat, but a slender body like yours . . . you'll always be beautiful, Rebekah." He leaned over and trailed kisses from her brow to her eyelids, down to her lips and throat, then took her breasts, teasing and suckling them until she arched up in his embrace, whimpering as her nipples hardened and thrust into his mouth.

When his hands swept lower, curving over her hip, then up across her belly, he could feel her tense. "Don't be afraid, Rebekah. I'll go slow. Let me touch you." He felt her relax as he held one warm palm on her flat little belly, then ever so slowly, in soft gliding circles, moved lower to the soft curls at the juncture of her thighs.

The sensations his hands and mouth were creating in her body rocked Rebekah to the core of her soul. Heat, shimmering and flashing, combined with a building ache that seemed to move downward from her breasts, and his hands followed as if he knew her most secret place that had suddenly come to life. She could feel the tingling frissons of pleasure when his fingertips grazed her nether lips and came away damp. Shame flooded her. What was wrong with her? But he seemed pleased, smiling and kissing her, whispering love words, praising her natural passion. Was it supposed to be like this?

"I can't wait any longer, Rebekah," he whispered as he sat up and began to yank off his boots and breeches.

Every nerve in her young body was thrumming with an unknown hunger while he undressed before her. She had seen his naked backside that day in the river and had often lain awake at night imagining how the rest of him looked.

But he gave her no time to look as he rolled down at her side and took her in his arms.

As he pressed his lips to hers again in a searing kiss, she could feel that hard, mysterious male part of him, no longer confined by his breeches, but hot and probing, pressing against the softness of her bare belly. His tongue tasted her, teasing her on to answer. When their kisses grew fevered and fierce, he took her hand and guided it slowly over the sinewy muscles and hair of his chest and belly, then lower to touch the heat, the hardness of his male member.

At first she flinched away in surprise. He murmured soft love words, coaxing her gently until she again let him place her palm around it. The sleek length was hot and velvety, like nothing she had ever felt before. She squeezed and he moaned, but when she let go, afraid she had hurt him, he urged her to continue, showing her how to stroke as well as squeeze, until he was trembling and crying out her name. She realized for the first time the power a woman had over a man.

Never before had a woman's touch made him respond like this, not even as a green, sixteen-year-old boy. Rebekah was reticent, constrained by a lifetime of modesty and religious scruples that had no doubt instilled in her the idea that love between a man and a woman was something ugly and sinful. But she was naturally passionate, already wet and creamy with wanting him, and she did not even know it. If only he could keep control and not spill himself before he brought her along with him.

"Now, my darlin', now . . ." he breathed against her mouth as he rolled her onto her back and positioned himself between her thighs, using his aching staff to spread the moisture across her velvety, swollen petals, easing his entry into her virginal sheath. Sweat beaded his face as he fought back the urge to plunge headlong into the softness beckoning him. Instead he moved with agonizing slowness, letting her stretch to accommodate him until he encountered the barrier of her innocence.

Rebekah felt the heat and the strange sense of being filled, yet not fulfilled, of reaching for some elusive need that burned brightly, coiled deep within her. When he stopped and grew still, she could feel his whole body trembling. She opened her eyes to stare up into his face, which was contorted as if he were in agony. Sweat beaded his brow, and she reached up to stroke it. Her slightest movement caused him to shiver anew and emit a low growl.

Yet she could not fight the instinctual urge to move, to arch up toward his invasion of her body, wanting to meld their flesh together even more completely. Her hips undulated upward, and he gave in with an oath that sounded more like an endearment as he thrust downward.

The sharp sting of pain took her by surprise. Her eyes met Rory's, and she knew why he had hesitated. But the pain brought with it a keening sweetness that drew her to writhe against him.

"Don't, Rebekah," he gasped, breathing heavily, trying once more to hold still, buried so deeply inside of her. "Give yourself a little time, and the hurting will stop."

"No, no time—I can't wait," she cried, her voice muffled against his shoulder as she clung to him, willing him to assuage the ache, somehow knowing that when he moved, it would be so.

And it was.

He felt the sweet heat of her enveloping him and was lost in her cries of surrender as he began to move in deep, slow thrusts, stretching her untried young body, feeling an answering hunger in her that he had never imagined. He encouraged her with love words, instructing her how to wrap her legs higher and lock her ankles behind his back so he could penetrate deeper. They were drowning in the vortex of ecstasy that seemed to be drawing them both under its spell.

She felt the low, stretching ache change as they moved, mysteriously building to a pleasure so intense it robbed her of speech, of every thought but that it continue. Yet she needed something more, something just out of her grasp, which beckoned her as she ascended to the heights of passion, making low, incoherent noises that she was unaware came from her own lips.

Rory struggled to hold on for her, but she was like a lioness, his wild golden love, so fierce in her demands that he felt himself toppling over the abyss, unable to stop the swift, boiling surge of glory in those last hard strokes as his seed spilled deeply within her.

Rebekah felt the change in his body, the stiffening of his muscles and the sudden swelling of his staff, as he drove into her with such splendid fury. The hunger that had been so elusive, so compelling, suddenly shimmered and burst deep inside her. Wave after wave crashed over her, convulsing her flesh, touching her very soul. All she could do was hold tightly to Rory as he collapsed on top of her.

The weight of his long, hard body pressing her to the warm, fecund earth felt right and good in spite of the discomfort. When he shifted and began to pull away, she clung to him. He rolled to his back, holding her nestled on his chest. Their legs were still entwined as he rained soft, light kisses over her forehead and stroked the silky cascade of hair falling around his face and shoulders.

"Ah, Rebekah, I love you more than life itself," he whispered. "I didn't mean to hurt you, but—"

She raised her head and gave him a tender kiss, interrupting his protest. "You didn't hurt me—at least, only for a tiny bit." Her eyes gleamed like emeralds in the moonlight. She felt wantonly bold enough to say, "It didn't matter, for what came after . . . is it always like that?"

Rory stroked the side of her face tenderly. "Not the pain. That only happens once—the first time for a woman—but the rest . . . it's always pleasurable, but never anything like what we just experienced. In fact, I doubt many men and women ever feel what we did."

"And will again?" She felt the heat flood her face. "You must think me shameless. Good women—"

"Good women love their husbands. We're pledged to each other, Rebekah, in love. There's no shame in that, no wrong in our coming together. Only beauty, what's natural and good. What God intended." He tilted her chin so she had to meet his eyes. "Do you love me?"

"Yes, yes, of course. More than anything, but . . ." She struggled to find the right words.

"But your family will never approve of an Irishman—and a penniless Irishman at that. Is that it?" He could not keep the bitterness from his voice.

She bit her lip. "They'll fear for my welfare, yes. Somehow I have to make them understand."

He could see that she was close to tears. "Don't cry, Rebekah. I never meant to hurt you. I'll make them understand that we love each other, that we're going to wed."

She shook her head and held him tightly, suddenly afraid for the enormity of what she had just done. She had given herself to him and knew in her heart that she'd do it again. She was weak and immoral. "You can't just walk up to Papa and ask to marry me. He'll refuse."

"And then you'll have to choose, won't you, darlin'? Him or me?" His voice was laced with scorn as he rolled up,

disentangling her arms and setting her aside. She clutched
for her nightgown, which was lying in a crumpled heap, and
began to pull it over her head as he seized his breeches and
donned them with swift, angry movements. Then he pulled
on his boots and reached for his shirt and hat as he stood
up. Planting the hat on his head, he began to button his shirt
and tuck it roughly into his trousers.

Rebekah sat huddled on her robe, looking like a forlorn
wraith in the moon-dappled, voluminous white cotton gown.
She hugged her knees and hid her face as sobs racked her
slender shoulders, all the more poignant for their silence.
"I—I can't choose. Please, don't ask me. I'm so confused,
Rory."

Sighing, he reached down and pulled her into his arms.
"Rebekah, think of us, of what we've shared, of our love.
Surely it's stronger than your family's prejudices against
me."

How could she explain her father's unreasoning aversion
to the Irish when she did not understand it herself? Rather
than admit her beloved father was flawed, she seized on the
more explainable, pragmatic objections of her mother.
"They'll want me to marry someone who can take care of
me, who has—"

"Who's rich like Amos Wells," he snapped, his arms
dropping from her abruptly.

"It's not the money—it's security."

"You'll have to make up your mind what's more important for you. Being *secure*"—he ground out the word contemptuously—" or being loved. I'll not keep skulking
around in the night after you, Rebekah. Either you love me
or you don't. You decide!"

Rebekah stood hugging herself, suddenly cold in spite of
the warm night air. He spun around and stalked away. She

watched him go, a black-clad figure vanishing through the dark bowers of the orchard. Tears streamed down her cheeks in silvery rivulets, but she made no attempt to call him back.

Virginia City

English Annie pasted a vapid smile on her carmined lips and swished her ample hips seductively as she walked across the bedroom. Her kohled eyelids drooped over unfocused blue eyes, an aftereffect of the opium she smoked regularly. All of Sauerkraut Schnell's girls used the drug to help them endure life in the sordid bordello he ran above the Howling Wilderness Saloon.

Annie really was English, from the Yorkshire countryside, but her wholesome good looks had begun to fade. Her brassy yellow hair was bleached, and her pale flesh grew more flaccid with the passing of each brutal winter in the mining camps.

"So, you came back to Annie, luv. See, didn't I say you would?" she whispered seductively in her heavy accent. She slid her hands beneath his jacket and began to unfasten his shirt. "I can do it for you, luv, you know I can," she crooned, pulling him toward the bed as her busy hands undressed him with practiced ease.

Her customer remained silent, letting her do all the talking as she plied his tense body with skilled fingertips and that eager red mouth. Ah, the things she could do with that mouth. He threw his jacket and shirt onto the chair by the bedside, wrinkling his nose at the sickly sweet smell of her opium pipe. Then, when she opened his fly and took out his phallus, he sucked in his breath, forgetting the squalid surroundings, the unwashed smell of the woman's body drenched in cheap perfume.

If only she *could* do it again. The others had failed. Every whore here knew it, whispered about it, laughing behind his back. It was all her fault, that icy bitch of a wife. She had done this to him. He forced himself not to think of her but to concentrate on what English Annie was doing instead.

She helped him off with the last of his clothing, and he stood naked before her. He had always been vain about his looks, his well-proportioned body and handsome face. Gazing in the wavy mirror on the wall, he studied himself and the whore in her garish red-sequined gown. She was overripe, going to fat but not quite there yet. Large white breasts spilled out of her black lace corset when she unhooked the top of her dress and let it fall to her waist.

She held up a doughy breast in each hand, preening for him, but he simply snarled, "Get on with it," and lay back on the bed, impatient for her to complete her strip and join him.

Annie sighed to herself as she peeled off the scanty dress, revealing black fishnet stockings held up by the garters of her black corset. She wore no underpants, but in this case it did not matter anyway. She would earn every dime he paid her and then some, but he did pay well. So far she had been able to satisfy him, even if it took more than the minimal effort she was used to expending. In a wilderness where any female was a rare commodity, Nevada men were normally randy and eager for a woman's touch.

She began her performance, admiring his body, oohing and aahing as she ran her fingers and lips across his skin, teasing him as her mouth drew nearer and nearer his sex. In spite of her nakedness, her breasts brushing across his chest, her hands and lips caressing him, his staff remained flaccid.

He seized a fistful of greasy yellow hair and forced her head down to his groin. "Get on with it, dammit!"

Annie began by stroking him with her hands, using every technique in her considerable repertoire, but she could quickly see that it was doing no good. He growled in frustration, his fists pounding the mattress. "Annie'll take care of ya, luv, never fear," she crooned in a singsong voice, her breath hot on his staff. Then she took it into her mouth and began to ply it with teeth and tongue.

He let out a few whimpering moans as the old familiar sensations danced at the periphery of consciousness. Almost. He was almost there. His hips began to arch up, jerking convulsively in a desperate attempt to speed the process along.

Annie increased her efforts, lips and tongue busily at work. Her hands cupped his testicles and he let out a strangled sob and surged to life for one fleeting moment. Then it was over. For that, at least, she was grateful.

"See, luv, I told you English Annie could do it for you," she said. Then she rolled from the bed and began to dress, turning her back on him. The whore did not see the murderous look burning in his eyes as he watched the jiggle of her fleshy body.

Henry Snead stood in the Flying W office, staring broodingly out the bay window at the vast empire of Amos Wells. The mountains were a hazy pinkish-gray on the distant horizon. The flat, grassy basin land shimmered in the afternoon heat as a zephyr blew in sudden gusts, stirring up dust and making the grass lie flat to the earth. He had been summoned by his employer and told by the housekeeper to wait in this lavishly appointed room.

Letting one large hand glide over the gold-embossed leather volumes that lined the wall, Henry thought about the future. He was general foreman now, and Wells had been pleased enough with his work to bring him into the manage-

133

ment of his silver interests. Hard-rock miners and cowboys were not all that different to handle. All it took was a few brains and a lot of grit. Henry Snead possessed both. Someday he would own a fancy house like this, and Leah would have all the silk dresses and fancy rigs she was always mooning about. Maybe it was time to ask Wells for another raise. Maybe not. More stock might be a better idea. Yes, that was definitely a better idea. In a few years Henry Snead planned to be a silver baron, too.

Wells entered the room, nodded affably to Snead, and motioned for him to have a seat. Then he slid into the big leather-upholstered chair behind his desk.

"You wanted to see me about something, Mr. Wells?"

Amos Wells steepled his fingers in front of his face, studying the younger man with cool, calculating gray eyes. "Yes. We've already discussed my calling on your sister-in-law."

"Yes, sir, we did."

"How does your wife feel about her sister becoming my wife?"

Snead suppressed the consternation he felt. He stroked his mustache, then said carefully, "Leah would be delighted to have you in the family, of course."

"Apples never fall far from the tree. Rebekah and Leah are sisters. If I'm going to marry into the Sinclair family, I want to know what sort of people they are. Tell me about your wife. Is she biddable?"

Henry spread his hands over the smooth chair arms. "Leah's dutiful, a good cook and housekeeper, although I have hired a Johnny to do the heavy chores for her. Those Chinese work really cheap. That seemed to please Mrs. Sinclair. My mother-in-law always wanted help, but with her husband being a preacher, well, they just couldn't afford it."

"So, the Sinclairs want better for their daughters, do they?"

"I expect all parents do," Henry replied reasonably, keeping his voice noncommittal. The last thing he wanted to discuss was Leah! Or the way the sisters detested each other.

"Well, considering the limited circumstances in which the Sinclair daughters were raised, they should both appreciate the niceties that prosperous husbands can provide for them. You do see the obvious advantages of the two of us being brothers-in-law, Henry?" Amos asked gently.

"Yessir, that I certainly do. What exactly do you want me to do, Mr. Wells?" Henry asked, leaning forward in his chair.

Wells gave a sharp bark of laughter. "Not one to beat around the bush, are you, Henry? That's what I liked about you when I hired you. That and your ambition. You talk to your missus about her sister. Make sure she's using her influence to see that Rebekah is favorably disposed to my suit. I want a beautiful wife to take with me to Washington, and I'll be inclined to great generosity toward her family."

"Generous enough to let me in on more mining investments?" Snead knew Wells was dangling a carrot in front of his nose, but damned if he'd go docilely along without bringing it out in the open.

Wells nodded solemnly. "Stock in the fastest-rising mining operations on the Comstock. Inside information for inside information, if you get my drift. . . . "

A smile of understanding was exchanged between the two men.

Wellsville

The back alley was dark and a Washoe zephyr tossed dust up in swiftly circling swirls, then skipped on, letting it settle against the sides of the buildings, piling up on sashes and filling corners with the reddish powder. Chicken Thief Charlie Pritkin stood in the shadows between two of the noisiest saloons in glitter town, his collar turned up against the stinging summer wind. The man was late for their appointment. Charlie needed a drink and wanted one of the soiled doves inside, but could afford neither until he was paid.

Suddenly the sound of boots padding firmly through the dust caused him to turn. His employer materialized from around the corner. "I been waitin' fer a spell." His voice was hoarse and surly.

"What have you to report?"

Charlie cleared his throat nervously, uncertain of how his benefactor would take the news he had to impart. "Miz Sinclair, she's been real busy the past few weeks. That mickey she seen at the fight, I heerd she met him at the park the next day."

"Imprudent, but harmless enough. I already knew about it. Go on."

"Well, he come over to her house a few days later, when her folks wuz out 'n she wuz workin' in th' garden." He wet his lips and plunged ahead. "Had 'em a real mud wrasslin' contest, right out in front a God and ever'body. Then she up and come to the river that Sunday to meet him, real private like."

"Did she lose her virginity before the box social at the park?"

Charlie scratched his dirty red cowlick and shrugged un-

136

easily. "I don't think so, but last night . . . well, he come to her house real late, 'n she snuck out to the orchard with him. I couldn't get too close, but they wuz in them trees a long time 'n when she come runnin' back inside, she warn't wearin' nothin' but one of them female nightshirts—all billowy and see-through."

His employer nodded, his face carefully hidden in the shadows. Only his eyes burned as he stared broodingly at his hireling. "Keep watch on them. I want to know everything that goes on between them—but I don't want anyone else to hear a whisper about this. You understand?"

As Chicken Thief Charlie Pritkin bobbed his head up and down, his employer tossed a double eagle to him, then vanished down the deserted alley. Charlie scratched his cowlick in perplexity. No figgering those fellows from the right side of town. He could have sworn his boss *wanted* the preacher's daughter to fornicate with that mickey boxer. Now what kind of sense did that make?

Rebekah lay awake in her lonely room, awash in misery. It had been three days since she had given herself so recklessly to Rory Madigan. She had scarcely slept, not at all that first night. In the morning, she had finally rolled from her tangled bedsheets and peered bleakly into the mirror, afraid she would see the evidence of her lost innocence stamped clearly on her face.

She had looked no different, just puffy-eyed from weeping and pale from lack of sleep. Yet inside of her everything was changed. She had pledged herself to Rory not only physically but with her heart, her very soul, as well. They had made solemn vows before God which should never be broken. But no legal words had been spoken before man, and if her family had any say in the matter, none ever would.

Rory was right. She would be forced to choose between him and them. How could she hurt her father and disgrace the Sinclair name by running off with a prizefighter? How could she remain and betray her vows by wedding Amos Wells? *How can I live without Rory?*

She had gloried in his touch, boldly followed his lead, and reveled in the pleasures of the flesh. Although her mother had never explained anything specific, Rebekah knew good Christian women were not supposed to enjoy the physical side of marriage. She had overheard Dorcas's discussion with Leah before Leah's wedding, and her sister had seemed to be in complete accord with that sentiment.

Why was she so unlike her mother and sister? What was wrong with her that she took such delight in physical love? She had actually hungered for Rory's touch. And, God forgive her, she still did. In spite of the shame and guilt that tied her insides in knots, she still ached with wanting her lover's arms around her, craved the bliss that his touch evoked.

If only there was some way for them to marry with her father's blessing. She sat up in bed, rubbing her aching temples. The banjo clock struck midnight, and the chimes echoed dolefully from the parlor below, each bong like a warning. What if Rory left Wellsville and returned to the prize ring? She had hurt him. She knew Rory Madigan was a proud man, but a poor one, and she had made it clear that material comforts and security were important to her as well as to her family.

Amos Wells had come calling again last evening. She had pleaded a headache and fled to her room, repelled at the very thought of fencing with him while her nerves were strung so tightly and she was riven with guilt and confusion. If only he were not complicating matters with his unexpected court-ship, she might be able to get her parents to view Rory in a more favorable light. He had a respectable job. Well, *almost* respectable, she amended, realizing that working around racehorses was not precisely something her father would countenance. But it was a steady job, and if he were willing to convert and let her father marry them, that should weigh heavily in his favor.

She must think of some way to get rid of Amos without angering him. Playing calm and aloof only seemed to pique his interest. Could she dare explain that her heart was already pledged? No, that course was too risky. The waiting game would go on as he tried to wear her down. And every time he came to call, she could not have girlish vapors and refuse to see him. But if she did see him, Rory would be jealous. He might think she had chosen Amos.

The clock finished striking, and the silence pooled around her, chill and foreboding. "I can't let him think I don't love him," she whispered desperately.

Without giving herself time to think, she got out of bed and began to dress quickly and quietly. She finished by don-ning an old bonnet with a wide brim that hid her face, not that any respectable person should be out and about to rec-ognize her at this ungodly hour.

Rory lay on his bunk with a book of poetry clutched in one hand, a glass of whiskey in the other. *Leaves of Grass*, which used to fascinate and enchant him, seemed as stale as yesterday's beer now. Even the bottle, once a certain source of oblivion, offered no solace. He could not even do a decent job of getting drunk. Every time he closed his eyes, he could see Rebekah, small and forlorn, with her virginal white night-gown puddling around her as she sat crumpled in the orchard.

He had been wickedly wrong to take her innocence—worse, he had been a fool to exchange vows of lifelong commitment when there were such formidable obstacles to overcome.

"If I had any sense, I'd ride out of here tomorrow and never look back. Those vows mean nothing to her. They shouldn't to me. Let her marry that rich old bastard and be the senator's wife." He sat up and placed the book on the floor, then reached over for the bottle beside it and uncorked it, preparing to pour another shot. The sharp creak of a rusty hinge, followed by soft, rustling sounds brought him out of his ruminations. He set the bottle down and reached for his Colt, then blew out the flickering lantern and moved quickly to the door.

Rebekah kept looking over her shoulder, but could see nothing in the darkness of the big stable. Horses nickered restlessly and stomped their feet dully against the straw-covered earth. She had the eerie feeling that someone was following her. But that was ridiculous; no one had been out on the darkened streets as she made her way furtively downtown to Jenson's place.

She let her eyes adjust to the dark interior. Thin streams of moonlight poured in through the cracks between the planks, and larger squares of light were cast from the high windows at the sides of the barn. Blinking, she made her way as much by feel as by sight, keeping the narrow stairs at the rear of the building fixed in her mind. About halfway across the stable, she heard the sudden click of a weapon being cocked and froze. Then a powerful arm encircled her waist, dragging her backward into one of the empty stalls.

Rebekah tried to scream, but a hand fastened over her mouth, stopping her outcry.

"You little fool!"

Chapter Eight

Rory crushed her against him, then spun her roughly in his arms as she crumpled, clinging to him and struggling for breath.

"You frightened the life out of me," she gasped.

"I could've shot the life out of you—me or one of Jenson's other hands. They're off in town for the night, thank God, or you might've been dragged into one of these stalls and raped."

His voice was low and tight with anger. There was whiskey on his breath. She could not see his face, only feel the leashed fury in him as he swept her into his arms and carried her up the narrow, rickety stairs to his quarters. He deposited her in the center of the small, dark room, then struck a match, lighting the kerosene lamp.

In the dim light he looked like a menacing stranger

when he asked, "What are you doing here?"

She moved back, edging toward the door. "It was a mistake. I shouldn't have come."

"But you did," he said, stepping between her and the door, barring her exit.

"You've been drinking."

"For all the good it's done me, yes." He looked into her eyes. They were round with fear, luminous and dark as emeralds. Her lips trembled, and she flinched when he reached out his hand toward her. "Ah, God, I'm sorry, Rebekah. I've the devil's own temper, and you were crazy to risk coming here. I was afraid for you. I could've shot you for a horse thief—and that's the best of the bad things that could've happened."

The tears choked her, welling up and overflowing as she sobbed, unable to blink back the shimmering droplets that clung to her lashes. "I had to see you, Rory. After the way we parted the other night—I couldn't let you leave thinking that I didn't love you. . . . "

"That you took shameless advantage of me and then cast me aside?" he whispered. A grin tugged at one corner of his mouth as he extended his hand, letting his thumb gently wipe away the trail of tears from one delicate cheekbone.

Suddenly he was Rory again, not the frightening, angry stranger who smelled of whiskey and held a gun. The tight knot inside her loosened, and she met his gentle smile with a hesitant one of her own. "When you put it that way, it does sound pretty ridiculous, doesn't it?"

Neither of them knew who reached out first, but suddenly they were embracing, their hands and lips soft yet hungry, seeking the warm assurance that their bodies gave.

"I could never leave you, Rebekah. I love you more

than life itself, but I don't like this sneaking around in the dark.''

''If only Amos Wells weren't so powerful—why does he want me, of all the women he could choose? I'm no-body—''

His lips stopped her words; then he brushed his mouth across her cheeks and eyelids, murmuring, ''You're some-body very special, Rebekah darlin', beautiful and bright and brave. The love of my life.''

The love of my life. When he held her, his breath warm on her as he kissed her and murmured his devotion, the world went away. Rebekah forgot Amos, even her own fa-ther and the consequences if she were found here with her love. ''I can't bear for us to be apart. I haven't slept since we argued and you left me in the orchard. Don't ever leave me. . . . ''

His mouth swooped down to claim hers. She opened to him, tasting the alien tang of spirits on his tongue. Rather than repelling her, it seemed only to add to his forbidden allure. No man but her Rory would ever kiss her, touch her, know the intimate secrets of her body. She returned the kiss, running her hands across his shoulders, sliding her fingers inside his shirt, hungry to feel his warm, smooth flesh and the crisp, springy hair on his chest.

Rory feasted on her lips as he deftly unfastened her dress and began to work it from her shoulders, letting his mouth travel over her skin as he bared it, inch by inch. Rebekah responded with a boldness that surprised them both, and delighted him. She let the tip of her tongue trace small swirls around his hard male nipples, making him tremble. His little Puritan was a passionate woman who would be a warm and loving wife. He finished stripping off her simple calico gown and mended cotton undergarments, then laid her back on his narrow mattress and knelt to kiss and caress her.

"You're so beautiful. I only wish this were eiderdown instead of corn husks. I wish I could give you silks and jewels—"

"Only give me yourself, beloved," she whispered against his lips, silencing him.

He tugged off his jeans and climbed onto the bed, covering her slender body with his own.

Downstairs in the darkness, Chicken Thief Charlie Pritkin crawled into one of the stalls, watching the flickering light coming from between the rough board walls of Rory's small room. This time there was no doubt that Madigan had despoiled the preacher's daughter. He wondered how his employer would take the news as he waited patiently for them to emerge. They were young and obviously randy. He placed his greasy hat over his eyes and lay back in the straw to catch a nap. Several hours had elapsed when he awakened to the sound of muffled footfalls and whispered voices.

"I'll see you safely home." Rory walked into the stall where he kept Lobsterback and began to saddle the big bay as he and Rebekah argued heatedly.

"But you can't come to my house either. What if Papa awakened and came downstairs to read? He does that sometimes when he can't sleep late at night."

"I should come courting in the daylight. This is no good." He yanked the cinch tight, and the bay snorted in protest.

Rebekah shook her head in misery. "We've already had this argument. Please, Rory . . . give me time. We'll think of a way."

"It's the damn money. If I could show your father that

I had cash to stand on, he'd have to relent. I'll go back to the prize ring. There's big money to be made in the mining camps."

"No! You'd be hurt or killed—and besides, that's money made from blood. My parents would never approve of your boxing."

"What will we do, then? It's too dangerous for you to come here, but I can't be without you." He paused as they walked the bay to the stable door; then he took her in his arms. They stood silhouetted in the moonlight, clinging together, oblivious of the rest of the world. After a moment, they broke apart and he swung onto the bay, then pulled her up in front of him and took off at a slow walk.

Her voice carried on the still night air. "The river. I'll come to your place by the river. It's close by my house, and no one will find us there. Since Leah's married, I'm usually left alone on Sunday afternoons and sometimes, if we finish supper early on weeknights, I can get away for a ride with Celia without Mama fussing too much."

"But what about Wells? He's been hanging around you like a bee at a honey tree. He'll give you no free time, Rebekah."

"I'll talk to my father about needing more time to think about Amos's intentions. If he thinks I'm feeling pressured or rushed just because of what my mother wants, he'll relent. I know he will—just be there for me. At the river. Please?"

"I'll try, Rebekah, but I have to find a way out of this—a way to get some money fast." She started to protest, but he pressed his fingers over her lips and continued, "If that means traveling some distance to win a big purse for a stake, I'll go. Your family need never know how I earned the money. I'll not hear another word about it. It fair eats my guts out to see Wells touch you.''

Their voices faded as they rode around the corner. Pritkin, who had slipped silently through the side door to follow them, realized he could not keep up on foot. But he had learned enough. More than enough. Maybe there was even a bonus in this.

Celia Hunt's big brown eyes nearly popped from their sockets when her friend explained about Rory Madigan. ''You can't mean it! Why, he's penniless—and he's Irish, for heaven's sake.'' She looked at the stubborn set of Rebekah's jaw, a sign she had learned when they were children. ''You're really involved with him, aren't you? Oh, Rebekah, you haven't let him . . .'' Her voice trailed off and she coughed discreetly, then peeked at her friend's flushed face. Rebekah's eyes would not meet hers, and she was nervously fidgeting in the balloon-backed armchair.

The two young women were whispering conspiratorially in the Hunts' rear sitting room while Mrs. Hunt held her weekly mission board meeting in the main parlor. Dorcas and Leah were in attendance, but as young unmarried girls, Celia and Rebekah were excused from what they considered an odiously boring activity.

''You *have* let him! Ooh, Rebekah! What was it like? Did you enjoy it? Tell me everything!'' Celia gushed excitedly.

''Shh. I can't tell you,'' Rebekah whispered, praying that Celia's squeals would not bring one of the servants in to check on them. ''It's very personal and private . . . and beautiful,'' she added with a defiant lift of her chin. ''But I do need your help to slip away and meet him.''

''I could get in so much trouble,'' Celia said.

''Since when has that ever bothered you?''

"You say you don't want Amos, but if we both ruin our reputations, he won't want either of us, and I *do* want him."

"As I said, all the more reason to help me be with Rory. If all else fails, we may have to elope once he's saved enough money. Then that would leave Amos for you."

"Oh, fiddle, why not? If you're that desperate, even willing to run away with him against your parents' will, I suppose the least I can do is stand by you."

"Celia, I knew I could count on you," Rebekah said, throwing her arms around her friend.

Over the next few weeks, Celia rode by the Sinclair place just after the supper hour and the two friends went riding. At first Dorcas fumed, but because of Rebekah's talk with Ephraim about needing time to think over Amos Wells's suit, her father allowed her the leeway.

On their latest excursion the conspirators headed toward the river, but before reaching it, Rebekah reined in and said, "You needn't wait for me. I'll tell my parents you rode home at dusk the same as I." *What a wicked liar I've become.*

Celia grinned and kicked her new palomino filly into a brisk trot, calling back over her shoulder, "Do enjoy yourself."

Rebekah slowed old Bessie Mae as she approached the trees, wondering if Rory would be there tonight. He was not always able to finish work at the racetrack in time to return to town before dusk. *Please let him be waiting for me.*

So preoccupied was Rebekah that she did not see Bart Slocum rein in his mount just after Celia departed. He watched her dismount and make her way toward the dense willows near the bend of the river, wondering what a high-toned lady like the preacher's daughter was doing out, leaving her girlfriend to ride back to town alone. He'd always had an itch for Reverend Sinclair's pretty little blond daughters, and now one had just dropped right into his lap.

He left his horse close to hers and stealthily raced through the tall grass to get ahead of her. "Wal, now, little yellow bird, whatcha doin' out all by yore lonesome?" He unfolded his lanky frame from where he was leaning against the trunk of a gnarled old willow and reached out for her.

Rebekah gasped in surprise as she snatched her hand from his grasp. "You get away from me, Bart Slocum."

"So you know my name, huh? Wouldn't think a good girl like you would—but then you ain't such a good girl 'er else you wouldn't be out here all alone, now would ya?"

"I'm not alone. I'm waiting for a friend—and you are not he," she said, trying to emulate the snotty voice Leah used when she wanted to give someone a set-down.

But Leah's social circles did not encompass men like Bart Slocum. His arm snaked out and grabbed her, catapulting her against his chest with a sudden thud, knocking the breath from her. "Now ain't you the unfriendly one. Who you meetin'? Cain't be nobody yer pa'd allow. I heard you was sparkin' with ole Amos Wells. He shore wouldn't have to sneak around."

"Let—me—go," she gritted out, fighting down panic. *Please, Rory, please come!*

In response, Slocum took a fistful of her hair and yanked brutally on it, until her face was tilted up for his descending mouth. She screamed, but he quickly stopped her cries with his fetid kiss. Her struggling only increased his excitement. For such a slim young thing, she had some real curves beneath her prim clothes! He reached up and tore her blouse open, revealing one creamy shoulder and the swell of a breast above her camisole. "Gawd, you are a lush peach just ripe for pickin'!"

"You'll go to jail—be hanged for this," she managed to cry out as he wrestled her to the ground.

"I don't think so. You tell 'n it'll go harder on you than me. You'll be ruined. Besides, you're no better 'n you ought ta be, sneakin' out here. You ain't gonna lose nothin' you ain't already lost."

Slocum wrestled her to the ground and held her pinned with his body atop hers, reaching down with one hand to unfasten his breeches. Just as he did so, Rebekah bucked up and kneed him in the groin as hard as she could. When he gasped and fell off her, she rolled to her hands and knees and began to scramble away.

As she raced through the willow thicket, she could hear him, cursing and panting, in furious pursuit. He was gaining on her! Then she stumbled and would have fallen, but Rory's strong hands were there as he suddenly materialized from beneath the curtain of a willow, running from where he had dismounted outside the trees when he heard her scream.

"Oh, Rory, I prayed you'd come," she sobbed as he shoved her behind his back, then advanced on Slocum, who quickly began to back up.

"Now, Kid, I ain't no boxer. You can't—"

Slocum's plea was cut short as Rory's fist connected swiftly with his jaw in a stiff left jab followed by a powerful right cross that sent Slocum flying backward onto the seat of his breeches, which were gaping open obscenely. He shook his head, sending blood flying from his cut lip as he struggled to his feet, trying to avoid the Kilkenny Kid's advance.

Rory gave him no opportunity. His fists delivered a flurry of punishing blows to his foe's face and body. Slocum never landed a single punch as he retreated, feebly attempting to stave off his infuriated opponent by holding up his arms to protect himself. His knees buckled beneath the onslaught, and he fell to the ground again, but Madigan simply took hold of his shirt with one fist and continued smashing his other into Slocum's face until it resembled a shattered watermelon.

"Rory, no. You've killed him!" Rebekah's pleas did not seem to penetrate the killing rage surrounding him until she threw herself across his back.

Gradually he came to himself and dropped Slocum's inert body to the ground. Breathing heavily, he turned to Rebekah and saw the horror in her eyes. Saints above, was it *he* she feared? He reached out one hand, palm open, to her entreatingly. "Rebekah, it's me, Rory. I'll never let anyone hurt you."

She looked at his hand which had so often caressed her with such gentleness. Dear God, his knuckles were bloody and swollen from the beating he had administered to Slocum. Then she raised her eyes to meet his, so dark blue, compelling her, imploring her. This was her love, who had rescued her as she prayed he would. She flew into his arms and he held her, soothing her with soft love words, crooning to her. She reached up when he tenderly brushed the tears from her cheeks and took one of his injured hands in hers, kissing the bruised knuckles, then holding them against her pounding heart. "Oh, Rory, thank God you came when you did!"

"This should never have happened," he said grimly.

"What if I had worked late?" He swore. "I almost stayed to give Jenson's new racer another time trial. If I had . . ."

"But you didn't," she replied, burrowing her head against his chest.

"It could happen again. We'll not be meeting like this anymore, Rebekah. The next time I see you, I'll be riding up to your house and asking your father for your hand." He stilled her protest and went on, "And when I do I'll have a large enough stake to be respectable."

"You can't box anymore, Rory. Please! It will only make matters worse with my father."

"Worse than this?" He gestured to Slocum's crumpled, unconscious body, then walked over and heaved the man across his shoulder. "I'll take him to town and make certain he understands that if he comes near you again—or breathes a word about us—this will seem like an exhibition compared to what I'll do to him then. Come on, I'll see you're safe on Bessie Mae before I ride into town with him."

In silent misery, she followed, unable to think of anything that could sway him from his course.

Amos sat arranging documents on his big desk in the Wellsville First Charter Bank when Henry Snead was ushered into the room. Snead, dressed nattily in a new black broadcloth suit and string tie, looked every inch his up-and-coming protégé. Wells smiled and offered a handshake. "Have a seat, Henry. Looks as if your new duties at the mines are agreeing with you."

"Leah complained a bit about the long hours, but then I bought her a new phaeton and matched team. That settled the issue," he added with a shrug of satisfaction, not wanting to let Wells know what a shrew his beautiful wife could be when she set her mind to it.

"Good, good," Wells replied dismissively, his thoughts elsewhere. He picked up a crystal paperweight and turned it over in his well-manicured hand, watching the facets of light reflect off its polished surface. "That matter of the Irishman we've discussed . . ."

"Mr. Wells, I know Rebekah's been foolish, but she's young yet. Blood will tell, and she's from a fine Christian family."

"I'm willing to overlook her youthful indiscretions—up to a point—but I don't want a public scandal, else she'll be of no further use to me. In fact, she would become a political liability." He set down the paperweight abruptly, and his chill gray eyes bored into Snead's murky dark ones. "I want you to arrange a job for Jenson's stablehand. What better way for him to make a lot of money than to be offered the chance to fight a London Prize Ring Champion in Denver?"

A slow smile tilted Snead's mustache up at its edges. "You have enough influence to get a backwater fighter like the Kilkenny Kid a bout with one of those fancy Brit boxers?"

"My dear Henry, I have enough influence to get an audience with Queen Victoria, if I were interested," he boasted. "It so happens one of my banking associates from Sacramento is quite the fight enthusiast, and he's arranging a match in Denver. The purse—what's being offered aboveboard, not to mention the side bets—is five thousand dollars."

"You don't think Madigan could win?" Snead asked, his dark eyes enigmatic.

"No, but in the most unlikely event he did, I think Rebekah's family would be so scandalized by her bloodied paladin returning to claim her that they would lock her in her room until she agreed to marry me.''

"I still don't see why it wouldn't be easier to simply tell the Sinclairs about Rebekah's association with the Irishman and be done with it.''

"That might eliminate him as my competition, but Rebekah would blame me if I did so—and more likely, she would simply run off after him. Far better if he vanishes in disgrace after being beaten senseless. But even if he wins, she'll see him through her father's and mother's eyes—a blood-soaked barbarian with an infamous reputation as a brawler. Then, when everyone else castigates her, I'll be there to console and forgive.''

"What do you want me to do?" Snead asked simply.

"I've made arrangements for a match with Archimedes Poole, who'll be in Denver next week. Beau Jenson owes me money. He'd love to get out of debt, and he'll jump at the chance to let the Kilkenny Kid help him do it. Talk to him discreetly and suggest that he might want to accompany Madigan to Denver. Once he knows how much money he could win, I doubt he'll need further convincing.''

Bart Slocum sat nursing a bottle in the back room of his brother's saloon. The whiskey burned his split lips and bloody gums as he swallowed, but the fire deep in his gut helped assuage his misery. There was not a place on his body that did not pain him. His eyes were swollen to slits and his nose so badly broken that the doc had just shrugged and said, ''Reckon you'll have to learn to breathe through your mouth, Bart.''

He would carry the scars from the beating that mickey

153

gave him for the rest of his life. He cursed and took a long pull from the bottle.

"Thet won't help—leastways it won't fer long. Naw, if'n I wuz you 'n I had a score to settle with thet mick, I'd do somethin' b'sides drink."

Slocum looked at Chicken Thief Charlie's greasy beard and calculating dark eyes. "You got somethin' in mind, Chicken, 'er you jist blowin' off hot air agin?" Pritkin was the town snoop, a petty thief. As far as the Slocum brothers were concerned, he was a general nuisance who annoyed paying customers by begging drinks.

"I got a job fer you . . . if you got the nerve ta do it." A crafty look came over his face as he pulled up a chair beside Bart and eyed the whiskey bottle.

"Whut kinda job kin *you* offer me?" Slocum scoffed.

"Feller's payin' real good ta follow th' Kilkenny Kid to Denver 'n see thet he don't come back. If Poole don't kill him in the ring, we do it while he's sleepin' off his beatin'. I figger ya might want th' chance ta use a knife on him. Course now, if yore skeered after the way he worked ya over . . ."

"Who'd pay you to kill thet dumb mick?"

Chicken Thief Charlie scratched his beard stubble and grinned guilelessly. "I ain't allowed ta say, but he pays real good." He pulled out a wad of greenbacks and flashed them in front of the startled Slocum. "You in? He'll pay a thousand—when it's done."

"Yeah, Pritkin, I'm in."

"Please, Rory, don't do this. Even if you could win, it isn't worth the chance." Rebekah's voice was thick with tears she struggled not to shed.

"It's our *only* chance. I can take Poole. I've seen him

fight. He's overrated and getting slower. That's probably why he was willing to take on an unknown. I'm grateful Jenson was able to get me the fight." Rory looked out on the river flowing so peacefully, as they argued in the very place where they had so often made love in the past month.

"You'll forgive me if I don't share your gratitude," she said angrily. She had been so overjoyed to receive his note, asking her to meet him at their old trysting place after more than a week of separation. She rushed to the river, thinking he had changed his mind and was going to welcome her into his arms. Instead, he had told her his "wonderful" news!

"It's five thousand, Rebekah. That's enough to buy a piece of land, run some cattle, and start breeding horses. We won't be rich, but if I work hard, in time I can make a success of it," he said earnestly.

"And if you fail, you can always go back to boxing. My father won't accept blood money won in a contest of chance as a marriage settlement."

"And because your father's lofty principles won't allow my grubby money, neither will you." His words had the bite of lashing fury in them, barely under control. He fought the urge to take her by the shoulders and shake her until her teeth rattled.

"You'll be beaten senseless and end up with nothing," she said, reaching out to him with a sob.

He stepped stiffly away. "Thank you for that vote of confidence in my boxing prowess, but I think I'm a slightly better judge of the issue than you. I can beat him. I know it." His eyes darkened with the strength of his impassioned feelings.

"What if you can? You'll come back to Wellsville, the

conquering hero with your face all swollen and cut up, waving fistfuls of dollars. I'm certain everyone in glitter town will be dying to welcome you.''

"But the good respectable folks won't. Rebekah, I may be a penniless Irishman, but I am a man and I have a man's pride. I won't beg and I won't pretend to be what I'm not to please your sanctimonious family or anyone else. I quit the ring and settled down, took a steady job, but I still wasn't good enough to come calling at your front door like Amos Wells. No matter what I do, I never will be, so there's no sense in us ever meeting again. Marry Wells and be done with it. It'll make your father happy!'' He turned and strode toward his big bay.

Rebekah stood frozen in shock for a moment, watching him walk away, out of her life. Forever. "Rory, no! We made solemn vows. We swore to love each other—and I do love you. I'll always love you, no matter what.'' She ran to him and fell at his feet, her arms wrapped around his legs as she crumpled onto the earth. "I don't care about the money. I'll go with you—now, anywhere you say. Don't leave me.''

Drawing a ragged breath, he turned and knelt by her side, pulling her into his arms and burying his face in the silky golden hair that tumbled down her back. "Don't cry, Rebekah, please don't cry.'' He cupped her chin with one hand and kissed the trickle of tears from her thick lashes. "I'll come back for you—win or lose. I swear on my honor I will. But I have to fight this fight. It's my one chance to amount to something—to prove to your family that I can take care of a wife. And I will win. Believe in me and wait for me. Then, if your family still won't accept us, we can elope, but this way there is a chance they might.''

She nodded, unable to speak for a moment. Her emotions had become so intense lately. She seemed to cry at the slightest thing. "We will have our chance," she finally managed to say. "Amos hasn't called in the past few weeks. Perhaps I've succeeded in discouraging him and he won't hurt my family when we marry." She met his level blue eyes, searching for assurance. And found it.

He studied her lovely face, cradling it in his hands. "I'll be back, Rebekah darlin'. And the devil himself won't keep us apart. I swear to you."

"I'll be waiting, Rory, I swear to you. Just keep yourself safe and hurry back to me."

He gave her that heart-stopping grin and winked at her. "Even before my cuts and bruises heal?"

She kissed the tiny white scar on his temple as she whispered, "I'll always love you, scars and all. Just come for me."

"I made a vow. I'll never break it as long as you love me."

"Then the vow is sealed for all time," she murmured against his lips as they sank to the soft grassy earth, locked in an embrace.

Chapter Nine

Denver had a look of permanence about it that none of the Comstock towns ever achieved. Although not possessing as large a population as Virginia City in its boom years, Denver in 1870 was growing steadily with five thousand residents. After earlier fires and floods, churches and newspapers, banks and mercantiles had all been rebuilt of sturdy brick and stone.

When Rory and Beau Jenson rode into town, they bypassed the imposing wide streets north of Cherry Creek and east of Laramie, where mansard roofs and Gothic spires were crowned by wrought-iron railings, all glowing like fairy-tale creations beneath the newly installed gaslights. Their destination was the unsavory district where prizefights and other illegal affairs were winked at by the local police.

''The Bucket of Blood has good whiskey, and Blackie Drago

will put us up with a clean room,'' Rory said to his employer as they stopped in front of the livery and dismounted.

"Y'all know Denver?'' Jenson asked, surprised.

"I've made a few friends, all on the shady side of the tracks, I confess. Drago's a countryman of mine. He runs the political machine in Denver and has something on just about every respectable man in town, even the Temperance Republicans,'' Madigan said with a grin, knowing that Jenson, a Democrat from Alabama, kept his politics to himself among the wealthy community leaders in Wellsville.

The Bucket of Blood Saloon had not changed in the two years since Rory had left Denver. It was big, raucous, and gaudy, with a three-foot-high beveled glass mirror running the length of a huge, intricately carved oak bar. The two piano players were still employed plunking out the latest renditions, as a motley assortment of rough miners and bullwhackers rubbed elbows with citified clerks and slick gamblers. Here and there a scarlet poppy draped herself across a customer, soliciting drinks and other activities that were conducted on the second floor.

"Do me eyes deceive me or is it himself, the Kilkenny Kid?'' a gravelly voice with a thick brogue called out from the stairs at the rear of the room as Rory and Beau walked through the door. The speaker was a dapper-looking little man with curly dark hair and a thin waxed mustache, dressed resplendently in maroon and black and sporting diamond shirt studs.

"Blackie, you old card shark, how the hell are you?'' Rory called out as the smaller man crossed the room to greet them.

They shook hands warmly and slapped each other on the back, an odd-looking pair, one slender and short, the other a head taller. Rory introduced Beau Jenson to Blackie Drago.

"So yer the one who got this fight for my boyo here. And

159

a grand catawhumping it'll be, too! I've matched the purse with side bets on the Kid here,'' Drago said.

"Another five thousand?" Jenson said, stunned. "Y'all really *are* certain Rory can take Archimedes Poole."

"Aye. I've seen this bucko fight. He's just hittin' his stride while Poole's past his prime. Beside, Poole's a Sassenach." He winked at Rory, and the two men chuckled as they all wended their way to the bar. "A pity it is that Steve Loring's up in the mountains making a freight delivery. He'd relish the chance to make a wager on your behalf."

"Loring?" Rory echoed, unfamiliar with the name.

"Ah, you haven't met Cassie's new husband. A right proper Philadelphia gentleman he is—and a decent sort, even if he is a Republican."

"Cass Clayton got married?" Rory made an invidious comparison between the red-haired, bullwhip-wielding owner of Clayton Freighting and his own proper little preacher's daughter. "That hellion female bullwhacker could blister a rawhide boot with her cursing."

Drago chuckled as he signaled Gus, the huge grizzled barkeep, to pour three cold beers from his best German keg. "Aye, that she still can, but I think she's met her match in Steve Loring. Now, down to the matter at hand," Blackie said, taking a deep drink from his foaming stein. Looking around, he lowered his voice. "Word on the street has it that Poole's slowed down. Using a one-two combination now, no more. Only a left jab followed by a straight right. The odds are still in Poole's favor, but closin'. Since he arrived in town and staged his first exhibition match the other night, I heard a wee bit of a rumor spreadin'." He winked and motioned for them to grab their beers and follow him upstairs.

As they climbed the steps, Rory said, "Just what sort of a rumor would you be talkin' about?"

"While I was at Poole's exhibition match, I happened to let it slip that you've a fearful dangerous left hook that could take the head off a grizzly. Oh, did I mention it was Denver's leadin' sports reporter who got this jewel of casual information from me?" he said, opening the heavy walnut door to his private apartment.

Beau looked puzzled. "But the left hook ain't yer special punch."

Rory grinned. "If old Archimedes has slowed down from fast combinations to using only the left jab–right cross, and he starts to fear my left hook, it makes him into a one-punch fighter."

"He'll keep his good right hand up high as a banner in a breeze, protectin' his jaw instead of bashin' in the boyo's brains," Blackie supplied as a dawning light of understanding spread across Beau's face.

"But does Poole believe the rumor?" Beau asked reasonably.

"That'll be up to me boyo here." He turned to Rory. "I've just planted the thought. It's yerself who'll have to be plantin' the fear. Wade in fast when the bell opens and attack with a hard left hook. But be careful, bucko. Poole can beat you just with his jab. Last year in Kansas City, he nearly knocked Gentleman Harry Harlow through the pearly gates with nothin more than a straight left. Old Poole's a big fellow with more power in his left jab than lots of top fighters have in their Sunday punch."

Rory nodded grimly and tipped back his glass. "I'll remember that."

"Three to one isn't a bad return on a man's investment. Bennett Ames is still takin' bets for Poole," Blackie said with a wink.

"Ames, you say?" Madigan grinned and pulled out his

carefully hoarded wages from the past weeks. "Added to the purse, this should give me quite a start on that ranch in Truckee Valley."

"So, yer fixin' ta settle down after all these years of bein' fiddle-footed since Ryan and Patrick died. Must be a female waitin' out in Nevada," Blackie said shrewdly. "I'll loan you an even thousand to fatten your bet, boyo."

Before Rory could reply to the generous offer, Jenson pulled out a money belt from his waist and began counting out bills. "If you're that all-fired certain, I'd be a fool not to throw in with y'all fer another thousand." Hell, he would be able to pay off that vulture Wells and own his livery free and clear!

The crowd was typical. Bare-knuckle boxing, being illegal across the country, always drew the unsavory elements as well as the thrill-seeking rich, but out west the assortment of humanity was even more diverse. Dozens of burning torches illuminated the motley spectators. Brawny miners in flannel shirts dwarfed fragile-looking Chinese, elegant in their silk tunics and pants. A somber Jewish merchant dressed in black stroked his beard as he made a wager with several scarred Basque sheepherders. Windburned cowboys with shooting irons strapped to their hips jostled wiry bullwhackers with whips coiled across their shoulders, the jagged metal poppers dangling menacingly as if waiting to be loosed on the crowd.

Here and there a nattily dressed gambler in a silk shirt and brocade vest took bets and marked his tally sheet, surrounded by young and old, rich and poor, all eager to wager on the contest. The twenty-four-foot-square ring was set up beneath the stars outside the city limits in a shallow canyon whose gently sloping walls allowed the big crowd a clear view of the proceedings from their seats on the rocky ground.

The ring floor was smooth dirt, hard packed from numerous earlier fights. Three stout ropes were held in place by four-inch square posts at the corners. As Madigan and Jenson watched, the torches cast flickering shadows across the crowd. Suddenly a huge roar went up, and the sports enthusiasts parted. The former champion from London walked toward the ring with his entourage. Archimedes Poole was a big man, his given name aptly fitting for a fighter known as a "scientific" precision boxer in his prime. But Poole at thirty-six was fast slipping out of his prime.

"Damn, he's a big galoot," Jenson said sourly.

"Ah, but look at the fat overlaying his stomach muscles," Blackie said with relish.

"At six-foot-three, he can carry the weight." Beau was reconsidering his rash bet. Still, Drago was the king of the Denver underworld, and his money was on Madigan. If only their rumor worked.

"Don't worry, Beau. You'll win your bet." In fact, seeing the giant ambling arrogantly around the ring, Rory was beginning to feel a niggling doubt or two, but he forced the thoughts aside. Blackie believed he could pull it off. *And so does Rebekah.* He could not let either one down, no matter what. As they made their way through the crowd, Rory reviewed all the information he could remember from January Jones, who had watched Poole box on numerous occasions and even "cornered" for him once.

"The bloke's got a wicked right cross. Uses 'is 'eight to advantage, 'e does," the little Cockney had said. Well, if Blackie's strategy worked, they could neutralize that right in round one. *Then all I have to worry about is the left.*

Poole had three inches on Rory and at least thirty pounds, but it was his reach that was most daunting, for Archimedes's arm length was several inches greater than the younger

163

man's. That was an advantage the long-limbed Madigan was used to having for himself against most opponents, even if they were taller or outweighed him. *Get him to guard against my left hook,* Rory repeated to himself like a litany as they made their way to the ring. Irish miners cheered as Rory passed, while other Denver locals looked contemptuously at the youth who dared challenge a London Prize Ring champion.

Flanked by Blackie and Beau, Rory climbed through the ropes and walked to the center of the ring, where the referee waited impatiently while Poole and his handlers played to the crowd. Once both fighters were ready, the tall, skinny Australian referee began to review London Prize Ring rules in a swift rote monotone.

Rory quickly surveyed the scarred veteran who once had been a passable-looking man before his nose had been repeatedly broken and his ears cauliflowered by countless blows. He remembered Rebekah's gentle fingertips exploring the contours of his own features so softly and lovingly, and he vowed he would not end his days as tired and battered as Archimedes Poole.

Feeling Poole's shrewd pale eyes measuring him, Rory ignored the other fighter and stared intently at the Aussie referee. As he did so, he clenched and unclenched his left fist, working the fingers like a piano player warming up for a big concert. Out of the corner of his eye, he saw that Poole had taken note of the seemingly unconscious gesture. Just then the referee finished. Both fighters returned to their corners, and their handlers climbed out of the ring. One of the fight promoters struck a crude iron triangle, signaling that the fight was on.

Instead of slipping into the familiar dance of a smaller, faster man circling his larger, more powerful foe to spy out weakness, Rory took the plunge and charged straight into Poole, taking the older man completely by surprise. Reflexively, the champion launched a hasty but sloppy left jab which slipped harmlessly over Rory's shoulder while the young challenger stepped inside, landing a stiff left jab to Poole's jaw. When the champion's head snapped back, Rory dropped down and crouched slightly, lowering his left shoulder, and dug a ripping left hook into Poole's midsection. It landed hard just under the champion's right floating rib.

Straightening, Rory attempted to capitalize by driving another hook toward Poole's jaw, but the older man, recovering skillfully, stepped inside the arc of the punch and used his right hand to partially block the blow, which landed on his tender, cauliflowered right ear. At this point, Madigan danced out of range and began to do what Poole had expected him to do in the first place, circle to his own right, keeping out of reach of the older man's vaunted right hand. But Rory noted with grim satisfaction that the champ was now carrying his right fist very high, with the elbow tucked close to his rib cage. If all continued this way, Blackie's scam—with a bit of help from his own frontal assault—would change Poole from a two-punch fighter to a one-punch fighter, for the champ could not throw an effective right from the defensive position he now adopted.

The action began to fall into the pattern Blackie had envisioned as the fight progressed, with Rory circling to his right, then moving in like a mongoose baiting a cobra, drawing the champ's left jab. Most often he was quick enough to get under it and slam his right into Poole's ribs, then follow with a stiff left. Although the left jabs to the jaw were often as not slipped or blocked by the old pro, the body blows began to do their inexorable work.

Poole became slower of foot and began carrying his left

hand lower. Then Rory ended his last body attack with a wicked right to the left side of the champion's face. Poole dropped down to one knee, signaling the end of the first round. By London Prize Ring rules, only when a man went down did a round end, regardless of how long or short a period that might be. The older man stumbled back to his corner for a blessed thirty seconds of rest. As the process repeated itself a dozen more times in the next half hour, the crowd began to grow restive and catcalls at Archimedes echoed from around the tightly massed wall of humanity encircling the ring.

"Whatsamatter, you limey—gonna let a mickey beatcha?"

"A good Irishman's worth a dozen Sassenach in my book!"

"Poole needs so many rest periods, I think the Kid there oughta give him a permanent one. Knock him cold, Kilkenny!"

As he sat in his corner during the round break, Madigan looked at the "old man," whose left side was now covered with ugly red welts turning to purple in the flickering torchlight. The left side of his face was grotesquely bloated, and his left eye swollen almost closed, but Rory, too, had paid a price. The ex-champ had landed enough blows to cut his left eye at the corner. Blackie worked quickly to stanch the trickle of blood from it. Rory had a troublesome "mouse" swelling beneath his right eye and his right hand, with which he had so effectively battered Poole, was almost totally numb. When he tried to unclench his fist, Drago quickly covered it and held it closed.

"Don't try it, boyo, until the fight's over. It's too swollen to open now. I'll use ice on it when this night's work is done."

"The old fox is a game one," Rory said with respect as he watched Poole.

"Aye, you been bangin' his ribs and the side of his head like a Salvation Army bass drum, but he's lettin' his neck muscles go limp and rolling with those overhand rights of yours."

"Get him to come to you," Beau interjected. "Punch him while he's moving into you."

"Aye, he's right, bucko. Without using his own forward momentum to get some extra power, you'll never keep him down."

Just then the thirty-second bell rang and Rory approached his nemesis, thinking about what his corner men had said. Suddenly, pain like fire seared his brain and lights went off like July Fourth fireworks inside his skull. As the crowd roared, he crashed to the dirt and rolled onto his side, terrified. What had happened? Seizing the rope, he tried to pull himself up but fell partway through instead. Three ringside parties, yelling encouragement, shoved him back into the ring and Beau half carried him to his corner.

"Jasus, he used his right." Rory shook his head, desperately trying to clear it.

"No. You walked into his left jab. Remember Gentleman Henry Harlow? But you've gone and cut a hog in the ass now, boyo," Blackie said with a wink. "He's comin' to you right enough. Slip some ice swabs up his nose quick, Beau." He slapped Rory on the back as the bell rang. "Practice runnin' backward until yer head clears."

Rory swore as he rose, muttering, "Don't hit me any more than that tough old bastard already has." He wobbled out of his corner and attempted to smother Poole's flurry of punches by grappling with the heavier man. The champion kept up his punishing barrage as Rory backed away. Then when they locked in a clench, Madigan emulated what the crafty old fighter had done so often and dropped to one knee, ending the round. Beau rushed out to help him back to his corner.

"Stand in front of me, Beau, and fan me with the towel," Rory commanded in a surprisingly clear voice. "Blackie, give me a sip of water. Did you boys see what I saw?"

"What, stars?" Beau asked wryly, already kissing good-bye to his thousand-dollar bet and paying off the livery.

Rory smiled, a grotesque parody on his battered face. "No. My head's cleared up—enough to see that the old boy's dropped that right hand. He's cocked it, ready to throw his famous straight-right Sunday punch. Now if I can—"

The bell sounded, cutting short Rory's words. He got up and wobbled out to the center of the ring. Poole snapped out his left jab. Instead of slipping away from it as he had done all during the earlier rounds, Rory acted addled and leaned away, exposing his chin. The consummate pro, Poole gave nothing away when he saw the opening, but moved forward, dropping his right shoulder to throw his killing Sunday punch. But just as he leaned forward to unleash it, Rory suddenly crouched, twisted to his own right, and drove a left hook at the oncoming champion.

The collision between Rory's left fist and the big man's jaw produced a sickening crack that was heard over the roar of the crowd. Poole stepped forward on his right leg, which simply crumpled beneath him. Fists falling to his waist, he toppled forward on his face—stone-cold unconscious.

For an instant, the crowd seemed to collectively hold its breath before erupting into wild cheers for the Kilkenny Kid. Madigan walked back to his corner and sank down on the stool Jenson slid through the ropes as Blackie shook his head sadly. "The end of an era, boyo, when a man like Archimedes Poole goes down. No offense to yourself, Rory."

"None taken," Rory replied through broken, bleeding lips, still seeing Poole's scarred face when he had entered the ring to the triumphant cheers of the fickle crowd. "I take no pride in any of this. On my parents' graves, I swear I'll never box again—not for all the gold between Cherry Creek and the Comstock."

"Let me help you, Kilkenny," Junie Killian said. The big, brassy redhead climbed through the ropes and took the chunk of ice from Beau's hands. She began to stem the bleeding over Rory's eye by applying it with practiced skill. "My da was a prizefighter. I used to do this for him."

"You used to do lots of things, Junie, but I think the boyo here already has someone to tend him—waitin' back in Nevada," Blackie said to the handsome madam who ran his bordello above the Bucket of Blood.

She ignored him and continued working on Rory's bloodied face, inspecting it with a practiced eye. "Nothing busted that won't heal."

"It'll take time. I don't want to return to Wellsville looking like this," Rory replied distractedly. The tremendous surges of adrenaline that had sustained him through the fight were gone now, but the pain from his beating had not yet set in. He was briefly, blessedly numb.

"I'll see to collectin' our winnin's while Junie here tends you," Blackie said with a wink.

"Rory, I can't stay in Denver," Beau interjected as the crowd surged noisily around them. "I got a livery to tend and a new racer due to run next Saturday at the track."

"I understand, Beau. You collect your winnings and head out. I'll be along once I don't look so polecat ugly."

"Even beat up, you ain't ugly, darlin'," Junie purred.

"I appreciate your help, Junie, but I think what I need to do right now is go back to my room and sleep—for about a week." He stood up and clapped Beau Jenson on the back. "I owe you, Beau, for getting me this opportunity."

"I reckon everything worked out for the best. You got you a real good stake now. What y'all figger on doin' with it?"

"Buying a piece of land up in the Truckee Valley. I might even be interested in some of your racing stock." Rory grinned through cracked lips. "I'd shake on that, but neither hand will unfist until I soak them."

Jenson thumped him on his shoulder. "I take it that means I done lost me the best horse handler I ever had."

"That it does, Beau, but I'll always be grateful that you gave me that job."

"You done earned every cent I paid you, son. Why don't y'all head back to the saloon? I'll see what's keepin' Blackie." Jenson waded into the crowd of well-wishers who began to cluster around their new hero, while Poole's handlers dragged him, semiconscious, out of the ring.

"The end of an era," the Kilkenny Kid said softly to himself as he saluted his fallen foe.

"Nearly ten thousand between yer purse and the side bets," Blackie said, shoving a stack of bills in front of Rory as they sat around the big walnut table in his private apartment. The din of the celebrating crowd downstairs was muted by the thick carpets and heavy paneled walls. Blackie Drago was a man of the people, a saloon owner and political boss, but he had acquired refined tastes over the years. He poured a round of excellent cognac and raised his crystal snifter in a toast.

"To new beginnings."

Jenson swallowed the aromatic brandy and coughed. Rory held his cognac gingerly between two badly swollen hands.

Soaking and ice had finally enabled him to unclench his fists, but they were badly hurt. He sipped the brandy cautiously through his sore lips, grimacing at the sting of the alcohol.

"Keep my prize money in your safe, Blackie. As soon as I can hold a pen, I'll write a letter to my lady in Wellsville, but I don't think it'll be any time in the next few days. Every nerve and muscle in my body is starting to ache like a bitch. Think I'll turn in now," he said, finishing the cognac and setting down the glass. He turned to Jenson. "I'll not be up to see you off tomorrow. Safe trip, Beau."

"Same to you 'n all the luck of the Irish, Rory," the beefy-faced older man replied as Blackie refilled his snifter.

"I've already had all the luck one man can ask for in this lifetime—even an Irishman." He left the two men and headed down the hall toward his room. The raucous sounds of celebration from below made him grin inwardly. Once he would have been down there in the thick of the crowd, swilling cheap liquor with a girl on either side and a deck of cards in his hand. Now all he could think of was getting back to Rebekah.

Engrossed in his own thoughts, Rory did not see Junie in the dark hallway. She unfolded her lush curves from her doorway as he walked past and placed her hand on his arm. "Need someone to rub yer sore muscles, darlin'?" She insinuated herself closer, rubbing one nearly bare breast against his chest. "I hear boxers are in need of some relief after a fight—they kinda hold everythin' in before." She wet her carmined lips with the tip of her tongue and smiled at him.

"I appreciate the offer, Junie, but all the relief I can handle right now is to fall sound asleep," he replied, gently disengaging himself from her fulsome charms.

He watched in mild amusement as she pouted and ran one hand down the curve of her satin-clad hip onto the black fishnet stocking revealed in the slit up the side of her costume—what little there was of it. Her hair was hennaed a harsh dark red that clashed with the vivid pink rouge on her cheeks. Her eyelids were weighed down with kohl, giving her dark eyes a slumberous, sly look. All in all, she was the kind of woman he was used to spending time with, nothing like the slender, delicate beauty of his quiet Rebekah. Pausing at his door, he gave her a brief nod good night and slipped inside. She stomped downstairs in her high-heeled satin mules to join the celebration.

In her snit, Junie did not pay any attention to the two men who watched the exchange from the bottom of the steps. "Glad thet whore didn't go ta bed with him," Chicken Thief Charlie Pritkin said, spitting in the general direction of the cuspidor. "I'd hate to cut a fine-lookin' piece like her."

"Madigan's enough ta handle by hisself. Just be glad we ain't got no screamin' female to distract us," Bart Slocum replied.

"Let's git it done," Pritkin replied, starting for the stairs.

"Shit! Give him some time to fall asleep first."

"You afraid o' thet mickey?" Pritkin scoffed.

Slocum's face darkened. "Hell, no, but I got sense. He jist beat a prize ring champ unconscious, remember?"

"I wuz there. He took lots o' raps hisself. He'll be asleep quick enough."

"At least we can use the window. He's probably locked his door," Slocum said, eyeing the side door to the saloon.

A crafty glint came into Chicken Thief's eyes. "Ain't no lock I cain't pick," he replied, chuckling.

Rory was just drifting off to sleep. He rolled onto his left side, brushing the stitches over his eye that Doc Elsner had so carefully sewn after the fight. Pain lanced through his skull, and he flopped flat on his back, gritting his teeth. Then he heard it—a soft click, the sound of a door latch snapping open. He turned his head and peered through the darkness at a slit of light widening as the door to his room slowly opened. Two figures slipped stealthily inside. Rory caught the gleam of a knife before the door closed silently.

Surely they couldn't think he was stupid enough to sleep with his prize money under the mattress! He waited tensely, thinking of his options. The gun he carried was in his saddle-bag across the room. No way to reach it. Over the din downstairs, no one would hear his call for help and Blackie's apartment at the opposite end of the hall was virtually sound-proof.

One of the assassins began to circle the bed. Rory could not let them surround him. He rolled off the mattress and launched himself at the nearest one, hoping to fell him with one surprise punch, but the room was dark, and his vision greatly impaired by the swelling around both his eyes. He struck the target, but the punch was just off center. The man doubled over but did not go all the way down.

By then the second fellow was on him with the knife. Rory whirled around, his stiffened muscles crying out in agony as he grappled with the man, one hand holding the wicked-looking blade just inches from his throat. He pounded his assailant's ribs and twisted the knife away from his own throat at the same time. As the would-be killer doubled over, the blade caught him full force, buried to the hilt at the base of his neck.

Madigan yanked it free and turned just as the other man recovered and charged him, knife raised. As the two blades clashed, Rory was at a distinct disadvantage. His swollen hand could barely hold his own weapon and was fast going numb. He had to finish this quickly. Trying to parry the other man's blade, he jabbed again with his left but missed. He was slowing down, his grip on his knife slipping away.

"Too late, mickey," Chicken Thief Charlie Pritkin said with a low, ugly chuckle. His knife slipped between Rory's ribs.

Madigan fell to his knees, Slocum's knife falling from nerveless fingers as he crumpled. Pritkin reached out to assure himself the job was done by slashing Madigan's throat, but footsteps coming down the hall deterred him. Perhaps someone had heard the fight and come to investigate. He sprinted toward the window, jumping nimbly over Bart Slocum's body. That one was dead meat. So was the Irishman. He climbed through the window and jumped to the soft ground below, landing with a thud.

Whistling jauntily, he rounded the corner of the alley and melted into the shadows. The job was done and he had no one to split the reward with. A good night's work all right.

Rory awakened as fierce, thrumming pain washed over every inch of his body, but none so wicked as that centered in his left side. He tried to move and grunted in agony.

"Easy, boyo," Blackie's voice said out of the darkness. "A good thing yer such a tough son o' the sod. We're hard to kill, us Irish."

"If one inch higher that knife had gone in, even an Irishman such as our redoubtable young friend here would have met his maker," a German-accented voice replied.

When Rory opened his eyes, the first thing he saw was Dr. John Elsner's thin, ascetic face as the physician worked on him. He was lying in his room on the bed while the doctor finished packing the knife wound in his side. Bright sunlight streamed in the window. How long had he been out? "The other two . . . where . . ."

"Two is it? We found one—that big ugly galoot in the

174

corner. Sheriff's comin' to fetch him away." Blackie motioned to the body shoved unceremoniously against the wall. "Lucky you pulled down that bedsheet and passed out on it. Doc here says the pressure from it saved your life durin' the night. Lucky, too, that Junie decided to check on you this mornin', else we might not have found you in time."

"I owe Junie one." Rory tried to raise his head and caught a glimpse of the dead man, who looked as if he were sitting up, asleep, but for the grimace on his face. "Bart Slocum."

"You know him then?" Blackie raised one eyebrow.

"You could say so. I beat him senseless after he tried to rape Rebekah."

"Then that explains the sneaky snake, attackin' you while you slept—with a helper to boot, you say."

"He's the one who did the damage, and got away." Every word was agony for Rory as the doctor finished his bandaging.

"My apologies, Herr Madigan, but I must bind the packing tightly to keep you from losing more blood," the gray-haired physician replied. "Do not move—even to roll over—until I check you in the morning. It is lucky to be alive you are." He shook his small, elegant head in wonder.

"The luck of the Irish," Rory said grimly. "How long until I'm able to travel, Dr. Elsner?"

The kindly old Austrian frowned with concern. "The beating you took in that fisticuffs exhibition alone would keep you down several weeks, but now, with such a deep stab wound . . . I do not think any vital organs were damaged, but it is a great deal of blood you have lost. I would not wish to hazard a guess for several days." He peered at Rory's pallor beneath the bruises. The young man was not out of danger yet. Even with luck, it would be several months before the Irishman was able to ride a horse. He knew his

175

young patient would not want to hear that now.

"I have to return to Nevada." Rory's jaw was clenched with pain and sweat beaded his brow. "I swore . . ."

"And that you will, bucko. In the meanwhile, you just get some rest. You'll be able to write the lady as soon as the swellin' is out of those hands." A twinkle came into Blackie's eyes. "Unless now, you'd be wantin' the likes of meself to write a love note for you?"

"I imagine I'll be able to manage in a few days," Rory demurred wryly.

Three days later, Rory was struggling over the words, eager to share his joy with Rebekah. They had the chance to begin a new life with a small fortune. Yet in explaining why he would be so tardy in returning to Nevada, he did not want to frighten her with Slocum's attack. He wrote a very sanitized version of the assassination attempt, leaving out the man Slocum had no doubt hired to assist him and the fact that one killer was still at large. Minimizing his injuries, he said that he would return in a month, good as new, finishing with his pledge:

"I'll come for you with all the love in my heart, Rebekah, my darling. We swore we would never be parted and we will not.

I love you always,
Rory

The letter went out on the evening train.

Broken Vows

Wellsville

Rebekah and her mother were out working in the garden while Reverend Sinclair made his customary morning trip to the post office to pick up their mail. Since it was Monday, he would spend the day at home working on some long-overdue correspondence. When he returned to the parsonage, Ephraim took the letters into his office and quickly perused them. Then one with a Denver postmark caught his eye.

Ephraim knew who was currently in Denver. He had over-heard the men at Wally's barbershop talking about the big prizefight the Kilkenny Kid had won there. Beau Jenson had returned day before yesterday with his winnings, and folks on the shady side of town were agog that the Irish boy who had beaten Cy Wharton had also been able to defeat some infamous Englishman in one of those barbaric gladiatorial contests.

That saloon-bred trash who had dared to shame his daughter by publicly bidding on her box lunch now had the te-merity to write to her. Surely Rebekah, in spite of her free-spirited ways, could not really have meant to encourage the scoundrel. Then he remembered a pair of blue Irish eyes set in a soullessly lovely gypsy's face framed by gleaming inky hair. *Kathleen!*

He squeezed his eyes closed and blocked out the vision of the beautiful Irish woman who had betrayed him. "No, I won't think of her. I swore an oath I would place that part of my life behind me forever," he murmured to himself, staring at the letter which seemed to burn in his hands. Should he give it to her? Surely she would see the folly of associating with these stiff-necked people. No. If he did, it

177

would go hard on her when Dorcas found out. *It would go hard on you, too,* his conscience accused him.

The truth. Dorcas hated the Irish with even more passion than he did, but she would turn her wrath on Rebekah first, and his daughter needed no more such harsh outbursts. He feared already that his wife's incessant complaints to Rebekah about her cool treatment of Amos Wells had led the girl to harden her heart against an eminently splendid match. Rebekah was headstrong enough to turn away Amos and run off with this Irish prizefighter if she were pushed too far. Better to let the whole matter drop. If his daughter knew nothing about the letter, she would probably never give Rory Madigan another thought.

"Now, if only Amos hasn't given up on her." His older, more experienced guidance was just the thing a reckless girl like Rebekah needed. She had none of Leah's practical sense. Of course, Leah had none of Rebekah's keen intelligence or soft heart either, he admitted with a fond smile. Still, his younger daughter must be saved from herself.

He took the letter to his wastebasket and tore it into tiny pieces.

Chapter Ten

Rebekah sat on the edge of her bed with her head between her knees praying for the spasms racking her to cease. She had thrown up almost every morning for the past several weeks, and hiding the evidence in the slops was getting more and more difficult. She had to hurry and perform the odious chore of emptying and washing the pails in both bedrooms every morning before her mother got to the task. It was no easy feat, since she felt light-headed and dizzy for the first hour or so after arising.

Dorcas had already made several comments about her failing appetite, and even her father was concerned that she looked so listless and pale. Her indisposition did make a legitimate excuse for refusing to see Amos Wells, but he had not been around for the past month—not since the week before Rory left for Denver. If only her love would return. It had been more than three weeks. She had heard nothing about the fight, but that sort of news was not respectable enough to be printed in newspapers and was confined to the rougher elements over in glitter town anyway.

At first she had attributed her malaise to fear over Rory's boxing match and simply missing his love and laughter in her life. In the few brief months they had shared, he had turned her world around and become the center of it. When she missed her courses the past month, she had thought little of it, considering the stressful situation she was caught in, but when again this month they did not come and the light-headedness and sick stomach began, she realized that something was amiss.

Dorcas had never said a word about women in a "delicate condition," but Rebekah had heard her friends, who had the benefit of younger siblings, say that missed courses and upset stomachs were two signs of pregnancy. At first she had been thrilled at the idea of bearing Rory's baby, secure in the knowledge that he would return for her, but then she realized that she would have to confess to her parents the reason for her unseemly rush to wed. Her mother's furious tirade would be bad enough, but just thinking about the stricken silence with which her father would greet the news wrung her heart.

For several weeks she had held to the consolation that with Rory behind her, they could weather her parents' censure, and once they were wed, everything would work itself out. But the trip to and from Denver should not have taken more than two weeks, unless something awful had happened to him. Remembering the savagery of the fight she had witnessed the first day she laid eyes on Rory, Rebekah shivered in terror. And that had only been an amateur bout with a big, clumsy local bully, not a professional fighting champion. Visions of Rory haunted her nightmares. She saw him lying bloody and battered, his splendid body and heart-stopping face beaten beyond recognition.

Rebekah had to know what had happened to him. Working up her courage, she decided she would go to the livery and ask Mr. Jenson that very morning. Slipping away to the livery was not nearly as difficult as Rebekah had feared, for Dorcas dispatched her to the mercantile up the street to purchase some sewing thread. When she arrived at the big stables, a small, narrow-faced youth was shoveling hay into one of the front stalls. She recognized Mort Logan. Although his family was considered poor white trash of the worst sort, he had always seemed like an industrious and sympathetic waif to her.

"Good morning, Mort. Is Mr. Jenson around?"

The boy tipped his battered hat awkwardly and said, "Yes'm. He's out back by the corral."

When she thanked him and headed through the big stable, he stared after her curiously. Rebekah tried not to look up the rear stairs to Rory's quarters, where she had so shamelessly gone to him in the night. Once she asked Mr. Jenson about him, Rory's boss would know that she had been involved with the Irishman. She only prayed he was chivalrous enough not to reveal it to anyone. Beau Jenson was not a member of her father's nor any other church in Wellsville, but he was a quasirespectable businessman, if one overlooked his association with the racetrack and the fact that he was from Alabama originally and voted a straight Democratic ticket. The best families of Wellsville were Northerners and Republicans.

When the big, beefy man saw Rebekah Sinclair approaching, his bulldog face reddened even darker. So this was the filly Madigan had taken such a beating for—a preacher's kid. Who would have guessed? He doffed his hat and smiled respectfully. "Good mornin', Miss Sinclair. What brings y'all to my livery?"

His eyes were shrewd but kind. *He knows!* She swallowed for courage as she nodded a return greeting, then plunged ahead. "You accompanied Mr. Madigan to Denver several weeks ago . . ."

"Yes, ma'am, I did," he replied, aware of the awkwardness of the situation. Surely her snooty family would never approve of a kid like Madigan sparking their daughter. "Rory won the fight—and a battle royal it was, too! You'd a been proud of him, Miss Sinclair."

"That—that was over three weeks ago. Did he say when he was returning? I mean, surely his job here—"

"Aw, he quit his job, ma'am. I warn't surprised none. He won the five-thousand-dollar prize plus several thousand more on side bets that his friend Blackie Drago made for him."

"Who is this Mr. Drago?" Rebekah asked, already dreading the reply.

Beau's face turned even redder as he realized that Madigan's plans may have changed regarding the quiet little preacher's daughter. "Blackie Drago's a real influential person in Denver," he began uneasily. "He's a sportin' man, if y'all take my meanin'."

Rebekah did, all too well. "You mean he's involved in saloons, gambling . . . and other things."

"Yes'm." Beau's face would have glowed in the dark, it was so fiery red as he thought of Junie Killian's attentions to young Madigan. "Well, anyways, Blackie knowed Rory from when the boy first come west. After the fight, even though he won, Rory was beat up pretty bad." She paled and he hurried on. "Aw, nothin' serious, but he said he just wanted to stay on at Blackie's place and heal up for a spell afore he come back to Wellsville. Said he wuz gonna write a letter explainin' it all to his, er, intended," he finished lamely.

"Well, as we can both see, Mr. Jenson, he's had a change of heart. I received no letter." He had left her. He was not coming back! Rebekah felt the world spinning away, and her own voice sounded thin and distant. Then everything went black.

The next thing she knew, she was sitting on a bench against the outside wall of the livery with Beau Jenson attempting awkwardly to hold her up and wipe a wet cloth across her forehead.

"Miss Sinclair, you all right? Y'all fainted dead away on me. Like to scared daylight out of me," he said as she stiffened and sat up.

Her reticule had fallen in the dust, and her hat had come loose from her head, leaving her hair straggling down her back. She must look a fright! What would Mr. Jenson think? "Please, I—I'm all right. I apologize for giving you such a start. May I ask you a very great favor?" He nodded, and his bulldog jowls shook. "Please don't tell anyone that I've made inquiries about Rory Madigan."

"Y'all got my word on that, ma'am, and a Alabama man never breaks his word," he said solemnly as he helped her stand up. "Y'all sure you're all right? Maybe I should see you home in one of my rigs."

"Thank you, but no. I'm fine. I really must be going now."

"Ma'am, give him a chance. I expect he needs a little time to get used to havin' so much money 'n all. But he'll be back. Just wait and see," Jenson said earnestly, praying he was right.

But Rebekah Sinclair did not have time. *Wait for me, Re-*

bekah darlin'. How could he do this after all the nights he had held her in his arms and loved her, after the sacred vows they had exchanged? He had sent no word of explanation. His face should have healed from the fight by now. Nothing was keeping him in Denver. Nothing but an old friend by the sinister name of Blackie Drago, who probably had enough whiskey and loose women to tempt the devil himself. Rory had confessed to her the profligate existence he had lived before coming to Wellsville. Apparently the bright lights of Denver had lured him back to it.

Over the next weeks, Rebekah's certainty that she was with child grew as surely as her certainty that the child's father would not return to claim it. She had to do something but had no idea what. The very thought of facing her mother's screaming tirade or her father's shocked anguish was more than she could bear. Sweet, giggling Celia would have no idea of what to do and would blame herself for helping Rebekah along the road to perdition. Leah was her only hope.

Although the two had never been close, Leah herself was expecting a baby. Perhaps her sister's joy in approaching motherhood would soften her heart. As she drove their old buggy out to the pretty ranch house Henry had built for Leah, Rebekah rehearsed how she would explain her desperate situation. They had relatives back in Boston. Perhaps she could go east and save her family from disgrace.

Rebekah choked back tears. What a watering pot she had become. Since she met Rory Madigan, it seemed she had cried more than she had in all her life. Leah and Henry were well enough fixed that she did not feel it would be impossible to ask her sister and brother-in-law for a small amount of money to see her on her journey. If only the relatives in Boston would take in an unmarried, pregnant woman.

"I'll never see my home again. Never see my father. I hate you, Rory Madigan! I'll never forgive you for your betrayal." She whipped up the old nag, and the rickety buggy gave a lurch as one wheel hit a rut in the road.

Leah's new house was quite the prettiest thing Rebekah thought she had ever seen, a confection of gingerbread trim, gabled roofs, and wide bay windows around the parlor and dining rooms. The Sneads had just moved in a few months ago, and Rebekah had visited only once with her parents. That day a proud Henry had announced that they were expecting a child—news that was greeted with unbounded joy. How differently her own pregnancy would be treated. Resolutely she climbed down from the buggy and picked up the gift she had brought—several tins of freshly baked raisin rolls, Leah's favorite sweet, and a jar of piccalilli she had made for Henry.

The Chinese boy who worked for the Sneads led her into the parlor with grave courtesy, then excused himself to go and inform the missus that her sister had come calling. Rebekah sat nervously on the lovely new Méridienne sofa and looked around at the cluttered room, filled with lace doilies and porcelain figurines. Two lamps sat on opposite sides of the room, and a bronze Seth Thomas clock ticked steadily from the handsome marble mantel.

Leah entered the room, looking pale and haggard in spite of the beautiful pink silk gown she wore. Her figure had grown fuller but she still laced herself, something that Doc Marston had told her only aggravated the discomfort of her pregnancy. Since she had always tended toward fleshiness, her present condition quickly took its toll on her voluptuous figure, but Leah Snead was not one to give up her appearance any sooner than she absolutely must.

Shirl Henke

"What a surprise, Rebekah," she said with no particular enthusiasm in her voice.

"I brought you some fresh-baked raisin rolls and Henry some piccalilli Mama and I put up last week." Rebekah handed the small basket to her sister, then followed as Leah headed toward the kitchen with it. "How have you been feeling, Leah?"

"I've been poorly, but that's to be expected in my condition," Leah replied tartly. "If you want some coffee, Won will make it for you. These days I can't abide the smell of it."

Rebekah shook her head. "No, thanks. I'm sorry you're not feeling well," she said sincerely. Leah had always been a complainer who disliked any small discomfort, yet she did look genuinely ill. Wanting to shift the conversation to a more positive note, she said, "Henry's really pleased about the baby."

"Oh, he's pleased right enough, I guess," Leah said bitterly. She dug into the sweet rolls, licking the gooey icing from her fingers. "My only consolation was to tell Henry that he'll have to sleep in the spare bedroom now that he's done this to me." Her cheeks pinkened after she realized what she had blurted out to her unmarried younger sister. At Rebekah's look of appalled surprise, Leah tossed her silvery curls angrily and took another bite from the roll. "You needn't look so shocked. It's a woman's lot to be miserable when she's in a family way."

"Maybe if you didn't lace yourself, you'd feel better," Rebekah suggested. Remembering the exquisite joy Rory's touch had brought her, Rebekah could not imagine how her sister, lawfully wedded, her union blessed by the Church, could feel so differently.

"I finally have all these beautiful gowns, and now I can't

186

even get into them. Besides, what would you know about it?'' Leah snapped pettishly.

''That's what I needed to talk to you about. . . . '' Perhaps this was not such a wise idea after all. Yet who else could help her? She took a deep breath for courage and said, ''I know more than you think, Leah—and I need your help. I'm with child, too.''

''Good God!'' Leah exclaimed, paling and dropping onto a kitchen chair. ''How could you *do* such a vulgar, immoral, disgusting thing? How will I hold up my head in the community? Mama and Papa will be disgraced. Papa might have to leave the ministry. Who did this? You've only had one serious—surely Mr. Wells didn't do this to you?''

Rebekah's knuckles whitened as she clenched the back of an oak chair. ''Of course not. I never encouraged Amos Wells to call.''

Leah gave a nasty bark of laughter. ''Well, I scarcely expect he'll be calling any more once he hears of this.'' Her eyes narrowed on her sister. ''Who is the father, Rebekah? Tell me. Maybe Henry can force him to marry you before we're all dragged down in the mud with you.''

''He left Wellsville. Left Nevada. But perhaps there is a way for our family to escape disgrace—if you and Henry would help me. I could go to Uncle Manasseh's, in Boston.''

''Don't be absurd! His wife Esther would die before she took in a fallen woman. You must get married. That's all there is to it. Who is this scoundrel? Henry could fetch him back if need be.''

''No! Rory doesn't care about me. He broke his solemn pledge to—''

''Rory! That—that Irish brawler who paid twenty dollars for your box lunch! Small wonder he expected something more than food for his money,'' Leah said cruelly, watching

Rebekah blanch. "So that's why he took a job at Jenson's Livery. To stay here in town and seduce you. Of all the men in the world—how could you, Rebekah?" Leah's face, so red with anger a moment ago, grew pale as the magnitude of the family disgrace struck her. "You must wed, but marrying that penniless foreigner would be as big a disgrace as remaining single." She rubbed her head, then glared at Rebekah, who stood with shoulders slumped, looking down at the kitchen table, unable to meet her sister's accusatory glare.

"There is no one to marry me," she whispered brokenly. *I couldn't bear anyone else to touch me after Rory's betrayal.*

"Let me think. I shall summon Henry. He'll know what to do. Perhaps if Amos Wells didn't find out about the baby—"

"I couldn't lie to him." Rebekah's head shot up as a shiver of fear raced down her spine. "Besides, he's not called for several weeks. I made it clear I didn't favor him."

"You'll come down from that prideful position quickly enough and do whatever we decide is best. Just let me discuss the matter with Henry."

Amos Wells came to call the next evening. He brought a bouquet of magnificent damask roses for Rebekah and asked her to walk out in the garden with him so they might speak privately. "Go on, go on," Dorcas called gaily. "I'll just arrange these in my best crystal vase." She turned to her husband. "You know the one, Ephraim, that your brother Manasseh gave us for a wedding present. Fetch it while these young people take a nice walk. I've baked some gooseberry pie we can all share when you've returned."

Amos held open the side door with a flourish. "After you, my dear."

Rebekah clutched her gray wool shawl around her shoulders and tried to force a smile. "Thank you, Amos."

They walked around the well-tended rows of vegetables. Rebekah could not bear to look down at the pumpkin vines and fat cabbage heads. *Where I fell in the mud and Rory . . . No! Don't think about it.* Amos's voice interrupted her unhappy reverie.

"I regret that business has kept me away from Wellsville so much the past weeks, but I thought perhaps it might be best to allow you time to discover your own mind and better consider my suit."

Discover my own mind. Oh, she had done that. For days—weeks now—she had done nothing but turn her own thoughts inside out until her stomach knotted in misery. What should she do? Tell him about the baby—and guarantee he would repudiate her? Or do as Leah insisted and gratefully accept if he proposed. "I have noted your absence, Amos," she replied carefully. The thought suddenly struck her between the eyes like a sledgehammer. What if Leah had told Henry, and Henry had told Amos about her pregnancy?

She stumbled on a pumpkin vine and Amos took her arm to steady her. "Careful, my dear. You could fall on those pesky vines," he said kindly.

No, her sister and brother-in-law would never have done that, for they wanted the match. And if Amos knew, certainly he would not have come calling with roses for her!

"I've given you time, but now I must go to Carson City to deal with the governor and the legislators. Securing an election to the United States Senate is not a simple matter. Then there are my mining and banking investments to consider. I fear I must have your answer soon, Rebekah. We could be married quietly by your father here in Wellsville, then have a gala celebration to announce our nuptials in the

189

capital.'' He stopped at the edge of the garden beneath an elm tree and took her hand between his, waiting expectantly.

It's all wrong. His touch felt cold, alien. There was none of the thrill, the tingling awareness that always flamed between her and Rory. But her Irishman was gone, off in Denver with his ill-gotten gains and his whores, leaving her behind to take care of herself and his child as best she could. Still, all she could manage was, ''Marriage is very serious, Amos. Let me discuss this with my father. I'll let you know my decision tomorrow . . . if that is all right?'' She looked up into his cool pewter eyes, reading nothing.

He smiled and raised her hand to his lips for a brief, chaste salute. ''I shall look forward to tomorrow.''

Rebekah sat huddled miserably in her father's study, unable to meet his eyes, her head bowed, her own eyes red and swollen from weeping. ''I'm so sorry, Papa, but I couldn't consider Mr. Wells's proposal without telling you the truth.'' She wrung her hands and forced herself to look him in the face. ''I don't think I can do as Leah suggested.''

''You mean you won't marry Amos?'' He had feared this as her story came pouring out, shattering his very soul. *Why, oh Lord, not only me but my favorite child as well, prey to those heathen Irish?*

''I mean that I must tell him about the baby. I can't enter into holy wedlock with a lie hovering between us. He'd learn the truth soon enough.'' Her face reddened, but she was too numb with misery to really feel embarrassment.

''Perhaps not,'' Ephraim began cautiously. ''Rebekah, there's an innocent life to consider here. That of your unborn child, a child destined not to know a father's love . . . unless we can provide one. Amos could believe the baby was his.

He would treasure a child—the heir his first wife was not able to give him.''

Rebekah looked at her father in shock. ''You—you actually mean lie to him—deceive him?'' she blurted out, appalled. Her father had taught her about morality and truth, honor, justice—every value she held sacred.

Ephraim read the horror in Rebekah's eyes. ''Put that way, it sounds wicked indeed,'' he said with a sigh as he combed his fingers through his fine silver hair. ''I've tried to think of what would save you from heartbreak and disgrace—and your child, who did not ask to come into the world under this stigma. And Amos, too, would be happier if he believed you wed him of your own free will, not because you needed a father for another man's child. I suppose some would call it sophistry, but you need tell no lies—simply omit the truth about who the father is. Certainly Amos would never think to ask.''

''But . . .'' Her cheeks reddened with mortification. ''But the baby will come sooner than the normal time . . . at least, I think . . .'' She could not look at her father now.

''A couple of months won't make that much difference. It isn't terribly unusual for babies to come sooner—and even when they do, often they can live. What if this whole sad mistake—or what seems a mistake with that Irishman—is really a blessing in disguise? Perhaps it's the Lord's own providence to see that you and Amos come together as man and wife.''

''You mean that it was meant to be—that Rory desert me this way?'' Her voice almost broke in anguish. ''How could a just or merciful God do such a thing?''

''Rebekah.'' His voice grew stern and he straightened up, pulling his hand away from hers. ''Do not blaspheme.''

''I'm sorry, Papa, but . . . I love him so much. We took

191

Shirl Henke

vows, pledged ourselves to each other before we . . ." Her voice choked off and she lowered her head, unable to bear the pain of Rory's betrayal as it lashed at her again.

"Think, Rebekah. What kind of vows would a man like that consider binding? Only those made before his own priest in his Romish Church. No others hold any fear of retribution for people like them." Ephraim hesitated as Rebekah stared out the window in mute misery. "There is something I have never told you or anyone else. It happened a long time ago, in Boston. Before I ever met your mother."

A cold sense of dread seized Rebekah's heart. "Does it have something to do with why you seem to hate the Irish so?"

His mouth softened a bit and he said softly, "You have always been such a bright, perceptive child, Rebekah. Yes. You see, I fell in love with an Irish girl. She was a servant in my friend's home—a parlormaid. The first time I saw her, I was bewitched by her blue eyes and raven hair. They're the devil's own handsome race, the Irish."

Rebekah's mind at once conjured up Rory's startlingly blue eyes and inky locks. Yes, they were indeed. Her father continued his tale.

"I was a young college student, just started in divinity school on a scholarship. As you know, our family was socially prominent but the money, even back then, was almost gone. I disregarded the pleas of my parents and my peers and courted Kathleen." He stood up and began to pace restlessly as his tale unfolded. "We—we became lovers, and like you and your Irishman, we pledged undying devotion. But she would not abandon her Romish faith and asked that I give up mine—convert for her. God forgive me, I almost succumbed. But your Uncle Manasseh found out about my trysts with her and told our father. When I was forced to

192

examine my feelings under his more mature guidance, I realized that I could not give up the vocation that I had worked a lifetime to enter.

"Neither did I wish to give up Kathleen. Her lack of social station, her being an Irish immigrant—meant nothing to me, even though my family would have ostracized me. I went to her and explained that I had a calling and that I had to answer to the Lord. I asked her to come away with me and marry in my church. We would weather the bigotry of the social elite of Boston. I would even risk being disowned by my family. I still had my scholarship and could finish divinity school at Yale. She cried and she pleaded. She tried to seduce me again—anything to keep me from my resolve. When I said no—and it was not easy—she refused to wed me, saying our vows were not blessed by a priest and were therefore not valid.

"She entered a convent. When I tried to intercede, to prevent her from locking herself away for the rest of her life, the good sisters there turned me away. Then her brothers came after me, waylaying me one night on my way home from classes. They beat me within an inch of my life and threatened me if I ever went to the convent again. She took her final vows. I've never seen her since."

Emotionally and physically drained, Ephraim sank onto the big chair behind his desk, shoulders stooped, head resting in his hands. Rebekah looked at him as the silence thickened around them. *He's still in love with her after all these years, and he doesn't even realize it.* That was why he hated the Irish when he was the soul of tolerance for all others. She rose, walked behind the desk, and placed her arms around his shoulders.

"Oh, Papa, I never understood. Now I do." *You never loved Mama. You couldn't.* This also explained Dorcas's bitterness. Her parents had always had a loveless, mismatched marriage. And she was doomed to repeat the same tragic cycle all over again. More broken vows. More heartache.

Finally Ephraim raised his head, and his eyes were filled with tears. "It will all work out for the best—you'll see, Rebekah. It did for me. I'd like to think I've made a difference with my work, serving the Lord. I've had a good and loyal helpmate in your dear mother, and I've been blessed with you and Leah. You can make a good life for yourself, too."

The pleading look in his eyes broke her heart. Never in all her life, not at the funeral of his best friend, not even when her grandmother had died, had she ever seen her father cry. *I'll settle for a life of giving love, never receiving it, just as you have, Papa.* "You have made a difference in so very many lives—too many to count. I'd be proud to be half the Christian and the person you are, Papa. I'll marry Amos."

He reached out and patted her shoulder, then pulled her into his arms for a fierce hug. "You'll see, Rebekah. It *will* be for the best."

The Howling Wilderness Saloon was busy that night. Virginia City was a town that never slept. The deep mine shafts employed heavy equipment to extract ore from rock hundreds of feet beneath the earth where temperatures soared up to one hundred and forty degrees. Miners worked in shifts, coming up at frequent intervals lest they pass out or even expire from the heat. The mining operations never stopped, going on twenty-four hours a day, seven days a week, when a new bonanza was discovered.

Breweries and distilleries were almost as lucrative as the mines. Saloons and their upstairs fancy houses never closed down either. All manner of men crowded into them to drink and disport themselves. The Howling Wilderness was an anonymous place where everyone pursued his own pleasures, and few were so foolish as to question other men about their reasons for being there.

He had grown to like it that way, like the smell of whiskey and sawdust downstairs and like the heady musk of cheap perfume and sex upstairs. As he approached the bedroom door for his prearranged assignation, he could feel himself getting excited. The thrill of the forbidden sent chills up and down his spine. English Annie would be waiting for him. He opened the door and stepped inside, then froze.

"You're not Annie."

A slender brunette with slitted eyes as old and hard as the ore being mined beneath them, stared unsmiling at him. "Annie got herself booted out. Too much 'o the pipe, ole Sauerkraut sez. She wuz doped out 'o her haid all the time. Couldn't keep up with traffic." She sized up his expensive clothes. He was attractive and even clean. A small smile softened the harsh planes of her mouth but did not reach her cold, dark eyes. "I kin make yew happy, sugar. They call me Magnolia. I'm from Alabama."

Her drawl was heavy but sounded more like East Texas than Alabama. He did not argue but closed the door, stripped, and sprawled on the bed. Her body was thin and angular, nothing like the soft pillowy flesh he was used to, but she was a whore—she had better know what to do.

Magnolia took off her robe without a flourish. Beneath it she wore only a lacy camisole. When she looked down at him, he was watching her expectantly. And his shaft lay shriveled and limp.

"Soo, yew one o' them boys whut's got the guilties over bein' here? Cheatin' on yer wife?" A mirthless laugh bubbled up in her throat, but after one look at his face, she swallowed it. She climbed on the bed beside him and went to work.

It was no good. *She* was no good. He cursed angrily and flung her aside, ripping out several greasy strands of dark hair in the process.

"Yew sonofabitch! I ain't no doped-up English Annie," she spat furiously, rubbing her scalp as she scooted off the bed. "Cain't get it up so yew take it out on me. I don't take no crap from no man—man, hah! Maybe yew ain't a man at all, sugar. Some woman geld yew—yer wife maybe?"

He struck her with his fist, slamming her against the rickety chair beside the bed, overturning it. She stumbled back, a scream welling up in her throat, her eyes enormous with fear as she saw the killing rage etched on his face. He was on her before she could get out the cry for help, the fingers of one hand tightening around her throat while he slapped her with the other. She kicked and tried to claw his eyes, but he threw her to the floor as his fury boiled over.

"You invoke my wife's name—you, a dirty whore! Call me gelded! I'll see you in hell!" He fell on top of her, knocking her arms aside, but not before her nails scratched the side of his face. Then his fingers tightened on her windpipe, and he squeezed and squeezed until she was still.

Chapter Eleven

The wedding was a small, private affair, for which Rebekah was grateful. Her father married them in front of the altar just a week after Amos proposed to her. Only her mother, Leah, and Henry were present.

She had debated about asking Celia, but decided it was unwise. Her friend knew how she felt about Rory and would be upset that Rebekah was marrying Amos. There would have been too many difficult questions about the hurried wedding. In a jealous snit, Celia might even have blurted out something perfectly dreadful to Amos. Rebekah decided that once they were safely settled in Carson City, she would write to her old friend and make up some excuse for what had happened.

No one in Wellsville could have any knowledge that she was expecting a child until well after its birth. This perfectly suited Amos's plans to travel from the capital to Washington once his election to the Senate by the Nevada Legislature took place. Their departure also provided the perfect reason for the hasty marriage. Amos wanted to take his new bride with him to meet his influential friends.

Of course Dorcas had been beside herself over the speedy wedding, altering Leah's wedding dress, and preparing a nuptial feast worthy of the exalted Amos Wells. Indeed, if it had been anyone other than Amos, Rebekah knew her mother would have balked at the simple, quiet exchange of vows. But the disgrace of her daughter's condition and the fact that Amos Wells wanted to wed her quickly before leaving for Carson City greatly mitigated her displeasure. In private, she spoke to her younger daughter only in curt commands, so shocked and disgusted with Rebekah's conduct that she could not even muster one of her famous diatribes.

Rebekah feared her mother would have disowned her if not for Amos's timely proposal. Ironically, now that Dorcas had achieved her cherished goal of having Wellsville's leading citizen in the family, she was so alienated from her daughter that she could find no joy in it.

The wedding meal had been sumptuous by Dorcas Sinclair's frugal standards, a crown roast of pork with sage dressing, green beans and creamed onions fresh from the garden, hot rolls, and rhubarb pie with ice cream for dessert. Leah and her mother had worked since daybreak preparing it. Everyone complimented them lavishly.

Rebekah was scarcely able to swallow a bite. She kept stealing covert glances at her new husband. He was an imposing-looking man, slightly above middle height and well built—trim for his age, she supposed. His clothing was expensive and expertly tailored, with a sapphire stickpin winking in his cravat. The immaculately barbered Vandyke beard added to his look of middle-aged elegance, as did the silver-streaked dark hair framing his well-molded features. Only the unsightly set of scratches on his left cheek marred the effect of perfect grooming. She wondered what accident might have caused them, then dismissed the thought. Probably he'd received them from some low-lying tree branch while riding.

Shortly after seven, Amos indicated that it was time for them to leave. While he, Ephraim, and Henry chatted amiably, Dorcas cleared the table. Rebekah, accompanied by her sister, went upstairs to change into a simple suit for their ride out to the Flying W.

"I would feel it my obligation to explain marital duties to you, but that obviously won't be necessary," Leah said nastily as she finished unfastening the buttons to her sister's wedding dress.

Stepping out of the layers of white satin, Rebekah felt like an utter hypocrite. White for purity. What a cruel joke. She had given up purity, innocence, honor—everything for a man who did not love her. The hostile silence between the sisters thickened while Rebekah donned the sensible tan twill suit she would wear on the long ride.

"I'm sorry for the worry I've caused the family, Leah." Rebekah did not want them to remain enemies. Soon she would be miles away from everyone she knew, living in a strange new city, then traveling all the way to Washington.

"You'd best be grateful for Henry's timely intervention, else this whole ghastly affair wouldn't have ended so well," Leah replied as she smoothed her white satin dress, irritated that it had been ruined by the alterations and was altogether too small for her ever to fit into again. Not that she wished to, but it was *her* wedding dress, after all.

"Leah . . ." Rebekah paused as her sister's words turned

in her mind. Surely it could not be! "Did Henry tell Amos about Rory—about the baby?" Her voice was a hoarse whisper.

Leah's eyes were cold with contempt. "I hardly think so. Why on earth would a man like Amos Wells want some dirty Irishman's castoff? He must've told him some malarkey about your regretting your earlier coolness and pining away for him. When Amos takes you tonight, just act like it hurts the way it did the first time you rutted with that prizefighter. Amos probably won't realize the difference." She shuddered with distaste.

Rebekah blanched and sank onto the dressing stool in front of her small vanity. She would have to sham virginity. Because of her revulsion over bedding Amos, she had blocked the whole thing from her mind. "What if he knows?"

Leah gave her a scathing look. "That, my dear harlot of a sister, is your problem to deal with, isn't it? You're married now, so I'd advise you to become a very good actress. Now, if you don't mind," she said sarcastically, "I'm not feeling at all well myself. My ankles are horribly swollen from working all day in the kitchen. I need to put my feet up and rest." Her hand went to her belly, now rounding noticeably enough to force her to abandon her corset. Leah was only in her fourth month.

Amos will know! All the fear and repugnance Rebekah felt came roaring down on her. It would be horrid enough just to endure another man's touch after Rory, but now she must also contend with her husband's deadly wrath once he realized he had been deceived. Even if she somehow managed to get through the sham of her "deflowering" tonight, her pregnancy would all too soon become apparent if she progressed as her sister had.

But Leah has always been more voluptuous. She watched

as her sister walked out the door and closed it with a firm click, leaving the bride alone with her terror and guilt. She looked down at her own still flat belly and slender body. Perhaps she would not grow heavy so quickly. But that was several months ahead. Right now she had to face letting Amos Wells strip her clothes off and do intimate things to her that she could imagine no one but Rory ever doing.

"Stop it!" She pressed her fingers to her aching temples. Somehow she would get through tonight. She had to for the sake of her unborn child. The baby was innocent and deserved a chance to be part of a real family, to have a loving father. Yet she could not imagine Amos as a doting parent. The cold flashes of controlled fury she had sensed in his eyes still made her stomach clench. But he had been smiling and genial on their various outings, always the chivalrous gentleman. Perhaps it would all work out. "It must, for your sake, little one," she whispered, holding her palm to her belly.

The Sneads were staying with the Sinclairs overnight so Leah could rest up. Good-byes between Rebekah and her family were constrained and mercifully brief. As Amos was bidding farewell to Dorcas, Ephraim quickly gave Rebekah a fatherly squeeze around the shoulders and whispered, "Everything will be fine—just do your duty and love your husband."

How can I? She nodded, unable to meet his eyes as Amos took her arm and assisted her into the large carriage that contained her few worldly belongings. Then they were off, two polite strangers, now man and wife. Conversation was stilted and desultory, as it had always been between them. He explained about his grandiose political aspirations and she listened, nodding in the appropriate places.

The drive to the ranch took longer than usual because an

early autumn storm came pouring down on them with deluging force, turning the dusty road to a quagmire in minutes. To Rebekah it seemed an evil omen, but she forced the thought aside. When they arrived at the Flying W, Amos helped her from the elegant covered carriage and guided her toward the front porch of the white frame mansion. A servant scurried down the steps carrying an umbrella with which he quickly sheltered her.

If she had possessed any romantic notion that her husband would sweep her into his arms and carry her across the threshold, it was quickly dashed. Amos strode up the steps with her on his arm. A tall, thin old man held the door open as the bridal couple walked into the foyer.

Amos made no attempt to introduce her, increasing her sense of isolation and foreboding. As he instructed the butler to take her bags to her quarters, a young girl with light brown hair and freckles came scurrying down the front staircase and bobbed a curtsy.

"This is your personal maid, Rebekah. She will see you to your room and assist you in changing. I shall be up within an hour."

"This way, ma'am," the girl said with a nervous glance at her employer as she gestured to the stairs.

Rebekah smiled at the pale, homely young girl and preceded her. "What's your name?"

"Patsy, ma'am. Patsy Mulcahey."

Irish. She should have recognized the accent. Indeed, it was quite common across the state, especially in the Comstock where the Irish comprised the largest group of miners, whose wives and daughters worked as domestics in wealthy households from the Truckee River all the way south to Eagle Valley.

Rebekah turned her attention to the ornate hallway at the

top of the stairs. Their footfalls were swallowed up in a thick Aubusson carpet with an intricate pattern. The walls were covered with an equally dark blue wallpaper with narrow maroon stripes. When Patsy opened the door to her room, Rebekah stepped inside her large quarters. A delicate settee and piecrust table were placed near the door. Beyond, a tambour desk sat near the window, which was hung with maroon velvet draperies. The dark blues and maroons were repeated in the satin bedspread and pillows. Every piece of furniture in the room was expensive and exquisitely designed, but as cold and soulless as Amos Wells himself.

Refusing to look at the bed, she swept her gaze to the door to the adjoining room. At least she would have some privacy and be allowed to sleep alone. *But first I have to let him touch me the way Rory . . .*

"Will you be wantin' a hot bath, ma'am?"

Forcing her thoughts away from the pain of Rory's betrayal, Rebekah smiled at Patsy. "No, I believe the pitcher and basin will do." *Best to get this over with as quickly as possible.* She began to slip off her jacket.

Patsy came forward, and her deft fingers set to work on the buttons at the back of Rebekah's blouse. "I've never had a maid before, Patsy. I suspect it will take some getting used to," she said as the girl assisted her in sliding off the blouse, then set to work on her heavy skirts.

When she was down to her camisole and pantalets, the maid seemed to sense her modesty and turned toward the luggage the butler had deposited beside the armoire. The two battered old valises looked frayed and pathetic sitting amid such opulence.

"My nightgown is in the smaller one," Rebekah said. While Patsy unpacked her things and laid out one of her two simple white cotton sleeping gowns, Rebekah quickly performed her ablutions behind the dressing screen. "How long have you been employed by Mr. Wells, Patsy?"

"Nigh onto two years. Since me da passed on 'n me brothers went to Gold Hill to work in the mines."

"You must've been very young," Rebekah said sympathetically. The girl looked no more than sixteen now.

"I was fifteen. Old enough, I expect." Her voice was brittle and guarded. She would not meet her mistress's eyes as Rebekah stepped from behind the screen with her nightgown on. "Here, ma'am, let me brush yer hair."

Rebekah took a seat in front of the big mahogany dressing table and gazed into the oval mirror at her pale, haunted face. If eyes were windows to the soul, then hers were cursed for all eternity, their hazel-green brightness turned into night-dark pools. She let her lids close, shutting out everything but the gentle, even strokes of the hairbrush.

"Yer hair's beautiful, ma'am," Patsy whispered. "Like old Spanish coins I seen once, when me family was travelin' west."

Used to invidious comparisons between her own dark blond hair and her sister's silvery beauty, Rebekah was surprised and almost blurted out that her hair was far too dark a shade for true beauty, but stopped suddenly. "Thank you, Patsy. You're very kind."

"So are you, ma'am, if I might be so bold as to be sayin' so. If you ever need anything . . ."

Muffled footfalls echoed down the hall. Then a sharp rap was immediately followed by the opening of the door. "You are dismissed, Patsy."

With a look of alarm in her warm brown eyes, the maid put down the hairbrush, giving Rebekah's shoulder a squeeze before she curtsied to Amos and left the room. The silence between husband and wife thickened as he drew nearer, inspecting her. She sat very still, waiting, her fingers clamped to the edges of the satin-covered chair.

Amos's cold gray eyes swept over her sheer, voluminous nightgown, noting the dainty stitches that mended it in several places. "Your wardrobe is sadly deficient, but I'll quickly remedy that once we get to Carson City." His hand glided over her hair, which hung like a cloud of burnished gold to her waist. "I have a well-trained maid at my city house. She'll know how to fix your hair more becomingly."

Rebekah could think of nothing to say. She wanted to draw away in revulsion but stifled the impulse, forcing herself to appear calm. Finally, she found her voice. "I'm afraid I'm not used to maids."

"You'll become accustomed to them," he replied dryly with an air of superior amusement. The chit was terrified. He debated the wisdom of bedding her. She did have a certain innocent allure that stirred his blood. He could see her potential for great beauty, the sort that made men's heads turn with envy, but cultivating those sophisticated qualities would take time. Still . . . her body was fresh, her face unmarred by paints. He felt himself growing hard.

"Get in bed," he rasped harshly and turned to his room. Inside, he ripped off his clothes, throwing them in a pile on the floor. When he reentered her room, she lay beneath the covers like a sacrificial lamb going to slaughter. A sense of power pervaded his body, radiating pleasure and promise.

Rebekah felt his presence even though she refused to look at him. Would he be naked? She could smell his cologne, an expensive, too sweet odor that blended with the Cuban cigars he smoked and the cognac on his breath. Not altogether unpleasant but alien and frightening. Nothing like Rory's scents. *I must put that out of my mind. Forever!* Then she heard the rustle of silk as he slipped out of his dressing robe and turned down the wick on the kerosene lamp.

Amos pulled back the covers with a snap, wanting to see if she would flinch, hoping she would. But she did not. She lay rigid, waiting to do her duty, just as Heloise always had. And he hated her for it. "Take off that shabby nightgown," he commanded, unable to keep the anger from his voice.

Rebekah sat up, scarlet waves of shame washing over her. She struggled with the buttons of the gown, remembering how tenderly Rory had unfastened them. *Stop it!*

Impatient with her slowness, yet excited by the pain he sensed in her, Amos reached over and seized hold of the gown, ripping the thin old cotton. "There. Let me look at you." His voice was scratchy, his breathing swift and erratic. He reached out one hand and ran it over the curve of her hip. She huddled with the tatters of her nightgown lying about her, fighting not to cover herself from his lustful gaze. Her body was too slender for his taste, but it was well proportioned. Young. Strong.

Feeling the long-dormant urge rush over him, he quickly shoved her onto her back and covered her, his knee pushing her thighs apart as he fumbled with his shaft, positioning himself to breach her. She lay still, unresisting. Her nether lips were dry; the sheath his fingers found and probed was tight. He felt himself growing soft, shrinking. Frantically he tried again to penetrate her, but the brief burst of lust that had inflamed him was gone, doused like a sputtering candle in a Washoe zephyr.

Rebekah bit her lips to keep from crying in pain and panic. The degradation of his rough, cold attack was worse than her nightmares. In spite of his soft, well-manicured hands, his touch was hurtful, almost as if he were desperate to get it over with. Well, so was she. But then he began to curse and rolled off her, sitting up at the edge of the bed with his back turned to her.

"Cold and proper as your mother's Sunday corset," he said scathingly, his voice choked with fury that he masked behind icy disdain. "I shouldn't be surprised that you can't excite a man. But that isn't why I married you. If you do as you're told, learn to dress and act the part of a senator's wife, we'll deal well enough together." He picked up his robe, slipped it on, then turned and looked down at her. His face was glacially serene, but a cold flame burned in his eyes.

Rebekah sat up and grabbed the sheet, pulling it over herself. Dazed and incredulous, she looked up at him as his words registered. He was not going to consummate the marriage. Perhaps he *could* not. There would be no way to deceive him about the baby! "I—I'm sorry, Amos. I'll try to please you—if you'll just give me another chance." She almost choked on the words, but she had spoken her marriage lines, pledging love and devotion—how much worse was this entreaty?

A facade of icy calm hid the burning humiliation he felt. She would pay. Oh, yes, she would. "I think not." He started to leave the room.

"Wait! Please, Amos . . ." If he wanted only an ornament, not a wife, then the whole sham had been in vain. She had to tell him about the baby and offer the only honorable recourse. Annulment. *Oh, Papa, you were wrong. My innocent baby will pay for my sins!*

Wells turned, his bearded face cast in sinister shadows. He stroked his Vandyke as he looked down at her upturned face.

"I've deceived you. I married you to give my baby a name and a father. I'll not contest an annulment," she blurted out before her courage failed her. She expected him to strike her. To fly into a black, killing rage. Or, enigma that he was, to simply stalk off in icy disdain, saying his attorney would handle matters.

Instead he laughed. It was low and ugly, a chillingly eerie sound that was far more frightening than if he had yelled and beat her. "So, the truth is at long last out. Your Irish swain left you saddled with a bastard."

In the flickering light her face went from fiery red to the color of bleached bone. "How—how did you—"

That awful laugh again. Dry, like crumpling paper. "I suspected you were smitten with the ruffian after the fiasco at the box social. Very unwise, my dear, but then youth and impulsiveness go hand in hand, I suppose. You will not ever let another breath of scandal touch you—not to mention another man, especially trash like Madigan."

"But surely you can't want me—not now, not after what's happened?" The taste of bile rose in her throat, choking her.

"Annulments are almost as politically disastrous as divorces. As I said, I don't need or desire you in my bed. The child can be an asset." It could also provide a way to keep her in line, but he did not mention that. "Yes, indeed. A man of my age is expected to have an heir. I do hope you are not so far along that it will complicate things. No matter. You're not showing yet. I can still whisk you away to Washington where no one will know exactly when we married."

Rebekah sat stunned, trying to take in what he was saying. "Then . . . then, you'll raise my child as your own?" Somehow the idea was far less reassuring than it should have been.

His eyes were as cold and gray as hoarfrost. So was his voice. "The child will carry my name, as will you. I shall expect absolute loyalty and obedience from you both." His hand snaked out and took her wrist in an iron grasp. "Don't ever defy me, Rebekah. If I hear so much as a whisper about your behavior, you'll live to regret it—more than you could possibly imagine.''

Abruptly he released her and quit the room. When the door closed with a sharp click, Rebekah let out the breath she had been holding. A shiver ran down her spine, leaving her shaken. *Make no mistake . . .* Her stomach knotted with fear and suddenly lurched in protest. She jumped from the bed and raced to the basin on the dry sink, where she was violently ill.

Wellsville

Rory rode down Bascomb Street, looking ahead to the narrow white steeple in the next block. Her house was next to the church. He resisted the urge to kick Lobsterback into a gallop. The ride from Denver had been taxing enough. After nearly two months of recuperation, he was still as weak as a newborn foal, and his side ached abominably. The fall day was mild and golden, but sweat beaded his brow and he still felt light-headed.

Doc Elsner attributed his symptoms to the massive blood loss that had almost cost him his life. He had lain in bed, restless and miserable for all those weeks, wishing desperately that he had been able to put a return address on his letters to Rebekah so she could answer them. But the Bucket of Blood Saloon was exactly the kind of place in which her family would expect him to reside.

He had stopped at a small hotel on the edge of town late last night to rest up, bathe, and change into the new suit he had bought in Denver. His wedding suit. Dismounting from Lobsterback, he patted the small ring box in his pocket. Most of his winnings were in a Denver bank, but he had splurged on the emerald ring and braided gold band. Rebekah might be a simple rancher's wife, but she would have a proper engagement.

After steeling himself for a tense scene with her parents, Rory was disappointed and somewhat uneasy to find no one at the parsonage or the church. Perhaps there was some emergency out at the Flying W, where Leah and her husband lived.

Rory headed to Jenson's Livery. Beau knew everything that went on in town. As soon as Rory reined in at the central corral behind the big livery barn, the portly owner came striding across the yard, his red jowly face creased by a concerned frown.

"Where in tarnation you been, Madigan? Y'all look worse than you did when Poole got done with you," he said, inspecting Rory's thin, haggard face.

Rory still had a way to go to regain the weight he had lost while lying bedfast at Blackie's. "It's a long story, Beau, but I did make it back. I'm looking for Rebekah Sinclair. No one's at the parsonage or the church. Where is she?"

Beau's eyes met Rory's, reading youthful excitement and hope. He hated to be the one to dash it to pieces. Of all the fool rotten luck. What had made the boy dawdle so long? What had made the girl run off with a cussed galoot like Wells? His gaze shifted, and he began to wrap the reins of the bridle he had been carrying around one beefy fist. "I hate to be the one to tell you this, Rory . . ."

The hairs on Rory's neck prickled in warning and his gut clenched. "Tell me what, Beau?" he asked guardedly.

Rubbing one big paw across his paunch, Jenson shifted from one foot to the other, then looked up into Madigan's wary face. "Miz Rebekah's gone and got herself hitched. Family's up in Carson right now for a big celebration with the governor 'n all the high muckety-mucks in the legislature.''

''She married Amos Wells.'' His voice was tight and cold. ''When?''

''Oh, it was a while back. . . . ''

''How long a while?''

Beau scratched his gray head until the hair stood out at spiky angles. '' 'Bout a month ago, I reckon.''

''That was barely a month after the fight!'' Rory's grip on his emotions broke. The pain of betrayal hit him with sledgehammer force. He seized a rough corral post and held tight. He didn't even feel the splinters dig into his hands.

''She come down here the week after I got back from Denver, lookin' to find out about y'all. Seemed real upset. I told her y'all won 'n wuz commin' back—''

''The lady obviously didn't see fit to wait,'' Madigan interrupted tersely, then spun on his heel and stalked away.

''Wait, Rory. Don't go doin' nothin' crazy now, hear? Where y'all goin'?''

''To Carson City—to join the celebration.''

Jenson cussed as he watched the young man ride off in a flurry of dust. ''What in tarnation happened? That little filly was all teary-eyed 'n faintin', 'n Rory looks so damned skinny he best get out of the bathtub afore pullin' the plug.'' Beau swore at the folly of impetuous youth.

Carson City

Rebekah stood in front of the mirror while Patsy fussed with her dress, an elaborate concoction of bright fuchsia silk, cunningly cut with a thick fall of delicate black lace across the low bodice. Her breasts, which by now had begun to

211

round out significantly, were enticingly displayed. Her waist was only slightly thickened.

"Hold tight while I hook the last of these buttons, ma'am," the little maid said, her face screwed up in concentration. After disparaging Leah's vanity for lacing herself while *enciente,* now Rebekah was doing the same thing. Amos insisted. Whatever her husband wanted came to pass. She was to look beautiful, smile, and be the gracious hostess for tonight's gala. All the most influential men in the state would be there. Their city house would be lit from the cupolas to the cellars. She could hear the orchestra Amos had hired tuning up their instruments downstairs.

What a consummate actress I've become. Rebekah would do exactly as Amos wished. He had already made it clear that defying him would lead to setbacks in her father's work among the poor Chinese in the mining districts—not to mention an end to any financial support for the church itself. Using her unborn baby as a pawn was a ploy he had not resorted to as yet, but Rebekah had learned that Amos Wells was utterly ruthless and single-minded. He would not hesitate to use a child, not even his own, much less the bastard of a worthless Irishman.

"There, ma'am. Yer all ready to go." Patsy stood back and inspected her handiwork with pride.

Rebekah had grown fond of the quiet little Irish maid and had pleaded with Amos to allow her to travel with them to Carson City. Even though Patsy was not as skilled as the maid at the city house, she was bright and eager to learn. More importantly, she was the one friend Rebekah could rely on in her new life.

Her parents were here for a visit, as was Henry. Leah had stayed home since she was showing too much now to travel or to be seen in public. As far as Rebekah's family knew, things were idyllic between Rebekah and her rich, seemingly indulgent husband. Amos had outfitted her with a wardrobe so splendid that even Celia would have been green with envy. Their city house at the edge of Carson was situated on a rise overlooking the broad, verdant Eagle Valley. The three-story brick mansion was filled with elegant Victorian furniture, crystal chandeliers, and Aubusson carpets. Rebekah Wells was the envy of every lady in the capital. And the most miserable.

Pushing all such thoughts aside, Rebekah allowed Patsy to fasten the clasp of her new diamond necklace, a wedding gift from her husband. The heavy three-strand choker, dangling earrings, and matching bracelet were too cold and gaudy for her simple taste, but like everything else in her life, the choice of jewelry was at her husband's discretion.

Just then a light rap sounded at the door, and Henry Snead's voice asked, "Are you ready, Rebekah? Amos is tied up with Governor Blasdel and asked that I escort you downstairs. He'll join you to make your entry into the ballroom."

Patsy opened the door, and Henry stood silhouetted in the hall, looking handsome but a bit uncomfortable in his tails and starched white shirt. His wavy brown hair had been meticulously barbered, and his mustache waxed to stand out prominently. Tugging at his tight collar, he bowed and grinned broadly.

"You look grand, Rebekah. Amos will be the most envied man in Nevada tonight."

"That's always been his goal, Henry," she replied softly, smiling for him as he extended his arm and she took it.

"I've sensed the tension between you and Amos even though you try to hide it. He isn't an easy man, I know, but

213

once he gets to Washington, you'll have a wonderful new life.''

She looked up into his concerned dark eyes. "You're a good man, Henry. And you know why I had no choice but to marry him. . . . '' Her cheeks stung, but she met his gaze forthrightly.

A look of alarm washed over his face. "Does he know?''

"I told him.''

"Not an altogether wise decision, do you think?'' Henry asked gently.

"I had no choice . . . there are some things too personal, too painful to discuss, Henry. But I do appreciate your being my friend.''

"You can always rely on me, Rebekah, I promise.''

They made their way downstairs through the glittering press of silver kings, cattle barons, bank presidents, and railroad magnates. The assembly was liberally sprinkled with newspapermen from over a dozen leading papers in northwest Nevada and politicians of every stripe. All the rich men had their ladies on display, but none equaled Rebekah's fresh young beauty. She greeted everyone with a smile and laughter, hiding her inner anguish.

"There you are, dear, and don't you look splendid!'' Dorcas gave her younger daughter an affectionate hug as if nothing had ever been amiss between them. She beamed with pride as she inspected Rebekah's glittering outfit.

Ephraim, always uncomfortable at such lavish gatherings, smiled wanly and placed his arm around her shoulders. "Your mother's right. You look wonderful, child.''

"And you look tired. Have you been getting enough rest?'' Rebekah scolded.

"No, he hasn't, and it's all the fault of those heathen Chinese up on the Comstock,'' Dorcas said crossly.

"Now, my dear, you haven't seen the wretched conditions under which those poor people are forced to live. I'm only doing a small bit to help—"

"More noble servitude, eh, Ephraim?" Amos interrupted, proprietarily taking Rebekah from her father's arm and pulling her to his side, playing the doting husband. When he raised her hand and kissed it gallantly, half the women in the room fairly swooned in delight.

"Aren't Mr. Wells and his bride just the most romantic couple?" one matron gushed behind her fan.

"Of course, he is practically old enough to be her father, but a girl can always use the steady hand of experience to guide her," her companion commented discreetly, wishing she were in Rebekah's place as Amos Wells led his bride into the grand ballroom to open the dancing with a waltz.

The host and hostess floated across the floor to the sounds of violins while the perfume from huge sprays of roses and lilies filled the air. Glittering crystal chandeliers at both ends of the enormous room gave off multifaceted light which reflected brilliantly on Rebekah's diamonds as she whirled in silken splendor, a fuchsia canary in a jeweled cage.

Outside the wide patio doors, the swell of the music was faint as Rory made his way across the formal garden. In the darkness at the outskirts of Carson, the mansion had shone like a beacon, every window filled with dazzling light and color. "Jasus, it's a damned palace," he muttered beneath his breath as he rounded the topiary and looked across the fountain. She had chosen well. The Flying W Ranch, the fanciest frame house in Wellsville, and a mansion like this in the capital. Still, some small part deep in his heart of hearts longed to find it was all a mistake—that Amos Wells had not made her his wife and swept her off here. He had to see her for himself.

Knowing he'd be refused entry at the front door and being too proud to sneak in through the servants' quarters, he had opted to cut through the estate's gardens. Once he reached a side entrance, he had no idea what he would do next. The lilt of the waltz drew him toward the laughter and gaiety, although he felt nothing but the hollowness of desertion and betrayal.

Two sets of double doors were closed to the chill evening air, but the beveled glass panes acted as windows, bringing the brilliance of the assembly out onto the patio. He drew closer, crossing the marble inlaid tiles on the steps until he stood with his face so close to the glass that his breath frosted one pane as he peered inside.

Rory had reached out to turn the knob and slip in when he caught sight of her. He froze. If he needed proof positive that Rebekah had chosen the life Amos Wells could offer her over his own paltry dreams, it danced before him in a cloud of fuchsia silk. Lord above, he had thought her beautiful in mended hand-me-down dresses with her hair hanging in wheaten waves down her back. But this—this defied imagining. Rebekah glowed like a goddess, dripping with diamonds, her hair coiled high atop her head in an elaborate coiffure of burnished gold. She was garbed in a billowing ball gown that bared an indecent amount of her creamy breasts, which once he alone had been privileged to see.

Now her coldly elegant husband held her in his arms, gazing down at that bounty while the crowd gawked and fluttered like a pen full of gaudy geese. Rebekah was smiling as serenely as Queen Victoria when another couple on the polished dance floor called out some sally, and her laughter bubbled out. He could not really hear it through the glass separating them, nor could he smell the sweet, delicate perfume of her scent, but both were achingly familiar to him

216

and always would be. He knew the sounds she made in the throes of passion, the scent of her when he had caressed her body, the taste of that sweet flesh, the touch of her silken skin. And he would never know them again.

"Not as long as I'm a poor Irish immigrant who boxes for prize. But one day, Rebekah Sinclair—Madame Wells—one day I'll have you again," he muttered fiercely. "I'll be rich, and you'll come crawling to me. I swear it before God!"

PART II

EPIPHANY

For there is nothing covered that shall not be revealed; and
hid, that shall not be known.

Matthew 10:26

Chapter Twelve

Washington, D.C., 1874

Representative Rory Madigan stood at the edge of the crowded room, watching the assembly of dignitaries. The gala at the British Embassy was his first big social event since arriving at the capital as the newly elected United States Representative from Nevada. Being a Democrat who had won his seat on the strength of Democratic governor Lewis Bradley's influence, he scarcely expected President Grant and the ranking House Republicans to pay him much attention. That suited his plan perfectly. Being in politics was a means to an end—justice for Amos Wells and revenge for Rory Madigan. Rory also needed to secure the government's timber contract and shipping franchise for Patrick, which meant playing the game the same way all the politicians did.

Patrick. Just thinking about the miracle of finding his

brother alive was enough to bring a smile to his harsh face. After leaving Carson City in the fall of 1870, he had invested his prize money with Beau Jenson in some blooded race-horses. He quickly gained a reputation as a trainer and had taken a string of his most valuable stock to San Francisco. At the auction, his best bay was purchased by the agent for a prosperous shipping magnate who owned a big warehouse on the Embarcadero. When Rory delivered the prize animal, he was stunned speechless to find that the magnate was his brother.

Patrick had not been aboard the whaler that had gone down in the North Atlantic. Instead he had shipped out on a vessel in the China trade and had returned to San Francisco with enough profit to start his own shipping business. He had traveled back to New York to the orphanage but had missed Rory by scant weeks.

Reunited, the two had spent the next several years increasing the scope of their business. Patrick's contacts up and down the Pacific Coast led to more lucrative shipping contracts, and Rory expanded inland, buying up timbered lands to provide lumber for the voracious Comstock mines and ever-expanding railroads. Soon his lumber operations in Nevada had grown so lucrative that he purchased a large ranch in the Eagle River Valley outside Carson City and began to enjoy his one abiding pleasure, breeding splendid racing stock. Patrick ran their office in San Francisco and Rory ran his end of their venture from Virginia City. But always he kept his eye on the ultimate goal—the destruction of Amos Wells. And *her*.

Since Amos had become one of Nevada's United States Senators, he and Rebekah had spent most of their time in Washington, with only rare visits to Carson City. Rory had not crossed paths with them, since he spent most of his time in Nevada. It did not suit his plan for them to meet yet, but she was never out of his thoughts. After four years, would she look different—be fat and faded as her sister had become? He doubted she would recognize him, for he had changed a great deal. An unholy smile, utterly devoid of mirth, flashed across his face. *Someday, Rebekah . . . someday.* He had learned patience over the years.

"You look like a hungry tomcat watching a robin," Dorothea Paisley purred, running one elegant gloved hand up his arm while patting her sleek ebony coiffure with the other.

The beautiful brunette was married to an older Senator, who had survived the vicissitudes of the war and wielded considerable influence in spite of being a Democrat in a predominantly Republican Senate. Dorothea was almost as knowledgeable about where the skeletons were buried in Washington closets as was her husband. She had been Rory's mistress for the past several months.

He made it a point to confine his affairs to older, sophisticated women, mostly the bored wives of politically influential men. Not only was the practice a useful source of information, but it also kept him free of emotional entanglements. How ironic that the once pariah Irishman without a cent to his name had now become one of the most sought-after bachelors from San Francisco to Washington. But marriage was not in his plans. Not now, not ever. He had pledged himself once and been betrayed. One broken vow was enough.

"I've been talking to Senator Harbridge's wife about the mining bill. If you want to come to my place later tonight, we can discuss it. . . . " She let her hand slip surreptitiously beneath his coat and felt his heartbeat accelerate. A smile curved her lips. "Until later, then. Horace won't be home all night," she added discreetly.

"Thea, pet, I shall look forward to our discussion," he said gravely, raising her hand in a brief salute. Suddenly he saw them and froze.

Thea sensed the change at once, as if an electrical storm had swept through the room, leaving Rory crackling with tension. "What's wrong?" Her eyes followed his to where Senator Wells had just entered the crowded room and stood on the marble stairs with his stunning blond wife. "Surely you've met your distinguished colleague from Nevada, darling," she said in a saccharine tone, clearly implying that it was the woman, not the senator, in whom he was interested.

"I've met Wells—and his wife," he replied tersely, his eyes never leaving Rebekah's face. The years had been more than kind to her. She had grown from an innocent nymph into a breathtaking woman. The contours of her face had taken on more definition. Her cheekbones seemed higher and more elegant, her mouth sensuous and fuller. There was a flair about her as she moved with grace and assurance, passing along the line of luminaries, even pausing while President Grant and his wife exchanged pleasantries with her and her husband.

A flash of rage welled up, white hot, almost bubbling over before he brought it under control. The sudden force of it took him completely by surprise. He had worked for years to learn how to bury his emotions and channel his temper, his pain, his hate toward one goal. Swallowing hard and clenching his fists, he took a deep, cleansing breath and forced a smile to his lips, a smile that did not reach his eyes. Perhaps she could be useful. How much did she know about her husband's crooked stock manipulations?

"If you'll excuse me, darlin', I have to renew an old acquaintance. As you pointed out, the Senator and I are colleagues now."

Rory left Thea in a frosty huff and started across the floor. He was stopped frequently by fellow congressmen and other politicians. He smiled and laughed genially as he made his way slowly to where Rebekah stood with two older women he recognized as cabinet members' wives.

Rebekah saw him almost as soon as she stepped into the room. She had overheard Amos and Senator Brockman discussing his recent election as Nevada's only member of the House of Representatives and wondered how long it would be before their paths crossed. *Rory.* He looked so different. Older, yes, but more than that. He looked elegant, cultured, at home in the expensive black superfine suit expertly tailored to his tall, lean body. She knew little about his business interests out west, but she suspected that if his wealth did not yet rival her husband's, one day it would. She felt it in her bones.

I wonder what Mama and Papa would say about his suitability as a husband now? She tried to look away, to ignore the way he threw back his head and laughed, that same old blinding white smile, the gesture with those graceful, long-fingered hands, the unruly curl of night-black hair that fell onto his forehead. It was all so painfully familiar.

She had lived in virtual isolation these past years, far from friends and family back in Nevada. Amos had insisted. It was another means of keeping her in line. Mostly he traveled back to Nevada alone, leaving her and young Michael at their Washington residence. As she had watched her son grow from infancy into a bright, cherubic child, she always saw his father in him, a daily reminder of all she had lost. Yet she adored her son with a single-minded devotion. He was her whole life, the one good and perfect thing to come after Rory's betrayal.

It was not fair that he should reappear in her life once

more, to disrupt it here. She shook as he drew nearer, realizing that he intended speaking to her. Her eyes swept the room, looking for Amos. He had vanished with several other senators into a smoke-filled corridor to discuss congressional business. She found herself actually wishing for once that he would reappear and save her from having to face Rory.

"Ooh, my dear, that devilishly handsome young rogue from your home state is coming this way. Surely you know Representative Madigan? He's been cutting a wide swath through the ladies around the capital, I can tell you," Bernice Gould whispered to Rebekah.

"He's still an Irish upstart, I don't care how pretty his face—and he's a Democrat," Bernice's friend interjected, as if belonging to the opposite party were tantamount to membership in the legions of Attila the Hun.

"I met Mr. Madigan several years ago," Rebekah replied, trying to steady her breathing and not stare as he drew closer. A predatory smile slashed across his face, and Rebekah felt time and the world slip away when he spoke.

"Top of the evening to you, Mrs. Gould, Mrs. Stowe. . . ." He hesitated just a moment before making his bow to Rebekah. "And Mrs. Wells. How good to see a familiar face from home. Would you honor me with this dance?"

Without giving her a chance to refuse, he swept her into his arms as the music started up, leaving the two matrons gaping in consternation. Gossip would soon fly thick and furious around the capital.

Rebekah stiffened as his arms went around her, but without creating a humiliating scene she could do nothing except dance with him. Amos would be livid when he heard. Just having him touch her, feeling his nearness, made all the old memories thrum through her body, as painful as a freshly lanced wound.

"Why are you here?" she asked before she could bring her chaotic thoughts into order.

"I'm the new congressman for Nevada. You do remember Nevada? Your home," he prodded sarcastically. "I know you've seldom been there in recent years. Life in Washington seems to agree with you."

"Wealth and power seem to agree with you." *God, he looked as ruthless as Amos!* The coldness in his eyes, the hard set of his face, were nothing like the young man who had loved her. He looked at her the way he would an opponent he planned to beat senseless in the prize ring. She missed a step.

"So, to the heart of the matter. Now that I'm nearly as rich and powerful as Amos Wells, do you think your family would approve of me?" His voice was silky, taunting.

Remembering her very thoughts when she first saw him across the room, Rebekah felt the heat steal into her cheeks. The nerve of the arrogant wretch! She would be the one to pay for his cruel little game when Amos learned of their meeting. "My family's approval no longer signifies. I wouldn't have you if you owned the whole damn Comstock!"

He felt her try to pull away, all stiff and breathless. The furious anger leaped between them like a flame in dry tinder. "Oh, no, you don't get off so easily." His voice was silky but low and menacing as he whirled them toward a set of open doors. "Think of the scandal if you stalked away from me in mid-dance."

She eyed the direction he was taking them, and her heart skipped a beat. "Think of the scandal if I don't!"

"Worried about gossip—or Amos? I imagine a man who

bought a wife would be rather unreasonable.'' He felt her flinch and knew he'd struck a nerve. ''Not a marriage made in heaven?'' He *tsk*ed sardonically as he slipped quickly behind the fronds of potted palms beside the door.

Rebekah twisted in his arms, now growing desperate. ''Let me go!''

''What are you afraid of, darlin'? That you might still enjoy my touch more than all his money?'' He swept her into the muggy Washington night outside the crowded ballroom and pinned her against the warm bricks of the embassy wall. ''I like your perfume. Expensive. French, isn't it? And this . . .'' His fingertips grazed the top of the elegant celery-green silk ball gown cut in simple, straight lines, unlike the billowing fuchsia finery in which he had first seen her decked out. ''Understated. Tasteful. When did you stop letting Amos select your clothes . . . and jewelry?'' he purred. The trespassing hand lifted the single strand of pearls gleaming luminously at her throat.

His touch sizzled through every pore, every nerve ending in her body, leaving her paralyzed, unable to think—only feel. And with that feeling came mindless remembrance—and yearning.

She stifled a sob, whether of misery or frustration, she—and he—could not discern.

Rory whispered a succinct oath and lowered his head, taking her mouth savagely, grinding his lips over hers, his tongue probing at the tight seam of her lips until she opened for his pillaging. He plunged inside and felt her tongue collide with his. Her mouth was as delicate and sweet as he remembered. He dug one hand into the elaborate coils of her hair, holding her head immobile as he worked on the kiss. His lips, his tongue, his very breath demanded a response to the brutal invasion. She could fight him, bite him, he was beyond caring as the taste and scent of her intoxicated him with unbearable hunger.

Rebekah felt the anger in his rough caress and remembered all the times in their past when he had been that angry, that possessive, and had taken her so. Always she had given in to him. But now she was married to another because he had betrayed her. *Fool, fool,* she heard a voice whisper as her hands stole up his arms and her fingers dug into his shoulders. She molded herself against him, letting his tongue duel with hers, thrusting and dancing that old familiar ballet.

Then his hot, seeking mouth shifted position, slanting across hers at another angle as he pulled her yet closer, pressing his lower body against hers, pinning her against the wall until she could feel every muscle and bone. The swell of his sex probed against her belly, bringing forth a pooling heat, so long dormant, to spread in radiating waves as her starved young body remembered love. Rebekah heard the piteous whimpering yet did not recognize it as her own until he broke off the kiss abruptly.

Rory was losing control, drowning, drawn into the vortex of past remembrance, sweet remembrance. He itched to tear away the wisps of silk that clung so lovingly to her breasts and savage them with his mouth, to shove up her skirts and feel the velvety heat of her envelop him once more. *Witch.* What had begun as an attempt to punish her was ending as an exercise in self-torture. He pulled away, tearing a few strands of golden hair that clung to his fingers.

They stood a scant foot apart, staring into each other's eyes, revealing even in the murky darkness of the moonless night more than either wished the other to know. Panting for breath, shaking, they moved farther apart in silence, Rebekah sliding along the wall, Rory stepping back. She felt the sting of her torn hair. One heavy coil fell onto her shoulder. Breaking the hypnotic spell, she reached up and began to straighten the coiffure.

Easier for a woman to compose herself than a man, he thought bitterly, grateful darkness shadowed the still rampant erection straining to be free of his tight dress breeches. Damn, but he ached with wanting her! And she had wanted him, too, he knew it. "Old Amos must be a neglectful lover," he said softly. "Perhaps I should have carried you into the British Ambassador's topiary and screwed you soundly."

The barb struck home. Even though he could not know about her husband's impotence, Rebekah gasped in outrage at his crudity. Pain drove her to fury. Her hand flew out, delivering a stinging slap that rang out over the music from inside the embassy. "Don't you ever come near me again, Rory Madigan—or so help me God, I'll set the police on you!"

"Don't make any more promises you aren't able to keep, darlin," he taunted.

Her eyes glittered with unshed tears. "You're a fine one to talk of broken promises, you cheap Irish trash. Everything my father said about your kind was true!" She watched the fury darken his blue eyes and his jaw clench. For a moment she thought he was going to strike her back. She braced for it, but the blow never came.

"You chose well—you're every bit the bitch to match a bastard like Amos. I'd wish you joy of him, but it seems he's given you little satisfaction." An evil smile curved his lips as he looked scornfully at her.

Rebekah turned away and dashed toward the sanctuary of the embassy, wanting to die of shame for her brazen display, for her weakness, for his cruelty. And most of all, for their lost love. As she stepped through the door, his voice cut across the void between them.

"We'll meet again, Rebekah. And you will come to me. That's one vow I'll never break."

Nevada, 1874

Virginia City had always been an unbelievably ugly place to Patrick Madigan's way of thinking. He looked at the steep mountains towering above the town, bare and bleak, as raw as the disfiguring holes the mines had gouged in the earth. San Francisco—that was his town, with its wide streets and steeply rolling hills, situated high above the aqua-green grandeur of the Pacific. The violence and gaudiness had been bred out of the city by decades of civilization and permanence. Permanence was a virtue he believed Virginia City would never achieve. Even with its big brick buildings, there was always a look of instability about the town that never slept. Perhaps that very insomniac frenzy indicated its tenous hold on existence.

"You've grown too whimsically philosophical, Patrick, my man," he chuckled to himself as he stepped away from the big bay window in the offices of Madigan & Madigan, Ltd. He had arrived yesterday to handle a timber contract for Rory while his younger brother was off in Washington. Would their parents ever have believed it—their youngest son a United States congressman?

Of course, Rory's election meant more work for both of them, but then work was all his brother lived for—work and revenge. Where had that carefree boy of childhood memory gone? After their parents and Sean died, Rory had been bewildered by the sudden tragedy, heartbroken to be separated from Ryan and him, but hopeful of their reunion. Their little

231

brother had always been the most buoyant optimist.

Something—someone—had changed him. Even though Rory had tried to keep it secret, on one rare occasion when they sat up and drank late into the night, he had let down his guard and had told Patrick about her. Rebekah Wells. The beautiful young preacher's daughter who had thrown him over for Amos Wells's wealth and prestige. His brother's pain was like a festering wound that healed over but remained putrid, eating away deep inside. Rory's obsession grew, an obsession to eventually bring Wells's empire crashing down about his ears—to utterly ruin the man. And the man's wife.

Patrick, too, wanted Wells brought to justice. But Patrick saw in Rory's hate a dangerous cancer that would destroy him as surely as it destroyed their common enemy. And Amos Wells was their enemy. The ruthless greed of the silver kings and their banking cohorts was responsible for their brother Ryan's death.

Ryan had died in a mine shaft explosion deliberately set by the men who owned controlling interest in the mine. The practice was not unusual, especially on the Comstock, where mining speculations had reached frenzied heights—or depths, depending on one's point of view. Patrick had always thought California politics none too clean, but as one wag had said, "If California in '49 was the vestibule of Hell, then Nevada in the '70's was the throne room of Satan himself."

Unscrupulous mine owners often suppressed the news of a rich strike so they could buy up all the market shares cheaply. To keep word of a new vein from getting out before they cornered the market, speculators would either hold the miners prisoner underground with bribes, or failing that, set upper-level explosives to seal off the lower reaches of the shaft temporarily. The word of such a "disaster" would further depress stock prices for the bankers and mine owners. Now and then, an explosion went awry, and the men trapped below were suffocated or gassed to death before help arrived to free them. Patrick had learned that was what had happened in the mine where Ryan died ten years earlier, but he had never been able to prove anything.

He had gone searching for his elder brother as soon as his ship docked in San Francisco harbor. He had located the Silver Lady mine where Ryan had been employed—two weeks after his brother had died in an explosion. Patrick had wandered numbly around Virginia City for several days as rescue workers dug out the bodies. While grieving, he had indulged in a bout of drinking in the local saloons. That was where he heard the whispers about how the owners, in collusion with the California banking crowd, had intentionally set the blast.

When the Silver Lady reopened, Amos Wells and his cohorts made a fortune. Patrick swore he would find proof one day, but first he wanted to return for the younger brother both he and Ryan had promised to retrieve.

By the time Patrick arrived, Rory had already left St. Vincent's, swallowed up in the boundless vastness of the West. Heartsick, Patrick had returned to San Francisco and set to work building his shipping empire. He hired agents to search for the youth, but Rory had vanished without a trace—until a cocky young horse breeder from Nevada delivered a fine racer to his town house one day four years ago.

If only Rory could forget his obsession with Wells's wife. He needed to concentrate on ferreting out evidence about Wells's criminal activities while they both were in Washington. Patrick misliked having Rory so near Rebekah during his term in Congress. What would happen if the two accidentally met? Or worse yet, what if Rory sought her out? He pushed the disturbing thought from his mind and sat down at his brother's big desk to dig through the piles of business correspondence.

"No sense borrowing trouble," he sighed to himself.

Washington

Rebekah sat in the center of her big, lonely bed, unable to sleep. Her jaw still ached from the blow Amos had delivered on the way home from the embassy earlier that evening, but not half as much as the other, more judiciously considered, blows he had given her in the privacy of her bedroom—blows to her body in places where no one would see them but Patsy. After all, she was his ornament, and one must not break such a beautiful bauble.

Bernice Gould had practically trampled her way through the press of guests to whisper to Amos about how his wife and the new Nevada congressman had danced so scandalously close and then slipped from the ballroom into the secluded garden. Amos was livid. She had lowered herself to consort with riffraff and made him a laughingstock. Her public display was even more heinous than if she had broken her marriage vows and let Rory do as he had so crudely put it—taken her right there in the ambassador's topiary.

She felt unclean, thinking of her husband's brutality and her former lover's cruelly mocking words—and fiery, punishing kiss. "He's right. I do still desire him. I would've let him do whatever he wished with me." She shivered and hugged her bruised ribs. Suddenly unable to bear being alone in her mockery of a marriage bed, Rebekah threw back the covers and rose. The pain from her beating made her wince as she drew on a robe. She walked over to the window of their big brownstone, which afforded a splendid view of the capital, but the beauty of the city did nothing to soothe her troubled spirit.

Rebekah tiptoed into Michael's room where his nanny slept on a pallet near the door. Amos had insisted on a wet nurse for him and then had hired a series of nurse-governesses, freeing the boy's mother for their arduous social calendar. At every turn, she defied him as much as she dared, slipping away from other duties to squeeze in precious moments with Michael. Kneeling beside his bed, she surveyed his beautiful little face.

He would be four years old in the spring and was already beginning to look like his father. Soon this baby bed would be too small. She reached down and gently ruffled his inky-black hair. How fortunate, at least, that Amos, too, was dark, else he might have disowned the boy. As it was, she feared Michael's growing resemblance to Rory would create problems eventually. Amos had threatened her with boarding schools in cold, distant Massachusetts.

"It's only a means of keeping me in line. He won't separate us, darling. I promise." She leaned down and kissed her son's forehead, then watched as he snuggled over on his side and sucked his thumb. *What would Rory think if he could see his son?*

The question came out of nowhere. She had not considered it since Michael was a newborn, but meeting Rory tonight had triggered all her old hopes and fears. He must never learn about the boy. Already Michael was a pawn in the ugly struggle between her and Amos. She would not let Rory try to use him as well. "I'm sure he doesn't give a damn about Michael. He's probably left a string of children from New York to San Francisco." She was only another in a long series of foolish girls who had succumbed to his charms.

Rebekah rose and went in search of some warm milk to

lace with laudanum. When she was desperate for sleep, she used the evil stuff sparingly. Amos had had the physician in Washington prescribe it for her nerves in a blatant attempt to addict her, which almost succeeded before she realized his scheme. She had grown so dependent that it cost her weeks of agony to overcome the craving. By sheer force of will, she succeeded. After that, he realized that his control over Michael was a sufficient threat to hold her in line. He did not need the laudanum.

But tonight she needed something to assuage her pain, which was far beyond the mere physical aches of her beating. Amos had beaten her before, although not often. The physical pain she could endure, but the sort that Rory inflicted with his cruel words—that pain she could not withstand. The worst of it was that after all the years and treachery that stood between them, she had come to heel like his creature.

I was his creature, but no more! She moved through the long empty corridors of the big house, headed toward the kitchen. The sound of several voices carried from Amos's study. It was late, nearly three a.m. Whatever kind of clandestine meeting her husband was having at this ghastly hour, she did not want to know. Amos was involved in all sorts of shady dealings with other members of Congress and high-ranking cabinet officials in President Grant's administration. She soundlessly passed the heavy walnut door, but then a stranger's voice froze her in her tracks.

"You're certain Madigan won't be a problem? He's been nosing around the capital ever since he arrived, asking discreet questions about your connection to the mining lobby."

"That Irish upstart! He's nothing, I tell you. A one-term congressman elected by his fellow mickeys. A fluke because Bradley won the governorship. They'll both be gone come next election," Amos pronounced.

"I just don't want any trouble in the meanwhile," another voice interjected. Rebekah recognized it as belonging to a senior congressman from California who was a crony of Amos's.

"Have you spread word about the new vein in the Kettle Creek Mine?" the stranger asked.

Amos chuckled. "Rumor has it the mother lode is ten feet wide and deep enough to mine to China."

"Good, good. How soon will it be safe to begin unloading that worthless Kettle Creek stock?"

"I'd wait another week or two. We're holding the miners underground—bribed them with free whiskey and whores. Everyone in the know will think there's a really big strike. I figure stock prices should triple in two weeks," Amos replied.

"Let us hope so. My banking friends in Sacramento expect to maximize this—er, investment in Kettle Creek," the California congressman added.

"Only be certain your new Nevada congressman and his troublesome brother don't get in our way. Patrick Madigan has had agents trying to link us to his elder brother's death for years. Now that he has a foothold in Congress through the younger brother—well, I don't like it." The stranger's voice was petulant. "It was an ill day when those two were reunited."

"If the Madigan brothers get in our way, we have ways to take care of them. Out west we know how to deal with troublemakers," Amos replied in an ice-cold tone. "Don't fret, Stephan."

Stephan! Stephan Hammer—an undersecretary in the Department of the Interior. So he was part of Amos's corrupt ring that got rich by manipulating mining stocks illegally. And they were threatening Rory—and his brother Patrick.

Patrick wasn't dead after all! Hearing the sounds of chairs scraping, Rebekah realized that the meeting was breaking up. She hurried around the corner and down the hall to the kitchen, where she sank onto a hard-backed chair and tried desperately to think.

Amos was utterly ruthless. She had always known that. And he had been involved in the death of Rory's brother Ryan. Had Rory set out to seduce her because Amos was courting her? It seemed farfetched, yet it was possible. Seeing him tonight made the deception easier to credit. He had been so cold and sarcastic, a distant stranger with newly acquired wealth and polish.

"Let them kill each other," she whispered in the still kitchen. But in her heart she knew her words rang false. Whatever else he was, Rory had never been a criminal. He fought his own battles. He would not stoop to hiring assassins. But Amos would.

Out west we know how to deal with troublemakers. Rebekah forgot about the milk and painkillers. She hurried back to her room to write a note.

Rory crumpled the brief, cryptic message in his fist. Why would she send him a message warning him that Amos was watching his activities? Be wary, she cautioned.

"I'm damn sure it wasn't for love of me," he said to himself bitterly, downing another swallow from the glass of brandy. He stared broodingly at the fireplace grate, empty of logs during the warm fall evening.

"Wells probably put her up to it—to scare me off. No doubt her penance for creating gossip by dancing with me. He probably even heard we slipped outside for an indiscreet amount of time." But Rory did not want to remember how she had felt in his arms again after all the years. He had sworn to make her beg, to come to him as a supplicant. If his loss of control the night before was any indication, he would never succeed.

"Damn you, Rebekah Sinclair!" He threw the balled-up note into the empty fireplace and drained his glass.

Chapter Thirteen

Wellsville, May, 1878

After the mourners offering condolences had departed, only the immediate family remained at the parsonage with Ephraim. Amos had urgent business in the capital and quickly made his excuses, instructing his brother-in-law to escort Rebekah to the Flying W the next morning. Leah and their two sons were staying at the parsonage with Ephraim for a few more days. As her sister bustled her young boys upstairs for bedtime, Rebekah watched enviously.

She has them with her all the time while little Michael is a continent away from me. The ache of loneliness filled Rebekah; the pain had been a constant companion over the years. She went into the kitchen to straighten up after her mother's funeral dinner, but found the church ladies had put everything in Dorcas's kitchen back in better order than her own daughter could have done. Ephraim had held up well during the last days, but only another who secretly grieved could recognize the anguish he held so deeply inside himself.

Standing at the kitchen window, she watched her father walk around to the opposite side of the church, where the graveyard lay. When he did not return as dusk began to settle, she went after him. Ephraim was kneeling at the side of his wife's grave.

"It's time to come in now, Papa," she said gently, placing her hand on his shoulder.

He seemed not to take notice for a moment. Then he spoke quietly. "I never loved her the way I should have. She always knew."

"You were a good husband, Papa."

"She knew about Kathleen."

Oh, Papa, don't... "Kathleen was in your past. Over and done with when you wed Mama. You never dishonored your vows to her."

"I was unfaithful. The Commandments don't pertain just to overt actions, Rebekah. I lusted in my heart for another, and that made me guilty of adultery."

"Then it never goes away, does it?" she said miserably. They both knew what she meant.

He seemed more frail and stoop-shouldered than ever as he rose and looked down at Dorcas's freshly carved tombstone. "No, it never does." He turned to her with anguish on his face, and their eyes met. "I've had a feeling for years that I made a terrible mistake about you and Amos."

She could not bear to tell him of the humiliating sham her marriage had been from the wedding night on. He suffered enough guilt over Dorcas. "You did the only thing you could. The mistake was mine," she said firmly.

He shook his head. "No. I scarcely consider a splendid

241

boy like Michael to be a mistake. We all take great joy in him.'' Her eyes shifted away from his and scanned the eastern horizon. ''Amos has always known.'' It was not a question.

They had not broached this subject since that fateful day in his study when he advised his frightened daughter to marry for the protection of her unborn child. Rebekah nodded her head, working up the courage to speak as tears welled up from deep inside her. She had been unable to cry when the news of her mother's sudden death from a heart seizure came; she had not shed a single tear during the endless days of the wake, nor at the funeral. Now, suddenly, grief overwhelmed her.

Ephraim took her in his arms and gazed heavenward, his heart breaking with every sob. ''Has he abused you or my grandson?'' His voice was quiet and terse.

Rebekah sensed the change in him. She had never seen her gentle father this way—like an Old Testament prophet. He must never learn the truth about her marriage. She knew he would blame himself. ''No, no. Amos treats Michael as his son and heir.''

''Yet he hasn't allowed you to spend more than a few weeks at a time with the boy since he was out of diapers. All those governesses, then the fancy Eastern boarding schools. I know it breaks your heart every time you have to send him away.''

''It's what Amos wants,'' she replied in listless misery. ''He was raised in boarding schools himself, and he wants me free to travel with him and be his hostess for political functions.''

Ephraim stroked her back slowly, trying to soothe away the despair, knowing he was helpless to do so. ''Perhaps if there were more children . . . having you and Leah helped your mother and me."

When she made no response, he sighed helplessly. "That is no fault of yours, Rebekah. Amos had no offspring with his first wife either. A man can be infertile as easily as a woman."

Thank God Amos could give her no children. If so, he would have disowned Michael. The thought made her blood run cold. "It's for the best, Papa. Perhaps, as you said once, it's God's will."

"Sometimes human beings assume too much and tamper with God's will," he replied enigmatically. Tentatively, he said, "Madigan's become an amazing success. Have you seen him in Washington?"

"Once, briefly, several years ago." That awful, hateful scene in the embassy garden was etched in her very soul forever. "He's changed. Money and power do that to a man. I never really knew him at all. I was a naive seventeen-year-old girl when I thought I did."

Ephraim sensed the bitterness in her voice. "God forgive me, I failed you."

"You did the best you could for me, Papa," she replied, trying to smile through the haze of tears as she gazed up into his beloved face.

It was starkly anguished as he replied softly, "Did I? Often, over the years, I've wondered."

Virginia City, June, 1878

Rory sat behind his desk, sleeves rolled up against the heat of the day as he reviewed some accounts from the various mines that purchased lumber from him. Business was still booming, but he knew from previous cycles of boom and bust that the beginning of the end was in sight for the Comstock. The Big Bonanza of 1873 had resulted in such extraordinarily high stock speculation that in January of 1875, a panic set in and the bubble burst. Thousands of investors had been ruined. Some mines closed down and others ceased to pay dividends. The number left had shrunk dramatically.

Within a decade, the frenetic cities of the Comstock would become ghost towns. Never directly involved in mining operations or speculation, Rory was unaffected. His timber business already had a solid base of customers on the California side of the state line who purchased lumber for housing. The ranch he had begun as a small sideline now shipped thousands of head of beef and horses to fill lucrative army contracts in a four-state area. He also owned half interest in Jenson's racetracks and had gained quite a reputation as a breeder of prize racing stock. His winning horses brought in fat purses from Denver to San Francisco.

After two terms in the United States Congress, Rory had stepped down. His attempts to incriminate Wells in Washington had come to naught, although the strange note from Rebekah during his first term had been prophetic.

Perhaps it was only a coincidence, but a few weeks after receiving that message, someone had taken a shot at him. It had been early morning, and he had been on his way home from an assignation with Dorothea Paisley when the bullet had grazed his shoulder. Rory had run down his inept assailant, but the assassin was killed in the fight that ensued. He was never able to learn if Wells or the lovely Thea's jealous husband was behind the attack.

In the three years after the incident, he felt he was making so little difference in Washington that he grew increasingly more disillusioned. If he was going to destroy Wells, it would have to be on their home ground—Nevada. The corruption of the Grant administration had been replaced by "business as usual" in the supposedly "reform" administration of Rutherford Hayes. Like his well-meaning and personally honest predecessor, the general, the governor from Ohio was no match for the entrenched system in the nation's capital. Since he had backed fellow Democrat and New York governor Samuel Tilden in his unsuccessful bid for the presidency, Rory felt his usefulness in Washington was over.

Amos Wells's banking and mining interests always seemed to survive the vicissitudes of the stock market. He grew richer during the lean periods when so many investors lost everything. However, Rory had been working with influential men in the corrupt Nevada legislature who elected the state's United States Senators. By the time Wells was up for reelection, Rory's wealth was at last sufficient to back another candidate, who had defeated Amos. But to ruin him for good, Rory still needed to blow apart the ex-senator's sterling reputation by exposing the illegal means he used to raise and lower the value of mining stocks—means which had cost Ryan Madigan his life. Then Wells would not only lose any chance to return to Washington, he would go to prison, possibly even hang.

Beau was late. Rory shoved back the ledgers impatiently and stood up, looking out the window. Then a familiar footfall sounded on the stairs to his second-story office overlooking bustling, raucous C Street. Beau Jenson's beefy red face appeared at the door. His jowls were slightly looser, and the paunch protruding over his belt had grown a bit, but otherwise the passage of eight years had changed him little.

Short of breath, Jenson fanned himself and sank onto one of the big leather chairs across from Rory's desk. "Hot as an Arkansas stump preacher talkin 'bout hellfire."

"Beau, you ought to take better care of yourself. Lose a

little of that gut you're carrying around," Rory said, pouring a tall glass of water, complete with the luxury of ice. He handed it to his friend.

"Y'all sound like my doctor," Jenson replied, sniffing the cold, clear liquid suspiciously. "Gone temperance on me since y'all backed that Republican for senator?"

"I'm neither temperance nor turncoat, but you know as well as I that a Democrat doesn't stand a snowball's chance in hell of getting enough votes in the legislature. Forget politics. What about that note you sent?"

A crafty gleam lit Beau's eyes. "Yer hunch was right, Rory—'bout watchin' the bets Wells's mine supervisors make at our track. Sly Hobart's in debt up to his ass 'n he's a tall sucker to begin with."

"I'm sure he knows about holding miners underground while Wells and his cronies buy and sell stock, but what specifically can he give us that will implicate his boss?"

Beau grinned and rubbed his jaw. "If'n I was to tear up his markers, he'd turn over some real interestin' readin'—instructions 'bout keepin' men below ground until certain transactions was done."

Excitement lit Rory's face. "These instructions wouldn't happen to be written by Wells's own hand, would they?"

"I dunno, but Hobart keeps a whole strongbox of illegal records, real secret like. Reckon he figgered to use 'em to blackmail Wells 'n his boys one day. Now he done found hisself a better use fer 'em. My boys can be real convincin' when they go to collect on a bad debt."

"Tell him I'll sweeten the bargain with cold cash if he can get me more evidence. I want proof Wells has used explosives to seal off men in those shafts when a big strike was uncovered—proof he's not just a thief but a cold-blooded murderer." Rory began to pace back and forth across the polished oak floor as his excitement built. "God, Beau, do you know how long I've waited to get a man inside his operation? We're so close I can taste it. He's going down, Beau—Wells and everyone around him."

"And I can see how you relish it," Patrick said from the doorway of his adjoining office. He had silently taken in the exchange between his brother and Jenson. Although he still spent most of his time in California, their business holdings had grown sufficiently that he also kept a suite in Virginia City, just as Rory had one in his building on the San Francisco waterfront.

Rory looked at Patrick and read concern as well as condemnation in his face. "Hello, Patrick. I didn't hear you come upstairs."

Beau's eyes moved between the two brothers. They were a paradox, with faces as alike as if they'd been stamped from a single mold, yet where Rory was Black Irish, Patrick had the fiery red hair of some distant Saxon ancestor. It was Rory who had inherited the volatile temper to match Patrick's hair, while his older brother was calm and methodical.

Smiling sadly, Patrick replied, "I've been at the bank for the best part of the morning. I only just now came to the office." He turned to Beau. "So you have some hard evidence now? When can you furnish it?"

They discussed how to handle Sly Hobart and set him to work spying for them. Finally, when the arrangements were made to the Madigan brothers' satisfaction, Beau departed with his instructions.

"Once we get enough evidence to send Wells and his friends to prison, it'll be over, Rory. At least, it should be."

Rory's eyes met Patrick's. "What do you mean by *should* be?" he asked, leaning back in his chair and placing his feet on his desk.

"You can't deceive me, Rory. Remember who taught you to bluff at poker?"

"That was Sister Frances Rose," Rory said as he toyed with a pencil.

"Don't play games, little brother. Your obsession with Wells is as much because of his wife as it is because of Ryan."

Rory scoffed, tossing the pencil across the desk. "And what if it is?" His voice held a dare.

"What are you going to do to her? She has nothing to do with Wells's murdering ways."

"You don't know her like I do, Patrick. Just leave her to me."

"I understand they have a small son. He'll need a mother once his father's gone."

Rory shrugged with seeming indifference. "She's had the boy in some fancy Eastern boarding school since he was scarce out of diapers. I doubt he'll miss her."

"She must've really hurt you." Patrick waited, hoping Rory might explain something of the canker that ate at him, but he could tell by his brother's closed expression that he would not do so.

"Since you've been courting your little German dumpling, you've grown too sentimental for your own good," Rory said, trying to change the subject. His brother's first wife had perished in a cholera epidemic three years ago, leaving him with two small children to raise. Now he had at last fallen in love again—with a sweet young German widow named Gerta Froelich. "How is Gerta these days? Busy planning the wedding?"

"Gerta is fine, and the wedding is all arranged for next month, as you perfectly well know. It might do you a world of good to start seeing some of the eligible young women in

San Francisco instead of dallying with the class of females who live here in Virginia City.''

"What a prig you've become, Patrick." Rory laughed mirthlessly. "The women in Virginia City are at least honest about what they do, unlike the fine ladies of my acquaintance from San Francisco to Washington."

"That's because you've always gravitated toward women you knew you could form no lasting relationship with—whores or married society belles. You deserve better, Rory."

"Ironic. Once I thought so, too. But I think I've found my own level. Maybe I like it that way. Be happy with Gerta, Patrick."

"And leave you to destroy yourself? You know I can't do that."

"You can't stop me."

"Rebekah Wells just lost her mother last month—"

"Small tragedy in that," Rory interjected sardonically.

"She'll see her husband imprisoned, and their fortune will be lost. Isn't that enough?"

"No. It is not." Each word was enunciated with quiet finality, dropping into the thickening silence in the large office.

Finally, Patrick sighed in defeat and closed the door between them, leaving Rory alone with his memories.

Carson City

Rebekah hugged Michael so tightly that he wriggled like a small fish, trying to get her to loosen her hold as she knelt beside him on the railway platform. The Virginia and Truckee Railroad train was preparing to leave the station.

"You're squishing me, Mama. I can hardly breathe!" Michael was tall for a seven-year-old, with a thick mop of curly black hair and wide blue eyes. Those eyes suddenly grew solemn when he saw his mother's tears. "Don't be sad. Miss Ahern will write you every week—and I'll be able to write in cursive myself real soon."

Millicent Ahern, Michael's prim young governess, cleared her throat, indicating that it was time for them to board the train. A small brown wren of a woman, she at least seemed to be genuinely fond of the boy. That was more than Rebekah could say for the succession of nurses and governesses who had preceded her over the years—all handpicked by Amos.

"Do write as often as you can, Millicent. I promise there'll be a letter every day from me," she added, kissing Michael. "You be a good boy, and maybe if your father can spare the time we'll be able to visit you this fall when we arrive in Washington."

"That's only if Father receives the federal appointment," Michael replied gravely. "I overheard Uncle Henry say he might not. What if you can't come to Washington?" A note of panic made his clear child's voice break.

"You must've misunderstood. I'm sure your father will get the post," Henry Snead said, ruffling the boy's hair affectionately. "You just be a good boy and study hard until your ma and pa can come east. All right?"

Michael looked at his uncle gravely. "I'll do my best, sir." Then he flung himself into his mother's arms for one last good-bye hug, no matter if she did squish him, no matter if he was trying so hard to act grown up.

Rebekah held her son tightly, looking up at her brother-in-law with raw anguish in her eyes. "I love you, Michael. Always remember how very, very much Mama loves you!" she murmured against his soft hair.

The conductor called "all aboard" for the last time, and

the train gave a great hiss of its steam engines. "We must go, Mrs. Wells." Millicent's voice was drowned out by the noise as she knelt and gently tugged on the boy's arm.

Rebekah nodded and released Michael into her charge while Henry signaled the conductor to assist them in boarding the last car. As soon as the governess and Michael disappeared inside the passenger car, Rebekah crumpled, letting the tears roll down her cheeks. Henry put an arm of brotherly comfort around her shoulders, feeling the great sobs that racked her slender frame.

"Now, Rebekah, you have to be strong," he said gently.

"It's just not fair, Henry. He's such a little boy to be sent so far. First Amos made him stay here with nurses and governesses while we were in Washington. Now while we're here, he sends Michael all the way to Massachusetts."

"Calverton's supposed to be the best boy's school in the country," Henry said placatingly.

Rebekah wiped at the tears with her hankie and looked him in the eye. "Would you send your boys all the way across country to school—however fancy it was?"

He shrugged helplessly. "No, no, of course not, but we both know Amos feels differently."

"Yes. Michael is his pawn to keep me in line. The only way I ever get to see my son is if I do exactly as he says. He knows the threat of keeping Michael from me will always work. When I married him, I believed I was doing what was best for my child. I've tried, Henry—I've honestly tried to be a good wife, but nothing will ever make this marriage anything but a travesty." She fell in step with her brother-in-law after the train vanished down the track. Over the years, he had become her only real friend and confidant.

"Your marriage isn't the only travesty, Rebekah. You know Leah and I haven't gotten on for years. If it weren't for the boys, hell, I don't know if I'd put up with her shrew-ish outbursts. And we started out being in love—or at least I thought we were," he added with a bitter laugh.

Rebekah had watched as Henry and her sister grew further apart, he working longer hours while Leah spent his money. "Sometimes I think there is no such thing as real love be-tween men and women—at least not the storybook kind mar-riages are supposed to be built on. I should've realized that from my parents' relationship."

"How is Ephraim doing? I haven't been very good about going to see him. Seems like whenever I go with Leah to Wellsville, we fight."

"I know how busy you are between the mines and the ranch, Henry. Papa's doing all right. Losing Mama so sud-denly with her heart seizure—well, it was a shock, but as I said, they were never really close." She paused, thinking of the Irish girl her father had loved and lost a lifetime ago back in Boston. *She still haunts him as Rory haunts me.*

"Leah takes after her mother. You, on the other hand, have your pa's gentleness, Rebekah. I know Amos hasn't been easy on you."

"I'll get by, Henry. It's Michael I fear for." She stopped and took hold of his arm. "Please, if I could presume?"

"Anything you need, Rebekah. You know you only have to ask," Henry replied earnestly.

"If anything were to happen to me, would you look after Michael? I know it's a lot of responsibility. You have your own two boys and all—"

"That's all right. I understand about Amos and the boy." His face reddened, and he looked away.

He's embarrassed. "We've never talked about the circum-stances of Michael's birth, but I know Leah told you Michael isn't Amos's son." Now it was she who did not meet his eyes. She could not reveal her husband's affliction to anyone. It was too humiliating to her as well as to him. "Amos wanted an heir. I don't ever think he'll do anything to harm Michael. It's just . . ."

"He has no fatherly feelings for the boy," Henry supplied. "I'll look out for Michael. Maybe when I'm in Philadelphia or New York on business, I can make a side trip and visit the boy at Calverton. Rebekah . . ." He paused, then cleared his throat and asked, "Do you ever think about him?"

She knew he meant Rory. "It would be difficult not to since his name has been in the newspapers almost every day, first in Washington, now here."

"He's certainly had a meteoric rise," Snead said angrily. "His older brother had already amassed a fortune in the China trade, but he never had political aspirations."

"Neither does Rory. He's refused to try for Amos's Senate seat or even run for a third term in the House. No, he doesn't care about politics. He just wants to ruin Amos. And my family."

"That dirty saloon trash! He—"

"That's exactly why he's so set on this revenge. Don't you see? My family thought he wasn't good enough for me." She let out a small, choking laugh. "I guess no one thought he'd amount to much, myself included. I never dreamed he'd be more than a struggling stockman with a small place. But I'd have settled for that."

He looked at her with shrewd dark eyes. "Are you still in love with him?" He drew his own conclusions even when she shook her head.

"I don't know. He betrayed me and now he's set out to punish me for a lifetime of slights and prejudices because of his Irish heritage."

"He's proven to be a man of weak moral fiber just like

your father predicted eight years ago," Henry replied.

"That doesn't justify our prejudices, Henry," she said with a heavy sigh. Then she swallowed and raised her chin. "Whatever else he is, he is Michael's father. There, I've said it out loud for the first time in eight years."

"Does it make you feel better, having it in the open?"

"No," she replied forlornly. "Not at all. In fact I fear . . . already Michael is starting to resemble Rory so much." She shuddered. "If Amos begins to think someone might guess, he'll banish Michael forever!"

"And then there's Madigan himself—would he be above using the boy to blackmail you?" His tone of voice already gave the answer.

She nodded. "I live in mortal terror of that, too. He must never see Michael."

"He won't. I swear it."

Her eyes filled with tears as they resumed walking toward the waiting carriage. "I'm so grateful for your friendship, Henry. Thank you."

Leah Snead was having one of her "spells," as her husband called them. She picked up a dainty, heart-shaped pillow from the settee and threw it furiously at his face. He ducked the harmless object easily but eyed the heavy crystal paperweight on her escritoire with considerably more misgiving.

"Now, Leah, put that blame thing down. What will the servants think? You know how they gossip." That was one plea that usually gave her pause.

"They already gossip—you and my slut of a sister have set enough tongues wagging from Carson City to Washington these past years!" Leah's face was pasty pale and blotched red by her temper. What had once been a smooth porcelain complexion was now prematurely wrinkled, with pockets of fat quivering beneath her eyes and chin.

Leah's delicate features had not withstood the years any better than had her voluptuous curves, now gone to pillowy fat. Her once tiny waist was now thickened after two pregnancies and a decade of eating rich foods. Her hair, once silver gilt, was faded and lank. *How could I ever have thought she was the more beautiful of the sisters?* Henry thought in disgust. Aloud he repeated what he had been telling her to no avail for the past six or seven years. "Leah, you have no call to take on this way. Amos asked me to escort your sister and their boy to the train station since he couldn't get away from his meeting with the stock buyers at the Flying W."

"*Their* boy! Ha! We all know whose boy the little bastard is. That's why Amos foists them off on you every chance he gets." Her eyes slitted with jealous fury.

His blunt, handsome features grew harsh with anger. "I don't ever want you to repeat that—I don't care that you and Rebekah don't get on. She's the boss's wife, and you've got to live with it." He turned and slammed out the front door.

Leah knew she had pushed too far. Seldom did Henry lose his temper. In fact, seldom did he pay her any attention. His usual manner of dealing with her was to let everything she said and did simply roll off his wide shoulders.

She had begun throwing temper tantrums to get his attention when she felt his interest in her waning. Not that she had ever enjoyed the intimacies of the marriage bed, but when she had been young and pretty, he had doted on her, taking her everywhere as his position in Amos Wells's empire grew in importance. Men fawned over her and women were envious. But that was before her looks faded.

Now everything had changed. Rebekah, always the plain

sister, had blossomed into a great beauty. Indeed, she seemed to grow more striking with the passage of every year, while Leah only grew grayer and fatter.

"It isn't fair. She sinned grievously and was rewarded with a rich husband, while I was virtuous and now I'm losing my husband to her wiles. Just like she ensnared that vile Irishman and Amos and every other man she meets!" Leah crumpled onto an upholstered armchair by the parlor window and sobbed as she watched Henry ride away, headed north to the Flying W.

She knew they were making plans to get Amos an appointment to the Department of the Interior now that the legislature had voted in another senator backed by that hateful Irishman. Even though her husband's fortunes were tied to those of Wells and his associates, a part of her could not help but rejoice that Amos's political star might be on the wane. If she had to be stuck in the Nevada backwater, let Rebekah be stuck here, too. *If only Amos didn't send Henry to squire her around so often*, a voice inside her head echoed fretfully.

Carson City, September, 1878

Amos steered her down the curving fan of marble stairs in the Sheffields' mansion. "I want you to charm the senator, Rebekah. He has President Hayes's ear, and you know how much I want that cabinet appointment in Interior. It's our entrée back to Washington."

A railroad builder of renown, the senior senator from Nevada was a political force to be reckoned with and everyone who was anyone in the state had received a command invitation to his annual birthday celebration. As they moved among the crowd, her husband smiled, laughed, pumped hands, and slapped backs, introducing her to dozens of influential men and their wives, but Rebekah's thoughts were far away as she greeted acquaintances perfunctorily.

Rory's note, which had arrived early that morning, was still etched in her memory:

Several years ago you sent me a message, warning me about Amos's threats against me. Now I'll return the favor. Your husband as well as you are in grave danger. Meet me in Sheffield's library during the presentation of the birthday cake.

Rory

Rory stood, partially hidden in the shadow of a wide pillar, looking down on the festivities from the second-story balcony that ringed the immense room. His eyes never left Rebekah's golden beauty as she glided, nodding and smiling, from man to man on her husband's arm. *The timing has to be just right,* he mused.

"You should at least have the courtesy to pretend I exist, darling," Thea Paisley said, using her long feathered fan to tease his jawline as she leaned provocatively against him. "After all, I did travel all the way from Sacramento just to be with you tonight."

He shoved the irritating feathers away as if brushing off an annoying gnat. "You traveled to Carson City because every rich, powerful man west of the Mississippi always attends Shanghai Sheffield's birthday parties. You wouldn't miss it for the world," he replied lazily, still not deigning to look at her.

She pouted, sticking out her heavy lower lip in a move that usually melted men to puddles. "I'm far more beautiful than that skinny stick. Whatever do you see in her, Rory?" She

nudged his arm with one lush breast as a reminder of the boun-
teous charms virtually spilling from her Worth gown.

"That, pet, is none of your concern." He turned to her at
last, offering her his arm. "Just smile and be—er, affectionate as is your usual charming wont." Raising one eyebrow
in a sardonic gesture, he winked at her, then led her toward
the festivities.

Rebekah knew Amos had seen Rory. She could feel his
whole body tense in anger when he danced by them with
Senator Paisley's wife clinging to him like a leech.

"Cheap, vulgar woman. Paisley's a fool to turn her loose
in public," he muttered beneath his breath.

Rebekah knew better than to bait him by replying, or to
let her eyes follow Rory's arresting figure. Dressed in formal
evening clothes that hugged every inch of that lean, muscled
body, he drew admiring female glances around the room. Not
yet thirty, he was already one of the richest men in a state
known for millionaires. The sapphire studs winking in understated elegance from his snowy white shirtfront and cuffs
attested to the fact.

While most of the elite were balding, toothless, or fat, he
was in his prime. A few premature silver hairs at his temples
only added to his mysterious air of brooding Irish charm.
Now that he had made his fortune, being Irish was no longer
a liability. In fact, the lilt of his accent seemed more pronounced as she heard him exchange jovial remarks with Senator Sheffield across the room.

By contrast, Amos, once so dapper and distinguished, had
deteriorated over the past years. His salt-and-pepper hair was
washed out and thinning now, and the thick muscles of his
barrel chest seemed to have slipped downward to form a
paunch that even the most expensive tailoring could not con-
ceal. Fleshy lines of dissipation from late-night drinking

marred his once handsome face, unmasking the cruelty within his soul.

Rory the ruthless charmer, Amos the cunning despoiler. Rebekah shuddered, thankful to have neither of them in her solitary bed. Let that Paisley witch fornicate with Madigan tonight! Yet she dared not ignore his request to meet him. What did he know about Amos that could place her husband in grave danger—and herself along with him?

Over the years, Rebekah had learned as little as possible about Amos's shady business practices and political chicanery. The less she knew, the better she could sleep nights. *As if I could change anything if I did know the sordid details.* Whether his fortune rose or fell, she was tied to him, with Michael an innocent pawn she would protect at any cost.

Shortly before eleven p.m., when Senator Sheffield's huge triple-tiered cake was wheeled into the room amid laughter and applause, Rebekah slipped away through the crowd. She prayed Amos would not miss her, nor the crotchety and keen-sighted old curmudgeon, Horace Sheffield, when he asked for help blowing out all those candles. Having been a frequent visitor to the mansion, she had no trouble finding the library at the end of the long hallway in the west wing.

The room was dark and silent when she peered in. Glancing up and down the deserted corridor to be certain she was not followed, Rebekah slipped inside and closed the door, then moved slowly across the thick carpet. Where was the blasted switch for the gaslights?

Suddenly a tall figure moved from behind one of the floor-to-ceiling freestanding bookcases in the center of the room. She jumped back and started to scream, but hard fingers covered her mouth and held her jaw immobilized as a man's muscled arm pulled her firmly against his chest.

"I doubt anyone would hear you over the racket down the

hall, but I'd advise against screaming. Think of the scandal if we were caught together in the dark.''

Rory's voice was a low purr. He held her back pressed against him as his hand slid down her throat and around the curve of her breast. She could feel the heat of his breath and see in the moonlight streaming through the window that once beloved hand, still sun-darkened and callused in spite of his elegant new lifestyle. How pale her breast looked in contrast. How achingly familiar the old tightening and swelling when he cupped the globe through its sheer silk covering. His throaty chuckle indicated that he felt her body betray her.

"Let me go, Rory.'' She was proud of the steadiness of her voice but could not stop her pulse from racing or her body from trembling.

He turned her around in his arms but did not free her. "I wondered if you'd come. The preacher's prim daughter on a moonlight tryst.''

"This is no tryst.'' She wriggled ungracefully free of his arms, which abruptly fell away as he reached over and turned up the lights. Blinking in the sudden brightness, she glared angrily at him. "I came because you said Amos and I are in grave danger—not to dally with you.''

His eyes swept over her. "A moment ago I could have sworn I detected quite a different response, darlin'.''

"Don't call me that. I'm not your darlin'. I never really was.''

"No, you weren't.'' Rory kept his expression sardonically cool and detached while he drank in her loveliness. The deep violet silk made her hazel-green eyes turn almost gray and brought out the bronzed highlights of her dark golden hair. She seemed to grow more beautiful every time they met. "Have you ever regretted your hasty bargain with Wells? Just think, if you'd waited a few years, I could've bought you Worth gowns and amethysts," he said as his hand caressed the delicate lavender stones encircling her throat, then trailed lower to where the largest oval stone nestled in the deep vale between her breasts.

She felt her heart accelerate until she was certain it would leap from her chest. Unwittingly she took a step backward, trying to break the spell. "If you lured me here only to add me to your string of conquests—"

His mocking laughter cut off her protest. "You were already one of my conquests. Or have you become such a staid society matron that you've blotted our brief liaison from your memory?"

"No, I haven't forgotten our *brief liaison,* as you so charmingly put it. Nor have I forgotten your threats back in Washington four years ago. I'll never come to you for anything, Rory Madigan." She started to walk past him, furiously angry for coming to humiliate herself in this cruel hoax of his.

His arm barred her way as he reached out and placed his palm against the end of the bookcase. Then he stepped toward her and pulled her into his arms again. "Don't be so certain of that. I happen to know your husband's political fortunes are on the decline. So are his business interests."

She stood rigidly within the circle of his arms, her nails biting into her palms as she struggled to regain her poise. "Amos has lost his bid for a second term as senator. I know you had a hand in it."

He shook his head reprovingly. "So little wifely concern, Rebekah. Could it be you have as much reason as I to want him brought low?"

"Why should you care about him or me? Why this vendetta, Rory? Just because you were a poor Irish Catholic and my family favored Amos Wells over you?"

He refused to give her the satisfaction of knowing how flayed he had been, returning to Wellsville with those rings in his vest pocket, learning of her marriage, watching her dance with Wells's filthy hands all over her. "Your family has sterling taste indeed. They favored a murderer."

She blanched. "Amos is many things . . . but murder . . . I don't believe you. You're just as filled with prejudice and hate as the good citizens of Wellsville were."

"I have far better reason for my hate. Remember when I told you my brother Ryan was killed in a mining explosion?"

Cold dread washed over her. "No! Not Amos." Her protest was desperate. She had seen her husband's cruelty and ruthlessness firsthand.

"Yes, Amos. Surely you've heard about the way speculators hold miners prisoner underground?"

She nodded. "To start false rumors about a big strike— or keep word of one from getting out until they buy up the stock cheap."

Rory could see from her expression of dawning horror that she understood. "I have proof Wells was involved in half-a-dozen explosions. Unfortunately, not the first one at the Silver Lady back in '64 when Ryan died, but more than enough others since then to send him to prison for life."

"No!" She put her hands on her ears as the room spun around her and a great roaring noise seemed to fill her head.

He pried her hands away and forced her to hear him out. "It's only a matter of time until the investigators sift through all the evidence. Once Patrick and I got our first piece of solid information, his whole filthy operation began to unravel."

She looked up into his face, once so beloved, still as handsome even though etched by the years and his bitterness. "I understand now why you hate him, but why me?''

"Perhaps I don't hate you, darlin'—any more than you hate me.'' He let one hand caress the elegant line of her cheekbone, then move to her lips and lower yet down her throat. His fingertips teased around the low décolletage of her gown, grazing sensuously over the creamy swells of her breasts. He could feel the pulse racing frantically in her throat and knew she felt the old pull just as he did. And resented it just as he did.

"Once Amos is in prison, you'll be penniless. I think we'll derive mutual pleasure when you become my mistress.''

Chapter Fourteen

Rebekah slapped him so hard that her hand stung. The noise echoed around the high-ceilinged room as she tried to move past him, but Rory was too quick for her. He seized one slender wrist and turned her around to face him. The red handprint stained his cheek. Her own cheeks were filled with high color from the fury his insult had generated.

"Let me go, you insufferable bastard!" She twisted under his hurtful grip.

"Not until I'm good and ready," he said in an implacable voice.

"I'll scream the house down, birthday celebration or not!"

He grinned sharkishly. "I doubt it. What would Amos say?"

"Why do you think I won't go to him and warn him about your plans to destroy him?" Foolish question! She berated herself the instant she blurted out the angry words.

"Perhaps for the same reason you sent me that note warning me about him four years ago in Washington. You were right. Someone did try to kill me. You know what your husband is. Could you still hold some guilty bit of tender feeling for me?"

He studied her with fathomless blue eyes, watchful, perhaps uncertain, she was not sure. "Don't be absurd!"

"Or perhaps you were only trying to frighten me away from dear Amos then. But now—now you must realize you're both in over your heads. His house of cards will crash down around him, and you'll be dragged under too, unless—"

"Why? Why do you want me now?" Her expression changed from anger to hurt bewilderment. He had thrown away her love, deserted his child eight years ago. What kind of cruel game did he play? Surely he had not found out about Michael! Panic welled up inside her. *He can't know!*

Rory watched the play of emotions sweep over her face and tried to read the truth. All he could see were the small golden flecks swimming in her green eyes. "You're quite an actress," he finally said with a sigh of disgust, releasing her wrist.

She stood rubbing it where his fingers had bitten into the tender white flesh, too afraid to move as her thoughts tumbled over each other in chaos.

"I'm sorry," he said softly, his hands gentle as he took her arm and raised it to plant a soft kiss on the bruise forming on her wrist. "Once your skin was golden from working in the hot Nevada sun . . . in a cabbage patch."

"Don't—please." His coldness, even his cruel, degrading insults she could endure better than the invading desire engendered when he evoked old memories. "Please let me go, Rory." *Damn, she was begging!*

"For now, Rebekah. Only for now," he said, placing one last soft salute on the inside of her palm.

She snatched her hand away as if he had scalded her and ran from the room.

When Rory's note arrived the next morning, she was having a late breakfast with Amos. Her husband had insisted on discussing their social agenda for the forthcoming weeks. Normally her routine was to rise at dawn, eat lightly, and go for an early morning ride before the heat of the day became oppressive. Amos, who often conducted late night meetings and drank to excess, slept late. Their paths crossed as little as possible except for the political events during which she was on display as his ornamental wife.

"What's that?" he said, frowning over his coffee as he poured an extra dollop of cream and stirred it.

She folded the note and slipped it onto her lap before her hands betrayed her trembling. "Just an invitation from Celia to go shopping this afternoon," she replied with feigned calm, praying he would not demand to see the invitation to a tryst with Michael's father.

"That fool woman is as scatterbrained as she was before she married," he muttered, uninterested in her friends.

"But she married Bryan Kincaid," Rebekah could not resist adding just to jab at Amos. Bryan was a vice president of the Central Pacific and one of the most powerful railroad men in the West. At least Celia's dreams had come true. But she spent most of the year in Sacramento, which meant they saw each other all too seldom.

"We have dinner at the Ormsby House with the Sheffields and Stephan Hammer tonight. Seven sharp. Don't dally shopping with Celia and be late." He started to rise, then paused, wiping his beard meticulously with his napkin. "Oh, do wear your diamonds tonight. That old bag of Sheffield's will be weighed down with hers."

Diamonds. She hated them. Cold, heavy, and as soulless as her marriage. "How fitting," she said flatly, nodding in acquiescence as he left.

What should she do about Rory? Once she heard the front door slam, she unfolded his note and reread his bold scrawl:

> Meet me at the stand of cottonwoods behind the
> racetrack at one p.m. You know there is a good
> reason not to disappoint me.
> R.

"A good reason," she repeated, balling up the note. Could he have found out about Michael? Was that his threat? Or did his monstrous arrogance simply lead him to believe she would be compelled to come because she still desired him? How could he possibly believe she loved him after what he had done? Why would he not when she trembled and melted at every touch, every brush of his lips against her skin?

"I hate him. But I must go—to protect Michael," she whispered as she rose and walked over to the sideboard where two candles burned beside the breakfast buffet. She slid the note into the greedy flames, then dropped it on a silver tray and watched it burn until only charcoal flakes remained.

Although Amos had not set spies on her in years, there

was no sense taking chances. When they were first married, he was convinced that a woman so wanton as to get herself with child outside wedlock would look for other lovers because her husband was unable to fulfill his marital duties. But that physical part of her was dead and gone, killed along with the love she had given Rory Madigan. No other man interested her. Within a couple of years, even Amos believed that she had shifted all her love to her son.

But that was before Rory had come back into her life. In Washington, her one brief encounter with him four years earlier had cost her dearly. Amos must never catch her again. She would call on Celia and arrange a shopping trip as cover for this meeting. How fortunate that Celia was indeed in Carson City with Bryan this week. How ironic that her past had gone full cycle to catch up with her—once again she would use her friend as an alibi while sneaking off to Rory.

"Damn them both—Amos and Rory. I'll see them in hell before they harm my son."

Rory patted the sleek bay filly, then turned her over to the handler for a rubdown. The magnificent two-year-old had been sired by Lobsterback. He had named her Scarlet Poppy. He grinned at the conceit, thinking of all the respectable ladies who frequented his racetrack, sitting in their reserved seats, all prim and cool while their husbands bet on the horses. Those same women slipped heated looks his way and came to his bed in the dark of the night. At least whores were honest about what they did and the reasons for which they did it.

Will she come? Rory really had no idea. His agents had discovered a great many things about her relationship with Amos Wells. Like many of the silver barons, he was unfaithful to his wife. Unlike them, he did not indulge in keeping expensive mistresses, but visited cheap bordellos. Whether or not he still visited his wife's bed was a mystery.

Had Rebekah turned him out of it for being an inept or selfish lover? Did she not want the encumbrance of more pregnancies? Their son was virtually invisible, having spent his entire life raised by servants and more recently attending exclusive private boarding schools. Neither parent was exactly doting from what he had learned. That fact struck him as peculiar. For some reason he could not fathom, Rory could not imagine Rebekah Wells as anything but a loving mother.

"You're creating fanciful pipe dreams, my man. Even if she hasn't taken other lovers, you know her for what she is," he muttered to himself as he strolled around the racetrack, heading toward the beckoning coolness of the secluded copse of cottonwoods. A small feeder to the Carson River flowed through it. The irony was not lost on him as he knelt on the grassy bank and began skipping pebbles across the clear running water. His thoughts skipped back over the years just as quickly, remembering other warm days on a sun-dappled riverbank. How young they had both been. And how stupid he had been to believe in love.

But you still want her. He tried to tell himself he only wanted revenge for the heartache she had cost him and the destruction her husband had cost the Madigan family. He had vowed to make her crawl to him, the once proud and prudish minister's daughter with her veneer of morality covering her greed. And she would. *But you want her*, the voice in the back of his mind taunted.

At the sound of approaching hoofbeats, he stood up and composed himself as Rebekah rode through the trees and reined in. She perched warily on her elegant mare as if ready to bolt at his first untoward move. He crossed his arms over his chest and inspected her with lazy, heavily lidded eyes.

"The riding habit is quite fetching. That shade of bronze brings out the highlights in your hair." It also clung to her soft curves like a lover's caress.

As he approached, patting her nervous mount and calming it with his magical touch, she worked up her courage to face him down. "You didn't send for me to compliment my dressmaker," she said tartly, unable to help noticing the crisp black chest hair visible above his half-unbuttoned shirt or the way his broad shoulders stretched the fine white lawn with his slightest movement.

"Whatever my reasons, you're here," he replied simply, reaching up to catch her by the waist and lift her from the sidesaddle before she could protest. "I was just thinking how we've come full cycle, trysting by a riverbank again after all these years."

Rebekah stiffened and pressed her hands against his chest, pushing away. "We're not trysting."

He arched one brow sardonically. "No, darlin'? Then what might you be doin' here?"

He was mocking her! "Your brogue has thickened over the years. Is that how you charm the women gullible enough to fall under your spell?" she retorted with cool amusement, turning away from him. Two could play at his game.

"I find the voters like it." He moved up behind her when she stopped at the edge of the stream.

"A pity women can't vote in Nevada then."

"Would you? Vote for me, that is," he whispered against her ear. He could see the pulse leaping in her throat. His nearness disturbed her.

"First dressmakers, then suffrage. What next? Surely you aren't going to try to rekindle a long-dead passion here in the grass?" She stood her ground, growing angry at his cat-and-mouse tactics.

"Long dead? I don't think so." Without warning, he spun her around and took her mouth in a swift, fierce kiss. As his lips slanted across hers, he dug his fingers in her hair, pulling the pins out with one hand while the other pressed her lower body tightly against his, rotating his hips in rhythm with his mouth. Let her feel his lust. He damned well knew she felt the same.

Rebekah gasped in surprise when his lips met hers, trying in vain to keep the old fire from swamping her senses, but all she succeeded in doing was opening her mouth for the invasion of his tongue. He thrust it with wicked skill, as he rocked her against him, letting her feel the bulge in his tight denims pressing into her belly.

So long. She had been so many lonely years without a man's touch, merely an ornament to be placed on display, admired and then returned to her sterile bedchamber.

His hot, hard body, so achingly familiar, robbed her of will, of breath. Her bones melted, and a mesmerizing languor stole over her. Rebekah gave in to it, to him. When his hand slid up and cupped her breast, she felt as if a lightning bolt had flashed through her body. Her hands pulled him closer, her mouth opened wider, her hips arched against his as the savagery of their coming together obliterated all else.

Rory felt her surrender and pressed his advantage, lowering them slowly to kneel on the soft, grassy earth as his fingers unfastened her jacket and delved inside to slip between the buttons of her frilly blouse. Then, unable to stop himself, he tore at the soft fabric in his eagerness to feel the velvety lushness of bare skin and taste the sweet pucker of pink nipple.

Her breasts were fuller than he remembered, and her flesh paler, like silk. When he teased one round globe with his tongue she whimpered, thrusting it into his mouth until he

271

suckled greedily, then switched to the other tempting mound. While he made love to her breasts, his hands continued stripping the elegant riding habit from her body. She helped him, shrugging off her jacket, blouse, and camisole before reaching up to tear at his shirt voraciously. When her teeth caught one hard, flat nipple, he let out an oath of pleasure. She ran her hands through his chest hair, then dug her nails into his shoulders and clung to him as he yanked her unhooked skirts over her hips and shoved the heavy linen to her knees.

They tumbled to the grass, kissing and caressing desperately as they discarded clothing. Rory's warm, clever mouth moved over her skin as he bared each new inch of it, pulling away her camisole and pantalets. Then he moved to her boots and stockings, kissing her long, slender white legs. She lay naked beneath his touch, her hair spread in golden tangles around her. He seized great fistfuls of it as he covered her with his body and kissed her lips rapaciously until she writhed and whimpered beneath him, eager for him to complete their joining.

Finally he rolled up, tugged off his boots, and finished the job she had begun by unbuttoning his fly. He could feel her glazed green eyes on him as he slid his denims off. He reached for her hand and placed it around his rigid staff, biting down on his lip to keep from crying out her name.

Rebekah sobbed aloud with the need to feel that hard, sleek manflesh inside her once more. "Please, oh, please, Rory." She pulled him to her, opening for him as he moved between her thighs.

He looked down at her flushed, beautiful face. Her golden head thrashed from side to side as her body arched in anticipation of his invasion. *Now.* Now was the time to scorn her, to taunt and humiliate her for betraying him, then to take her by force when her ardor had turned to ashes. But he could not do it. Sweet Mother of God help him, he could not do it. He ached with wanting, and that wanting demanded that she come to him as inflamed as he was.

Rory lowered himself to her and plunged inside the soft wetness beckoning him. At once he felt the almost virginal tightness of her sheath. She stiffened and cried out in pain, even though her hands held him fast. He had hurt her. Murmuring sweet words of love and reassurance, he clamped a steel control over his raging desire. Blood pounded through his body. Every fiber of his being screamed that he appease his need with savage ferocity. But her still, soft body, so yielding in spite of her hurt, held him in check. How long had it been since she had lain with a man? Surely years.

Cursing Amos Wells for a fool, he rained kisses down her throat and breasts, then took her mouth once more in a deep, sensuous exploration. Gradually she came back to life under his gentle wooing, returning his kiss, her body softening and stretching to accommodate his.

Rebekah was taken completely by surprise at the tight, burning pain that followed his first thrust into her. She was so desperate for this mating, she ached with the wanting of it, little knowing that her body, like a flower denied sunlight, had dried and shriveled from deep within after all the years of neglect. But he waited, buried deeply inside her, feeling her hurt, giving her time to open and bloom for him once again. And like the miracle of spring renewed, it happened. His soft touches and lush kisses worked their magic. She felt herself taking him deeper yet, stretching and yielding, drawing him to move once more within her. Wrapping her legs around his hips, she arched up with a joyous cry.

Rory smothered it with his mouth as he began to move once more, withdrawing ever so slowly, then plunging down into the slick heat of her welcome. Her hunger was so fiercely sweet, so desperately demanding, it unleashed a maelstrom of passion in him. With no other woman had he ever felt this blind, mindless bliss.

Together they rode the storm, giving and taking, hungry, building toward a culmination beyond the stars. When it swept over her, she stiffened, feeling the old, never-forgotten rhythm of her body's release rippling through her. His body answered, pounding harder, faster, deeper, until his staff swelled in one final hammering burst of indescribable ecstasy. Then he collapsed on her slender body and they held on to each other, panting and shaking with the aftershocks of passion.

His weight pressed her into the soft grassy bank but she pulled him tightly to her, wanting the closeness, the hard, heavy feel of his body joined full length to her own. *Let it last. Please . . .* She could not think beyond the drugging lethargy of satiation to what she would say to him or he to her.

Reality finally began to soak into Rory's consciousness as an autumn wind rose, blowing cool air across his sweat-sheened back. He raised himself on his arms, shaking his head to clear it as he looked down and met her dazed eyes, their changeable green now almost hazel with golden flecks dancing at the centers. He withdrew from her and rolled onto his back, reclining on his elbows, head dropped back, face tilted up into the dappled sunlight filtering through the rustling cottonwood leaves.

''This wasn't what I planned . . .'' What should he say? *I intended to seduce and humiliate you?* ''Nothing is turning out as I expected. We need to talk, Rebekah.''

Rebekah struggled to sit up. Muscles she had not used in eight years cried out as she moved. Gradually his words registered. He had not planned to make love with her—or had he simply not intended to be swept into the madness of their passion? Shame washed over her like a tidal wave, guilt beyond bearing. She had broken her marriage vows. Even though Amos Wells had never been a true husband to her, he was still the man to whom she legally and morally owed her allegiance.

"Coming here was a mistake," she said, her voice barely audible, so overwhelming was the tight knot of pain building inside her.

He turned and looked at her as she gathered her scattered garments and began putting them on with clumsy, trembling fingers. "Rebekah, your marriage—"

"My marriage won't go away, Rory. For better or worse, I am Amos Wells's wife. Nothing can change that. Only now I'm an adulteress."

He could hear the choked tears in her voice. "Presbyterian guilt," he said with a sigh. "Your marriage was a mistake. There are ways to end it."

"Divorce?" Her head snapped around and she looked at him for an instant with a shocked expression. "Surely if you're still Catholic, you wouldn't suggest it—but of course, I forgot. You don't want to marry me, only install me as your mistress once you've gotten rid of Amos."

"Consider the bright side. He might hang," Rory replied flatly, reaching for his pants. He quickly slipped them on and stood facing her as she fastened her heavy riding skirt and fumbled with her blouse, too badly torn to button. He could see she was fighting to keep a tenuous grip on her emotions. *Would you marry her?* The thought flashed into his mind. He had never dreamed of it over the bitter years, but suddenly he was no longer certain.

"You don't really want me, Rory. You only want to use me in your twisted vendetta against Amos." She used his sarcasm to fuel her anger. "You want to destroy everyone connected with your brother's death. Did you come to Wellsville to seduce me because Amos planned to marry me? Was I a part of your revenge even then?"

"Don't talk crazy. I didn't even know about Wells and Ryan when I met you. Wells is a monster—and no kind of husband. I could tell that when I made love to you, Rebekah. Leave him—now." He reached out, trying to take her in his arms, but she backed away, slapping at his hand.

"No! I can't. In case you didn't know, I have a son to consider." At least she would know now whether or not he knew the truth about Michael. She studied his face and held her breath expectantly.

Her angry rejection, while no surprise, still stung. "I've heard about the boy. You're such a devoted mother hardly anyone in Nevada's ever seen him, least of all his parents. Governesses and tutors are raising him. Isn't he back east somewhere right now in boarding school?"

Misery and guilt choked her. Her sins against Michael were now compounded by her adultery with his father. But at least it would seem there was one small blessing. Rory did not know Michael was his son. "It's what Amos wants," she said woodenly, turning to go.

The pain in her eyes was real. He could sense it in his gut. No one, not even Rebekah, could be such an actress. "Rebekah, wait." This time he took her arm firmly and held it fast, forcing her to turn and look at him. Their eyes locked as he struggled to find the right words, but before he could, the loud pounding of hoofbeats interrupted them.

Her bereft expression turned to one of blind panic. "Someone's headed right toward us! If I'm caught here with you like *this*—"

"Ride across the stream and head around the trees to the

north. I'll stop whoever it is.'' He tossed her up onto her mare and slapped the horse into a trot, then quickly walked out of the copse of trees toward the approaching rider, cursing the ill timing of it all.

"Mr. Madigan,'' Jem Butler called out. "We been looking for you everywhere. One of the new colts has sprained his leg—er, at least that's what the fellas at the stable think.''

"I'm coming, Jem,'' he yelled to the youth, who was apprenticed as a trainer at his Carson City racetrack. As he made his way back to the big stable that housed some of his most valuable racers, Rory's mind was far more concerned with what he would do about Rebekah Wells than with the problem at hand.

He did not see the shadowy figure emerge from the copse of cottonwoods and watch his retreating figure.

Amos Wells sat in his cluttered office, staring at the message in his hand as the blood boiled in his veins. His sallow complexion was mottled beet red, and his whole body shook with rage. "Cheap, wanton trash—frigid in my bed, then going back to that damned mickey like a bitch in heat!'' He held up the report and took a lit cigar from the ashtray beside his chair, holding the rosy tip to the paper until it caught. If word of her escapade ever got out, his chances of getting the federal appointment would be ruined.

As he leaned back and watched the paper smolder in the heavy brass ashtray, a plan began to take shape in his mind. He had swallowed his bile and used that bastard of Madigan's as his heir, allowing him the privileges of the Wells name and position since there was no way he could hope to have a son of his loins. Over the years Michael had proven a good tool to keep Rebekah in line. He would prove so once again. Smiling, Amos rose and called for his secretary to take a message over to the telegraph office. Michael Wells was coming home from school for a visit with his beloved family.

Rebekah spent a desperate afternoon, pacing like a caged lioness in her room, emotionally spent and racked with guilt. How could she have fallen to the ground with him? They had rutted in the open like a pair of animals! What if that rider had discovered them? Shame washed over her as she sank onto her bed and gave in to the tears that had been burning behind her eyelids since she had returned to Amos's big city house.

Amos. Her husband. The man who held her fate and that of her son in his hands. He had warned her about the terrible retribution if ever she created a scandal. *Make no mistake.* Not only would she suffer, but so would Michael. Hunched in a small ball of misery, she closed her eyes and tried to picture her son's cherubic little face, but an adult version of it kept appearing in her mind's eye. She saw Rory. Her love. The man who held her heart. In spite of all he had done to her, she could not stop loving him. But for all she held sacred—her honor, her child's very life—she must never see him again.

He's just using me. It's a blessing he doesn't know Michael is his. Yet try as she might, Rebekah could not blot out the memories of how his wild loving had gentled when he felt her pain, how considerate he had become. And what of afterward? His cold and accusatory remarks had cut her to the quick, but then he had realized his power to wound her. *What was he going to say when we were interrupted?*

"No!" She sat up in bed and covered her ears, shaking her head. It was madness even to think about it, about him, about all they had shared and lost—and found again in one golden afternoon. She must put it all behind her and try to go on with her life. Yet forgetting the splendor of his touch was impossible. Her body cried out for his. She was still young and passionate; she wanted more children, a real marriage, a real father and brothers and sisters for Michael. Then a horrifying thought struck her. She could once again be carrying Rory's child! Yet all Rory offered her was the shame of divorce compounded by the ignominy of becoming his kept woman.

What was she now but Amos's kept woman? A possession to be placed on display for every man to watch and no man, including himself, to touch. Her head ached, and she looked a fright. Dinner at the Ormsby House Hotel tonight was important to Amos's political aspirations. If she appeared in this state, he would demand to know why.

Rebekah slid from the bed and reached for the bell pull, summoning Patsy, then went to the dry sink and poured cool water into the basin. She would soak her tear-ravaged face and have Patsy fetch her some fresh cucumber from the kitchen to bring down the swelling. As to the rest, she would try not to think of anything until she recovered her equilibrium.

By the time Patsy had finished her ministrations, Rebekah looked like a new woman—at least on the outside. Inside she still quaked with guilt and confusion, but when Amos watched her descend the spiral stairs of their city house that evening, his look of proprietary satisfaction indicated that he was pleased.

She had taken particular care with her appearance, touching a hint of kohl to her eyelids and rouge paper to her pale cheeks. Patsy had dressed her hair in an elaborate series of coils entwined with dark blue silk ribbons, piled high on her head and drawn severely back from her face, emphasizing her dramatic features. Her gown was a rich royal blue brocade trimmed with delicate silver stitching around the low neckline and sleeves. She wore his diamonds.

"Splendid, my dear," Amos said indulgently, taking her gloved hand and tucking it in the crook of his arm with almost fatherly affection. "You'll have every man in Carson City lusting after you. Perhaps you already do."

The shift in his tone of voice alerted her even before his words registered. She faltered as he handed her into their waiting carriage, then clutched her ermine cape tightly about her shoulders to keep her hands from trembling.

Amos climbed in beside her and took his seat. When the carriage began to move, he stared across the cramped interior, studying her frozen features with his cold pewter eyes. The smile that curved his lips turned her blood to ice. *He knows! But how?*

"Cold, my dear?" he asked in that overly solicitous voice again. "Your new ermine wrap should keep you quite warm—as if you weren't hot-blooded enough already."

Rebekah felt the hard buttons on the carriage seat upholstery pressing into her back. *Damned if I cower from him!* "Stop playing with me, Amos. Say what you intend to say and be done with it."

He feigned a look of wounded bewilderment. "What? Is your conscience perhaps bothering you? It wouldn't have anything to do with Rory Madigan being here in Carson City, would it? One of his prizewinning thoroughbreds will race tomorrow against Senator Sheffield's best at that track he owns. You are familiar with the track . . . near the small stream that feeds into the river a few miles up."

"You set men to spy on me again," she said flatly. Dear God, the humiliation of it was unbearable! Something so private, so beautiful as those few stolen moments, now tarnished irretrievably.

"Let's just say I know. Everything. Although I found Michael useful, he is the only heir I wish. You had better not provide me with any more of Madigan's by-blows or I will be forced to take retribution. We've already discussed how unpleasant that would be."

He watched her as he spoke, enjoying the terror in her eyes, seeing her face grow gray and her body tremble. He wanted to hear her plead. But she regained her composure and sat as regally poised as a queen, showing no signs of breaking. His fury boiled over. "You swore to be a faithful wife! What would your beloved father say were I to tell him his harlot daughter compounded the sin of lying with a man before marriage by crawling back to him again, breaking her oath to me? Me—your lawful husband!"

"You are my legal husband, Amos. I'm sorry I have dishonored my marriage vows. It will never happen again," she replied softly. His tirade did not terrify her the way such vicious outbursts, with their accompanying violence, had in the past. Perhaps she was beyond fear, beyond caring. *Perhaps I have no soul left.* But then his next words brought that fear blossoming back like a mine shaft explosion billowing up from the bowels of hell itself.

"I've sent for Michael." At last he could sense the reaction in her that he desired. He calmed and continued, "He should arrive within the week. You didn't want him so far away. I thought perhaps a reunion of mother and child would help . . . soothe matters."

His voice was oily now, making the hair on the back of her neck stand up. "Do what you must to punish me, Amos. I'm guilty. But if you harm a hair on that innocent boy's head, I swear I'll kill you!"

"Don't make threats you can't keep, my dear. Michael is my son by law—for as long as I care to recognize him."

Rage washed over her, overshadowing her own guilt. She leaned forward in the seat and faced him with blazing eyes. "If you ever so much as touch a hair of Michael's head, I'll tell the world Michael is your son *only* by law!"

He recoiled in shock. "Don't be absurd. You're over-wrought." Then he recovered his poise. "So overwrought, my dear, one might even say you were emotionally unstable. What would happen to Michael if his mother were so un-balanced that I had to commit her to an asylum?"

"You've already done your worst to me, Amos. I'm doomed and I accept it. But I know your political concerns could not survive the gossip of my accusations. After all, you're over fifty years old. Michael is your only child. The merest hint that he isn't yours would really start tongues wagging."

"You'd actually subject your son to such ignominy?" He tried to scoff, but there was an edge to his voice that betrayed fear.

"Anything—even being called a bastard—would be better than to have Michael live under your hand as I have. I've already told you I'm bound by my own past sins and my vows to you. But Michael is innocent! Touch him and you'll pay."

The cold finality of her words chilled him to the bone. He stared at a dangerous and unexpected enemy as if seeing her for the first time. This would take careful consideration—as if he did not have enough on his plate already, he thought bitterly, his mind racing ahead to tonight's gathering. Once he secured the Washington appointment, he would send the boy off to Europe and then deal with his faithless and dan-gerous wife once and for all.

Chapter Fifteen

Virginia City, one week later.

The cloyingly sweet odor of opium hung in the air, overlying the stench of sour sweat on unwashed bodies. Rory walked down the dark hallway strewn with refuse and knocked on the last door.

The voice bidding him enter still carried the heavy accent of her native Yorkshire, but it was scratchy and weak from disuse now. Here in this cheap place she worked around the clock and was paid only in the opium which let her mind drift in a dream world even as it wasted her body. English Annie did not care. In the years since she had come to Nevada, she had been on a continuous downward spiral. She had begun at the fanciest parlor house in Virginia City. Now she eked out a wretched existence in the lowliest crib. She would die here soon, but not soon enough.

Shirl Henke

Rory studied the skeletal woman reclining on the rumpled, greasy sheets. Although the room was dimly lit, the flickering shadows could not hide the ravages to her face and body. Graying hair in filthy snarls hung about bony shoulders. She brushed a wisp from her eyes with a yellowed, shaky hand. "You got the token, luv?" Her pale, watery eyes squinted.

Two bits. A quarter to purchase a token at the door. The price of English Annie's services. He tossed two of the house's copper tokens on the table beside her bed where her opium pipe lay. "I only want to talk to you, Annie. Years ago, when you worked the Howling Wilderness Saloon, you had a regular customer—Amos Wells," he began.

Her eyes narrowed. "How'd you learn that, luv?" A frisson of alarm penetrated the drugged haze of her mind.

"From a man named Sly Hobart. He's a mine supervisor who works for Wells. He knew you in the old days, same as Wells."

"So?"

"Tell me about what happened to a girl called Magnolia. She worked at the Wilderness around the same time as you. In fact, she was murdered in your room about eight years ago." He could see the fear in her eyes now as she clutched her pipe with white knuckles. "I'll buy you enough opium so you won't have to work for a week, Annie. Just tell me what you know about Magnolia."

"If he ever found out—"

"He won't know who told me. I'm going to see he hangs," he interrupted.

She gave a choking laugh. "Hang a rich man like Amos Wells for killing a down-'n-out whore?"

"He killed my brother, too. Make no mistake, Annie, Wells is a dead man. I want to know everything you've heard about what happened that night at the Wilderness."

"She died the night after I left. . . . "

By the time Rory paid English Annie and got out of the fetid air inside the crib, he was sweating and sick to his stomach. Sweet Holy Mother of God! Rebekah had married that vicious, sick pervert. What might Wells have subjected her to over the years? No woman, no matter how selfish she was or how she had betrayed him, deserved a man like Amos Wells. The very thought of that bastard putting his hands on Rebekah, sleeping beside her, made him ill.

As he rode back to his office, he thought about how to extricate her from Wells's clutches as quickly as possible. It might take months yet for Patrick's agents in Sacramento to gather all the evidence about illegal stock transactions. Sly Hobart had not yet given them what they needed either. Although he was certainly a better prospect, Rory was afraid to wait too long. Until every shred of information was exhumed and catalogued, they dared not move against Wells. He had to get Rebekah free now. He would write her, asking her to meet him again.

She had been upset about breaking her marriage vows and mistrusted his motives for seducing her, but she still felt something for him—something a lot more compelling than simple guilt over the way she had betrayed him. Her desire for him was as strong as ever. *As strong as yours is for her.*

Pushing the disquieting thought and its implications away, he composed a message and dispatched it to Carson City by rider, confident that she would agree to see him.

"You've done what!" Patrick's blue eyes blazed in amazement. He combed his fingers through his long red hair and paced back and forth in front of Rory's desk, casting incredulous glances at his brother.

"I've asked Rebekah Wells to be my mistress. I don't see

why that's so incomprehensible. She's a beautiful woman."

"She's the calculating bitch who cold-bloodedly threw you over for that murdering snake Wells with all his ill-gotten wealth! You're confusing lust with hate, Rory. A dangerous business. Once Amos is gone, she'll be punished enough. Leave her to heaven."

A strange look came into Rory's eyes. Haunted and uncertain. "What if it isn't hate . . . or even lust?"

Patrick cursed in Gaelic and gave his younger brother a baleful look. "Even worse! You're still in love with the heartless Jezebel. She'll destroy you, Rory. Forget her."

"After what I learned about Wells yesterday, I can't leave her with him. God, the bastard might strangle her the way he did that poor whore in the bordello—and who knows how many other women?"

"If she's survived the past eight years, I think that highly unlikely. Forget her."

"Maybe the best way to do that is to keep her in my bed for a while."

"What you need is a good, decent woman for a wife. You're nearly thirty years old. Have you no thoughts of a family?"

A crooked grin spread across Rory's mouth, lightening his mood. "You've scarce been wed a month. The honeymoon's not over yet. Just wait before you start urging me to join you in connubial bliss. I've no desire for a wife."

"Yet you'll take Amos Wells's wife. What of his son? Have you given a thought to him?"

"Wells has scarce been a doting father. They boy lives back east in boarding school. He won't even know about Amos's disgrace, much less learn about what passes between his mother and me."

"You're getting in over your head, Rory. Let the past lie.

My men will soon have enough to bring Wells and all his cronies to justice. Let it end there. Go out to that ranch you've built in Eagle Valley and raise horses.''

''Perhaps someday, Patrick.'' The finality in his voice indicated that the subject was closed.

Rory waited through the afternoon, too nervous with anticipation to concentrate on the mountain of paperwork piled on his desk. Finally the messenger from Carson City arrived. He broke open the letter eagerly, recognizing Rebekah's precise, elegantly slanted handwriting.

Rory,
  What passed between us the other day was a regrettable folly on both our parts. I am deeply ashamed of my actions and take full responsibility for them. My duty is clear. I must remain with my husband. You must proceed with your vengeance. We always were on opposing sides of every issue. There can be nothing between us.
  R.

''Nothing between us!'' He swore and balled up her missive. The self-righteous, stubborn little fool. He had to get her away from Wells.

The trip from Virginia City to Carson was a brisk few hours' ride. By the time he entered the verdant Eagle Valley, Rory's anger had cooled. He had calmly thought out a course of action. Although a Democrat, he had cultivated a number of influential Republicans in the capital, mostly through business dealings over the years. Social occasions had provided the opportunity to reinforce those acquaintances by charming the politicians' wives.

One such connection was with Bryan Kincaid, the California railroad magnate. His flighty little partridge of a wife, Celia, had at first been wary of her friend's former lover. However, in the past years Rory had sufficiently impressed her with his wealth and refinement to cause her to consider him in a completely new light. Celia had always been a romantic at heart. He was certain he could enlist her aid in setting up a tryst with her old friend.

Reno

Ephraim watched the train pull into the station with mixed feelings. He was always eager to see his grandson Michael, yet the terse note he had received from Amos asking him to meet the train in Reno and bring the boy to Carson City troubled him. Why couldn't Rebekah have come for her son, even if her husband was tied up with important business affairs and unable to accompany her?

He knew their marriage had never been happy and blamed himself for his daughter's suffering—even more for the loneliness of young Michael, who had been deprived of both parents' love for so much of his young life. He had wrestled with his conscience over Rory Madigan for years, ever since the penniless drifter had turned into a wealthy, respectable businessman. Perhaps he should not have interfered between the Irishman and Rebekah.

"It's all past now. Too late. Amos has legal claim over Michael, and nothing can change that," he murmured to himself. If he told Rebekah about Madigan's letters, it would break her heart and alienate her from her own father. These days he felt both she and young Michael needed him too much to risk that. He suffered the pangs of conscience in bitter silence.

"Grampa!" Michael's voice was shrill with excitement as

he leaped down from the train and raced across the platform, flying into the old man's arms. Millicent Ahern approached at a more sedate pace and stood back as grandfather and grandson were reunited.

"I do believe you've grown at least a head taller in the past few months," Ephraim said as he inspected the boy after a big hug. "How is that new school?"

Shoving a black curl off his forehead, the boy shrugged. "It's all right, I guess." His eyes scanned the platform. "Where's Mama?"

Ephraim could hear the fear and uncertainty in the boy's voice. *He never asks for his father.* "Your mama couldn't come, but I'm taking you to Carson in my carriage. You'll be with her and your father by tonight." He prayed he was right. Amos's note had been vague about the reasons Rebekah could not meet the train.

"Why did my father have me sent down from Calverton at the beginning of the term?" Michael asked.

"Well, he didn't say," Ephraim replied.

"I wish I never had to go back," the boy blurted out suddenly. "It always rains in Massachusetts—except for when it snows. I'd rather be home in Nevada with Mama and you."

Ephraim's heart wrenched. If only he could talk some sense into Amos; not that he hadn't already tried, but he would try again. "Someday you'll be able to stay here—if you still want to after you've made a lot of fine new friends back east," he replied to the lad.

"Oh," the boy said, suddenly fidgeting uncomfortably but meeting his grandpa's eyes, "I wanted to tell you in person how sorry I was about Grandma."

"That's all right, son. I appreciated your condolence letter."

"But I wanted to be with you for the funeral," the boy replied earnestly.

"There was no way you could've traveled so far so quickly." Ephraim hugged the boy again. It had always been a bitter regret that Dorcas had not favored Rebekah's son as she did Leah's boys. To his wife, Michael had been a symbol of her daughter's sins, tainted by Rory Madigan's blood. Although Michael knew nothing about that, he had always sensed, with the uncanny ability of bright young children, that his grandmother did not love him as she did his cousins.

"Do you miss her?" Michael asked, unable to squelch his boyish curiosity. Miss Ahern began to reprove Michael, but Ephraim signaled her gently with one hand. "It's all right. Yes, I do, Michael, but it was the Lord's will that she be taken. We must accept that."

"Just so the Lord doesn't want to take you," the boy said fiercely.

How lonely for a father's love he is. "Never fear, son. I expect I'll be around for a while."

As he exchanged pleasantries with Michael's governess, Ephraim secured the bags from the porter and had them placed in his battered old carriage for the long ride to the capital. Always bright and curious, Michael began to chatter and ask endless questions. Ephraim's misgivings about the summons faded. He settled down to enjoy the rare treat of having his grandson home.

The weather was dazzling, cool and cloudless, a perfect autumn day in Nevada as they rode south toward the capital. With any luck, they would arrive in plenty of time for supper.

Rory Madigan, too, made his way to Carson that golden fall afternoon. He had enlisted Celia Kincaid in his plan. Tomorrow she was supposedly having an intimate tea as a farewell before she and her family returned to Sacramento.

Rebekah would, of course, attend. But there would be no other ladies at the Kincaids' hotel suite, only Rory, waiting to talk with her.

He had to convince her of the danger if she remained with Wells. The man was far more than merely an unscrupulous businessman who would kill for profit. He abused and killed women to feed his own sick perversions. She would have to believe him. Sweet saints, had she already been subjected to Wells's brutality? Perhaps that was the reason behind her terse, hurtful note to him last week.

"I can protect her from him. She has to trust me." Of course, Rebekah had little enough reason to trust him these days, he admitted. Her own guilt and his bitterness were enough to make her tread warily. As he considered what to say to her tomorrow, he rode up a broad, tree-lined street on the outskirts of the city.

Without consciously realizing it, he had headed for the neighborhood in which Amos Wells's elegant city house was located. *Are you hoping for a glimpse of her?* some inner voice mocked. He was acting like a lovesick schoolboy! Perhaps Patrick was right to be worried about his obsession with Rebekah Wells.

Just as he was about to rein in Lobsterback and turn to avoid her street, Ephraim Sinclair's battered old black carriage came around the opposite corner. Rory remained in the shadows of a tall alder tree, watching the old man pass by, busily engaged in a laughing conversation with a young boy. *Rebekah's son.* What was he doing at home? Something was naggingly familiar about him. A primordial urge led Rory to follow the carriage.

A drab-looking spinsterish type sat in the backseat of the open buggy. He dismissed her as some kind of nursemaid, pitying rich men's children raised by servants. When the carriage approached the big horseshoe-shaped driveway of the Wells mansion, Rory eased his bay into the cover of a stand of dense pine trees and dismounted. Not knowing why he felt so compelled, he stealthily cut through the shrubbery. When the carriage pulled up and stopped in front of the house, the boy jumped down. He was tall for his age, Rory thought curiously. He waited until Rebekah's son turned so that he could see the boy's face close up.

The breath rushed from his lungs as if he had been gut-punched in a prize ring. He was staring into a younger version of his own face—the mirror image of an old daguerreotype his parents had had taken of him back in Ireland.

Blessed Virgin, he's mine! Rory stood frozen behind the juniper bushes, staring at the boy who was so near him he could almost reach out and touch him.

The child knelt in the grass and scooped up a fallen bird's nest. "Look, Grampa! Baby birds were once hatched in this!" He jumped up with his treasure and ran across the drive toward the porch, clutching the nest as he asked, "Where's Mama? Is she home?"

Blood pounded in Rory's ears as he watched Ephraim and the governess follow his son up the wide stone stairs. *His son!*

Then Rebekah appeared in the front doorway and knelt, clasping the child in her arms. "Michael, you're home. How I've missed you!"

Michael. She had named his son after him, yet she had deserted him and given the child to Amos Wells. Was the name some sort of ironic jest, or did the illustrious Wells family have a Michael in their family tree? "Damn you, Rebekah!" he ground out savagely, thinking about the ruthless and brutal Amos Wells raising *his* son. Thank God Wells had spent no time with the child. The farther away Michael could be kept from a madman like Amos, the better.

"I'll get you back, Michael. Both you and your mother, I swear it!" He had to think, to regain his self-control before he foolishly gave way to impulse and ran into the house to confront Rebekah and her sanctimonious father. That would frighten Michael and accomplish nothing.

He took a deep breath, then looked down and realized he was holding on to the rough branches of the juniper so tightly that he had ground splinters into his palms. His hands were scratched and bleeding, but he did not feel anything. He turned and made his way to Lobsterback. There were a great many things for him to consider before he met Rebekah in the morning.

While Rory made plans outside the mansion, inside his son was getting reacquainted. "Uncle Henry. Good evening, sir," Michael said with his best boarding school manners as he greeted the tall man with the mustache who stepped out of his father's study into the hallway.

Rebekah smiled at Henry as he returned his nephew's greeting. For some reason, Michael had never been as fond of Henry as she would have hoped, considering that his two boys were close in age to her son, and Henry was around a great deal more than Amos. But perhaps that was the difficulty. Hank and Jed *had* a father while Michael always sensed that he did not. *He has a father in name only who's brought him home only to blackmail me,* she thought in misery.

"Good evening, Henry. What brings you here—more business with Amos? I thought he was tied up at the capital," Ephraim said as the two shook hands.

"I've been in the Comstock towns the past week or so.

Just stopped by to check on Rebekah and see this young man here.''

"Isn't Father coming home tonight, sir?'' the boy asked. The question had become perfunctory. He knew it was expected that he ask about his father, but the austere man with the cold gray eyes who always seemed to stare at him as if he'd done something wrong made him uncomfortable. He was just as well pleased to have his mother to himself and his father off on business.

"I'm afraid your father has a dinner meeting that will last past your bedtime,'' Henry said, ruffling the boy's hair awkwardly. "You'll see him tomorrow.'' He turned to Rebekah. "If you'll forgive me, Rebekah, I do have to meet Amos and Stephan at the Ormsby House.''

"Of course. Give Undersecretary Hammer my regards,'' Rebekah replied as Henry made his way down the hall.

Ephraim took in the scene with mixed emotions. In the past years, Rebekah and Henry had become closer as both their marriages deteriorated. Leah was jealous of her younger sister and accused her and Henry of crazy things he knew to be totally false. Rebekah did need a friend, the Lord knew, but he wished Henry had not been drawn into Amos's circle of business associates, even peripherally.

Recently he had been hearing some alarming rumors about the way Stephan Hammer and Amos Wells made their money. If they lured Henry with promises of illicitly gained wealth, Ephraim feared his son-in-law would be tempted. And Leah would be at fault, for her love for expensive clothes, houses, and servants had grown insatiable. Rebekah's words broke Ephraim's troubled reverie.

"You must be tired, Papa. I've had the maids prepare your room and draw a bath before dinner.''

"Do I have to take a bath, too?'' Michael made a face,

still clutching his bird's nest in two small, grimy hands.

Rebekah eyed his sweaty little face and dusty, travel-stained clothes. "I think it might be best, don't you?"

Sighing, he nodded. "Knew you'd say that."

Rebekah rose early and spent the morning playing with Michael. Amos had returned home late last evening and departed again early, leaving word via his manservant that he would be in the Comstock for several days. He made no inquiries about Michael other than to ascertain that he had arrived on schedule.

"If I had known Michael would be here today, I'd never have accepted Celia's invitation," she said to her father as she slipped on a pair of kid gloves.

"The two of you have been friends since you were in pigtails, and she's leaving for Sacramento tomorrow. Go and wish her godspeed. I'll tend to my grandson until you return," Ephraim replied, peering out the window at the boy playing in the big swing that hung from the gnarled branch of an old cottonwood tree in the backyard.

Rebekah, too, watched him with a wistful expression on her face. "It seems he gets to play so seldom. I fear all they do in that awful school is dress him up in uncomfortable clothes and make him stand at attention."

Ephraim smiled sadly. "I think you exaggerate, but I do wish he could live with you until he's older. Perhaps Amos had him brought back with that intention in mind," he said hopefully.

Rebekah's expression hardened. "No. He had another intention altogether, Papa." She turned and picked up her reticule. "I'll only stay long enough to bid Celia good-bye."

Ephraim watched her leave with troubled eyes.

*   *   *

295

Celia observed Rebekah's carriage pull up in front of the hotel, then dropped the curtain and looked nervously over at Rory. "I hope I'm doing the right thing."

His eyes were unreadable. "You are. More than you could ever realize."

With one last wary glance his way, she turned and fled the parlor of her suite by a rear door.

When Rebekah knocked, a hotel maid opened the door and ushered her inside, then bobbed a curtsy. "Good mornin', mum," she murmured, then left before Rebekah could reply.

She was a bit late. Odd that none of the other ladies had arrived yet. She peeled off her hot gloves and called out, "Celia?"

"Celia's not here."

Rebekah dropped a glove as she stared aghast at Rory, leaning indolently against the door frame between the suite's parlor and hall. She struggled for composure as her thoughts whirled. If Amos found out . . . "What are you doing in her suite?"

"That should be pretty obvious. You and your friend were ever good at matchmaking." He glided like a predatory mountain lion, blocking her retreat via the front door.

Damn Celia and her harebrained ideas! "I can't stay, Rory. We have nothing to talk about." She tried to step around him. His question froze her to the ground.

"No? How about Michael?" His voice was deceptively soft.

She had seen his lightning Irish temper ignite a dozen times over the years, but this was different. The hairs on her nape prickled in warning. She tried to frame a reply, but her tongue stuck to the roof of her mouth as he stepped closer. *He knows!*

The tension between them was palpable. She looked into his beautiful blue eyes—Michael's eyes, only they weren't Michael's eyes, alight with childish laughter and love. These were ice cold with fury held under monumental control.

"Yes, Michael. My son. Tell me, did you name him after me? Was that your idea of some sort of cruel jest, Rebekah?"

Finally anger overrode her speechlessness. "Cruel! You're a fine one to accuse me of cruelty! You—"

"You've let that degenerate bastard Amos Wells raise my son."

"I had little enough choice in the matter. At least he gave Michael his name."

"His name? Or his wealth? That was your choice. I offered you the Madigan name, but it wasn't good enough. Wells had the money and the power you wanted."

"That's a damnable lie. I never wanted to marry Amos!"

"I'm sure you repented your bargain soon enough in spite of the glittering life he bought you. Diamonds are so cold when you're alone in bed, aren't they, darlin'?" His fingers reached up and glided mockingly along her cheek.

She flinched and slapped his hand away. "You're every bit as despicable as Amos."

He looked down at her with contempt. "And every bit as rich—now. But it took me years to catch up and you couldn't wait, could you?"

"No! I couldn't. I was seventeen and pregnant. You deserted me for the bright lights of Denver." Her voice sounded hurt and bitter, weaknesses she did not want to reveal to him.

"You knew I was coming back," he replied defensively. "I took a fearful beating. Then—"

"I'll just bet you did," she lashed out furiously. "I begged you not to go. Maybe I knew all along you'd never come back for me.''

"Such faith in my love, Rebekah?" His rhetorical question was delivered in a sardonic tone of voice.

"I was alone—"

"And along came Amos, dangling diamonds in front of you—never mind that you were giving away my child to that pervert!" His control was breaking as he answered her anger with his own. "I thought I'd never forgive you for marrying my brother's murderer, but now I've found out the real depth of your greed—to take my son away from me and give him to Wells. Tell me, does Amos know the boy isn't his?"

Her ashen face was answer enough.

"What sort of mother would let her son be punished by a sadistic son-of-a-bitch like Wells?"

Rebekah advanced on him, her nails curving into claws as fury roared in her veins. "For all his faults, Amos has treated Michael as his son and heir. He's never abused my son. He never will," she said flatly.

Rory studied her with a jaded expression on his face. Sweet Virgin, how he wanted to believe her! But dared he?

"I arranged this meeting to warn you about him. You damn well might die—he strangled a woman over in Virginia City eight years ago. It isn't safe for you to be around him. You have to get away. I can offer you protection. Bring Michael—"

"All you want is my son!" she gasped in outrage as his calculating plan became clear to her. "You don't give a damn about me—you only want Michael!"

"That's crazy. I can keep you and my son safe from Wells. He's dangerous, I tell you."

"He'd never dare harm Michael. I told you, Michael is his

only heir.'' The words sounded hollow, even to her own ears, but she could trust Madigan no more than she could Amos. Perhaps less, for at least Amos had become a known quantity.

"He let nursemaids raise Michael while he had you on display in Washington. Has he hidden my son away because he couldn't bear to see the resemblance to me?''

The barb struck home, for Rebekah had often thought as much, but she refused to give him the satisfaction of admitting it. ''Just because you've found a son who's your mirror image, you can't walk in and take him away after all these years.''

"Some devoted mother you are,'' he said scornfully. "I'm surprised the boy recognized you yesterday, he sees you so seldom.''

"You followed my father—you were spying on us,'' she accused him.

A look of pain flashed across his face, but he quickly masked it. "Not spying. Just a lucky coincidence. I saw Michael in Ephraim's carriage. I wanted to take a closer look.''

His pained expression confused her. Even though he did not love her, perhaps he did care about his son. "The resemblance between you is uncanny. It grows greater with every passing year,'' she said softly. A wistful look had replaced her earlier anger. "I . . . I didn't think you'd care.''

He stiffened. "Not care? He's my son,'' he ground out furiously.

She threw back her head and stuck out her chin pugnaciously. "Surely you have bastards from coast to coast by now.''

He took her by her shoulders, prepared to shake her teeth loose. "There are no others! I'd never let a child of mine go unacknowledged.'' He saw the look of doubt in her eyes. "I've always been scrupulously careful about taking precautions with women—but everything was different with you. I intended to marry you.''

''I don't believe you,'' she said stubbornly. *He only wants Michael.*

''I don't give a damn whether you do or not. It really doesn't signify since I've withdrawn the proposal. But make no mistake, Rebekah. I will have you, and I will claim my son.''

''You can't! No matter how much he resembles you, Amos Wells is his legal father. You have no rights. You gave them up when you left me eight years ago.''

''Once Amos hangs for his crimes, we'll just see about my legal rights. I'm the one who has the power now, Rebekah darlin','' he said mockingly. ''I swore you'd come to me and you will.''

''I will not.'' She stood close enough to feel the heat of him, the fury he had once again banked under such cold, calculating control.

She refused to back down from him when he reached out and pulled her into his arms, but her body remained rigid. ''Down at the river last week you gave in quickly enough,'' he taunted.

''That was a mistake. I told you I never wanted to see you again.''

''In a note. You were afraid to see me again. Afraid I'd get you to succumb again. You've become a coward, Rebekah. That must come from living with a man like Amos Wells.''

''Yes, I suppose you're right . . . I am.'' She bit her lip, feeling like the coward he had named her—but not for herself. For Michael. In spite of her threats to Amos, her husband might still succeed in harming the boy. Send him to Europe. Enroll him in one of those ghastly military academies. Have her declared an unfit mother and deprive her of her right ever to see her son again. Exposing his own sexual inadequacies would be small compensation for Michael's suffering. She wanted to trust Rory's protestations that he cared for her as well as Michael. She wanted to accept his offer to take them both away. But she could not trust Rory. She simply had to survive and pray he was telling the truth about Amos's imminent fall. Only then would her son be safe.

Rory tried to read what went on behind her troubled eyes. He wanted to trust her, to love her, to offer her marriage when Wells was disposed of. But that would be baring his soul to her as he had done eight years ago. He could not take that chance.

And still he could not release her. Slowly, feeling her passive resistance, he lowered his mouth to hers for a parting kiss.

Only to prove a point.

Liar.

Ignoring the mocking voices inside his head, he kissed her, letting his lips brush hers, his tongue rim her mouth, then tease the tight seam until it parted. With a groan he plunged inside, tasting, exploring, feeling the velvety glide of her tongue dance with his.

Her mind screamed no, but her body capitulated as she answered his kiss. He molded her flesh against his from head to toe, crushing her breasts against his chest and pressing her pelvis against his. She could feel the pressure of his erection grinding against her belly and gloried in his male vitality and her own answering feminine fire. God, but she wanted him, ached for him. With a muffled cry, she wrapped her arms around his neck and moved with the rhythm he had set between them.

Rory almost succumbed. They were alone. He could take

her here on the thick carpet just as he had down by the river. But he had proven his point. She would be his again. She *was* his. This was not yet the time or place to reveal his own hunger, his weakness. He reached up and pulled her hands from his shoulders, holding her by her wrists.

His eyes mocked her, and she reddened in shame, unable to hold up her head. Dear God, if he released her, she feared she would sink to her knees in front of him! "Please go," she choked out.

"A minute ago, your body was telling me to stay," he mocked.

"Just go." When he released her, she bit the inside of her lip, drawing blood, just to stand straight and face him. "Get out."

"I'm going. But I'll be back for you and my son."

As soon as he closed the front door behind him, she sank onto her knees and wept for all that could have been between them, but most of all she wept for Michael. Could Rory love his son?

Could he love you?

"No, no, no . . ."

Chapter Sixteen

Virginia City

Sly Hobart slipped in the back door of the Howling Wilderness Saloon and found the small table hidden in the alcove, just where Rory Madigan had said to meet him. He squinted into the shadows and saw the tall figure, his chair tipped back with seeming indolence against the wall.

"Madigan?" Hobart whispered nervously. The usual assortment of miners, whores, cowboys, and a variety of Eastern slickers were all too busy drinking and gambling to pay any attention. Still, it made him nervous to meet with Wells's enemy.

Rory lowered his chair back onto the floor. "Yeah, I'm Madigan. Get out of the light and sit down. You left word with Patrick that you had inside information about Wells's latest stock deal."

Hobart grabbed a chair and shoved it toward the darkest recess of the corner. His narrow face was as furtive as a weasel's. He grinned nastily, revealing pointy, tobacco-stained teeth. "Soon I'll have enough to stop the whole bunch of 'em—Wells and that fancy Washington politician Hammer. Shit, even ole Shanghai Sheffield's involved. They're planning to spread rumors the Alder Gulch Mine has just struck another bonanza."

"That should drive up the price of shares," Rory' said dryly.

"It'll make 'em worth ten times what they are now. Truth is, the mines are plumb gone bust. I been down in 'em. There ain't nothin' left but the smallest sprinkles of cheap-grade silver. Cost more than it's worth per ton to bring it out."

"But they plan to sell out after they've driven the price sky high." Madigan's voice was disgusted.

"They been holdin' the miners below ground, too," Hobart added with relish.

At once Rory's expression shifted from jaded to implacable. "Do you know who and where? I want times, places—everything."

From across the crowd, a pair of crafty eyes studied the two men engaged in such an intense conversation in the corner. Chicken Thief Charlie Pritkin had been following Sly Hobart for several weeks, ever since he had seen him in conversation with Patrick Madigan at Jenson's Racetrack. Sly was a luckless gambler who owed big money to Beau, who was a partner of the Madigan brothers. A man didn't have to know comere from sic 'em to figure the mine supervisor was selling information to pay off his markers.

He felt nervous about getting near Rory after his brush with death in that Denver saloon. The damn mickey should be dead! Slocum sure enough was. But the Irishman had not seen his face in the dark. He'd be safe enough, and his employer paid better than ever lately. Pritkin moved through the crowd and edged against the wall by the alcove so he was hidden around the corner yet able to hear the exchange between the two men.

"You got that old whore to talk?" Hobart asked.

"Annie told me about Amos's penchant for beating up women," Rory replied flatly. "He killed one right here, upstairs in her old room."

"Shit. I always knowed he was a mean bastard."

"I can't exactly depend on English Annie's recollections in court," Madigan replied sarcastically. "You said you have some hard information about this stock deal."

"I seen a hidden wall safe in his office in Carson. Never mind how I found out," he added with a sly chuckle. "Filled with stocks and deeds of transfer, all sorts of written proof about how he's made deals and with who."

"Sounds rather careless," Rory replied dubiously. "That sort of evidence would incriminate him, too."

"You wanna know what I figger?" Hobart went on without expecting an answer to the rhetorical question. "You know how I been collecting information about him, keeping his handwritten instructions, stuff like that?"

"To blackmail him someday," Madigan supplied the answer. "You think he's done the same thing."

Hobart shrugged. "Might be to bleed a feller like that high 'n mighty Hammer, or maybe it's a way to keep him or one of the others in line. Could be he's gonna use 'em to force his way back into politics."

Rory leaned forward. "Can you get me those papers? I'll not only forgive your gambling debts—I'll pay you ten thousand extra."

Hobart's eyes gleamed with avarice. "It'd be hard. Might

305

take a few weeks. I don't exactly get invited there real often," he added dryly. "But I reckon I can get in sometime. Lots of stuff on Wells there."

Rory stroked his chin consideringly, thinking not only of Amos Wells, but of his wife. Wells most probably used Michael the same way he did those incriminating documents—to keep Rebekah in line. *Amos Wells is legally his father.*

Deep in thought, Rory did not notice when Chicken Thief Charlie Pritkin slipped past the alcove and headed to the bar to celebrate the money he would shortly collect.

Eagle Valley

For several days Rory agonized over his bitter confrontation with Rebekah. He replayed their conversation in his mind, realizing that he had handled the matter badly. She was afraid of him, thinking he was using her only to get his son—and that he wanted the boy to use as a pawn the way Amos had always done.

"But he's my son, dammit," he raged to himself as he pounded his fist against the unyielding walnut desk in the study of his new ranch house. The two-story white stone building was grand indeed, but all that his money had been able to buy meant nothing now that he had a son he could not claim and a woman who still haunted his dreams, sleeping or awake.

Her accusations troubled him deeply. The more he had time to consider their parting eight years earlier from her point of view, the less of a crass monetary betrayal it seemed. She had been only seventeen, raised in a rigorously strict religious environment with parents who hounded her to make an advantageous marriage to Amos Wells. Who could she have gone to when he was hundreds of miles away in Denver? How terrifying it must have been to find herself expecting a child with no husband.

Of course, he had pledged to return for her and had sent three letters during the time he was recovering from the attempt on his life. Perhaps she never received them. He would certainly not put it past her conniving parents to have destroyed the letters. And he was gone long enough that she could have believed he would not return.

Over the years, Rory had never given much thought to the senselessness of that attack on him. He'd just assumed Bart Slocum and the mysterious companion who escaped after stabbing him were stupid cutthroats after revenge and his prize money. But now their attempt on his life took on far more sinister implications. What if Amos Wells had dispatched them to get him out of the way, then arrived like a knight in shining armor to propose to Rebekah? Had her family known she was pregnant? They would have moved heaven and earth to make her wed Amos if they knew.

It was ironic. If his suspicions proved true, Rebekah had every reason to be as bitter and mistrustful of him as he had been of her. He had believed her to be a shallow fortune hunter. What if she believed he was a faithless philanderer who had seduced and deserted her and left his son at the mercy of a miserable cur like Amos Wells?

Rebekah had been fighting tears when she defended her separations from Michael, separations Rory was increasingly certain were forced by Wells, who used the boy to blackmail her. Now it could appear to her that he was doing the same thing. She did seem to care deeply for her son. If only she were telling the truth about Wells never harming her or Michael.

All this may be a fool's wishful thinking. I never have gotten her out of my mind. It's as if she's robbed me of my very soul. Although it was only late afternoon, Rory poured a glass of fine Irish whiskey and took a sip, savoring the mellow burning as it traveled to his gut, soothing the confused thoughts that tormented him.

The key to the tangle lay with Michael. Whether he was right about Rebekah's reasons for deserting him or not, Rory was determined to have his son. And in so doing, he just might learn a great deal about Michael's mother. He smiled and raised the glass in a salute as he gazed out the window at the big corral.

"Here's to you, Rebekah darlin'."

Carson City

"Please, Mama, please, can—may I go to the market with Miss Mulcahey?" Michael's young face was alight with excitement, which he tried to contain.

His precise speech and struggle to restrain his natural boyish enthusiasm made Rebekah's heart ache. *He's being robbed of his childhood by tutors and boarding schools.* "If you promise to do just as you're told, I suppose it will be all right," she conceded, eliciting a shout of glee that would bring reproof from Amos if he heard it. But her husband was upstairs changing for the reception Hiram Bascomb and his wife were giving that afternoon. She, of course, had to accompany him and could not go to the market with the servants, a chore she normally enjoyed.

The market was a colorful hodgepodge, typical of Nevada, a state in which the foreign-born outnumbered natives. Italian and Slovak grocers vied with German butchers and French bakers. Jews, Serbs, Mexicans, and Chinese all hawked their wares amid the overflowing stalls. Rebekah's xenophobic mother had always hated Carson and Reno, not to mention the raucous Comstock towns like Virginia City, all filled with such heathen foreigners. Over the years, as she had broadened her horizons by traveling across the United States, Rebekah had come to appreciate Nevada's diversity. She wanted Michael to grow up in an environment without Dorcas Sinclair's intolerance.

Pressing several coins in her son's small hand, she kissed him. "That's to buy yourself a sweet at Mr. Silverstein's confectionery. You be sure to mind Miss Mulcahey."

"I love you, Mama! I wish I never had to leave you or Nevada again." He hugged her, then dashed off to the kitchen, not seeing the tears that glistened in her eyes.

Rory had been following Michael's routine for several days, waiting to approach the boy when his mother was not with him, but there had been no opportunity until this afternoon. He watched as the wagon pulled around the house from the servants' quarters. A small Chinese man drove the team and several domestics, including an imperious-looking Frenchman who he knew to be the Wells's cook, were chattering as they rode in the buckboard.

Michael sat beside a mousy-looking little maid, his small face lit with excitement. Rebekah had allowed him to go for an outing at the capital market. He followed at a discreet distance, his heart hammering in his chest. What would he say to the seven-year-old son he had not even known he had until a few short days ago?

Michael loved going to the market. If only his mother could have come, too, it would have been a perfect day, but her young maid was very nice. She had asked him to call her Patsy, saying Miss Mulcahey made her feel too old. She didn't correct his grammar or try to teach him lessons the way Miss Ahern always did, either. Patsy giggled a lot and told him wonderful stories about growing up in Ireland in a family filled with brothers and sisters. Michael thought wistfully about having lots of brothers and sisters. How wonderful that would be. Once he'd asked his mother why he didn't have any, but it had seemed to make her so sad, he never brought it up again.

"Now mind, don't be wanderin' too far," Patsy instructed her charge.

"I'll only go as far as Mr. Silverstein's confectionery. I want to buy a peppermint stick with the money Mama gave me. Would you like one, Patsy?"

"Bless yer soul, but I think not today—sweets give me the toothache, you know. But you enjoy an extra one fer me," Patsy replied, smiling as he scampered off toward the candy shop.

Michael secured his treat, then meandered down the busy street, gawking at the sights and listening to the magical sounds of foreign words. Two Chinese merchants were passing time with a game of dice while a fat German woman haggled with an Italian greengrocer over the price of his cabbages. Then Michael saw the most beautiful matched team of milk-white horses hitched to a carriage across the street. Unable to resist, he stepped out into the dusty thoroughfare intent on looking at them close-up. He stood entranced, sucking on his peppermint stick in the middle of the road.

"Golly, they're beauties," he breathed. Dared he approach and pat them? As he debated, Michael did not see the wagonload of beer casks and its whip-wielding driver rounding the corner from the opposite direction, headed straight toward him.

Rory had been working up his courage to approach his son when the scene unfolded in front of his horrified eyes. He jumped from the porch of the apothecary shop where he had been standing and raced down the block, yelling Michael's name. The boy turned in his direction just in time to see the cloud of dust the runaway horses were churning up as their drunken driver sawed ineffectually on the reins. Michael's eyes rounded with terror, but before he could react, Rory was there, sweeping him into his arms and leaping clear of the flying hooves.

They landed in the thick reddish dirt by the boardwalk of the mercantile as the team and wagon thundered by. Rory shielded his son with his body until the danger had passed, then rolled over with Michael in his arms. He placed the breathless boy on his feet and knelt beside him. They both coughed from the dust. Rory trembled.

"Michael, boyo, are you all right?" He clutched his son by his slim shoulders, holding him at arm's length, barely able to speak. *I could've lost him forever.*

"Yes—yes, sir. Thank you for saving me," the boy said between coughs. Then his eyes focused on Rory curiously. "How did you know my name?"

Before Rory could answer, Patsy Mulcahey fought her way through the gathering crowd, screeching like a banshee. "Michael! Are you all right, lad! They said you'd near been run down!" She seized her charge by his arm and turned him to face her, then hugged him. "I told you a hundred times niver to cross a street by yerself." She tried to sound stern but failed. "What were you doin'?"

"It was the white horses, Patsy. I wanted to see them better. They're so beautiful."

"They near got you killed by them other brutes."

"But this man saved me," Michael said, remembering Rory, who still knelt quietly behind him. "This is Patsy Mulcahey, Mister—?" He waited for the stranger to give his name.

As Rory stood up, Patsy looked from the dark stranger's face to Michael's and back. Her eyes widened.

Before she could say anything, Rory quickly smiled and answered, "A pleasure to meet you, Miss Mulcahey. I'm Rory Madigan."

"Sure and you are," she said in wonder. "I've seen you from a distance—durin' yer election campaign for the Congress. My brother Gabriel was one of yer organizers in the mines."

"Gabe Mulcahey's sister. I should've recognized you," he replied, hoping he had just made an ally in the Wells household.

"Aye, Irish family resemblances are easy enough to spot," she replied, glancing at Michael. So much made sense now. Her mistress's desperate unhappiness married to a mean one like Amos Wells, and his coldness and lack of interest in his only son. She studied Madigan with shrewd brown eyes. "Mrs. Wells as well as meself will be wantin' to thank you for savin' the boy."

She knows. The more time he spent around Michael, the more people would begin to remark on their resemblance, which only promised to grow stronger as the lad grew older. It would not matter once Amos was out of the way. But for now, he must be careful.

"No thanks necessary. I'm just grateful I was here." He had a good feeling about Patsy Mulcahey. Turning on his charm, he decided to test the waters. "Gabe was one of my best campaign workers. I could always depend on him."

"Yes, Mr. Madigan, and you can be dependin' on me as well," Patsy replied with a soft smile.

Her meaning was not lost on Rory. "I appreciate that, Patsy. Please, a countrywoman like yourself should call me Rory." She blushed and nodded. He turned his attention

312

back to Michael. "You like horses, eh?"

"Oh, yes sir. I sure do!"

"It just so happens I own a whole ranch full of them in Eagle Valley, and even part interest in the Jenson Racetrack outside of town. I have a pony or two just right for a lad your size. It so happens one of them is pure white, too."

"A white pony! Really? My father has a big stable but no whites and no ponies." His expression saddened for a moment as he added, "Of course, it really doesn't matter because I'm not allowed to ride his horses anyway. The grooms are too busy to take me out."

Anger churned in Rory's gut. A seven-year-old boy who'd never been on a horse! The servants had no time. What the hell was that bastard who called himself Michael's father doing that he couldn't devote a minute for his supposed heir? "Maybe one day I can teach you to ride. But first I have to convince your mother."

Patsy chuckled knowingly. "With yer gift of the blarney, sure and she'll be agreein'."

"What's blarney, Mr. Madigan?"

Rory struggled to explain. "Well, it's charm, I suppose— a way with people, to get them to like you and do what you want them to."

"Will I ever have it?" the boy asked, his big blue eyes round and guileless as he stared up into his new friend's face.

Rory fought the tightening in his throat and ruffled his son's hair. "Yes, Michael, I believe you already do. Now, how about my buying you another of those peppermint sticks? It seems you dropped the one you were eating in the dust."

They walked back to the confectionery, and while the boy went inside to make his selection, Rory took the opportunity to talk with Patsy.

313

Shirl Henke

"Yes, to your unspoken question. He is my son."

"If I hadn't seen you two right together 'n you holdin' the lad for dear life, I might not o' realized the truth o' the matter." There were unspoken questions in her eyes, but Patsy would not presume to ask. It was obvious to her that he cared deeply for his son.

"I never knew he existed until a few days ago," he said simply.

"Ah, sir, how sad for you . . . and for Miz Rebekah, too. There's niver been any love lost between her 'n that devil man she married."

Rory's face darkened ominously. "Wells won't be a problem much longer. He's going to prison—maybe he'll even hang if we're lucky."

Patsy paled and crossed herself. "I always knew he was a bad one. Gabriel said he was in on some awful minin' accidents that wasn't accidents, if you take me meanin', sir."

"Aye, that I do, Patsy. My brother died in one of those 'accidents'."

"Amos Wells can't be brought to justice soon enough," she replied fervently.

"Patsy, I'd like to spend some time with my son. I do have that white pony I mentioned. Is there a time when Wells will be gone? I could bring it around and take Michael for a ride."

Her brow furrowed. "He keeps crazy hours now that he's not a senator. Up half the night with his political cronies, meetin' at the house. But sometimes he spends all day at the capital. I suppose I could send you word . . . but what about the missus?"

"I'll handle Rebekah, but I don't want Amos turning his anger on her or my son."

"You don't have to worry about the servants tellin' himself. They're all loyal to the missus. They hate him, he's that vile to everyone.''

''Just let me know when the coast is clear.''

A note arrived the next morning, indicating that Amos was off to visit with several of his mining supervisors in the Comstock District and would not return until nightfall. Rory had instructed his foreman to bring the white pony to town the preceding evening. He was at the front door of the Wells city house before noon.

Cue Ging opened the door and bowed respectfully before the well-dressed gentleman. ''Mr. Wells not at home.''

''I've come to see Mrs. Wells,'' Rory replied.

''Who is calling, please?''

He grinned. ''Just tell her it's the man with Michael's white pony. I'm sure she'll know.''

Upstairs Michael had heard the horses' hooves in the drive and dashed into his mother's sitting room at the rear of the house. ''It's him, Mama! Mr. Madigan! And he brought it! He really brought it—the most beautiful white pony in the world!''

Rebekah bit her lip and tried to smile at her son's joyous little face. *This is what he always sought from Amos—time, attention, love.* Love? Did Rory love his son? According to the way Michael and Patsy sang his praises last night, he had indeed saved Michael's life and risked his own to do it. *Even if he loves Michael, that doesn't mean he wants you,* she reminded herself.

''A pony? I don't know, Michael. You've never ridden before.'' *And Amos will be furious if he hears Rory has been here.*

''Aw, please, Mama. Come meet Mr. Madigan. He's really

a nice gentleman. Patsy says he was a United States Congressman. You'll like him.''

Before Cue Ging could announce Rory, Rebekah followed her babbling, excited son downstairs like a prisoner walking to the gallows, trying desperately to put on a brave facade. Inside, her heart was hammering and the metallic taste of fear dried her mouth. Rory was insane to come here so openly. But then, she should have known he'd come after Michael. Cue Ging stood at the front door, holding it open as the boy dashed out and raced up to where Rory was holding the pony in the drive.

"You brought him! Oh, he's ever so beautiful!'' Michael reached up to rub the velvety nose.

"He's yours . . . that is, if your mother says yes,'' he added, turning to Rebekah, who stood frozen on the front step.

He looked devastatingly handsome, dressed in black. That color seemed to be his trademark now and accented his dark good looks, from the flat-crowned hat shoved carelessly back on his head to the leather vest and the breeches that hugged his long legs. His white shirt made a snowy contrast and was unbuttoned to reveal that disturbing thatch of dark hair curling on his chest.

"Hello, Rory,'' she said softly, forcing herself to draw nearer. "I understand you saved Michael's life yesterday. You know how grateful I am.''

"Then you'll repay me by letting the lad ride the pony,'' he said with a blinding white smile.

"He's so small to be riding alone—''

"He won't be alone. I'll be with him. I breed these Welsh ponies especially for children. He's gentle and well-trained. He'll be safe enough.'' He looked into her troubled eyes and said softly, "Don't be afraid of Amos. It won't be long now."

She nodded mutely. What was there to say? She should feel some twinge of guilt for the feelings of hope that Rory's statement brought. She wanted to see her own husband in prison. Or dead, God forgive her. Yes, dead. *I'm a wicked person.* "Be careful, Rory," was all she replied.

Rory helped Michael onto the pony and began to lead it around the driveway, showing the boy how to sit properly, hold his feet in the stirrups, and use the reins to guide the pony. Shortly he mounted Lobsterback, and the pair rode slowly down to the street.

Rebekah stood watching them until they disappeared beyond the trees. What would Amos say if he learned of the excursion? *Make no mistake* . . . She shivered. The servants would never tell him. To the last one, they had become loyal to her over the years and intensely disliked her husband, who was overbearing and inconsiderate, often venting his temper on them without reason.

But the capital was a close-knit community, and both Amos and Rory were well-known political figures. Even if no one saw them today, it would not be long before tongues would wag. People could not help noticing the resemblance between Rory and Michael.

Rebekah hoped and prayed Rory was right about her husband's fate. *Stop him soon.* But how could she ever explain the truth of Michael's paternity to her son? That question and the confusing and unresolved nature of her own relationship with Rory Madigan were enough to send her upstairs in search of her headache powder. *Dare I trust him?*

Amos Wells rode fast and hard toward Carson City that afternoon, more frightened and more furious than he could ever remember being in his life. Sly Hobart was dead—killed by a high-powered rifle right in front of his eyes when the two of them walked out of the mining office at the Silver Star. The second shot had grazed his cheek. He would have been shot as cleanly as his mine superintendent if one of the miners hadn't knocked him aside in a split second.

Who wanted him dead? The question—and a long list of obvious answers—dogged him on the way home. He was tempted to head for the Flying W, but it was farther away and he wanted to clean out all his papers from the office here. Were Bascomb and Sheffield backing out of the bank merger, or trying to double-cross him out of it? Or was it that snake-in-the-grass Hammer, now on his way back to Washington after refusing to support his cabinet aspirations with that mealymouthed reformer Rutherford Hayes?

Well, he had the goods on all three of them and more. But he needed protection until he could get his hands on the evidence and confront those bastards. It might be best to get Rebekah and the boy safely out of harm's way as well. He had enemies who would gladly stoop to kidnapping to try to obtain a hold over him.

"We seem such a loving couple," he snickered bitterly to himself as he rode up Stewart Street. His thoughts were interrupted when an old crony from the state legislature pulled up in his buggy and greeted him.

"Afternoon, Amos. You on your way home?" Graham Elden asked, spitting a noisome lob of tobacco from between blackened lips.

He looked happier than a flea in a doghouse. Something was afoot, a sixth sense warned the already agitated Wells. Elden owed him a favor or two. "Afternoon, Graham. Yes, I'm just on my way back from inspecting some mining property."

A crafty light shone in Elden's narrow eyes. "Just thought you might be interested to know your boy was out ridin' this mornin' with Rory Madigan. I thought it wuz real peculiar, him bein' a damned Democrat and doin' his best to see you didn't get them votes in the legislature for reelection to the Senate."

Amos felt poleaxed. "Madigan took my son riding?" He couldn't keep the croak from his voice and hated the smug, crafty look on Elden's face. *Does he know?*

"Yessir, he did. Brought the lad one of the fancy leetle horses he breeds out at his ranch. Glad I run into ya. Figgered you'd wanna know. Me, I'd never let my boys go near that mickey scum. Can't imagine what Mrs. Wells was thinkin', beggin' yer pardon for saying so."

"I'm obliged, Graham," Amos replied coldly, then kicked his horse into a trot. As if he did not have enough to worry about, now Madigan had come after the boy!

Then the thought hit him. *Madigan.* It could be the damned Irishman trying to kill him. Yet somehow he knew it was not Madigan's style to ambush him. A proud son-of-a-bitch like that mick would confront him head-on. It didn't matter. He'd kill both Rory and Rebekah for being so indiscreet.

Rebekah was reading to Michael when she heard the sound of Amos's angry voice downstairs. Quickly she closed the storybook. "Go down the back stairs to the kitchen, Michael. I'm sure François will have some scones and jam for you. Tell him I said to let you eat your fill."

A frightened look darkened his eyes. "Mama, is Father mad—angry about something?"

Rebekah shook her head. "It's probably just politics," she lied, trying to soothe the child. Amos had never shown Michael his vicious side, and she wanted desperately for it to

319

remain that way. "Please, hurry along now," she said, shoving him out the door and down the servants' steps. Then she composed herself and walked back into her sitting room.

Amos came through the door, his face mottled with rage. "You bitch. You stupid, ungrateful little bitch. I took you in, gave your bastard a name, treated you both like royalty. And you repay me by making me a laughingstock right here in the capital!"

"Amos—"

"Amos!" he mimicked nastily. Seeing the fear in her eyes made the bile in his guts rise. "You let Madigan ride out in public with his brat. The resemblance can't be missed. Graham Elden picked it up as soon as he spotted them. By week's end, the whole state of Nevada will be smirking about Madigan's bastard!"

"Don't you ever call my son that again!" Rebekah stood with her fists clenched, heartily sickened by the whole sordid mess in which her innocent child had been caught.

"Don't you presume to tell me what I can say," he growled as his hand lashed out, striking her a ringing blow to the cheek and knocking her back onto the settee. He fell on her, seizing her dress by the neckline and ripping it halfway down the front.

Rebekah saw the crazed light in his eyes. *Dear God, he's going to try to rape me!* She clawed at his face, raking a bloody set of furrows down his cheek.

Amos hissed in pain, letting her go, the moment of lust passing as quickly as it had sprung up. "I told you if you ever crossed me again, the retribution would be unspeakable."

"It has been. Every minute of every year married to you," she whispered, rolling away from him and seizing a poker from the hearth. "Get away from me, Amos, or so help me God, I'll use this!"

He backed off, daubing at his bloody cheek. "I think not. Consider what will happen to your son if I have to have you put away. A wife who threatens her husband with a poker and attacks him?" He *tsk*ed nastily as he watched her heaving breasts and saw the terror in her eyes. "Yes, you know I could have you committed. No one would blame me. And then what would become of poor Michael? Legally, he's mine. If I sent Madigan's bastard off to Europe, no one would blame me for that either."

"If you even try, I *will* kill you!" she shouted.

He cursed and turned to the open door. "You'd have to stand in line. Have your things packed. Tomorrow I'm sending you both to the Flying W until this gossip dies down. Then we'll discuss young master Michael's future." He stormed out of the room and down the hall.

Rebekah clutched the poker, her knuckles white against the black iron as she made her way down the hall to the head of the stairs. She did not release it until she saw Amos stride furiously toward the front door and heard it slam behind him. Cue Ging and the parlormaid stood at the bottom of the steps looking up at her. Patsy came tiptoeing from behind a door down the hall and gently took the weapon from her hands.

"Let's be gettin' you into a nice hot bath, ma'am."

"Michael—"

"François's keepin' him busy in the kitchen. You don't want him seein' you like this."

Shame washed over Rebekah. She reached up to her bruised cheek, already starting to swell, then pulled together the torn pieces of her bodice and nodded.

She soaked in the tub, holding an ice-filled compress to the side of her face, while her mind twisted and turned back

321

on itself. How could she free Michael from Amos's power? She damned Rory for coming back into their lives this way. After watching his son from afar and saving his life this morning, he should have let well enough alone. If he was telling the truth about Amos's imminent arrest, there would be time enough later for him to come forward and spend time with Michael.

"I can't go to that isolated ranch with Amos. God knows what he has planned for Michael or for me." *Make no mistake . . .* She threw down the ice pack and sat up, shivering in the steamy bathwater.

After repairing her appearance, Rebekah went to tuck her son into bed. She had carefully powdered her face to hide the bruise and pasted a bright smile on her lips.

Michael studied her with round blue eyes. "I heard the yelling. Why was Father so angry? Doesn't he like Mr. Madigan?"

"No, Michael. They're political enemies. It's all very complicated."

"But he was yelling at you. It was my fault. I was the one who went riding with Mr. Madigan. He should be angry with me. I tried to come upstairs, but François wouldn't let me," he said, choking back tears.

Rebekah hugged him, stroking his dark curls. "No, none of this is your fault, darling."

"It was mean of Father to yell at you." He reached up and touched her cheek. "He hurt you, didn't he? I hate him! I wish he wasn't my father!"

"Oh, Michael, you can't understand now. Maybe someday . . ." She crooned low, holding him close. Impossible dreams flashed through her mind. "Just finish your milk and go to sleep." She reached for the cup of warm milk with honey in it and watched as he finished sipping it slowly.

"I love you, Mama. He won't send me away from you again, will he?"

Her eyes grew hard as she stared into the inky darkness outside his bedroom window. "No, my darling, he won't ever separate us again. I swear it."

Rebekah waited until Michael was sound asleep before she went to her own room and tried to get some rest. Ever since Rory Madigan had come back into her life, sleep had become a rare commodity. She felt drained, physically and emotionally, caught between two ruthless and powerful men. Amos cared nothing for her and Michael—only for what they symbolized. They were political assets providing respectability to cover up the sordid and brutal things he did in the back rooms of Comstock bordellos.

Just thinking about the ghastly crime Rory had described Amos committing made her blood run cold. She recalled the scratches she had raised on his face in their earlier struggle. Dear God, he had had similar wounds on his face the very day they were married! Could he have come to his wedding night straight from that poor dead prostitute's bed?

Rory was right—she needed to take Michael and escape. She considered Rory's bitterness against her, the repeated accusations about her selling herself to Amos for wealth and prestige. Could he have intended to return to Wellsville? Had he, only to find her wed to his enemy?

"He promised days. I waited a month. No." She shook her head and rubbed her aching temples. There was no hope of sleep. Throwing back the covers, she slipped from bed and began to dress. Amos was gone, probably attending more political meetings or even carousing with some whore. He would not return tonight.

"I have to get some fresh air. Clear my head. Perhaps then I can sleep." She checked on Michael, who was fast

323

asleep. Patsy's room was adjacent to his on one side and Millicent Ahern's was across the hall. Although the governess was a fine tutor, she lacked the Irish maid's caring warmth. Michael certainly responded better to his friend Patsy than he did to Millicent, whom he deferentially called Miss Ahern. *Perhaps it's the kinship of their Irish blood,* she thought sadly.

Feeling it safe to leave him briefly with those two guardians, Rebekah tiptoed downstairs and slipped through the big deserted house to leave by the rear door adjacent to the stables. Just as she stepped into the kitchen, Cue Ging appeared, standing by the pump with a glass of water in his hand.

As always, he was quiet and unruffled, simply bowing to her as if being dressed to ride at midnight was an ordinary occurrence for the lady of the house.

"I feel in need of some fresh air, Ging. I'll return shortly. Please go back to sleep."

"Yes, missee."

Rebekah awkwardly began saddling her mare Buttermilk, but before she got farther than the bridle, Ramon, one of the liverymen, awakened and politely insisted on finishing the job for her. Although he did not ask, she could see the worried look in his eyes. *Everyone in the house knows Amos and I had that disgraceful fight.* She felt sullied and humiliated.

If not for Rory, Amos would have been able to convince her she was deficient as a woman, lacking the ability to fire a man's blood. If nothing else, Rory had certainly shown her the carnal side of her nature. She recognized Amos's sickness for the ugly thing it was, separate from her. At least she owed Rory that. And he had given her Michael.

With that thought bringing a wistful smile to her face, Rebekah pulled on her gloves and thanked Ramon as he helped her mount. Slowly she rode down the wide street toward the river beyond the city house.

The clock chimed midnight as Amos sat toiling at his desk in the spacious office with its view of the capitol building. How proud he had been as a newly elected United States Senator to open the elegant office right beside the legislature which had selected him for the high position. Of course, during the six years he served in Washington he'd returned infrequently, until the last year of his term, when he had to wage the campaign of his life for reelection.

"Damn that mickey bastard!" It was all Madigan's fault that he had lost his bid for a second term. But the other seat would come vacant in 1880, and he hoped old Shanghai Sheffield would not run for reelection. By God, he would be back in Washington then! Hammer had failed to secure him the appointment to the Department of the Interior, but being a Senator was really more prestigious.

However, he could have no scandal over Rebekah and Madigan's bastard. Why had he failed to see how much the boy was coming to look like his real father? The fact that he scarcely ever glanced at the boy or gave Michael a moment's attention did not occur to him. He only knew he must keep both mother and son under lock and key until he could deal with Madigan. And that had to wait until he had found out who was trying to kill him.

The stocks and bank ledgers were there. But a few particularly valuable items were at the ranch house, including a small fortune in cash he had skimmed on the last several stock deals. Now all he had to do was stay alive long enough to find out who his enemy was and dispose of him.

The first order of the day was to secure the items in his hidden safe at the ranch. He had made discreet arrangements in Virginia City to hire several bodyguards. They should arrive in the morning. Then he would take his happy family to the Flying W and lie low.

So intent was Amos on his plans that he did not hear the click of his office door as it was unlocked. The intruder quietly replaced the key in one pocket and withdrew the small pistol. A stroke of luck, being able to secure it. Perfect. The shadowy figure moved stealthily toward Amos, whose back was turned as he reached into his open safe to extract the last of the documents.

Some sixth sense caused Wells to turn just before the pistol was cocked. His eyes widened in utter amazement as he looked down the barrel pointed lethally at his heart. "Not you! Don't be a fool—"

The shot rang out, deafening in the silence of the night. Amos Wells was slammed against the wall. He was dead before he hit the floor. The intruder quickly scooped up everything on the desk and cleaned out the safe.

Chapter Seventeen

"Are you absolutely certain he's your son?" Patrick Madigan's expression was filled with disbelief as he stared at his brother. The two men were sharing a pot of coffee in Rory's suite at the Ormsby House Hotel.

Rory pulled out the faded and dog-eared old daguerreotype of himself as a young boy and handed it to Michael. Setting down his coffee cup, Patrick picked up the picture. "This is you with our parents, back in Galway."

"Michael is the mirror image of that picture. He was born in Washington exactly seven months after Rebekah married Amos Wells. I've had the dates verified." Rory's set look brooked no opposition. "He's mine, Patrick."

The elder Madigan sighed. "I suppose it's possible. But legally he's still Wells's son. You'd better tread warily until we've netted our prey, Rory. This could become very ugly if it got out.''

''I assumed the reason for your surprise visit was to let me know about how things were progressing in Sacramento.''

Patrick's worried eyes studied his brother. ''We should have indictments against Sheffield and Bascomb and the rest of their group in a week or two. The last I heard, Stephan Hammer had flown the coop back to Washington. He's going to be harder to convict because of his political connections there.'' He picked up the old photo and toyed with it, then looked back at Rory. ''What are you going to do about her once this is over?''

''Perhaps I was wrong about her.''

''Don't leap into marriage with her just to get your boy, Rory,'' Patrick cautioned.

Rory shook his head and smiled sadly. ''That may not be an option. Rebekah blames me for deserting her. If she's telling the truth, she has no reason to trust me now. To her, I'm no better than Amos. He uses Michael to blackmail her—I'm sure of it.''

''I can see how she might think you only want your son—not her. What *do* you want, Rory?''

Shrugging, Rory sighed. ''Hell, Patrick, I don't know. . . . '' He swore and shoved his chair back from the table. ''That's not true. I want her. I've always wanted her. After eight years, she's still in my blood. Even when I hated her, I loved her.''

''And now you don't hate her anymore,'' Patrick said quietly. ''Be careful, Rory. She may be the one who hates you.''

''I have to settle this. I'm going to face her and tell her everything.'' He stood up.

''Don't be a fool. Wait until Wells is out of the picture.''

"I don't dare. You saw those reports. The man's insane. He's already killed one woman—"

"A prostitute. He won't dare harm his own wife."

"You don't know that. Once he learns that we're behind his destruction, he could turn on Rebekah and my son. I can't chance it. I'm going to get them away from him today. While I took Michael riding, I read a great deal between the lines as he described his family life."

"Being seen in public with the boy was most imprudent, Rory."

"You're beginning to sound like Rebekah's father, Patrick—a dismal prospect indeed," Rory replied, giving his brother a slap on the back. "As long as you're here, why don't you see if you can run down Sly Hobart."

"Hobart's dead. That was one of the first things I learned when I arrived in Nevada. My agent wired me that he was shot outside a mine yesterday morning. Amos Wells was with him. Someone tried to shoot him too. Unfortunately, his aim was bad."

Rory swore and headed for the door. "Then his confederates are on to us—they must know we're after Wells. He's become a liability to them. If Hammer and the rest want Amos dead, Rebekah and Michael could be in jeopardy, too." Patrick blanched. "I never considered that, but you're right. Wait, Rory—I'll go with you."

"No time. I want to explain to Rebekah myself," Rory called out as he closed the hotel room door.

At the Wells's city house, Rebekah had packed two small valises—one for herself and one for Michael. They could not take much, and they needed to hurry before Amos returned. He had stayed out all night, not an unusual occurrence. But after his threat, she knew he would either come for her and Michael or send someone to escort them to the Flying W.

329

She and her son must be gone before that happened, and she could not involve the servants, who would suffer if they helped her.

After riding around for several hours last night, she had formulated a desperate plan. If they could simply vanish for a month or so, surely Rory would have Amos arrested and held for trial. Once her husband was publicly ruined and his sordid past revealed, she could return without fear of reprisal. Where to go had been the problem. The first place he would look was her father's house. But she had cash enough to buy them train tickets to Sacramento. Celia's husband was wealthy and powerful. She would simply have to throw herself on her old friend's mercy and hope for the best.

Rebekah slipped into Michael's room and awakened the sleepy boy. She guided him from his bed into her room, whispering that he must remain very quiet. He was too disoriented to protest. A few of the servants were up, but if she and Michael slipped out the side door with their bags hidden in her cape, no one would realize they were not coming back until it was too late.

"Mama—"

"Shh. Don't say anything now, dearest." She had him sit on her bed and began to dress him hastily. "You and I are going on a secret adventure. It will be great fun, but you must do exactly as I say." She shoved his arms through his shirtsleeves and quickly buttoned the front. Just as she was about to lace up his shoes, she heard Ging's voice raised from downstairs, arguing with someone. Rory!

"Wait here in Mama's room, Michael. Don't come out, no matter what," she instructed, urging him to lie back on her bed and doze.

"Is that Mr. Madigan?" Michael asked, rubbing sleep from his eyes.

"I—I'm not sure, but you must promise to stay here. Please. I'll come back as soon as I can."

Reassured when he nodded solemnly, Rebekah flew down the hall toward the front stairs. Rory had already bypassed Ging and was climbing the stairs two at a time. "Rory, what on earth—"

"We have to talk, Rebekah. Now. You and Michael are in grave danger." He took her arm and headed down the hall.

"There's a sitting room here," she said, stopping at the first door on the right.

He opened it and ushered her inside, then closed the door and turned to face her. "I'm taking you and Michael away from here—to my ranch."

A cold look came into her eyes. "A most peculiar coincidence. Amos has similar plans. Why, Rory?"

"It's all very complicated. Someone—one or more of the men who are mixed up in Amos's crooked dealings—has tried to kill him. I don't want you in the line of fire."

Rebekah remembered Amos's words during their fight. "He mentioned something about that yesterday. He knows you took Michael out for that ride. He was furious."

Rory approached and noticed the mark on her face for the first time. "He's hurt you. I'll kill that son-of-a-bitch myself!" His fingers touched her cheek gently, in spite of the anger radiating from him.

She pulled away. "He won't ever get the chance to strike me again. I grabbed a poker and ran him off last night. I can take care of myself—and Michael."

"You're both leaving with me."

"No. There'll be enough scandal as it is. I'll not have Michael hurt any more than he already is."

331

"You don't trust me, do you, Rebekah?" he asked gently, forcing himself to be calm.

"Why should I? You deserted us eight years ago without so much as a word—"

"I wrote you."

"How inventive. Did you give any reason for your delay?" she asked sarcastically. "Beau Jenson tried to cover for you, but he let slip that you were staying with a sterling character named Drago. Blackie Drago, isn't it? In a saloon and fancy house."

He ignored her tone. "Two men jumped me in my room at Blackie's place the night after the fight. I nearly bled to death from a knife wound, but as soon as I could hold a pen, I wrote and explained what had happened. It took me nearly two months to heal enough to return to Nevada. But I wrote three times, Rebekah. One of those letters had to have reached you."

"I received nothing," she said flatly, but a doubt began to niggle at the back of her mind.

"Then your parents must have intercepted them. The envelopes would've been stamped from Denver. Your mother or father—"

"No!" She turned away from his matter-of-fact accusation against her family. If true, it had cost them eight years of their lives.

He watched her struggle with doubts, her whole body trembling. "Your mother hated me with a passion, Rebekah. You said so yourself."

It was Papa who always went for the mail. She refused to consider it. The betrayal was simply too painful to contemplate. "I don't believe you. You deserted me like another in your long string of conquests and left me to live a life of hell with Amos—and believe me, Rory, it has been hell."

She was rewarded by the look of stricken anguish in his eyes.

"I'm sorry, Rebekah. I had no idea—"

"What you really mean is you had no idea about Michael. About how much he would resemble you. Now you want him. Well, it's too late. You can't have him. He's mine. Once Amos is in prison, I'll be free and my son will be safe. If you really care about us, see that Amos is arrested."

He took her shoulders in his hands and held her, fighting to keep his patience. "I know you're bitter. I guess you have every right to be—but so do I. I came back to Wellsville and learned you were married. I even went flying after you. I stood outside the ballroom doors on the patio and watched you dancing in his arms, dressed in fuchsia silk and diamonds."

She felt her heart skip a beat. "You . . . you were there the day of the governor's ball?" She had worn a fuchsia gown and that garish choker. She hated the dress and wore the diamonds as seldom as possible. Looking up into his face, Rebekah read stark pain. "You must have despised me then," she said softly and read the truth in his eyes. "Is this all part of your revenge, Rory?"

Unable to stop himself, he gathered her in his arms. She did not resist as he held her, stroking her hair. Then he tipped her chin up and kissed her softly. "It's over and done. Neither of us was to blame for what happened then. Wells was— and your family."

"No! You have no proof—"

As she pushed angrily out of his arms, a sharp rapping on the door interrupted.

"Sheriff Sears, Mrs. Wells. Your houseboy said you was in here. This is official business."

Rebekah gave Rory a horrified look, her eyes flashing around the small sitting room. There was no place he could hide even if he were so inclined, and she was certain he was not. The issue was quickly resolved as August Sears opened the door and stepped inside. He was a tall, thin man, gone to paunch around the midsection, giving him the unfortunate appearance of a candy apple on a stick.

He doffed his hat and nodded nervously at Rebekah, then looked past her at Rory Madigan. His pale eyes widened in recognition, but he quickly turned his attention back to the woman. "I don't know no way to do this 'cept to get on with it, ma'am. I come to arrest you for the murder of yer husband."

Rebekah felt the breath leave her body. "Murder! Amos is dead? How? When?"

"What's going on here, Sears?" Rory asked, moving beside Rebekah and helping her to a chair. "Explain what happened to Wells."

Sears looked from the powerful former Congressman to the widow. This was developing into one hell of a pickle. "Wells was shot late last night in his office across from the capitol. The Mexican woman who cleans the building come to work early. She found his body 'n come running to get me."

"Why on earth do you think Mrs. Wells had anything to do with it?" Rory asked.

The sheriff pulled a small .32 caliber Colt pistol from his coat pocket. "The gun is yers, ain't it?" He already had verified that it was.

Rory looked at Rebekah's chalky face as she nodded woodenly. "Yes, it's mine. My husband bought it for me several years ago, when he was traveling a great deal and I was alone in a big house in Washington. I haven't seen it in months."

"Is this the gun that killed Wells?" Madigan asked.

"Shot him clean in the heart, from the doorway by the look of it."

"Then there was no struggle." The sheriff shook his head. Rory could believe Rebekah guilty if Amos had struck her again, tried to attack her, but this was cold-blooded murder. "Was anything missing from his office?"

Sears shrugged. "Can't rightly say, but I found this here laying next to the body." He pulled a dainty white kid glove with pearl buttons from his pocket. "I can ask your maid if it's yours."

"I'll save you the trouble. It is, but I didn't know it was missing," Rebekah replied quietly.

"Doesn't this all seem a bit pat, Sheriff? Mrs. Wells had no reason to kill her husband. Someone has rigged this evidence," Rory said with a dismissive gesture.

Sears ignored Madigan and narrowed his gaze on Rebekah. "You 'n the mister had you a real bad fight last night, didn't you? Looks like he must've hit you." His gaze fastened on her swollen cheek. "That makes a pretty good reason for me. I been checkin'. Thet chink downstairs and yer greaser stableboy both say you went out last night—for a midnight ride." He waited expectantly, uncomfortable but dogged in his determination to close what appeared to be a straightforward case.

Rebekah started to reply, but Rory cut her off. "Yes, she did—with me. We spent the night together. I brought her back just a little while ago."

Sears's eyes widened in shock, then flashed from the man to the woman. She gasped and looked up at Madigan with horror in her expression. "He's just tryin' to get you off the hook, ma'am, but I know you done it," he said stubbornly.

"I did not kill Amos, although God knows, he gave me

335

reason enough,'' Rebekah replied, meeting the sheriff's pale eyes steadily.

"You have no real proof, Sears. Just her gun and a simple piece of apparel, either of which the killer could have stolen from this house. You can't arrest her with no more to go on. I'll have my attorneys at the courthouse before you can escort her there."

Sears's bony shoulders slumped in defeat. "Yer a rich, powerful man, Mr. Madigan. I know there was bad blood between you 'n Amos Wells, too. I'll leave it be fer now, but this ain't over." He nodded to Rebekah, then turned and stalked out of the room.

"Michael is in my room. He'll be frightened being left alone so long." Rebekah started for the door, but Rory placed his hand on her arm, detaining her.

He looked at the sensible twill suit she wore. "You were running away, weren't you?"

"I told you, Amos planned to send us to the Flying W. I couldn't allow it. Why did you lie for me, Rory?"

He tried to read the expression in her fathomless green eyes. Dark and bewildered, they swam with gold flecks. She looked so vulnerable that it squeezed his heart. Masking all emotion, he replied, "Simple. I'm your alibi. In return, you'll bring Michael and stay safely at my ranch until this whole mess is cleared up."

"The scandal is bad enough now—Amos murdered, the sheriff thinking I shot him in cold blood. Even if I didn't care about my own reputation, I won't have my son subjected to the ugly things that people would say if I moved in with you as your mistress."

"They'll figure out soon enough he's my son. As to your reputation, it'll be as secure as I can make it—with the protection of my name. You'll be Mrs. Rory Madigan."

Rebekah flung his hand away and stepped back, struggling to suppress the hurt surging through her. "How convenient. One might even be tempted to think *you* killed Amos. This is a very tidy way to get legal control of Michael, isn't it?"

"If I said I wanted to marry you because I still loved you, you wouldn't believe me," he replied in a weary voice.

"No, I wouldn't. Your original offer to make me your mistress rang a lot truer," she snapped bitterly.

"A lot has happened since then to change my mind."

"Michael has happened! He's all you want, and you can't have him." Her voice had a ragged edge to it. She needed time to think. *Amos is dead! You're free! You could marry Rory!* Thoughts tumbled about in her mind.

"Yes, I want Michael—and you. And I'll have you. I'm the only thing standing between you and the Ormsby County Jail right now. Frankly, Rebekah, you don't have any choice."

"You miserable, manipulative—"

"Tut, my dear. You don't want to say things to your prospective husband that you might one day regret." A hint of humor glinted in his eyes. Her show of temper was far easier to handle than that look of dazed hurt and accusation.

"What if I refuse to marry you?" she shot back furiously.

"Auggie Sears isn't very bright, but he's real stubborn. Without my vouching for your whereabouts, he'll be on you like a cougar on a lame doe. What would happen to Michael if his mother were in jail? I know you care too much for him to allow that."

Rebekah stared at him. "You're as ruthless and cold as Amos. And you're using me just like he did."

Rory gritted his teeth at her stubbornness. "That isn't true, but we don't have time to argue it now. I want you and Michael safely out of Carson City."

337

As he opened the door and escorted her down the hall, Rebekah said tightly, "You seem to have everything figured out. What kind of an explanation will you make to a seven-year-old boy? I won't let you frighten him with all that's happened, Rory."

"We'll just say that we're going on a trip. I suspect you've already prepared him for that." He watched the color stain her cheeks as she looked away. "I gathered as much," he said dryly.

"Just so you don't tell him his father is dead—"

"Wells is not his father," Rory snapped, then took a calming breath and added, "We won't mention it now. In a few days, when other matters are sorted out, we'll explain to him."

She stopped in the middle of the hall and faced him belligerently. "Explain what? That Amos was not his real father? That *you* are? Do you have any idea how shattering such a revelation would be to a small child? His whole world is being turned upside down."

Rory ran his fingers through his hair and stared up at the ceiling, trying to gather his thoughts. "All right. We won't tell him anything until we can agree how to do it."

"Including the fact that I'm marrying you the day after my husband's death?"

"Including that," he conceded.

"Let me take him to my father in Wellsville." She saw the dark flash of anger in his eyes before he masked it. "He's devoted to his grandson. Now that Amos can't come after us, Michael will be safe there—and I can tell Father about Amos's death. . . . " She paused and wet her lips nervously. "And that we're getting married. Please, Rory, I don't want him to hear it from strangers. He'd be devastated."

"I suspect he'll be beside himself anyway when you tell

him, but it won't change our agreement, Rebekah," he warned. "I suppose he could keep Michael overnight while we go to Virginia City to be married," he added grudgingly.

On the ride to Wellsville, Michael chattered excitedly, delighted that his new friend was coming with them and that he and Patsy Mulcahey were going to spend the night at his grandpa's house. As Michael plied Rory with the hundreds of curious questions seven-year-olds seemed to always have on their minds, Patsy watched them with genuine fondness. She easily joined in their laughter, as if seeing the two of them together was the most normal thing in the world. Rebekah wished she could take everything in stride half so well as her maid.

But her own thoughts were fixed on facing Ephraim. The closer they came to town, the greater her panic grew. Only by watching the warm exchange between father and son was she able to gain some consolation. Rory did seem to be good with Michael.

How could he not love his younger self? How alike they were. The physical resemblance was augmented by their quick laughter and bright, incisive minds. Once word of her appallingly hasty remarriage got out, no one would doubt for an instant whose son Michael truly was. *I'll be branded a shameless adulteress.* What would Ephraim say about such public disgrace? How could she face her father?

All too soon, Rory's fancy open carriage pulled up in front of the small white house on Bascomb Street, and Ephraim Sinclair's tall, stoop-shouldered silhouette appeared in the front door. When he saw Madigan with them, his expression grew troubled and his face pale.

The old man walked across the yard, and Michael went barreling into his arms. "Grandpa! You'll never guess what! I'm here to spend the night, me and—that is, Patsy and I," he corrected himself, "are going to spend the night. Mama has to go somewhere with Mr. Madigan. Have you met him? He brought me the keenest white pony and took me for a ride. He says I'll get to ride it again at his ranch!"

As the boy chattered on, Ephraim's troubled hazel-green eyes rose to meet his daughter's. Something was badly amiss; he could read it in her face.

"Father, why don't you show Patsy and Michael where you keep those cookies the guild ladies bring you every few days? When the two of them get settled inside, I have to talk with you."

Rory did not touch her, but as he stood by her side, his very presence was proprietary. He knew Sinclair sensed it and felt the old man's animosity. He nodded coolly. The sooner Rebekah faced her father and laid this out in the open, the better. He did not expect it would be a pretty scene.

"I know where the cookies and milk are, Grandpa. I can show Patsy," Michael crowed.

"I'll be takin' him inside, if that's all right with you, Reverend, sir," Patsy said uneasily, eager to get the boy away from the storm she could sense brewing.

Ephraim nodded. As soon as the maid and her charge disappeared inside the house, he turned to Rebekah. "Perhaps it would be best if we went inside the church."

"Yes . . . I suppose," she said. Guilt and sadness mingled as she remembered that it was in that very building where she had made her vows to Amos. And in the orchard beyond it where she had earlier made heartfelt ones to Rory. Her whole body trembled, and she found breathing difficult.

Once they reached the narthex of the small frame church, Rory quickly outlined what was going on, beginning with Amos's involvement in illegal mining practices and imminent arrest prior to his mysterious murder and the fact that the sheriff had come to arrest Rebekah.

When Rory had finished explaining everything, Ephraim glared at Madigan. His own guilt was swept aside for the moment. "You're blackmailing my daughter into marriage."

"You're a fine one to accuse me of that," Rory replied with cold contempt. The barb struck home.

The old man crumpled as he turned to his daughter. "I'm sorry, Rebekah. So very sorry."

She could see the tears gathering and hated Rory Madigan for this final humiliation to her father's already shredded dignity. She hugged him. "Don't—don't blame yourself. Everything will be all right. Rory and his brother have agents gathering evidence against Amos's associates. They'll find out who killed him and it will all end. Michael . . . Michael was never close to Amos. In time he'll accept Rory."

"He's my son, Sinclair. Don't you think I have the right to give him a father's love—the love Wells never did?" His jaw clenched and his eyes bored into those of the old man, daring him to protest. *You destroyed those letters, you old son-of-a-bitch!* He ached to accuse Sinclair, but Rebekah was so emotionally overwrought that he knew it would be folly to open that Pandora's box now. *Someday, Sinclair,* his eyes promised.

Ephraim's expression made it clear that he understood the unspoken threat, but he ignored Madigan's bitter question. Turning to his daughter, he said, "We could get a lawyer, Rebekah. We could fight this if you don't want to marry him. I don't want you forced into a second marriage against your will."

She patted his hand, then squeezed his gnarled fingers as if they were a lifeline. "No, Papa. Michael would find out that I was accused of killing Amos. I'd have to go to jail. It would be awful. It's better for him this way."

341

"What about you, girl? You know what folks will say—marrying your husband's enemy the day after his death."

"Those kind of people don't matter. I'll take care of Rebekah."

"You'd better, Madigan, or you'll have me to answer to. I've made mistakes, but I'm through seeing my children pay for them." There was a ring of the old authority in Reverend Sinclair's voice as he faced his tall young nemesis.

"Come on, Rebekah. We have a long drive to Virginia City."

The first time she wed, her father had blessed the union. Now he was to be denied even that opportunity. She knew how painful it was for him to think of a Roman priest performing the ceremony. She refused to consider Rory's hateful accusations against him. Wordlessly, she hugged Ephraim and let Rory guide her from the cool interior of the church back into the bright sunlight.

After swift good-byes to Michael, with promises to return the following day, the bridal couple set out for Virginia City. Rebekah endured Rory's preoccupied silence for miles, but the turmoil of her own thoughts was too disturbing. She needed distraction from considering the possibility that he was right about her father. Had Ephraim destroyed his letters? Her father had seemed more shaken and guilty than he had angry, almost as if he were defeated by Rory Madigan in some sort of turnabout justice.

No. It can't be true. She rubbed her temples and tried to put the thought out of her mind. There was enough to consider in beginning this marriage. *If I said I wanted to marry you because I still loved you, you wouldn't believe me.* His words haunted her. Had he been trying to tell her the truth? Did he really care for her, not just want Michael?

She smoothed the practical twill traveling suit, perfectly

fine for a train trip, but hardly a wedding dress. "Is this suit all right?" She felt the blush heat her cheeks as he turned distractedly to look at her. "I mean, will it be suitable in St. Mary's Church?"

Her question took him completely by surprise. "We're not getting married in church," he replied.

"But I thought—it's the only Catholic church in the area. I assumed that's why we were going to Virginia City. . . ." Her voice trailed off in confusion.

"I have a friend there who's a judge. He can marry us and be trusted not to tell anyone until this whole mess is cleared up. He can also take care of the legalities of giving Michael my name." The moment he added the latter, Rory saw the stricken look in her eyes and realized he had made a mistake.

"Then you'll have everything the way you want it, won't you?" she snapped back. "Legal claim to your son without the encumbrance of marrying me in your church. Catholics married by a priest can't ever get divorced, can they?"

"They also can't get married, unless both parties are Catholic. And it takes three weeks for the banns to be read before a priest will perform the ceremony." He waited until that sank in, then said, "Anyway, what makes you think I'd let you escape with a divorce?"

Rebekah was confused by his blasé answer. Did he really care about her or was this his way of getting her to make a fool of herself? Whenever he looked at her, touched her, she melted like a puddle of wax at his feet. But this time she must guard her heart. Too much was at stake—not only her life, but Michael's as well.

"So, there will be no divorce," she said, staring straight ahead, her voice chilly in the hot, dusty air.

"But there will be a marriage. A real one this time, Rebekah.'' That drew her attention from contemplating the horizon. He grinned. ''I'll be your husband tonight. And you'll be my dutiful, obedient wife, won't you, darlin'?'' She jerked her face forward again and he chuckled low.

The pink in her cheeks gave away her discomfiture, but she refused to allow him the satisfaction of a reply.

Dusk fell over Carson City that night as the four men sat around a big mahogany table in the opulent senatorial offices of Shanghai Sheffield. The old man pointedly glanced from one associate to the other, measuring each one until he could feel them squirm beneath his ice-blue eyes. One shaggy, snow-white eyebrow rose as he gestured to the large number of documents spread out across the table. ''We're missing several rather vital pieces of evidence. Not to mention a fortune in negotiable securities. I know Amos had them in his safe.''

''Not the one in his office here. It was open when I came in. Everything was spread out on his desk,'' the Senator's associate said.

''You should have beat the truth out of the fool before you killed him. He was hiding enough evidence to hang us all twice over,'' Sheffield snapped.

''I gathered up everything in the office. And I've checked the study in his city house. Nothing. Are you certain he left nothing in the Wellsville bank?'' the killer asked the man seated next to him.

''Nothing in his old office or in the vault,'' Hiram Bascomb replied nervously, dabbing the sweat from his upper lip with a limp linen handkerchief.

''It seems to me,'' the fourth man at the table said from the shadows, ''that leaves only one other possible place—

unless he entrusted a hoodlum like Sly Hobart with such valuable materials.''

''Hell, no. Wells was a liability and a fool, but even he wasn't that stupid,'' the killer replied in disgust. ''I took care of Hobart.''

''But not before he did us all material damage by turning over his information to those accursed Irishmen,'' the man from the shadows replied.

''I can handle the Madigan brothers.''

''First things first. We must have the rest of those documents that Amos hid,'' Sheffield cut in. ''Where do you think they are—the ranch?''

The man in the shadows nodded to the killer. ''I think we had better decide who will pay a visit to the Flying W. And in the meanwhile, we really must make plans for dealing with the Madigans as well.''

''Pritkin can handle Patrick. I'll take care of Rory Madigan personally,'' the killer replied grimly. If Pritkin had done his job eight years ago, none of this would have happened, but the Senator's associate was not about to reveal that gaffe. It was a long way from Nevada to Washington, but soon Amos Wells's murderer would be making the big step up.

Stephan Hammer stepped out of the shadows and smiled at him. ''I'm sure we can rely on you.''

Chapter Eighteen

Virginia City

A second marriage. A second desolation in the exchange of vows. This time the ceremony was not even in a church but before a civil official. Her marriage to Rory Madigan had been brief and even less adorned than had been the travesty with Amos. She was wed in a dusty twill suit and sensible low-heeled boots. Her hair was windblown and she wore no jewelry. There had been no time to purchase a ring.

Perhaps it was better that way, Rebekah thought bitterly as she sat gazing into the mirror at her own haunted eyes and pale, hollow expression. She had exchanged vows with Rory once before when she truly believed in them and thought he did too.

But fate and Amos Wells had intervened. Now she and Rory were wary strangers, reunited because of Michael and perhaps because of revenge. She continued brushing her hair methodically, too emotionally drained by the past twenty-four hours to think straight. There were a great many things she did not want to think about at all. Rebekah let her eyes wander around the room—her bridal suite. It was large and elegant, darkly masculine, rather like its owner.

Rory's private quarters were in the Virginia City headquarters of Madigan Enterprises, and his offices were on the floor below. The bedroom had been decorated with meticulous taste. In an era of gaudy clutter, the clean lines of the heavy oak furniture and wall coverings of blue silk were subdued and soothing. Yet the very massiveness of the chairs, table, and bed made her acutely aware that this was a man's domain.

The bed. Her eyes were drawn to it. Of all the times they had made love, not once had it been in a real bed. And this was a grand one, custom made to accommodate his long body. The coverlet was deep royal blue, and the soft plump surface was piled high with feather pillows. A bed made for pleasure.

Rebekah looked away from it quickly. After the hasty ceremony, Rory had taken her for a lavish meal in the dining room of the International Hotel, but she was too nervous to do more than push the exquisite roasted lamb around in its juices on her plate. After that he had escorted her to this big brick building and shown her to their night's accommodations. Then he had excused himself, saying he had to send some business wires and would have hot bathwater brought up for her. He had been cool and polite throughout the day, remote and unreadable, not the mocking and embittered man he had been earlier. But he was certainly not the laughing, loving Rory of her youth either.

Rebekah set down her hairbrush and wandered over to the

big oak armoire standing against the far wall. One door was partially ajar. Some inner craving to know more about her enigmatic husband made her open both doors and peer inside. Expensive custom-tailored suits, all in conservative dark colors, hung in a row, flanked by several pair of those tight denims that molded so scandalously to his long legs.

One massive drawer just below the suits yielded a dozen silk shirts, mostly white with a bright smattering of blues and reds thrown in. Expensive clothes but nothing personal. *I'm snooping.* Well, why shouldn't she? After all, she was his wife now. She pulled open a narrow drawer beneath the shirts and found it filled with beautiful men's jewelry, a sapphire ring, a ruby stickpin, diamond shirt studs, several pairs of gold cufflinks set with various precious gems. A fortune left lying about, casually unlocked.

She was just about to close the drawer when the dull gleam of an old locket caught her eye. It was a woman's piece and stood out amid the costly glitter, for it was cheaply made of base metal. Rebekah pulled the chain out from beneath one velvet-lined jewel box and found a tattered picture caught in it. When she held the old daguerreotype up to the light, her breath caught. One of the figures was Michael!

No, it could not be, of course. It was Rory at Michael's age, staring solemnly into the camera, surrounded by three older boys and a dark, handsome man with a mustache and neatly trimmed beard. A soft yet strong-looking woman with lighter hair stood proudly behind her brood. His family, who had died all those years ago. The locket was engraved "to Maureen with my heart's devotion, Michael."

He had lost so much—his homeland, his parents, his brothers, and then even his only son. Tears stung her eyes as she quietly replaced his worn treasure in the drawer and closed it. What love there must have been in that close-knit

Irish family, which was so unlike her own. Her parents had not been in love as Maureen and Michael had been. In many ways she and Leah had paid a price for their sad alliance. Rebekah had always felt that if Dorcas had not been so bitter over Ephraim's lost love, she might have been able to love her own children better.

"But Papa loved me," she repeated aloud like a litany. Her good and gentle papa had tried all his life to atone for his mistake of falling in love with the wrong woman. "And I've spent these years atoning for loving Rory just as surely."

A sharp rapping on the bedroom door interrupted her disturbing reverie. She opened it to admit a burly black man with a ready smile. "Your hot water, Mrs. Madigan." With a polite nod, he headed straight to the bathing room adjacent to the master suite as if long accustomed to the chore. Rebekah supposed he was on the payroll of Madigan Enterprises. She still found it difficult to believe that the impoverished young man who had dreamed only of a modest ranch had become one of the wealthiest tycoons in the western United States.

She thanked the man and let him out after he had filled a claw-footed tub of dazzling white porcelain which sat in the center of the bathing room. It was the most enormous bathtub Rebekah had ever seen. A rack stacked high with fluffy white towels sat on one side of the tub, and a low marble-topped table filled with a variety of scented soaps and bath oils was positioned at the opposite side.

Opening one of the vials of oil, she recognized an expensive French fragrance. All of the exclusive bath products were imported. As she selected a delicate lemon-scented bubble bath and poured it liberally into the tub, she reflected on her husband's rise to such luxury and power. If he had not

349

lost her, would he have achieved all of this? Would he have preferred to live as a simple stockman in the Truckee Valley with her as his wife for all those years?

Don't torture yourself by asking questions you'll never have answers for, she chided herself. As she laid out a plain batiste nightgown and matching velvet robe of pale green, both wrinkled and in need of pressing, Rebekah realized how dependent she had become on Patsy and the other servants over the past years. Within minutes, her travel-stained clothes lay in a heap behind the tub, and she slid into the heavenly warmth of the fragrant water.

But you'd give up every luxury if things could be as they were when you first loved Rory Madigan. She tried to ignore the voice in her mind and lay back, exhausted, in the tub.

Rory quickly wrote out the instructions for his timber mill and waterfront warehouse foremen and dispatched the wires, but as the telegrapher sent the simple business messages, he stood at the counter and agonized over how to tell his brother that he had married Rebekah, not to mention the circumstances under which he had forced her to comply. Always a cautious man, Patrick would be upset with his precipitous actions. Sighing, Rory set a simple declaration of facts to paper, addressed it to his brother in Carson City, and shoved it at the operator along with payment. Then he stepped out into the brisk evening air. The chill of autumn came early in Nevada's high elevations.

Virginia City's crowded streets and raucous noise did little to distract the preoccupied man as he walked slowly back to his office building, where his bride awaited him in their private quarters. *My wife, Mrs. Rory Madigan.* He should have been the happiest man alive. Eight years ago he would have been, but now he was not at all certain what he felt. Certainly

none of the triumph of revenge in forcing her to do his bidding. He had fulfilled his vow after a fashion, although the
idea of marrying her had been furthest from his mind when
he had watched her dancing in Amos Wells's arms. But she
had come to him against her will and now lay waiting for
him in his bed.

Against her will. "What did you want, boyo?" he scoffed
beneath his breath. "For her to fall into your arms in gratitude the minute Wells was dead?" She had suffered, but so
had Michael and so had he, dammit! Even if she refused to
face any other fact, the reality of the sizzling passion that
flared out of control between them was one she could not
deny, one he would not let her deny. Sweet Blessed Virgin,
he ached with wanting her. She had felt guilty the last time
after their angry, explosive coupling. Then it was a betrayal
of her personal sense of honor, her marriage vows to a man
utterly devoid of honor or the smallest shred of decency.

Now she could claim no refuge in that guilt. She was his
wife and he would have her passion. *But will you ever again
have her love?* The thought haunted him as he walked up
the steep flight of stairs to the second floor.

He let himself in, then walked quietly across the sitting
room to the bedroom door. When he opened it and scanned
the dimly lit room, he saw only the empty bed. Panic seized
him for an instant. She could not have fled into the wild
streets below that were filled with riffraff from around the
world! Then he heard the soft sound of water lapping against
the tub and saw her nightclothes spread across a chair.

Feeling like a fool, Rory slipped off his jacket and used
the bootjack beside his armoire. Quickly and quietly, he undressed and then donned a wine-velvet robe and tied the sash
casually. He did not plan on wearing it long. How thoughtful
of her to remain naked in her bath for him. Smiling, he

351

opened the unlocked door and looked at the woman in the tub.

His breath escaped in an agonized whoosh and he was too dazed to draw another as he looked down at his wife. Rebekah was asleep in the tub with her head leaning back on the rim, exposing her slender throat. Thick golden lashes lay against the translucence of her cheeks, shielding those wide green-gold eyes. Her lips were slightly parted, soft pale pink. She looked vulnerable, delicate, and so lovely it made his heart ache just to gaze at her.

Heavy masses of dark gold hair pinned carelessly atop her head glowed like polished amber. She had used the bath salts, and the tub was filled with a white froth of bubbles giving off a tangy lemon essence, her signature when it mixed with her own unique scent. He would recognize it and her in pitch blackness. His woman. His wife. Her body was partially covered by the white bubbles. Even her pale, slender arms and hands, draped elegantly along the edges of the tub, bore traces of the lacy froth. One pink nipple and the top of a knee peeked out from beneath the cover. Her beautiful body was all the more tantalizing and alluring because it was partially concealed.

Just looking at her made him rock hard. He fought the urge to rip off his robe, pluck her from the water and take her right there on the bathing room rug. Quietly he walked over to the tub and knelt beside it, taking one soft, glistening hand and raising it to his mouth. Her eyes flew open as he blew away a series of small bubbles, then softly kissed her fingertips while the tiny spheres drifted on the air and popped one by one.

"Rory." Her voice was hoarse, startled.

"Shh," he urged as he continued his path over her wrist and up her arm, his breath warm on her wet skin as he blew away bubbles and kissed a trail up to her shoulder. She watched him in silent surprise, unresisting.

When his dark head bent lower, and those piercing blue eyes could no longer mesmerize her, Rebekah gave in to the heat and languor and closed her eyes, letting his touch soothe her. Then his other hand reached out and flicked over the nipple that protruded from its cover of bubbles. Again her eyes flew open. A surge of pure fire streaked through her body, and her breast swelled and began to throb in his hand as he cupped it. He brushed aside the foamy blanket and uncovered her other breast. When he blew away the froth, it pebbled into a hard crest before his fingers even touched it.

"A lush pair of treasures hiding beneath the surface," he whispered hoarsely, as he stroked and cupped both breasts. She moaned softly and arched involuntarily against his caress. He filled his hands with the slick globes, splaying his fingers around them, sliding below them, over her ribs, then lower to the delicate curves of her waist, lifting her forward in the tub.

"Put your arms around my neck," he commanded hoarsely.

"I'll get you wet," she whispered inanely, but her arms, dripping and shedding bubbles, encircled the soft velvet of his collar, pulling him closer until their lips were scant inches apart. She could feel his breath and smell the male essence of him, a faint touch of expensive tobacco mixed with a hint of Irish whiskey. Honest masculine smells, no sweet colognes to mask the heady musk of his excitement. How long ago, yet how well she had learned to recognize it.

His lips brushed hers teasingly. After a few exploratory passes, he felt her fingers pulling away his robe and her nails digging into the muscles of his back. He slanted his mouth fiercely across hers, and his tongue rimmed the seam of her lips. She opened for him and he plunged inside, tasting her, feeling the answering quest as her tongue darted against his, then twined with it.

He growled low in his throat as he pulled her up against him, cupping her silky little buttocks in his hands while he continued kissing her feverishly. Rebekah felt his hands gliding all over her wet, slick body. In spite of her leaving the warmth of the water, the heat was building beneath her skin. His heavy robe was sopping wet in front and the wine-red velvet covered with a fine froth of bubbles.

She suddenly felt the urge to see those tiny glistening spheres in the dark pelt of his chest hair. Her hands slid down to the belt at his waist and tugged it free. He obliged her instantly by shedding it with one swift shrug.

She reached down into the pile of bubbles surrounding her hips and brought a handful up to his chest, blowing them onto it.

"So, you want me dressed like you are," he whispered seductively. Before Rebekah could do more than press her hands into the hair on his chest, he kicked away his robe, then climbed into the big tub facing her. "I always wanted to do it in this tub, but I must confess, I never thought of using bath salts."

He reached for fistfuls of billowy white froth and began to pile them on her shoulders, working the glistening stuff down over her breasts, pausing to expose the hard pink nubs of her nipples by blowing on them. Then his hands glided lower to the curve of her hips.

Rebekah responded, playing in the dark mat of hair on his chest with a foaming lather, then moving over his broad shoulders and down his biceps. When her hands shifted back to his torso and followed the black arrow of hair in its descent over his belly, she felt him tremble. Then she felt the hardness of his staff brush her thigh and instinctively sought it, taking it in her hands and stroking it in her slick palms until he cried out her name and pulled her against him for another fierce kiss.

"Faith, keep that up and I'll be adding more oil to the waters," he murmured raggedly into her mouth. Then he lowered them into the froth and laid her back against the rim of the tub. Kneeling between her thighs, he raised one leg and kissed the knee, then the other. When he took her mouth again, she clung to his shoulders, returning the kiss. He cupped her buttocks and raised her lower body to meet his thrust. She locked her ankles behind his back and held on as he impaled her with the hard length of his phallus.

Rebekah thought she heard him murmur curses, or love words, as he trembled, buried completely inside of her. His invasion stretched her, filled her, yet she craved more, clinging to him and crying out, unable to stop the writhing undulations of her body as he began to thrust in and out. Even with her eyes squeezed shut in bliss, she could picture the glitter of bubbles on his staff as he stroked her aching flesh.

Her velvety sheath contracted around him the instant he penetrated her, wet and eager, yet so small and tight that the pleasure nearly drove him over the edge. He steeled himself to keep control, then felt her arch against him, rolling her hips hungrily. Red exploded behind his eyes in a haze of ecstasy. His body pummeled hers with swift, hard thrusts, oblivious to anything but the blind drive to climax.

His desperation mirrored her own as she moved with him in the wild, sweet dance, drawn to that burning culmination awaiting her just another stroke away, and another. . . . Each one grew more fierce until she thought she could endure no more of the frenzy, the pain-pleasure of her hunger. Then his staff swelled within her on one final, deep thrust and he shuddered, holding her tightly against him. In that instant the dam broke and a hot surge of shimmering, breathless ecstasy bathed her, releasing her body and soul.

Rory could feel her body clenching rhythmically around his, squeezing out every last drop of his seed in her own fiercely sweet completion. Her flexing sheath added to and prolonged his violent explosion until he was utterly drained and weak. He fell back onto his heels, holding her against him. They were both oblivious to the water, which had now grown chilly.

Her head fell against his shoulder, the golden curtain of her hair shrouding them both. She had lost the pins during their wild coupling. He reached up with one dripping hand and touched a shining curl, sighing her name.

" 'Tis fearful cold in here, darlin', and getting cramped," he finally managed, lifting her away from him so he could stand and climb out. Then he reached down and swept her out of the tub, depositing her on the carpet.

Rebekah stood still, suddenly aware of her nakedness and the chill air as goose bumps rose on her skin. She shivered. He immediately wrapped her in a large towel and massaged her dry. She felt too shy to say anything, so she just stood there, clutching the towel around herself. When he took another and dried himself off, she did peek from beneath the shield of her lashes, watching the smooth ripple of his lean muscles. He finished quickly and tossed the towel away. Then he picked her up and carried her to the big bed, where he pulled back the coverlet and had her recline in the center of a pile of pillows.

Without hesitation, he climbed onto the bed beside her and lay looking down at her with troubled eyes. Slowly, reverently, he pulled away the towel shielding her nakedness. He was becoming aroused again. She could feel the tumescence of his erection pressing against her hip as his hands glided over her cool, damp flesh. His touch quickly began to warm her.

"You're so beautiful . . . and you're mine. I can't bear the thought that a pervert like Wells ever touched you." The words slipped out before he even realized what he had said, but at once he could feel her stiffen and pull away. "Rebekah—"

"*You* can't bear it! How do you think I felt?" She pulled the sheet up, covering herself, placing a barrier between them. She shivered in revulsion as the memory of her first wedding night returned. "I was terrified to have him touch me." A small hiccup of hysterical laughter bubbled up in her throat. "But you don't have to worry that you've bought damaged goods—Amos never consummated our mockery of a marriage. He couldn't, although he humiliated me enough in the trying that awful night." She buried her face in the bunched-up sheets and cried. "That's why I had to tell him I was pregnant. I married him to protect my baby, and it was all for nothing!"

Her muffled words seared his guts like acid. "You said he never hurt you or Michael," he whispered brokenly, afraid to touch her, to offer comfort or apology.

Her shoulders stopped shaking and she raised her head. Her eyes met his squarely, accusatorily. "If he had hurt Michael, I *would* have killed him, but he never did. He needed an heir to prove his virility. As for me"—she shrugged stiffly—"mostly he paraded me around like an ornament, or ignored me."

"That isn't how you got that bruise on your cheek," he said softly, reaching out to brush it with gentle fingertips.

"If you hadn't come back into my life, he wouldn't have reacted as he did."

357

"He knew Michael was mine—that you were mine. No man could ever forget that. That's why he sent Michael so far away to boarding school."

"I couldn't stop him. He *owned* my son. Now you do."

There was a dare in her voice, and it nettled the guilt buried deeply inside him, along with his own righteous sense of betrayal. "I won't be spendin' the rest of my life doin' penance for the sin of losin' you and Michael eight years ago, Rebekah." Anger brought back the brogue he had spent years erasing. "Neither of us is to blame. Your family separated us—"

"You keep accusing my father of manipulating our lives," she lashed out. "What are you doing now? You've forced me to marry you. You have legal control of Michael. Amos is dead. What more do you want?"

"I'll show you what I want—what you want, too, only you're too stubborn to admit it." He seized the sheet she clutched to her breasts and yanked it away with an oath, then covered her body with his.

His mouth ground down on hers, demanding a response. At first she resisted, but when his hands caressed her breasts and glided over her hips, his lips gentled and his tongue danced along the closed seam of her mouth. With a small cry, she opened for his kiss and her arms pulled him closer. Her thighs parted and she welcomed him, but Rory did not plunge in as he knew she expected.

Instead he trailed hot, wet kisses from her mouth to her throat, then lower, pausing to suckle and caress her breasts as she writhed, calling out his name, digging her fingers into his night-black hair. His head moved down to her belly. His tongue dipped into her naval; then his lips continued on their downward course. When she realized his destination, she tried to pull him away but he nuzzled the silky gold curls at the juncture of her thighs.

"No," she protested weakly, but the heat of his mouth found her and she lay still, paralyzed by the shocking ripples of pleasure his caress called forth. This was unnatural, surely sinful, wicked . . . bliss!

Rory sensed her acquiescence, then the increasing tension of renewed hunger that his gentle licks and kisses were eliciting. Her body arched taut as a bowstring. Then he felt the first rhythmic swelling of her orgasm. Her cries were sweet to his ears as he laved her with kisses, then raised his head to watch the soft pink stain her skin from her face and throat across her breasts and belly. "Look at me, Rebekah," he commanded as he positioned his hard, aching staff at the still quivering portal of her femininity.

The keen breath-robbing release ebbed slowly, and Rory's voice, low and hoarse, brought her back to earth. Dazed green eyes fluttered open and she gazed up, meeting the hungry intensity of his dark blue gaze. What had he done to her? It was unimaginable. The look of utterly male possessiveness on his face was tempered only by his own stark hunger. Instinctively her hips arched up, welcoming him inside her body, wanting to claim him as he had her.

But his desperation quickly dissipated as he slowed the rhythm of his thrusts, holding her hips and molding them to him in lazy, languorous strokes. "We have all night," he whispered hoarsely.

She did not answer with her voice, but the building heat deep inside her compelled her body to answer for her. Gradually she came alive under his caresses, and his thrusts grew in response, deeper, swifter, harder until they were both lost in the maelstrom once again.

When it was complete, he gave her no chance to move

away, but rolled them to their sides, holding her closely to him, and yanked the bed covers up over them. Feeling the softness of her body melded against his, he quickly fell asleep.

Rebekah stared out across the room, her eyes wide open. The hard muscles of her husband's arm held her fast, and a slight rasp of his whiskers grazed her shoulder as he moved in his sleep. *This is the first time we've ever spent a night together. We're really married. At last.*

But why had he married her? He lusted for her, but did he love her? He loved Michael, and he had married her. Perhaps she should be satisfied with that much and leave the rest to sort itself out. Someday the three of them might become a family to make up for the one he had lost as a child.

Carson City

Patrick received Rory's telegram that evening and read the terse message with incredulity. "That damned fool! He's let that woman get her hooks into him just because of the boy." Of course, he had to admit that if Rory was right about the resemblance, there could be no doubt of his paternity. But Patrick Madigan had no reason at all to trust Rebekah Wells. She had far too strong a hold over his brother for him to like this sudden marriage, even if Rory had been the one to force her into it—*especially* because he had forced her.

Early the next morning he would go to Virginia City to meet his new sister-in-law. He had a number of things to tell Rory which he dared not send over the wire. Their day of reckoning with Ryan's murderers was at hand.

Just after dawn the next morning, Patrick walked out of the hotel, deep in thought as he headed down Musser Street toward the livery. When Rory had not returned from his early morning visit to the Wells residence the day before, Patrick had been worried about his brother and had gone to investigate. Upon his arrival at the mansion, he was informed that Amos had been murdered and the sheriff had evidence that Mrs. Wells was the culprit. But Rory had provided her with an alibi—one Patrick knew to be a blatant lie. Wells's death greatly complicated matters. If his cohorts wanted him dead, might they not want Rory dead as well?

Patrick did not like the way things were developing, not one bit. So engrossed in family problems was he, he almost did not see the glint of the shotgun barrel in time. Just as the blast belched forth from the alley, he dove into the dust, rolling as he pulled a stubby .41 caliber pocket revolver from inside his suit jacket. When he heard the second barrel of the shotgun being cocked, he fired in the direction of the sound before he could even see enough to take aim.

The second blast from the scatter gun went wild. Patrick's slug had hit the assassin squarely in his chest. He dropped the shotgun and slid down against the rough cedar planks of the building, where he lay slumped on one side in the narrow alley. A stray beam of sunlight penetrated the gloom, revealing his straight red hair and a thin hatchet face frozen in a death grimace.

Patrick leaped to his feet and scrambled over to examine the man, then cursed when he realized the killer was dead. When a crowd quickly gathered and Sheriff Sears elbowed his way through it, Madigan swore some more. This would really delay his ride to Virginia City if he did not do some fast talking.

Virginia City

Rebekah awakened, disoriented at first. Then she felt the heat of Rory's body cocooning her. He lay beside her with his head propped up on one hand, staring possessively down at her. *My husband.* Remembering the wanton passion he had unleashed in her last night, she felt her cheeks flame with heat. In all the times they had made love he had never done *that* to her. And she had allowed it—no, she had loved it, every shocking, thrilling moment of it.

As if reading her mind, he grinned and winked. "Morning, darlin'. I trust you slept well. I sure did." He touched her bare shoulder and let his fingers trail down to the tip of one breast, which rewarded his boldness by puckering into a hard little nub.

She tried to squirm away. "Rory, we have to talk . . ." His hand trespassed further, while his other arm held her fast.

"We can talk later," he said as he leaned down and claimed her lips in a languid good-morning kiss.

By the time they had finally risen from the badly rumpled bed, there was a commotion from downstairs. Rory threw on a pair of denims and a shirt. "Peal should be here with bath-water for you in a few moments. We need to get back for Michael," he said as he pulled on his boots.

Just then a sharp rap on the outside door drew his attention. "What the hell—"

"Rory—it's Patrick. I have to talk to you," his brother's muffled voice called through the heavy oak door.

"Wait here while I see what's wrong," Rory instructed Rebekah.

She paled. Patrick was the one who had first uncovered Amos's involvement in their brother's death. How would he feel about Rory's hasty marriage to the Widow Wells? Somehow she knew his reaction would not be favorable. There was so much left unsaid and unsettled between her and her husband. *We need time.*

Rory vanished out the door, and the hulking black man arrived a few minutes later with buckets of fresh hot water.

While Rebekah performed her morning toilette, Rory took Patrick downstairs to his office and ordered coffee for the two of them. Then his harried brother explained about the attempt on his life earlier that morning.

"You think it was Sheffield's doing?"

Patrick shrugged. "Sheriff identified my assailant as one Chicken Thief Charlie Pritkin. Quaint, isn't it?"

Rory swore in amazement. "Pritkin was a drunken hard case from Wellsville. He used to hang around the glitter district. I saw him a lot when I worked at Beau's livery. I wonder . . ."

"You think he was involved in the assault on you eight years ago?"

Remembering a dark hotel room above the Bucket of Blood Saloon, Rory nodded. "Too bad he isn't alive to tell us." Then he added with a grin, "Not that I'm unhappy you proved a better shot than he. I'd hate to be the one to have to face your wife—"

"Speaking of wives, let's discuss yours. I know you wanted the boy, but couldn't it have waited?"

"Yesterday morning Sears was going to arrest Rebekah. You know I couldn't let that happen," Rory replied defensively.

Patrick studied him with intent blue eyes. "You're still in love with her after all these years. That's dangerous, Rory. Maybe she did kill Wells."

"Don't be an imbecile. Leave that to the sheriff. Rebekah

363

and I will work out our problems ourselves.''

The finality in Rory's tone made it clear that the discussion about Rebekah was closed. ''There is another reason I came here.''

''I had hoped so, since I scarcely expected you to join us on our honeymoon,'' Rory replied dryly.

Patrick ignored the jibe and explained. ''Before he was killed, Hobart gave a satchel full of papers to one of my men. I finished going through them yesterday. We have enough evidence to arrest Sheffield and Bascomb right now. If only that snake Hammer was around.''

''Nothing on him?'' Rory leaned forward across his desk.

Patrick ground his teeth in frustration. ''No. But I think he may not have left Nevada. He could be hiding out in Carson, waiting to see what happens when the dust clears.''

''What have you done about arresting Sheffield and Bascomb? That might flush him out.''

''As you've made abundantly clear, the local sheriff in Carson is not reliable. I'm afraid I need your help, Rory. Who can we trust to round up these weasels before they slip the trap? After the attempt to kill me this morning, I'm afraid they're already wise.''

''I have contacts in the capital. I'll talk to the governor. He can order the federal marshal and his deputies to arrest Shanghai Sheffield and Hiram Bascomb while I nose around for Stephen Hammer. Where is Hobart's evidence?''

''In our safety deposit box in the First National Bank in Carson,'' Patrick replied, handing Rory a key. ''As soon as I looked through it, I knew not to take any chances with it until I could locate you.''

''And I had to go and spoil your plans by running off to get married,'' Rory said wryly. Then he became serious. ''Patrick, they tried to frame Rebekah for Wells's murder.

She could still be in danger. So could Michael. I want you to take her to her father's place in Wellsville and pick up my son—''

''May I come in?'' Rebekah's voice sounded nervous yet determined from the other side of the office door.

Rory ushered her in and watched with amusement as she and Patrick sized each other up. ''Patrick, may I present my wife, Rebekah. Rebekah, this is my rapscallion elder brother.''

Rebekah looked into a pair of dark blue eyes, identical to Rory's, set in the same finely chiseled face, different only because of the bright red of his hair. No wonder Michael was the mirror image of his father! The family resemblance was uncanny. ''I'm pleased to meet you, Patrick, and so happy Rory found you alive after he'd given you up for dead so long ago,'' she said softly.

Rebekah was not what Patrick had expected. Oh, she was heartbreakingly lovely with her golden hair and green eyes. She was dressed in an elegant rose-linen traveling suit that accented her slim curves perfectly. His brother had always gone for strikingly beautiful women. But there was a vulnerability in her that touched him. She must have loved Rory once. Perhaps she still did. Patrick hoped so for his brother's sake and for Michael's.

He took her hand and raised it to his lips in the same endearing European manner Rory had first charmed her with eight years ago on the Wellsville bandstand. ''I'm rather happy not to have drowned, myself. My felicitations on your marriage. I only wish it could've been eight years ago.'' Patrick was not certain what he expected her reaction to be, but he studied her intently.

''You don't trust me, do you, Patrick?''

Her forthright question pleased him. Perhaps this could

work out after all. "I'm not sure, to be perfectly honest, but I have hopes."

"You'll have time enough to take each other's measure as you ride to Wellsville," Rory interjected, taking Rebekah's arm possessively and showing her to a chair across from his desk. Then he explained what had transpired in Carson.

"You think Michael could be in danger?" she asked when he had finished.

"No. I don't think it's him they're after. But for some reason they want you disposed of. Maybe they think you were privy to Amos's schemes. Whatever their reasons, you and Michael have to get out of harm's way. I have to return to Carson. Patrick will take you to get our son, then to my ranch in Eagle Valley."

"That's a long ride out of the way. It would be closer to just take us to the Flying W. My sister is nearby, and once we're safe there, Patrick can return to the capital and help you," she said, turning from her husband to his brother.

Patrick nodded. "It makes sense, but I don't think I'd leave you alone until we know those men are all in jail."

"I agree," Rory added. "You stay with her, Patrick."

"I'm ready to leave now, Rory."

Taking her in his arms, he reassured her, "Michael will be all right. You both will."

"Take care of yourself, Rory," she whispered, reaching up to touch his cheek tenderly.

He kissed her palm and pressed it back against his face. There was so much yet unsaid. He tried to read her fathomless eyes and saw—what? Love? Or did he only imagine it?

Broken Vows

Ephraim sat alone on the porch. He could still hear the echo of Michael's laughter, so boyishly happy. *Was I ever that young? That carefree?* At the moment he felt old far beyond his sixty-one years. Madigan had won. He had Rebekah as his wife and he had claimed his son. Was this in truth the Lord's judgment against his own presumption in meddling with other people's lives?

"I should never have destroyed those letters. Rebekah had the right to choose," he whispered brokenly as he stared out across the sunny backyard. Would he ever have the courage to confess to her what he had done? It had weighed more and more heavily on his conscience as the years passed.

He had known the first time Rebekah and Amos returned from Washington that all was not well in their marriage. The way Amos kept his wife separated from Michael over the years only confirmed his worst fears. And the haunted sadness in his daughter's eyes ate into his soul.

When Rory Madigan had returned and begun his meteoric rise to power, Ephraim lost his last excuse for destroying those letters. Now the Irishman was back in their lives to stay. "Sooner or later, old man, you'll have to tell her. . . . " He only prayed that Madigan really cared for Rebekah and Michael.

The sound of a rider pulling up distracted Sinclair from his troubling reverie. He stepped down from the side porch and walked around to the front yard.

Henry Snead dismounted and approached.

"Morning, Henry. What brings you here so early? Leah and the boys—"

"They're fine, just fine," Henry hastened to reply, quelling the older man's alarm. "It's Rebekah I'm concerned about." Henry turned his hat nervously in his big hands. "Amos is dead, Ephraim. Someone shot him at his office in Carson. The sheriff thinks Rebekah did it."

"I know," the old man answered quietly. At Henry's startled expression, Ephraim hastened to add, "She told me all about it."

"Then she's here?" Henry's voice was filled with relief. "When she and Michael disappeared from Carson with Rory Madigan, I was worried sick. I need to see her to finalize arrangements for Amos's funeral."

"They were here. Michael spent the night. Earlier this morning, Rebekah and Patrick Madigan came for him."

Snead blanched. "I don't understand. What have those damned Madigans to do with our family?"

The sadness in the old man's hazel-green eyes was soul-searing. "You know as well as I the answer to that, Henry," Ephraim replied gently.

His son-in-law's face turned dark red. "That's all in the past."

Sinclair shook his head. "No, not any longer. Rebekah has married Rory."

Snead's red-faced embarrassment turned to furious incredulity. "Amos isn't even cold in his grave! The day after his death! What will people think? What the hell was *she* thinking?"

"You sound like Leah, Henry," Ephraim reproved.

Henry had the good grace to flush once more. "She can't have thought this out. He must've forced her. Why did you allow it?"

Ephraim explained how events had unfolded, ending with Patrick and Rebekah coming earlier that morning to collect Michael. "He's taking them to the Flying W. They'll be safe there. Rory went back to Carson to see about some urgent business.''

''Well, I'll feel better after I've talked to Rebekah myself. I'm not without influence in Carson. I could protect her and Michael from the Madigans—if she wants me to, that is.''

''You've been her true friend, Henry. I've always appreciated that. I know it's not right to speak ill of the dead, but Amos made a hard life for my daughter. She relied on you.''

''She still can,'' Henry replied earnestly. ''I have to go back to Carson—Amos's affairs are in shambles, and his business partners will be moving in like vultures after a kill. I'll protect Rebekah and Michael's interests. Maybe I'll have a talk with Madigan while I'm at it. If Rebekah's made a mistake, we can extricate her from it.''

Ephraim shrugged. ''I don't know, Henry. Maybe we've meddled enough in their lives already. . . . '' His voice faded away.

Henry just patted him on the back fondly. ''Don't worry. This time I'll see that things turn out all right, Ephraim.''

As the younger man rode away, his father-in-law watched mutely, the war inside him still raging. Finally, he walked over to the church where he had spent so much of his life. It was time—long past time—for him to pray.

Chapter Nineteen

The Flying W Ranch

The sun was shining gloriously, and the zephyr winds were still that morning. Rebekah watched Michael and Patsy riding ahead of them and marveled at how well the boy handled his new pony. Rory had arranged for one of his hands to bring the beautiful white to the ranch, much to Michael's delight.

"He's a natural rider," Patrick said, watching the way her eyes never left her son. "Just like his father. Rory always did have a way with horses, like our da."

"Rory said your father was head stableman for an earl. Why did he leave Ireland? Surely there was security in his position."

Patrick's face, so startlingly similar to Rory's, took on a faraway expression as he remembered the past. "It's difficult for you, born and raised in this country, to understand. There we could never have been anything but menials. Oh, we had a decent roof over our heads and food enough to eat. In Ireland not many are so fortunate. But our parents wanted more.''

"The streets of America aren't always paved with gold," Rebekah replied, remembering the tragic circumstances the Madigans had encountered in New York.

"No. But here a man can breathe free, and everyone has the chance to look for his own pot of gold—even an Irishman.''

"You and Rory certainly succeeded. Has it been worth all the sacrifice?''

Patrick studied her. "I'd trade every cent Madigan & Madigan Ltd. has to have our parents and Sean and Ryan alive again. But I can't undo what's in the past. Neither can you.''

Her expression became guarded as she tried to read the meaning behind his enigmatic remarks. "Do you believe that I betrayed Rory? That I married Amos Wells for his money?''

"You are forthright," Patrick replied, laughing softly. "Once, not very long ago, I would have answered yes. Now . . . I don't honestly know. I've only heard Rory's side of what happened eight years ago, or what he knew of it. The Madigans aren't the only ones who have made sacrifices, are they, Rebekah?''

She could feel those piercing blue eyes, so like Rory's, on her. "Rory had gone to Denver, and I received no word from him for nearly a month. I was expecting Michael, and my family thought it was providential when Amos offered me marriage. I won't lie to you and say I didn't feel bitterly betrayed by your brother. I hated him then . . . especially when I realized what kind of monster I'd been forced to marry.''

''Wells must've arranged all of it—sending Rory to Denver, the attempt on his life, all to have you.'' The waste of all these years saddened him beyond measure. ''The question now is, do you still hate my brother?''

Her expression was guarded when she turned to face him. ''No. But I can't trust him either.''

Patrick's bark of laughter had a ring of frustration in it. ''You can't *trust* him? He gave you an alibi when you were accused of murdering Wells, and then he married you.''

''Yes, he did,'' she replied simply. ''It was the only way to get Michael. He offered to make me his mistress before he knew about his son.''

Patrick swore beneath his breath. ''You've been frank with me. I'll be the same with you. Rory planned revenge not only against Amos but you as well. He was obsessed with what he believed was your betrayal. But believe this, Rebekah.'' He reached out to her and reined in their horses. ''Even when he thought he hated you, I could always sense something else—something deeper than the hate. He couldn't stop loving you. That's what really ate him alive, what drove him. And that's why I was so upset when I received his wire saying he'd married you. There were other ways to get his son back—if that was all he'd wanted to do.''

''Beginning with letting me go to prison for killing Amos.'' She sighed in confusion. ''I don't know, Patrick. He's changed so much. When I saw him for the first time in Washington four years ago, the old laughter in his eyes had died. He's hard, ruthless.''

''And you've had more than your share of experience with

372

that kind of man. You can't believe Rory is like Amos Wells and his minions."

"No. But there are things he's said . . . things I've said. We've hurt each other too many times. I don't know if all of it can be undone." Thoughts of her father's possible complicity in their separation almost surfaced. She quashed them. Rory had always told her that one day she would have to choose between her father and him. After all these years, it might come to that yet.

Patrick watched her struggle with her inner torment and wished he could offer some sage advice that would smooth the way for them, but he had none. As they once more kicked their horses into a trot to catch up with Patsy and Michael, he described Rory's rise in business and politics, hoping it might enable her to understand how driven and lonely his brother had been.

"All these years and all the money and power he's amassed, yet my brother never married. He's wanted no woman but you, Rebekah. Believe that."

"Perhaps that very single-minded obsession is another reason why I should distrust him," she replied sadly.

Wellsville

Ephraim Sinclair struggled with his conscience all through the day. By evening, he had made the most painful decision of his life—even more agonizing than the parting from Kathleen back in Boston. He must confess to his beloved younger daughter what he had done. First thing tomorrow he would ride out to the ranch and get it over with.

"No more rationalizations or excuses. My own blindness has caused such hurt, it may never be undone," he murmured to himself. The empty house echoed his words as he walked

373

through the shabby parlor and into his small, cluttered office. Although never elegant, the house had been kept immaculately neat while Dorcas was alive. Now the ladies of the church guild took turns bringing him his meals and tidying up. Their efforts were well intentioned, but Ephraim had always been prone to absentmindedness, strewing his books and clothes about. How Dorcas had scolded him, he thought wryly, following him around as tenaciously as a bulldog, picking up after him.

"Ah, Dorcas, I sinned against you, too, in my blindness." The silence closed in on him. Twilight eroded the light, but he did not touch the lamp on his desk. Finally, unable to bear his loneliness, he decided to ride out to Leah's place. With Henry in Carson, his elder daughter and her boys would be glad of some company. Henry left them alone too often.

Ephraim knew there had been trouble between Leah and Henry. He had always turned a blind eye, as he had to so much else, hoping they could work it out, or live it out as he and Dorcas had. Leah had always been unreasoningly jealous of her husband's friendship with Rebekah. When he realized how desperately unhappy Rebekah was with Amos, Ephraim had been grateful for Henry's concern. He should have tried to explain to Leah that her mistrust was unfounded.

If he could not help Rebekah, perhaps he could do something for Leah. Or at least listen to her troubles. After tomorrow, Ephraim feared Rebekah's outpouring of confidences to her father would cease forever. Even though he had grievously wronged his younger daughter, he had always favored her. There were amends to be made to his elder daughter and no better time for doing so than the present.

When he pulled up in front of Leah's fancy gingerbread house, the place was brightly lit. He climbed down from his old buggy and headed toward the front porch, where one of the small army of servants was waiting with the door open.

"Miz Leah will be pleased to see you, Reverend," the man said. "She's putting the young masters to bed. I'll have cook bring you some dinner—"

"No, James, thank you. I'm not hungry right now, just in need of some company."

"Very good, sir. I'll send word up—"

"Let me do that myself. I'd enjoy helping her tuck in Hank and Jed." Ephraim headed upstairs.

An hour later, he sat across from Leah in her elegantly furnished sitting room. Dorcas's silver tea service was on the turret-top table in front of them, its contents cooling and ignored as Ephraim told her about Rebekah's marriage to Rory Madigan.

"I can't believe she's done such a thing." Leah's eyes grew round, and her face reddened with indignation, making her resemble her mother even more. Over the years her weight had continued to increase, and her once silver-gilt hair was now the same dull, streaked gray Dorcas's had been. "Amos dead one day and Rebekah running off to get married the next. It's positively barbaric. And to marry that—that Irishman! Whatever possessed her?"

If Ephraim had hoped to oil the waters, it was evident that his plans would come to naught. Leah had always been as obsessed with social propriety as her mother. "She had good reason, Leah." He explained about Sheriff Sears's absurd suspicions that Rebekah had killed her husband and the way Rory Madigan had rescued her—with the proviso that she wed him in return. "He forced her into the marriage, Leah. But the ceremony was performed in secret. They won't release the news until a respectable time has passed. She and Michael are staying at the Flying W for the present. That

375

should cause no gossip until the mystery of who killed Amos is solved.''

"For all I can see, my sister may very well have killed Amos just so she could have her Irishman now that he's rich," Leah snapped.

"Leah, that is a shameful thing to say!"

"You always defend her! So does Henry! Everyone loves her best. If she's so innocent, then why did the sheriff try to arrest her in the first place?" Tears threatened to spill down her plump cheeks. Her eyes grew puffy and narrow when she blinked the salty droplets back.

"Someone tried to make it look as though she were guilty. That awful gun Amos bought her was used to kill him. One of her gloves was found lying beside his body."

Leah had begun to stir an extra lump of sugar into her cold tea as he spoke. The spoon dropped from her fingers with a clatter. Her face turned the color of old parchment, and her skin looked just as stiff and wrinkled. She swallowed and looked around the room, frantically, like a wild creature caught in a trap.

"Leah, child, what is it?" Ephraim took his daughter in his arms and held her as she rocked back and forth, sobbing desperately.

Carson City

Horace "Shanghai" Sheffield had spent his youth in the China trade dealing in opium. When he made his fortune and entered politics, he made much of the former fact and totally buried the latter. He was now an elder statesman. In recent years, he had begun to contemplate retirement from the Senate to enjoy the money he had made from imparting misery and death. But he found that the cycle of busts and bonanzas on the Comstock had dissipated his fortunes even more quickly than opium wasted its victims.

His frivolous and expensive young wife had done her share to deplete his fortune. In fact, she was in San Francisco spending more money right now. But his risky mining speculations and dealings with dangerous men like Stephan Hammer and bumblers like Hiram Bascomb had him pacing the floor late at night. He raised one shaggy brow and fixed the always sweating weasel Bascomb with his most intimidating glare. "You're positive Hobart gave those papers to Madigan?"

"*He* told me so—and you know he's always been right."

Sheffield cursed. "And now when Madigan has everything he needs to ruin us, that bungling flunky Pritkin goes and gets himself shot! We've got to get our hands on every scrap of information Hobart gave Patrick Madigan."

"Well, er . . . that might be difficult. He placed everything in his safety deposit box in the First National Bank."

"Then we have to get rid of those damn Madigans immediately. They're becoming more of a liability than Amos ever was."

Sheffield leaned back in his big leather chair and steepled his fingers as Bascomb sat across from him trembling like the miserable worm he was. Perhaps it was time to get rid of this weak link, too. He needed to discuss it with Stephan and—

A hard-looking gunman barged into his private office, interrupting their clandestine meeting.

"Who the hell are you?" Sheffield asked, inspecting the big man's fancy Colt and unshaven visage. A shock of greasy yellow hair hung across his low forehead, and pencil-thin dark eyebrows drew together over opaque light eyes. Killer's eyes.

His uninvited guest smiled evilly, revealing dull yellow teeth. In a rusty-sounding voice, he replied, "Your business associate hired me to dispose of a couple of problems for you." He closed the door, then looked at Bascomb with eyes as dead and cold as a three-day-old fish. "Who's this?"

Bascomb daubed at his brow and upper lip with his handkerchief. "I'm Hiram Bascomb, President of the Greater Sacramento Trust Bank." He tried to sound authoritative, but his voice broke.

Sheffield turned to Bascomb. "Pay a visit to your dear friend Sam Pfeffer at First National in the morning. See what you can do about getting those papers from Madigan's box."

"But—"

"Don't argue, Hiram. Just do it." Once Bascomb had sidled out of the room, Shanghai turned to the gunman. "Hammer sent you?"

"I've done a few jobs for him over the years."

"You got a name?" Sheffield asked sourly. Damn, this man made *him* sweat!

"Yeah. But it don't matter. What does is the Madigan boys. Patrick got away, but his baby brother's back in town."

Sheffield squinted his beetle brows together. "Rory Madigan—here?"

"Rode in this afternoon and took a room at the Ormsby House. Then he paid a call on the federal marshal."

Shanghai was sweating in earnest now. "That means you don't have much time."

"Don't need much time. I was told you'd have my money ready soon as the job was done." The killer grinned at the senator. "Five thousand for each brother, the younger one first." He dared the old man to argue.

Sheffield did not, although it infuriated him that Hammer would stick him with paying the assassin. It was just like that bastard to handle things this way. "You stop Rory Madigan from getting to that safety deposit box. Bring me the key." He smiled thinly. Perhaps this would make things a little easier. The killer nodded and started to leave, but Sheffield stopped him as he reached for the doorknob. "I have more work for you."

"Bascomb?"

"Bascomb for openers. Get rid of him and Madigan. After that, I want you to take care of someone else. . . . "

Rory watched the deputy marshal hand a furiously protesting Stephan Hammer over to an amazed Sheriff Sears, who put him under lock and key. Prior to checking into the hotel that afternoon, the younger Madigan had made a furtive visit to the First National Bank by the back door. There he had met the governor and the state's attorney. Together they had gone over the evidence stored in Patrick's safety deposit box. Warrants were issued for the arrest of all the conspirators involved in the mining fraud—Hammer, Sheffield, Bascomb, and half-a-dozen lesser men on the Nevada–California state line.

"We won't get anything out of Hammer," Rory said to the marshal. "He has friends in Washington who will most likely save him."

"So does ole Senator Sheffield," the marshal replied. His deputy nodded in agreement.

"This here whole thing is crazy, you ask me," August Sears interjected, even though no one had.

"Just keep watch on our illustrious guest," Rory replied. Then, turning to the marshal, he said, "I think we should pay a midnight call on the Senator."

His young deputy chuckled. "That old boy will sure be pissed. At his age, he needs all the beauty sleep he can get."

The three of them departed, leaving a bewildered Sheriff Sears to attend to the strident cries of the undersecretary issuing from the rear cell in the Ormsby County jail.

As they headed to the Sheffield mansion, Rory realized that the more he tasted of it, the less he cared for his long-sought vengeance. Rebekah and Michael were of far more concern to him. What could he say to convince her to trust him, to give their marriage a chance? Yet as he thought of her, he kept returning to the evidence planted at the scene of Amos's murder.

Who among the conspirators wanted not only Wells dead but Rebekah out of the way? Something just did not add up. *At least Patrick is with them. They're safe.*

After leaving Senator Sheffield's office, the gunman headed to the rendezvous he had planned with his employer in a cheap hotel on the outskirts of the city. He knocked and was admitted to the dingy interior.

"You were right," the killer said without preamble. "Sheffield plans to double-cross you."

"You know what to do, Kelso," his boss replied.

The gunman slipped out into the night, moving with amazing stealth for a man of his size. Within ten minutes, he was climbing in the kitchen window of the Senator's mansion. Locating the old goat should not prove difficult. *I can just follow the sounds of his snoring*, he thought with a sneer. He moved soundlessly down the hall and into the front foyer, then climbed the thickly carpeted spiral stairs to the master suite. Pausing outside the door, he withdrew a wicked-looking knife from his belt, then turned the brass knob with a low click.

As Rory and the federal officers crossed the grounds of

Sheffield's place, they heard a bellow of rage coming from inside.

"I'll take the back door—you, Billy, take the front door," the marshal commanded.

Without waiting for instructions, Rory headed for the big glass doors at the west side of the mansion. By breaking a windowpane, he let himself in more quickly than the marshal and deputy who pounded for entry, then waited for sleepy servants to admit them. Madigan took the stairs two at a time, nearly knocking the elderly butler over as he passed him. With his gun drawn, he slipped up to the open door of Shanghai's bedroom suite and peered inside.

One gaslight was barely lit, casting eerie shadows around the room, which was in shambles. Senator Sheffield had put up quite a fight. The pier table was overturned and two lamps were shattered across the thick Turkey carpet, which greedily soaked up the blood pouring from an evil slash across Sheffield's throat. He lay in a grotesque sprawl with a gun clutched in his hands.

"Tough old buzzard," the deputy said, coming up behind Rory.

"Not tough enough. He was awake. I imagine that surprised his assassin," Rory replied, his eyes sweeping the scene for signs of the killer.

"He's the one who looks surprised," the deputy said, studying the strange grimace on the old politician's face as he knelt beside the body.

Rory was already sprinting down the hall. He could hear sounds of a struggle coming from the rear of the house. When he reached the kitchen, he saw a big man running out the back door. The marshal was slumped on one knee, holding on to a table, shaking his head doggedly. The servants had all vanished.

"Are you all right?" Rory examined the grizzled law-
man's body for signs of injury.

"He just used his Colt to club me aside the head. Go after
him, Madigan."

"Right, but send your deputy to arrest Bascomb right
away! I have a feeling he's next on the list, and he's our
weak link—the one who'll talk once he's in jail and frightened!"

As the marshal nodded in understanding, Rory took off
out the door after the assassin.

A dim quarter moon sent small slivers of light to illumi-
nate the dark grounds. A dense stand of pines obscured his
view to the north. Rory stood still in the backyard and listened, then heard the crunch of gravel near the senator's orchard. He started running as fast as he could in the darkness.
Moving swiftly through the trees, he sighted a shadowy figure ahead of him. As the killer turned and fired, Rory dove
for the protection of a fallen log. The slug missed him by
inches.

Rory returned the shot, but it was too late. The killer had
disappeared among the peach trees. Madigan followed cautiously, using the shadows for cover. Then he heard the click
of a hammer being cocked and spun around just in time to
hear the roar of the blast.

The Flying W Ranch

Early the following morning, Rebekah awakened with the
sun. She sat in her big, empty bedroom, staring out the window at the dawn. She had scarcely slept the night before,
tossing and turning in the cold, lonely bed—as if spending
one night in Rory's arms had made her unable to rest without

him! She rubbed her aching head and gazed out, seeing nothing.

Everything in her life had changed with Amos's death. He would never again threaten her or Michael. "I suppose Papa was right about how we break the commandments. I've certainly murdered Amos in my heart a thousand times. And I would've pulled the trigger without hesitation if he had ever touched Michael."

But that part of their lives was over and done. Now she was Rory Madigan's wife, and that fact presented a whole new set of problems. What might they have said to each other yesterday morning if Patrick had not interrupted them? "If only I weren't so vulnerable." *If only you weren't so in love with him,* an inner demon tormented her.

Yet there was a chance that he loved her, too, now that he knew she had not deserted him for Amos's wealth and position. Perhaps he could forgive her and even her family for their prejudices, although in her heart she doubted it. She would still have to choose between him and her father.

"Don't be a fool, Rebekah. He hasn't asked you to convert. He doesn't want to marry you in church," she chided herself. Then the memories of their wedding night rushed back to her—the passion, the wild, incredible pleasure he had given her. But that very pleasure had brought out a wanton response in her that revealed her weakness. She could still see the gleam of predatory male satisfaction that blazed in those dark blue eyes after he had brought her to that singular climax and she lay open and vulnerable before he took her again.

He had placed his mark on her for all time. She would always love him, whether or not he still loved her. But that was of secondary importance. The innocent victim in all this was Michael. She would never let anyone use her son again, not even his own father.

As if the thought had summoned him, Michael came running through her bedroom door with a squeal of delight. Although he did not know Amos was dead, the boy was relaxing, acting like a normal child, as if he could sense that the fearful authority figure had been removed.

"Mama! Remember, you promised. You and Patsy and Mr. Madigan were going to take me on a picnic out by the pond today!" Excitement danced in his eyes as he jumped onto the bed and into her open arms.

She squeezed him to her, and this time he did not protest, but returned the hug with gusto. *He senses that he's free.* Rebekah tousled his hair and forced down the lump in her throat. "I imagine we can have that picnic, but I'm not certain if your . . . that is, if Mr. Madigan can come along." She had almost said "your uncle!"

"Aw. I really like him—almost as much as his brother, the other Mr. Madigan. Rory. That's an Irish name, isn't it, Mama?"

"Yes, son, it is."

"Grandpa doesn't like Irishmen—or at least he didn't used to—but he likes Patsy. Is that because she's a lady?"

Rebekah smiled sadly. "Maybe your grandpa has changed his mind about Irish people." *He loves you, and you're Rory's son.*

Refusing to worry about what was ahead, Rebekah seized the promise of the bright new day. "Let's get washed up and dressed. We'll have some breakfast, then we'll see about packing up a picnic lunch."

Michael grimaced at the prospect of morning toilette, but quickly brightened when he remembered his new treasure. "Can I ride Snowball?"

"Of course, he's your very own pony. Now let's get cleaned up."

"Yuk." The boy sighed but wriggled from the bed and headed resignedly to the washroom down the hall with his mother behind him.

When they came downstairs, Rebekah heard conversation in the front parlor. She recognized Henry's voice and then Patrick Madigan's.

Henry's tone was guarded and hostile. "I was concerned about Rebekah and Michael. They vanished suddenly with your brother. When Ephraim told me that she and Rory—"

"Good morning, Henry," Rebekah quickly interrupted before her brother-in-law blurted out that she and Rory were married. She had spent the past day trying to decide how she could explain that fact to her son. "I'm so happy you're here. I know Papa was concerned for Michael, but everything will work out all right, given time." Her eyes implored him to drop the subject of her marriage as she held on to Michael's shoulder, ushering him into the parlor in front of her.

Henry gave her a relieved smile. "I'm certain it will, Rebekah," he replied gently, reaching down to pat his nephew on the head. "Morning, Michael."

"Good morning, Uncle Henry," the boy replied politely. "We're going on a picnic," he added, turning from his uncle to Patrick, working up the courage to invite his new friend to join them.

"Why don't you head to the kitchen and see if Patsy and the cook have started frying chicken for our basket?" Rebekah shooed the boy off down the hall, then turned to Patrick and Henry, who stood like two fighters about to square off in the prize ring.

"I came as soon as I could, Rebekah. What the hell have you done, marrying that bastard? He probably murdered

385

Amos just to get control of the boy.''

"Now I'd be watchin' what I say, bucko," Patrick said, stepping menacingly forward. His soft brogue only heightened the threat radiating from his tall, lean body.

Rebekah stepped between the two big men. "Will you both stop this bravado at once," she commanded in a steady voice. Heavens above, the last thing she needed was for Henry and Patrick to have a brawl! Men could be such idiots at times. "My reasons for marrying Rory are my own, Henry, and to even think he would shoot Amos the way the sheriff described is ridiculous. Rory Madigan is many things, but a cold-blooded killer is not one of them. We all have to think of Michael," she added as a reminder to them both that their nephew was just down the hall.

Henry sighed and ran blunt fingers through his thick brown hair. "I'm sorry, Rebekah. It's just that this whole thing is such a shock. Your father made it clear that Madigan blackmailed you into marrying him. You don't have to stay with him. I'll help you—"

"You'll be stayin' out of it and lettin' Rebekah and Rory settle it between themselves, is what you'll be doin'," Patrick interjected.

"I appreciate your concern, Henry, but Patrick is right. Rory is my husband now, and we'll have to work out our differences. He has a right to know his own son."

"You haven't told Michael?" Henry asked, aghast.

Rebekah shook her head. "He doesn't know Amos is dead or that Rory and I are married. We have to think through how to explain everything to him." Her eyes met Henry's levelly. "You know Michael had no reason to feel close to Amos. I don't think his death will be as much a blow as . . . the other things."

"He already loves Rory. I could tell it by the way he

talked about him all day yesterday,'' Patrick said. ''It's natural, Snead.''

''If he's such a loving father, then why isn't he here with his boy?'' Henry asked.

''Rory has important business in the capital,'' Patrick began cautiously.

''And you want to join him, I know,'' Rebekah said. ''Go, Patrick. Michael and I will be safe here. Henry could stay with us.'' She turned to her brother-in-law. ''That is, if you have time?''

''Of course. I came out to see if you were all right and to tell you I authorized Fortner's Mortuary to prepare Amos's body. Under the circumstances, I thought a private service would be best. We can return to Carson tomorrow to take care of that. Amos has a bevy of lawyers to handle his estate. I expect that when they get it straightened out, they'll be in touch. Meanwhile, there are two new stud bulls down at the barn that I should check on and there's always plenty of paperwork for the Flying W that Amos has no doubt left in arrears,'' Henry replied.

Patrick looked from Snead to Rebekah. Her expression was one of implicit trust, perhaps relief, that a member of her family had come to help her. He disliked Snead, but even though the man had worked for Wells, there had been nothing in the evidence to implicate him in the deadly dealings with the conspirators. In fact, when Wells and Sheffield were arranging the blast that killed Ryan, Snead had not yet met either man. Patrick was too close to Rory, and his friendship with his new sister-in-law was too fragile to presume she would prefer his company over Henry Snead's.

Still, he could not leave her and the boy alone with anyone who was connected with Amos Wells. Perhaps the best thing would be to watch Snead while he was not suspecting. ''If

387

you're certain you don't mind, it would be wise for me to hightail it back to Carson," he said to Rebekah.

She took his hand and squeezed it fondly. "I think we shall become good friends, Patrick. Be careful and watch out for Rory."

"I expect everything will be in hand by the time I arrive," he said reassuringly, "but I'll send him directly here to collect you as soon as the legalities are taken care of." He returned her squeeze, then released her hand and nodded curtly to Snead.

Rebekah and Henry watched Patrick ride off. Then he turned to her with a smile and said, "How about some breakfast? You could use some fattening up, and Michael is always hungry."

Down the road to the south, Patrick reined in behind the cover of a stand of pinion pines and looked down on the layout of the Flying W. He waited a few moments, then began to circle around to the west, keeping out of sight of the ranch house. When he neared the west side of the big, two-story structure, he dismounted behind an outcropping of rock and tied his horse, then climbed up to watch and wait. He was not certain for what.

In an hour or so, Rebekah and Michael, accompanied by Patsy Mulcahey, headed down to the corral. The maid carried a hamper filled with picnic treats. In a few moments, they rode off. Patrick debated following them, then decided they would be safe enough since two of the cowhands accompanied them. He would wait to see if Henry Snead was up to anything.

When Snead left the house shortly and headed toward the barn, Patrick worked his way to a side window. Snead entered to the angry bellowing of a bull, confined near several dozen cows. There was nothing unusual in the conversation between Henry and the bull's handler. Patrick crouched outside the barn until his quarry headed back to the ranch house.

The big gunman watched from across the corral, hidden behind the rocks where he had found Patrick's horse tethered. Kelso's yellow teeth showed as he grinned evilly. All he had to do to get this Madigan was wait until he returned to his cover. "Like shooting fish in a barrel," he muttered as Patrick neared the rocks once more. He was spying on Snead. The thought made the killer laugh.

Patrick settled down in the rocks. "It's going to be a long day," he sighed.

As the butt of the gunman's pistol came crashing down on Patrick's head, Kelso replied, "Longer than you'd ever imagine, Madigan."

Rebekah sat under the shade of a pine tree watching Michael skipping along the edge of the pond. The jagged mountain peaks gleamed rusty bronze in the distance, and heat shimmered across the valley floor. Her son's infectious laughter sounded like music in the peaceful afternoon air, but the rich lunch she had just eaten was not sitting well. After a sleepless night and the day's enervating heat, she had a throbbing headache as well as indigestion. Rebekah leaned back against the tree and closed her eyes, then opened them again quickly. Visions of Rory's mocking smile were always hovering.

If only she knew what to say to him, how to make him understand what she herself did not fully comprehend. And even if they could work out some sort of relationship, how could they help Michael accept it? It was one thing to like the charming man who brought him a pony, but quite another to have that man come into his life and in the space of a heartbeat marry his mother and become his father.

Rebekah did not honestly think Michael would grieve over Amos's death, but that in itself might eventually make the boy feel guilty. Imagine his added bewilderment when he learned that he was not truly Amos's son, but Rory's.

Patsy approached the picnic blanket and knelt down beside her mistress. "It's that tired you look, ma'am. Yer worried about the mister, I know."

If Patsy had been shocked over Rebekah's unseemly haste in remarrying, she had never betrayed a hint of it, but acted as if it were the most natural thing in the world for Michael's parents to be reunited. Rebekah only wished things *were* that simple. She smiled feebly. "I didn't sleep well last night," she replied evasively and then blushed when she realized what the remark implied.

Patsy clucked sympathetically. "I'm thinkin' it might be best if you went back to the ranch and rested before dinner. The mister might arrive by then."

"I don't want to spoil Michael's outing," Rebekah replied, watching her son. Randy Ziegler, one of the older men who had worked for the Flying W for years, helped Michael mount Snowball and began to walk beside them, showing the boy the finer points of how to handle his treasured pony.

"We'll look out for Michael. Not to worry. I'll have him home in plenty of time to wash up for supper."

Her pounding head, and the thought of the powder back at the ranch house that could soothe it, decided Rebekah. "Let me tell him to mind you before I go," she said, climbing wearily to her feet.

In less than an hour, Rebekah slipped quietly in the kitchen door. The old cook was taking his siesta before starting dinner. No one was about as she mixed a spoonful of headache powder in water and drank it down with a grimace.

Perhaps a nap would give her the strength to face Rory

tonight, assuming he came for them by tonight. As she started down the hall, she heard sounds of papers rustling in Amos's study. Smiling to herself, Rebekah approached. Poor loyal Henry was at work on her late husband's books. She opened the door and stood frozen in amazement at the sight that greeted her.

There, spread out on the desk, were dozens of bundles of paper currency in huge denominations and stacks of mining securities. Henry was facing the wall behind Amos's desk where the safe—a hidden wall safe even she had not known existed—stood open while he pulled the last documents from it.

Rebekah started to back out of the room, but he turned too quickly, pulling a hidden gun from inside his jacket. ''Come in, Rebekah. I regret your catching me like this, but I would have had to dispose of you quite soon anyway.''

Chapter Twenty

Henry's tone of voice was matter-of-fact, his expression regretful. He acted solicitously toward Rebekah in spite of the unwavering gun he pointed at her. His words simply would not register at first. She stared dumbly at him as he walked over to her and gently pulled her into the room, closing the door behind her. That was when she saw Patrick's body lying slumped across the chair in the corner.

"You've killed Patrick!" She tried to pull away and rush to him, but Snead held her fast, shaking his head.

"No, he's quite alive. Observe the rope binding him. We'd have no need to tie and gag a corpse, although I'm afraid my assistant, Mr. Kelso, did strike him harder than necessary." He shoved her down into the chair in front of the desk, then slipped his gun back into the hidden holster under his jacket and continued going through the money and documents on the desk.

Rebekah's mind raced frantically, trying to make sense of the insane nightmare unfolding in front of her. "You were one of the partners in Amos's illegal stock manipulations."

"Not at first. It took me a while to gain his confidence before he let me in on their really lucrative ventures. Arranging for you to marry him was a decided point in my favor. No easy feat to accomplish either," he added with a sigh.

It was as if a great fist had slammed into her chest. "*You* sent Rory to Denver for that fight," she choked out.

He shook his head. "No, that was Amos's idea, after I began feeding him snippets of information gleaned from the man I hired to follow you and your Irishman. However, Amos would've been content to let Madigan return, thinking your family would turn the bloody ruffian away when he tried to claim you. But I knew you a bit better than Amos ever did. I wasn't inclined to take a chance." He fingered a bundle of thousand-dollar bills.

"You hired those men to kill Rory in Denver, not Amos." She could still scarcely take it all in.

"Amos wanted you—and Michael." He nodded at her gasp of shock. "Oh, yes, I knew about his impotence. You weren't the only one I set spies on. I knew the only way he could get an heir was to have Madigan do the job for him, then conveniently drop from the picture. A pity the mick had to return from the dead, as it were—he and this one here." He nodded to the pale, unconscious form of Patrick. "The Madigan brothers have caused us all no end of grief in recent years. I always planned to kill Amos one day." He smiled sadly at her. When he resumed, there was almost an apology in his voice. "I rather thought you'd consider that a favor of sorts."

"But why make it look as if I did it?"

His shoulders slumped as he placed the last bundle of money into a heavy leather satchel. "I regretted having to do that, Rebekah, but Amos had become a liability to the men he worked with. He'd grown careless and arrogant. But more than that—a matter they didn't know about— Amos was withholding money from them." He patted the satchel. "As I said, I've made it my business in the past decade to learn all his secrets. After all, he was my kinsman by marriage."

Rebekah's heart sped up and she curled her fingers into fists, willing herself not to panic. "And if I was out of the picture, all Amos's estate would go to Michael and you would surely be appointed his guardian."

"But then you had to go and ruin everything by marrying Rory Madigan. I underestimated you, Rebekah."

"You underestimated Rory," she said flatly.

"Since he and Patrick began their little vendetta against Amos, I always knew that sooner or later I'd have to deal with them. Then Amos's carelessness caused him to implicate Sheffield and Bascomb, even the high and mighty Stephan Hammer. You can bet they were glad to have me on their side against the Madigans, but I alone kept my name out of their deals."

"I suppose Amos stole more than enough to compensate you for that," she said, nodding to the securities and cash on the desk. "But you're still underestimating Rory."

"I think not. My assistant, Mr. Kelso, and I have devised a plan to take care of everything. I'm only sorry you had to get in the way."

Absurdly, she believed him even as the icy chill of his words sank in.

"As I said, Rebekah, I've grown genuinely fond of you and Michael over the years. I'll take good care of the boy. Leah can raise him right along with our sons. He'll want for nothing."

He was so sincere with his monstrous promise. "Please, Henry—you can't just kill us."

"Unfortunately, I have no choice. Can't say I'll feel bad about the Madigans, but you . . ." He studied her fondly, the corners of his mustache turning up in that sad smile he'd given her so often over the years. "I married the wrong sister, you know. Should've seen how much promise you had instead of being blinded by my wife's voluptuous charms. But what's done is done," he added with a brisk shift of mood, snapping the satchel closed.

Rebekah scanned the room, looking for a weapon. Henry was a big man, and somewhere on the premises his hired killer lurked. How could she outwit them by herself? Patrick was injured, unconscious, and bound. As Snead walked around the desk, she said as calmly as she could, "You can't get away with this, Henry. Take the money and leave Nevada—run. Rory and Patrick went to the governor. Rory is helping arrest Senator Sheffield and all the others right now. They'll implicate you."

"I'm afraid not. Mr. Kelso took care of Sheffield and Bascomb last night. Hammer is too smart to talk. Besides, being a high-ranking federal official, he knows he can buy his way out, and after the unfortunate deaths of his friends, he'll want nothing more than to get the hell out of Nevada and never return."

"But Rory—"

"Madigan tried to stop Kelso. He's dead, too," Snead

said, watching her reaction carefully.

Black spots floated before Rebekah's eyes as she struggled to breathe. *No! I would know if you were dead, Rory. Surely, I would know. . . .*

Just then, a hulking giant with a lethal-looking Colt strapped to his hip walked into the office. "The coast is clear, boss," the hard-looking stranger said in a raspy voice.

"You carry Madigan. I'll escort the lady. Oh, Rebekah, I'd advise you against screaming. The only men around to hear you are the old cook and a stableboy. I don't think you'd want their deaths on your conscience, now would you?" he asked gently.

"What are you going to do?" She forced out the words, trying not to recoil when he took her arm and moved toward the door. Kelso picked up Patrick and slung the big Irishman across his shoulder as if he weighed no more than Michael.

"You're still under suspicion for your first husband's death. When you and your second husband's brother abscond from the ranch with all Amos's money from his secret safe . . . well, it won't take much to convince Sheriff Sears that you and Patrick planned the whole thing."

They headed to the kitchen with Kelso preceding them to the back door, carrying Patrick. Rebekah shook off Henry's hand and walked calmly ahead of him. As soon as they were inside the room, she saw what she had been praying for—the small, sharp paring knife the cook used to cut vegetables from his garden out back. It lay in the shadows on a small corner table beside the door with his apron carelessly thrown beside it. How could she slip it inside her skirt pocket without Henry noticing?

When Kelso opened the back door and started to maneuver Patrick through it, Henry's attention was diverted. Rebekah stumbled against a kitchen chair and fell forward toward the table, crying out as if it were an accident. Before Snead could reach over to catch her, she had concealed the knife and straightened up. She did not have to pretend the shivers of terror when she looked up at him as if expecting that he would strike her. *Just don't look at that apron that fell onto the floor,* she prayed. "I . . . I felt a bit dazed," she murmured.

As solicitous as the old friend she had always believed him to be, Henry smiled and took her arm. "Be careful, my dear. I know you're frightened. It won't be much longer and this will all be over."

Carson City

The search for the killer had proven fruitless. Rory sat in his suite at the Ormsby House, pinching the bridge of his nose, exhausted and frustrated. His shoulder kept a steady throbbing beat in time with the pounding in his temples. When the man who murdered Sheffield had shot him in the orchard, he'd fallen, striking his head against the trunk of a peach tree.

By the time the marshal found him, their quarry was long gone. Against his will, the semiconscious Rory had been taken to the doctor, then driven back to his hotel, where he passed out on the bed. By the time he had awakened, it was late morning, and the news the governor's aide brought him was not good. When the deputy had arrived at Hiram Bascomb's house the night before, the little banker was as dead as Shanghai Sheffield, probably shot by the same assassin. A thorough search of Carson City yielded nothing.

Wells and his cohorts were all dead. All but one—Stephan

Hammer—and he was securely held in the Ormsby County jail, refusing to say a word except to express outrage and indignation at being detained. Perhaps he had hired the professional who took care of his fellows, but something just did not fit.

"I'm missing something. What would a man like Hammer have to gain by framing Rebekah for Amos's death? If he was afraid she knew about Amos's illegal associations, why not just have her killed along with the others?" He looked at the breakfast tray a maid had brought earlier. He had no appetite, but maybe some food would fortify him so he could think straight. Then he'd ride out to the Flying W and discuss the whole debacle with Patrick. Between the two of them, with Rebekah's help, maybe they could make sense of the puzzle.

Just as he was finishing the last bite of steak, a loud rapping sounded on the sitting room door of his suite. Rory shoved the plate away and reached for his gun. He walked slowly to the door and unlocked it, standing clear as he yanked it open. The last person on earth he expected to see was Ephraim Sinclair.

The reverend took one look at the pistol barrel so near his face and stiffened, but did not step back. "I have urgent information I need to share with you," he said in a low, weary voice. "I've spent the night asking the Lord for guidance."

"And he sent you to me?" A sardonic smile swept over Rory's face as he lowered his gun and motioned for the old man to come inside.

"You're Rebekah's husband. A part of this family now. And I . . . I don't know where else to turn, what to do."

"Sit down, I'll get you some coffee. It should still be fairly hot." Rory looked at the old man's haggard face. Something was badly amiss. A moment later, he shoved a cup of strong black coffee into Sinclair's hands and sat down across from him, unconsciously rubbing the bandage on his shoulder. Damn, he was still groggy from whatever that doc had given him last night. Shaking his head to clear it, he said, "Maybe you'd better tell me what this is all about, Reverend Sinclair."

The old man's shoulders slumped as he carefully set the cup and saucer down on the table beside his chair. "Last night I went to have a talk with Leah. You know how angry I was that you'd forced Rebekah to marry you. I suppose that's part of the reason . . . Anyway, the rest can wait. The issue now is who killed Amos."

"What could you or Leah know about—Snead!" Rory jumped up abruptly. "It was Snead, wasn't it?" He cursed his own obtuseness as Sinclair nodded, a bewildered expression on his face. Rory continued, "It all makes sense. He worked for Amos and was in with the others. He just hid his trail more carefully."

"But why did he implicate Rebekah? He's always been her champion against Amos," Ephraim asked plaintively.

"With Rebekah out of the way, all Amos's estate would go to Michael. His uncle would have been the logical one to act as my son's guardian and executor—if I hadn't gotten in the way. But how did you find out what Snead had done?"

"The gun—Rebekah's gun. Leah found it while she was going through Henry's desk the day before Amos was shot. She just assumed he'd taken it to clean or repair it for her sister. He was always doing errands for Rebekah. That was one of the things that drove Leah to such jealousy. . . . " His voice faded away.

"I don't expect swiping one of Rebekah's gloves was any difficult feat for him either," Rory said angrily. "Does Leah have any idea where he might be?''

''He came by my place late yesterday after Patrick and Rebekah left with Michael. He acted concerned that Rebekah had run off with you and told me he was going to confront you here in Carson when I explained where you were.'' His eyes moved to Rory's bandaged shoulder, revealed through the front of his robe, which hung open to the waist. Sinclair blanched. ''He tried to kill you!''

Rory strode across the room and gathered up his clothes. ''Go to the federal marshal's office on Stewart Street. Tell him everything we've discussed. He can start the search here for Snead. I'm going to the Flying W to see that Rebekah and Michael are safe.''

''Surely if your brother is with them . . .''

''I hope you're right! Go for the marshal,'' Rory added, as he threw on his clothes.

The Mud Pots near Pyramid Lake

The heavy blanket covering her was suffocating. Patrick still had shown no signs of awakening as they bounced along the rocky ground headed toward the flat sink in whose center lay the magnificent blue-green Pyramid Lake. The area was surrounded by russet-brown volcanic cliffs and the domed, twisted deposits of sediment called tufa rock. It was a wildly beautiful place that Rebekah had always delighted in visiting, but its very desolation would now seal her doom if Patrick did not awaken to help her in the attempt to overpower Snead and Kelso.

Kelso had brought an old spring wagon around to the rear of the house. He had put Patrick's unconscious body in it and she was instructed to join him. The thug had covered them and then driven off. Henry followed at a distance sufficient to keep any possible witness from associating him with the wagon, yet close enough to keep watch so she could not jump free and run for help.

Sweat ran in rivulets over her body, soaking her dress. Every breath she drew in the fetid heat was burning and painful. She felt the knife in her fist and squeezed it for courage, debating about cutting Patrick free. If he did not regain consciousness and Henry decided to remove the blanket, her last element of surprise would be lost when he saw the rope removed. Yet alone against the two armed men, with only her small weapon, what could she do anyway?

Kill Henry. The thought settled in her mind and repeated itself over and over with every turn of the creaky wheels. Yes, failing everything else, she must do that. Even if Kelso shot her, she would stop Henry from gaining guardianship of Michael. *Papa will take care of Michael if we're all dead.*

In the back of her mind, she still held out the faint thread of hope that Rory was not dead. But with every mile they drew nearer to the mud pots, Rory's help was further away. She had listened as Henry explained to Kelso how she and Patrick were to vanish. The vast basin area between the Carson and Humboldt sinks was scattered with mires of muddy water that bubbled up like small volcanic eruptions from deep beneath the earth. In places there were literally acres of the deadly morass. The mud pots could swallow up man and horse alike.

She and Patrick would vanish without a trace in a boiling cauldron of mud. Kelso would drive the wagon across the Utah border, and its trail would be lost in the zephyr-driven sands of the high desert. Most people would assume what Henry planned for them to assume—that she and Patrick had run off with Amos's money. Would Rory believe it? No, but that was because he trusted his brother, not her. *Please be there for Michael, Rory.*

Rebekah continued her attempts to prod and nudge Patrick without alerting Henry. She could hear the muffled hoofbeats of his horse beside the wagon now. Then Patrick groaned softly and moved a tiny bit. Now or never, she had to cut him free and take her chances. Slowly, carefully, she slid the knife close to the ropes binding his wrists. He lay on his side with his back to her. Several minutes later, she had him free but still he did not regain consciousness. Rebekah whispered to him in a low, desperate voice, trying to rouse him and explain their danger. Kelso had probably given him a concussion!

Then the wagon slowed and came to a stop. Rebekah pulled Patrick flat on his back with his hands still partially hidden beneath him, praying she could reach Henry before the men saw that she had cut Madigan free. She sat up and kicked off half of the covers, leaving them on her unconscious brother-in-law. Henry was dismounting ten feet from her while Kelso climbed down from the wagon seat and watched.

Rebekah coughed and looked around, trying to accustom her stinging eyes to the blinding late-afternoon sunlight. They were at the edge of what looked like a fantastical landscape from Dante's *Inferno*. Acres of yellow-ochre and bronze-red ooze spread to the east, with small treacherous paths of firm ground threading between the cauldrons of bubbling mud. Steam hissed in sibilant geysers, filling the air with a stench of sulfur . . . and death.

Not giving Henry a chance to realize her intent, Rebekah leaped from the wagon and ran to him, the knife hidden in the folds of her skirts. Just as she drew up in front of him and fell to her knees, seemingly in supplication, hoping he would reach down to pick her up, Kelso yelled out a warning.

"Madigan's been cut free!"

Henry reached for the pistol in his shoulder holster, but Rebekah rose up like a she-bear. She butted him in the stomach and knocked him backward to the ground, then came at him with the knife clenched in her fist. Snead struggled to recover his wind and roll free of the demented woman who was on top of him.

Rebekah slashed at his throat, narrowly missing but opening a long, ugly gash across his right shoulder and down his arm before his left fist slammed against the side of her head. Even while the pain lanced through her in black waves, she held fast to the paring knife as the force of his punch sent her flying into the yellow mud. Rolling up, Rebekah tried to clear her head and gain purchase in the hot, squishy mud pot as Henry came after her.

In the struggle, he had dropped his revolver and stopped to pick it up as she scrambled deeper into the maze of steaming, muddy earth.

"You won't get far, Rebekah," he called after her with maddening calm, then began following her with the same relentless, inexorable patience he brought to every task.

Kelso cursed as he pulled Patrick's inert body from the wagon, only to have the big Irishman come to life just as his feet hit the ground. Still dazed, Madigan tried to swing at the gunman but only grazed him. Kelso shoved him back and started to draw his gun. Patrick grappled with him, seeing blurry triple images of his foe as he concentrated on making his arms and legs obey his commands.

If only he could hold on. Patrick could hear Henry's taunts to Rebekah in the distance. He had to help her, but his knees felt like rain-soaked ropes and his hands were unable to still the gunman's hand as it moved the deadly weapon nearer his head. He threw his whole weight on the man, hoping to topple him over backward, but it did not work. Patrick started to go down, still holding on to his enemy's arm. Then, suddenly, the gunman was yanked free just as a shot roared from his weapon.

Rory leaped at Kelso from Lobsterback's saddle. As Patrick and the gunman fought over the weapon, he had been unable to get a clear shot without endangering his brother. He knocked the killer free of Patrick in the split second before the bullet from Kelso's Colt would have taken off Patrick's head. Unfortunately, the impact of landing caused his own gun to fall from his holster. Kelso turned with a snarl of surprise as Madigan buried a hard right in his midsection. The force of the blow knocked his gun away but also sent pain lancing up Rory's injured shoulder. Gritting his teeth, he ignored it. Kelso grabbed his belly, staggering backward, but did not go down.

As Patrick dropped to the ground, his head spinning and his ears ringing with his exertions, his brother began to methodically pound his much larger opponent. Kelso was slow, but he was tough and muscular and had a significant height and weight advantage. With a bull-like bellow, the killer charged. Rory's lightning series of left jabs slowed his advance and dazed him, but he kept on coming, his big meaty right fist raised for a Sunday punch.

Rory slipped past the powerful but clumsy swing, then landed several more wicked hooking blows to Kelso's floating rib before retreating. His gun lay in the dust only a few yards away, but he knew he'd never reach it before Kelso could grab his, which was even closer.

I can't outshoot him. I sure as hell have to outfight him. He closed with Kelso again, this time following his swift left jabs with a hard right cross that dazed the killer. Rory could hear Snead and Rebekah out in that hellish sea of boiling mud, yet he dared not take his eyes from Henry's hireling. Patrick was too dazed to go to her. A patch of the reddish slime lay directly behind his foe. If he could only get the gunman to back up and step into it. There was but one way. His jab smashed into the big man's face again and again, driving him backward.

The big brute started to slip just as Rory came forward with a long right. The blow grazed Kelso's jaw, doing no serious damage, but knocking him off balance. As the gunman went down, his right foot came out to trip Rory, who rolled to the ground on top of him. The two men slid around in the mud, punching and gouging as the sulfurous slime flew all around them until they were covered in it.

Henry could see that Kelso had his hands full with Madigan. In spite of his size, Kelso was no match for a professional like the Irishman. Snead abandoned his pursuit of Rebekah and began to make his way back to where the two mud-soaked gladiators were battling, raising his pocket revolver to get a clear shot at the Irishman.

Rory regained his footing enough to scramble away from Kelso, back onto dry ground, hoping he could reach the nearest gun, but the big killer was right behind him. Madigan whirled around before Kelso could seize hold of him and hunched low, delivering a hard hook to his foe's crotch. Then, as Kelso doubled over in surprise, Rory's right uppercut landed squarely on his jaw with such force that Madigan felt it clear up to his injured shoulder. Ignoring the pain, he closed in for the kill with a sweeping left hook that brought Kelso to his knees.

When the brute pitched back into the mud and began to

sink, Rory made a run for the gun Kelso had dropped, but Snead was too close.

"I don't think so, Madigan," he said calmly, raising his weapon and taking aim.

"Rory, no!" Rebekah screamed, trying to distract Henry. She slipped and slid, her skirts dragging through the mud as she made one last desperate lunge for her target.

Snead turned in surprise, having completely discounted his troublesome sister-in-law. He swung his gun toward her, but her right hand came up with the paring knife arcing for his throat. This time she caught him cleanly across the carotid artery. Blood spurted out like a plume of crimson mud from a geyser. He dropped the revolver and staggered back, toppling into a deep mud pot. One strangling gurgle got past his lips as he flailed in the dark yellow slime which quickly bubbled up around his thrashing body.

Rebekah stood trembling, her eyes transfixed with horror on Henry Snead as his lifeless body was sucked down into the cauldron, leaving behind an ugly pinkish-gray stain.

"He's going straight to hell, just the way he deserves," Rory said as he took Rebekah in his arms and turned her from the grisly scene.

"Oh, Rory, I knew you couldn't be dead!" She threw her arms around him and held on tightly, burying her face against his mud-smeared chest. "He told me—he said Kelso had—"

"Shh, don't think about it. It's all over now," he soothed as she trembled in his arms.

"I k-killed a man."

"You saved my life—and Patrick's and your own." He held her tightly. "Oh, Rebekah, if I'd lost you. . . . " He, too, trembled as he guided her away from the maze of bubbling mud holes.

"Patrick's been hurt badly," she said, looking over to where he had fallen by the wagon.

Patrick was struggling to stay on his feet, Rory's gun clutched firmly in his hand as he tried to focus on Kelso, who was crawling slowly from the mire, choking and cursing. The dazed Patrick had to hold on to the wagon with one hand to remain standing. He could see three Kelsos in front of him, but he held the gun steady until his brother dragged the defeated killer to the wagon.

"Let's use the rope he tied me with on him," Patrick said as Rory shoved Kelso against the wagon.

"See," Rory said, turning to Rebekah, "it takes more than a little cosh on the head to keep an Irishman down."

She let out a small hiccup of relief. "That's only because there's nothing between an Irishman's ears to hurt."

"I only see two of him now. That mean I'm recovering?" Patrick asked as he handed the gun to Rory.

Rebekah helped Patrick sit down in the shade of the wagon, then examined the huge lump on his temple, which still oozed blood. "Thank God, you Irish are a tough lot," she said with relief and amazement.

Rory tied Kelso up and shoved him into the wagon, then knelt beside his brother and his wife. "Let me see that thick skull."

Rebekah realized for the first time that her husband was bleeding too. A long slash of red trickled through the thick yellow mud plastered to his right shoulder. "Henry said Kelso shot you—he did."

"Just grazed me, but I went down. Luckily for me, he couldn't stay to finish the job."

"How did you find us?"

"I learned in Carson that Henry was behind everything. When I arrived at the Flying W, Michael and Patsy were frantic. They came back to the ranch house and you were missing with no explanation. I searched the grounds and found a stableboy who said he saw Henry ride off behind a wagon driven by a stranger. I knew he had to have you, and I guessed he'd taken Patrick, too. Luck of the Irish that the wind was still today, else the wagon tracks would've vanished." He looked from his wife to his brother in profound gratitude that they were still alive.

Rebekah said worriedly, "Let me wrap your shoulder. It's bleeding worse."

He stood patiently as she ripped off a piece of her mud-soaked petticoat and began to wrap it around his shoulder. "I've heard mud packs are supposed to have mineral salts in them for healing," he said, raising one eyebrow dubiously.

"Then we should both be healthy as oxen," she replied.

"Smear some of it on my head, why don't you?" Patrick interjected as Rory helped him into the wagon. All three laughed, purging some of the tension after their brush with death.

"Are you sure I shouldn't drive for a while?" Rebekah asked for the third time since they had begun the long, slow ride back to the Flying W. Patrick was asleep in the back of the wagon. They had traveled for nearly an hour. "You're hurt and bleeding," she persisted.

"You're hurt and bleeding too, I think, only it's on the inside, Rebekah," Rory said as he studied her haunted expression. He knew what having to kill a man did to any decent, God-fearing man, much less to a woman raised in a religious home such as Rebekah had been. Even worse, she had killed her sister's husband, a man she had believed to be her friend.

"Oh, Rory, how could he have done all this?" Her voice

broke and she leaned into his body as he encircled her shoulders with his arm. "For all these years, I thought he was my closest friend . . . and then, there he was in Amos's office, pointing that gun at me, explaining how he'd set spies on us, hired those men to kill you in Denver. He conspired to separate us from the beginning. And he was so calm, almost apologetic when he spoke, as if he regretted the inconvenience to me!''

He could hear the pain and bewilderment in her voice and knew it was best that she talk about all that had happened. "Henry wanted money more than anything—money and power. I suppose he had always been jealous of Amos, who was an easy man to dislike. Some men are just . . .'' He groped for the right words. "Ruthless yet passionless at the same time.''

"He told me he'd raise Michael with his own boys. But I knew that when Michael came of age, he'd be in the way just as we were.'' She shuddered and fought back the sting of tears.

"Cry, Rebekah. Let it out, darlin','' he said softly. "We've lost eight years together, and you've lost someone you thought was a friend.'' She sobbed, great racking shudders tearing through her. Rory held her close to him as the wagon bounced its way west, back to the Flying W Ranch where Michael waited.

They had the rest of their lives to make up for the mistakes and tragedies of the past.

Chapter Twenty-one

Rebekah did not want to stay in Amos's big, garish ranch house that night, but there was really no choice. Darkness was approaching, and Patrick's injury was too dangerous for him to travel farther. Rory helped his groggy brother into one of the guest rooms upstairs.

Rebekah quickly put a frightened and exhausted Michael to bed and sat with her son until he drifted off to sleep, secure in the knowledge that she was indeed safely by his side again. Once he was resting comfortably, she left Patsy to watch him, then went downstairs where Rory was explaining to Ephraim all that had happened.

"I'll go over to Leah's place and tell her Henry's dead. It's my duty, and it'll come better from me," the old man said quietly to Rory. Then he looked up and saw Rebekah standing in the doorway with a stricken look on her face.

"I killed him. Oh, Papa, Leah will never forgive me," she said in a raw, anguished voice, her hands clenched into fists at her sides.

"She won't know, Rebekah. There's no reason to further burden her with that knowledge. I'll tell her that Patrick shot him to save your life." *How good you've become at dissembling, old man,* he chided himself as he took Rebekah in his arms and patted her back.

She raised tear-filled eyes to meet his. "Leah and I were never close . . . I always regretted that, but now she'll need help."

"I'll see that she and her boys are provided for, Reverend Sinclair," Rory said quietly.

Ephraim nodded. "That's generous of you, Mr. Madigan."

"It's my duty to offer what I can easily afford. After all, we're family now." He met Sinclair's eyes and read resignation and acceptance in them. This was not the time to push for a showdown with Rebekah's family. He knew how hard it was for Rebekah and her father to accept Snead's crimes and how guilty Rebekah felt for killing him.

"I'll stay the night with Leah. I expect she'll be needing me. Will you be all right, Rebekah?" Ephraim studied her pale but composed face. She had always been the stronger of his girls.

"I'll be fine, Papa. Just take care of Leah and the boys."

Rory put his arm around her waist proprietarily. "We can talk when everyone's up to it." He and his wife watched as the reverend left in his small black buggy, heading for Leah's house.

Once Ephraim was gone, Rory turned to Rebekah. "I have to deliver Kelso to the sheriff in Wellsville along with Snead's satchel full of money and securities. It'll be safer locked up in town until the marshal from Carson can come

411

for it. I'll bring Doc Marston back here to look at my brother.'' He smiled at Rebekah's muddy, disheveled appearance. ''I think you should relax in a big tub of hot water and soak off that medicinal mud while I'm gone.''

She sniffed him. ''Look who's talking. Are you certain you can ride that far with that wound reopened?''

''I'm fine. As I said, it's just a scratch. Patrick's the one to worry about.''

''At least let me rewrap it with clean linens,'' she protested.

''No time. It's getting dark already. Clean yourself up, then look in on my brother. I'll be back as soon as I can.''

''At least take one of the hands with you. Even tied on a horse, I don't trust Kelso.'' She shuddered, just thinking of the big brute Rory had beaten into submission with his bare hands.

''All the fight's out of him for a while,'' Rory replied grimly.

''I never believed I'd be grateful that you were a boxer, but I was this afternoon.'' Without being aware of it, she raised her hand and brushed one of his mud-smeared cheeks tenderly.

Rory grinned in that old cocky way she remembered from eight years ago. ''He never laid a mitt on me.'' He took her hand and moved it to his lips, placing a warm, soft kiss in her palm. ''Take care of yourself. I'll be back as soon as I can.'' He pulled her against him for a long, thorough kiss, then headed for the door.

As she watched him ride away, Rebekah realized that there was much left unsaid and unsettled between them. He had legally claimed his son. Now with Amos's financial empire crumbling, she and her whole family were beholden to her husband. He said it was his duty to care for Leah and her boys. But Rebekah did not want to be just another duty to Rory Madigan. Her pride simply could not bear it. She had spent eight years as one man's ornament. Never again. She wanted to be Rory's wife.

"No, you want more. Admit it. You want to be his love, not just his wife. You want the three of us to be a real family," she whispered, hugging herself. Dare she hope that he wanted the same things? No matter what her heart's desire, she would not risk Michael becoming an innocent pawn in a struggle between his parents. She had protected him from Amos; she would protect him from Rory if need be.

Rebekah had not missed the silent exchange earlier between her husband and her father. Rory still felt Ephraim was involved in their separation eight years ago. What if it was true? After all the shock and losses he had suffered, Rebekah could not turn away from her father, even if he was guilty. Would Rory ask that of her?

Someday you'll have to choose, Rebekah.

She was too weary to think straight. Rebekah went to the kitchen and asked the cook to heat water for her bath. Tomorrow would be time enough to face the future.

When Rory returned with Doc Marston, it was nearly midnight. The physician examined Patrick, who he said had a mild concussion which should not prevent him from returning to Carson City in a few days, even returning by train all the way home to his family in San Francisco within the week.

Once assured his brother was safe, Rory slipped into Michael's room to check on his son.

When he emerged, Rebekah was waiting in the hallway.

"I've had a bath drawn for you. When you're through, I'll rewrap your shoulder."

"Doc already looked at it." He shrugged, then smiled at

her. "But I'll not turn down your medical attention. Bring your supplies to our bedroom, wherever that is."

She wet her lips nervously. "Rory, I think it wise if we don't sleep together until we've had a chance to explain to Michael—"

"Michael's fast asleep. He won't know a thing. But I won't deceive him, Rebekah. I'm your husband and his father. He deserves the truth."

"He's a little boy! How can you expect him to take all this in—the man he thought was his father is dead, me remarried, you appearing suddenly as his real father?" Her voice had taken on a hysterical edge. "We have to settle things between us first before we involve Michael."

"There's nothing to settle," he said firmly, taking her by her shoulders. "You're my wife, and we both could use a good night's sleep."

She sighed in defeat. "All right, but . . . please, let it be anywhere but the master suite. I can't bear—"

"Obviously," he said, drawing her into his arms. "I don't relish Amos's ghost hovering over us as we sleep." He tipped her chin up and brushed her lips with his, softly.

She waited in a guest bedroom across the hall from where Patrick slept. It was small but had a good-sized bed with clean linens. Doc Marston left her a supply of fresh bandages and ointment for tending to Rory's injury. If the old Wellsville physician had any thoughts regarding her hasty marriage to Amos Wells's foe, he kept them to himself. Rebekah was certain few others would be so disinclined to gossip.

Rory found her sitting nervously on the edge of the bed, fiddling with the medical supplies when he returned from his bath. She was wearing the same pale green robe she had taken to Virginia City on their wedding night. He smiled, remembering that she had never been given the opportunity to wear it then.

Rebekah felt his eyes on her before she saw him standing in the doorway. He had just come from his bath and was clad only in a pair of clean denims, barefooted and bare chested. His hair was still damp, and that one errant lock fell across his forehead as he leaned against the oak sash, his gaze dark and hungry. Heat suffused her body, staining her cheeks and pooling low in her belly. She could not meet his eyes, but was unable to keep her own from sweeping down his tall, half-naked form.

The angry red slash across his shoulder stood out from the other old wounds, long scarred over. The deep, puckered white one around his side just above the waistband of his pants must have been from the assassins Henry had sent to kill him in Denver. She shivered, thinking of how close he had come to dying in order to fulfill a cold-blooded killer's designs.

His lips curved into a quietly amused expression. "Like what you see?" He stepped into the room.

Rebekah shot up off the bed, the trance broken. "Your shoulder should be tended," she said too quickly, her breath coming in unsteady little gasps. She ignored his innuendo and bent over the small bedside table where the bandages lay. "Sit down so I can look at it."

"Seems you were doing a pretty fair job of looking from where I stood," he replied as he obeyed her command. Her fingertips felt soft and cool as they spread the healing ointment across the throbbing flesh wound.

"It must be painful."

"Doc hardly had to stitch it once he got the bleeding stopped. I've had worse."

"Like this one?" Her hands grazed the big scar on his side. "Henry's men did that."

He could hear the pain in her voice. "No more of the past, Rebekah. We've lost these years, but we have a chance to start over. You and I and Michael."

She wrapped his shoulder carefully and tied off the strips, trying not to tremble when she touched him. "Rory . . . about Michael . . ."

"Shh. Not tonight. You've been through so much." The pads of his thumbs caressed the dark circles beneath her eyes. As she lowered her lashes, he kissed her eyelids tenderly, then began to unfasten the belt of her robe and slide it from her shoulders. "Just lie back and go to sleep."

He tucked her in and put out the light, then peeled off his denims and climbed into the bed beside her. Gathering her into his arms, he curved his big warm body around hers and fell fast asleep. Lulled by the comfort of his presence, she too slipped into a deep, exhausted slumber.

Rebekah awakened as she felt the tickle of whiskers brushing against her neck and shoulder. Then Rory's warm mouth began to trail soft kisses down the curve of her spine. When his hand reached over to unfasten the front of her nightgown and cup her breast, the last drugging vestiges of sleep vanished. Frissons of pleasure shot through her, making her feel languorous and willing to let him work his magic on her body. But with wakefulness came the realization also of where they were and all that had happened, and not happened, since their marriage.

She squirmed away from his grasp and scrambled free of the sheets, grabbing her robe from where he had thrown it on the floor beside the bed. Pulling it on, she felt better able to think clearly. "We have to talk, Rory." But then she made

416

the mistake of looking down at him as he reclined casually on the bed with the sheet barely covering his naked body. How bronzed and sinuous his flesh was against the whiteness of the bed linens. How blue and piercing his eyes as he stared at her, waiting for her to continue, arrogantly amused with her discomfiture.

"Michael could come searching for me any moment. We have to talk about him," she began nervously, turning away from the disconcerting sight he presented.

Sighing, he slid from the bed and padded over to where his denims lay. He began to pull them on as he said, "What is there to say, Rebekah? You know we have to tell him the truth—Amos wasn't his father. I am. Do you really think the idea will make him unhappy?"

"I'm not certain," she replied, wringing her hands as she paced. "He missed a father's love with Amos. But not liking the man he believed was his father is one thing. Finding out he's dead is another. And that I've married you so soon— it's all too complicated. He's only seven years old."

"And a very bright, quick seven years, from what I've seen. He'll be all right, Rebekah. He'll trust me. But will you?" He studied her agitated figure, willing her to look at him.

She turned and met his eyes. "What is that supposed to mean?" she asked defensively.

"You know," he replied softly. "You're the one who's confused and afraid. Don't ascribe your own motives to your son. You still think it's possible that I could've deserted you when you were alone and pregnant, don't you?"

"No . . . I don't know what to think. . . ."

"You mean you don't like the other alternative. If you admit I'm telling the truth, that when I was unable to return for you I wrote to you and explained, asked you to wait, then

417

that means your parents—probably your beloved father—destroyed my letters.'' He waited for her to confess her fears.

She whirled angrily, the pain of so many betrayals over the years clawing at her. ''It always comes down to your stubborn Irish pride, doesn't it? You can never forgive my father for thinking you unworthy. You want me to choose—him or you. It isn't fair, Rory. My father and Henry were the only ones I could rely on before Amos was killed. They were my bulwark, my protection—they were there for Michael. Now Henry has betrayed me. And you want me to believe my father has betrayed me, too. I can't do it!''

''I want you to face the truth!'' His bitterness broke through the patience he was struggling to maintain. ''I lost seven years out of my son's life. I can't get those years back, but Michael will damn well know now that I am his father and I'm here to stay!''

''Even if he has to give up his grandpa to have you? You don't love your son half as much as you hate Ephraim Sinclair!''

''That's a bloody lie!''

Outside the bedroom door, Michael listened to his mama and Mr. Madigan argue. The sound of their rising voices had led him to the end of the hall in his search for her. Their exchange amazed and confused the boy. Surely Mr. Madigan, who had been so laughing and kind, would not hurt his mother. He knelt beside the keyhole and peered in.

They stood on opposite sides of a rumpled bed, she in her robe, he half naked. Could they have slept together in that big bed? Only married people did that, his friend Paul had said. Michael had always wondered why his father and Mama never slept together. But now, if Mama had slept with Mr. Madigan, he knew that was wrong. And they were arguing over *him*. Mr. Madigan said he was *his* son! And the man he believed was his father was dead!

418

Michael could not bear the angry words being hurled on
the other side of the door. He had to get away. Mr. Madigan
was angry with Mama and with Grandpa, too. And Mama
was crying. Why had Mama married Amos Wells if Rory
Madigan was his real father? Was it all his fault? He ran
down the carpeted hall, away from the shouting. They were
yelling at each other just as Mama and Father had—but no,
Amos Wells was not really his father. Somehow Michael
knew that part was true. But did it matter if his real father
was angry with him and Mama, too? All he could do, it
seemed, was cause the grown-ups to argue.

He ran downstairs and into the kitchen, where the cook
was busy beating biscuits for breakfast. The fat old man
looked down at the boy and saw his tear-streaked face.

"Yew 'pear to be a mite upset. Mebbe some fresh sweet
milk 'n warm biscuits with honey'd help out," Joe said
kindly. His rheumy eyes squinted merrily and he smiled, revealing several missing teeth. Over the years since old Amos
had married, Joe the cook had only laid eyes on the young
master half a dozen times since Michael was old enough to
be sent away to boarding school. Still, he guessed the boy
must be upset to know his pa was dead, even if Wells had
been a mean and neglectful man.

Michael didn't really feel hungry, but the sympathetic
smile of the old man made him feel better. "I—I'd be much
obliged for some biscuits. I could take them with me down
to the corral. I'm going to see my pony," he added, wiping
his runny nose on his sleeve. Miss Ahern would scold, but
he did not care.

"Reckon I kin fetch a few carrots fer yew ta feed ta yore
pony. Mr. Madigan give him ta yew, didn't he?" Joe asked,
seeing if the boy wanted to talk.

Michael's heart constricted as he remembered the angry

stranger upstairs arguing with his mama. "Yeah, he did."

"Yew miss yer pa?" Joe asked as he placed a small sack full of carrots on the table.

"No! I don't need a father," the boy replied, grabbing the sack and heading for the back door. "I'm going to see Snowball." With that he was gone, leaving the old man scratching his shiny bald pate in puzzlement. Maybe it was best to leave the boy to grieve with his pet for a while before awakening his mother.

Michael headed to the barn where Snowball was stabled. The saddle was too heavy for him, but he had learned how to bridle the pony. He'd seen other boys ride bareback and thought it looked like fun. But fun was the furthest thing from Michael's mind as he ran into Snowball's stall.

"Here boy, have a carrot," he said. When Snowball was finished with the treat, Michael struggled with the bridle.

Upstairs in the ranch house, Rebekah and Rory faced each other, their angry epithets all spent now. He rounded the bed and reached out for her. She tried to pull away, but he held her firmly by her shoulders.

"This is no good, Rebekah. I don't want your father standing between us. Not after all we've survived just to be together. I love you. I want us to be a real family—you, me, and Michael. I'd like to have brothers and sisters for him, wouldn't you?" He waited with his heart on his sleeve.

She swallowed the lump in her throat, wanting desperately to throw herself into his arms. How long she had waited for this declaration. She read the earnest love in his eyes and knew he meant every word. "I love you, too, Rory. More than anything. I will choose you over my family if I must . . . but if my father did do what you believe . . . couldn't you forgive him? It would mean so very much to me."

He looked into the fathomless depths of her eyes and read the pain and the longing reflected in his own. "You've suffered more than I, Rebekah. You were the one who was forced into that nightmare of a marriage with Amos Wells. If you can forgive, how can I not?"

She could see the tears glistening in his eyes, and her heart turned over. "Oh, Rory, my love, tell me nothing will ever separate us again." She melted against him.

He enfolded her in his arms, feeling the weight of the world drop from his shoulders. "Nothing will ever separate us from each other or Michael. We'll go slow explaining to him about Amos, about us. He's young and resilient. He'll accept, Rebekah." In his heart, Rory prayed that the boy's self-righteous old grandfather would be half so willing. *I'll meet him halfway.* Hell, he'd do whatever it took and he knew it.

"Let's go see if Michael is awake," she said at last and there was a joy, a new sense of freedom in her heart that she had not felt in years.

Just then they heard the sound of a carriage pulling up in front. "That must be your father." At the flash of concern in her eyes, he smiled and said, "Don't fret. I'll talk to him and make my peace, Rebekah. You see to Michael." He kissed her softly, then headed downstairs, shrugging on an old shirt he had borrowed to replace his own mud- and blood-stained clothes.

Ephraim was waiting in the kitchen, where he had just poured himself a cup of Joe's inky coffee. The old cook was out back gathering fresh eggs from his chickens for breakfast. The two men greeted each other warily as Rory helped himself to coffee also.

"How is Leah?" Rory asked.

Ephraim sighed. "She took it better than I expected. I

guess she's suspected something was wrong for a long time now. She wants to take the boys and go back east to spend some time with my brother Manassah and his family. They may decide to live there permanently. Leah has always put a lot of stock in what folks think. The scandal of Henry's killing Amos and all the rest . . . she wouldn't bear up well under that, not well at all.''

Rory nodded at the old man, who looked so broken and defeated. *He's losing a daughter and two grandsons, and he's afraid I'll cost him Rebekah and Michael too.* "Ephraim, we need to make a new beginning." The reverend's eyes met his with surprise, and perhaps hope.

"I want that very much, but first there is something I have to—"

"Rory—Papa! Michael's gone!" Rebekah came running into the kitchen, her face pale and distraught. "He must've awakened early and dressed by himself. Patsy thought he might have come downstairs."

"Maybe he's out with Joe gathering eggs," Ephraim said.

The three headed out the back door just as the fat old cook was waddling up the porch steps, egg basket clutched in one meaty red fist.

"Have you seen Michael?" Rory asked.

Joe scratched his shiny pate. " 'Bout half hour 'er so ago. He come into the kitchen. I give him some carrots fer his pony. He'd been cryin' 'n didn't say much. Just that he wanted ta talk ta Snowball. Is everthin' all right?"

Rebekah gasped and looked at Rory. "What if he overheard us arguing?"

Rory's face was grim. If the child only heard the first part of their conversation, how might he have interpreted it? "I'll check the corral. Rebekah, you and your father search around the grounds."

Within minutes they had discovered that the boy and his pony were both missing. "But how could he have ridden off bareback?" Rebekah asked incredulously, wringing her hands.

"He's a natural with horses. It's in the Madigan blood," Rory replied as he threw a saddle on Lobsterback. "I have the hands all searching. He can't have gotten far, Rebekah. Don't worry. We'll have him back safe in a little while." He swung up on the big bay and headed out.

Ephraim put his arm around Rebekah's trembling shoulders.

"We were arguing about how to tell him . . . about Amos . . . and that Rory is his real father," she said haltingly.

Reading between the lines, Ephraim knew there was more. "Rory knows what I did, Rebekah. He figured it out as soon as he learned why you were forced to wed Amos," he said gently. "I committed a terrible, unforgivable sin." His voice was raw with anguish as she turned to him.

"Oh, Papa, you of all people, a minister of the Lord, know there's no such thing as an unforgivable sin." She placed her arms around his waist and hugged him.

"The Lord forgives, but can you? I caused so much pain when I destroyed those letters. You all paid the price for old hurts and hates that I've let fester inside since my youth."

"Don't, Papa. It's over and done with now. You made a mistake, but you did it out of love for me. You were . . . misguided, perhaps, but you always wanted me to be happy. You tried to protect me, I know that. Rory and I talked it over. He said he'd forgive you, too."

"Yes, I believe he will. I've misjudged Rory Madigan. He was the man for you all along, wasn't he, Rebekah?"

She smiled through her tears. "Yes. And now that we're back together, we'll be a real family, and you're part of it too. If only we can find a way to explain to Michael," she said as worry rushed over her again. "With the wind up, there are no tracks for the men to follow. Where could he have gone?"

A sudden light flashed in Ephraim's eyes. "Rebekah, I may know! There's a place where I took him a few times. We called it our special place. Let me try—" He hugged her, then rushed out to where his shabby old buggy stood and climbed aboard it.

Rebekah could not bear to stay behind, but if Michael should return home, someone had to be there waiting for him. "Oh, please, Lord, please keep my son safe," she prayed more fervently than she ever had in her life as she watched her father drive off.

Ephraim took the old road across the ranch that headed southwest toward Wellsville. Ever since Michael had stayed with him as a very little boy, the two of them had shared a special hiding place that Ephraim had discovered years earlier. It was in pretty rough foothills, so he had not felt the cave was suitable for girls. Leah would have hated it, but now he realized that Rebekah would have been delighted with it. Leaving the buggy at the edge of the rocks, he began the climb up.

By the time he reached the summit by the small, shallow cave overlooking the valley, Ephraim was sweating in the morning heat. Snowball stood patiently at the entrance. The minister said a prayer of thanks as he called his grandson's name.

He found Michael sitting on the cool floor of the cave by the old, burned-down ashes of their long-ago campfires. "Would you mind some company, son?" he asked as the boy rubbed a grimy little hand across his eyes.

"Hi, Grandpa. I sort of guessed you'd find me."

"Maybe you hoped it'd be me," Ephraim said as he sat down beside the boy and they gazed out on the valley spread below them. The view was spectacular, but he knew the boy was thinking only of his parents.

"I guess I did. I don't know." He scratched circles in the dirt with a stick, refusing to look up into his beloved grandfather's eyes.

"You want to talk about why you ran away?" Ephraim prodded gently.

"They were fighting—over me. He's my father, not Amos Wells, isn't he?" He dared to meet his grandpa's kindly hazel-green eyes, and the old man nodded.

"Yes, son. He's your pa."

"But Mama married Amos Wells. He never liked me. I could tell. I don't think anyone likes me. All I do is cause trouble. They were yelling at one another. It was all my fault." Michael began to hiccup, and Ephraim put his arms around the boy.

"No, no, son. It wasn't your fault at all. Sometimes, even people who love each other have arguments."

"If they love each other, then why didn't they get married? Why'd he leave us?"

Ephraim steeled himself to do the most difficult thing he had ever done in his life. "He didn't leave you, son. He went to Denver to earn enough money so he and your mother could get married. But then . . ." His voice broke and he hugged Michael. "Some very bad things happened, and in part I was responsible."

Ephraim told the boy the whole story about how Amos Wells and Henry Snead had conspired to keep Rebekah from marrying Rory and how he himself had destroyed the letters the boy's father sent to his mother. When Ephraim finished the rest of the story leading up to the near-tragic events of the preceding day, he was trembling. He looked down into the small, trusting face of his grandson.

Michael digested all the incredible facts for a moment. Finally he said, "Then my father was mad at you because you didn't give Mama his letters. He wasn't mad at me?"

"No, Michael, he's never been angry with you. He loves you very much—and your mother, too."

"Is that why they got married?" he asked innocently. Any idea of lack of propriety in Rebekah's sudden remarriage was lost on the boy.

"Yes, son. That's why."

"If they aren't mad at me, do you think they're mad at you?"

"I deserve it, Michael, but no, they've forgiven me for a terrible mistake and I'm grateful. But above everyone else, you're the one I should beg forgiveness of." His thin, gnarled hand caressed the boy's face, searching.

Michael threw his arms around the old man's stooped shoulders. "Oh, Grandpa, I could never be mad at you!"

Ephraim Sinclair closed his eyes tightly, squeezing out the tears as he hugged his grandson and offered a fervent prayer of thanks for the Lord's goodness shown through this small child.

Rory was making one last sweep to the southeast when he saw the carriage with Snowball tied to the back of the battered old rig. He tore across the dusty ground to meet Ephraim and his son. "Where did you find him?"

"Pa?" Michael asked uncertainly as his father leaped from his horse and reached for the boy.

"Yes, Michael, I'm here, I'm here," Rory said as he hugged Michael.

"I told him everything, Rory," Ephraim said quietly. "He'd overheard a small bit of your argument with Rebekah and misunderstood. Now he knows the real reason why you've been separated until now."

Rory nodded with respect as he met his father-in-law's forthright gaze. "Thank you, Ephraim. I think from now on things are going to be fine for all of us. Is there room enough in that old rig for three?"

The old man grinned. "Tie that big red devil to the back with Snowball and climb aboard."

Patrick was up and about by dinnertime that evening, and Doc Marston pronounced him well enough to travel by train the next day. Ephraim bid Rebekah, Rory, and Michael good-bye, promising to visit them at their new home in Eagle Valley. He headed for Leah's place to help her and the boys prepare for their journey east.

Bright and early the next day, Patrick departed for the train station in Reno. He would return to Carson and see the end of the Madigans' quest for justice.

Rory took his wife and son, along with Patsy Mulcahey, and rode away from the Flying W for the last time. They were leaving all the sad and bitter memories of the past behind them. The big ranch with its garish house would be sold as soon as a buyer could be found. They stopped at Leah's for a very strained and brief farewell between the sisters.

That night, two doting parents tucked their son in his new bed in his new room at their very own home—a home, Rory explained carefully, in which Michael would spend the rest of his childhood. No more governesses or boarding schools, ever again. He would attend the Eagle Valley public school just like all the rest of the local children.

"Tomorrow, can I ride Snowball bareback again? I kinda liked that," he said sleepily.

Rory looked at Rebekah's worried expression and chuckled. "Well, I expect it might be better if you used a saddle for a little while yet—unless of course, I'm with you to catch you in case you fall."

"Aw, I won't fall. I didn't yesterday. . . . " Then he looked up at the ceiling, having just finished saying his prayers and added, "Well, only one time. But I'll practice real hard if you'll teach me, Pa."

Rebekah ruffled his hair as Rory chuckled. "I'll teach you."

They tiptoed from his room and down the hall to their own spacious master suite. The ranch house, like his place in Virginia City, was decorated in a bold masculine style with heavy, rough-hewn furniture and polished hardwood floors. Although everything was done in impeccably good taste, from the Argon lamps to the silk wallpaper, Rebekah decided it needed a woman's touch.

"Your home is beautiful, Rory," she said when he closed the bedroom door.

"After I commissioned the architects to build it, I was never very interested in it. At first it was just another symbol of success. Success! What a joke. I was alone and the place was so damn big. . . . "

"You're not alone anymore," she whispered, coming into his arms.

"Maybe I built it for you and could never admit it to myself. It's your home, now, Rebekah. Do what you want with it."

"I want to live in it, to put down roots."

He grinned. "How about planting a garden? I was thinking of a cabbage patch and some pumpkins. . . . "

She pummeled him laughingly, and he scooped her up in his arms and whirled her around. "You're right, Rory. This is a big house, and Michael is just one little boy. How about filling the place up with brothers and sisters for him?''

All laughter died as he framed her face with his hands and gazed into her eyes. "And for us. Nothing would make me happier."

He kissed her softly, and she clung to him as he carried her to the big canopied bed, an exact match to the one in Virginia City in which they had spent their wedding night. This time there was no hesitation, no tension or fear, nothing to hide from one another. They loved and they trusted as they had in the glorious innocence of their youth that very first time they had exchanged vows.

He began by unfastening the small pearl buttons down the front of her dress, kissing her skin as he peeled away the soft fabric. "You're so pale and delicate from city life. I want you all golden, the way you were when we first met."

She chuckled, her own hands busy opening his shirt and massaging that wonderful black pelt of hair on his chest. "You want the mud from the cabbage patch too?"

He nuzzled her ear. "I want whatever you want," he whispered into it. By this time he had the pink batiste dress in a puddle at her feet and was busily engaged in unfastening her lacy camisole and petticoats.

"You know what I want, Irishman," she whispered. Her lips grazed his shoulder as she slid his shirt off, pausing carefully over his injury. Then she pressed her lips to the scars that marked his body, beginning with that most recent one. He had the tapes of her petticoats undone, and his hands cupped her small, rounded derrière as he pulled her pantalets over her hips. Then he took the tip of one delicate breast in his mouth and suckled on it until she arched against him and moaned, pulling his head closer.

Rory lifted her and placed her on top of the bed before stepping away long enough to shed his boots and slide off his breeches. He could feel her eyes on him, devouring his body. "Wanton little witch," he breathed as he lowered himself into her open arms.

They rolled across the bed, kissing and caressing as their bodies melded together, arms and legs entwined. Then he rolled her on top of him so her hair fell around him in a glorious, rich golden curtain. She leaned forward, and their mouths met in a deep, slow, probing kiss. Their tongues danced, tracing outlines across the other's lips, then plunged deeply, entwining, thrusting, tasting.

His hands cupped her breasts, and his thumbs circled and teased her hard pebbly nipples. She writhed frantically, arching into his hands as frissons of pleasure lanced through her body, settling low in her belly. He broke off the kiss and raised his head to suckle one pearly globe suspended like ripe fruit before his hungry eyes. She let him feast for several moments, savoring the heat of his mouth moving from one breast to the other. When she could bear the sweet torture no longer, she rose, pressing her palms against his chest and arching her back so her hair fell behind her, brushing against the hard, pulsing length of his phallus. She shook her head, and the weight of her long mane teased his rigid staff until he gasped aloud in a mixture of curses that were really endearments.

His hands pushed up against her breasts, causing her to throw her head back even further. She looked like some Valkyrie, pagan and glorious. "Where did you learn that, you inventive little tease?" he muttered breathlessly as he slid his hands down from her breasts to her hips. He raised her and arched into the soft, wet heat of her body, impaling her slowly, watching the expression of rapture wash over her face as he completed their joining.

Rory guided the rhythm in slow, lush strokes, holding her

hips cupped in his hands. They stared deeply into each other's eyes, communicating in the sweet intimacy of sex and love. Gradually the tempo increased as the pleasure built to a molten inferno. Sweat sheened their bodies in the warm night air.

Rebekah buried her fingers in the hair on his chest. Her hands glided up to his shoulders, then framed his face. He took her hair, wrapping it around his fists, and pulled her to him. They licked and tasted of each other's skin, letting their lips caress, coming nearer and nearer until they met in a hard, hungry kiss. She was out of control now, spiraling ever upward into the ecstasy that seized her and would not let go. Then she felt his staff swell and pulse deep within her, spewing his hot seed against her womb as he shuddered and cried out her name. The waves of her release gradually subsided and she collapsed onto him, limp and utterly satiated.

Rory wrapped his arms around her and stroked the silken curtain of her hair, breathing in the scent of lemon combined with the musky warmth from their lovemaking. She brushed his face and throat with soft, lethargic little kisses.

"This is the way we were, darlin'. When we first vowed our love to each other in your father's orchard," he murmured.

"Only it's better now, more complete. We're both grown up. We've learned to understand, to forgive. I feel a communion with you beyond anything I ever felt ever before." She raised her head and gazed into his eyes, trying to read their dark blue depths.

He caressed her cheek. "I felt it, too. Ah, Rebekah, we have the best of it all now and the rest of our lives to enjoy it."

A few moments later, as she lay against his chest listening

to the steady thrum of his heartbeat, he murmured, "I have something for you."

She pressed a soft kiss against his chest and whispered, "I think I can already guess what."

He chuckled wickedly. "That, too, but there is something else." When she began to wriggle over him, he forgot what it was, forgot all words as the sweetness of their love obliterated all words, all conscious thought.

Much later, as Rebekah dozed, Rory gently disentangled himself and tucked the sheets about her, then pulled on a robe and crossed the big room, stopping in front of an oil painting on the wall. He pressed the frame and it swung forward, revealing a safe.

As he opened it and withdrew a small object, Rebekah awakened and watched with a puzzled expression on her face. When he turned back to her, she scooted up to the edge of the big rumpled bed and sat lost in the tangle of covers. He knelt down in front of her and offered her the box.

"I bought these eight years ago in Denver," he said simply.

Rebekah opened the velvet lid with trembling hands and gazed at the exquisite rings nestled inside. One was a beautiful square-cut emerald engagement ring and its mate a heavy, braided-gold band. Inside the wedding ring was engraved, "Rebekah and Rory, forever love." Tears filled her eyes as she whispered, "You brought these with you to Wellsville when you came back for me."

He nodded as he took them from the box and slipped them on her finger. "I wanted to throw them away at first, but I never could. Then I vowed they would be a reminder of the revenge I'd one day take against you and Amos. I really kept them for now, only I never knew it until these past few days.

You are, you always have been, you always will be my wife, Rebekah.''

''Oh, Rory, and you my only husband, forever.'' She leaned forward, and their lips met briefly. Then he held her hand as she raised it for the rings to catch the light. Clasping his hand in both of hers she brought it to her lips and said in a low, almost hesitant voice, ''There is one thing I would ask . . .''

''Anything.''

''To be married in church. It can be in your church, I don't care. I only want us and our children to receive the Lord's blessing.''

For a moment, Rory seemed to consider, his expression grave. ''Well, darlin',' '' he began in a wretched imitation of his own brogue, ''sure and that's a fine idea, and one worthy of an Irish politician—if it's your own da who'll be performin' the nuptials.''

With a sob of pure joy, she threw her arms around him. ''Yes, oh yes, my love!''

Epilogue

The First Presbyterian Church was crowded to capacity for the occasion. Beaming with happiness, Reverend Ephraim Sinclair waited to perform the sacrament. Music from the organ rose, and the congregation joined in singing a hymn of thanksgiving as Celia Kincaid, flanked by Patrick Madigan, stepped up to the altar with the precious bundle. Standing beside them, Rory and Rebekah each held one of Michael's hands as he stared in rapt fascination at his Grandpa.

"Is he gonna cry?" the boy whispered, looking from one parent to the other.

Rebekah put her fingers to her lips with a smile, urging him to be quiet, but Rory leaned down and whispered, "I don't think so. He's too happy.''

"Happy just like all of us," Michael replied. His eyes returned to the chancel, where his grandfather asked the ritual questions of Celia and Patrick.

The godparents made their pledges clearly for everyone to hear. Then the minister's voice rose sonorously over the assembly as he leaned over the font and touched the infant's head with water. "I baptize thee, Ephraim Patrick Madigan, in the name of the Father, the Son, and the Holy Ghost."

Michael's baby brother blinked up at his grandfather with surprise, then gurgled in contentment. Although his namesake did not have tears in his eyes, Ephraim did, but no one seemed to notice.

Author's Note

One Sunday afternoon about two years before we began this book, Carol and I brainstormed a plot outline for a tale of broken vows between two young lovers, separated by fate and the villainy of family and foe alike. We knew Rebekah would be a prim and proper preacher's daughter who surprised even herself with her attraction to a shockingly unsuitable man, a foreigner of some sort and of the Roman Catholic faith to add an extra element of conflict between them.

But where to set this story presented a challenge. After some general background reading, I stumbled on the colorful and raucous era of the Comstock Bonanza in 1870s Nevada, a land of "Restless Strangers" as Wilbur S. Shepperson called them. Nevada's foreign population outnumbered the native born, creating a unique backdrop for characters like the Madigan brothers, January Jones, Cue Ging and Patsy

Mulcahey, not to mention the return of that incorrigible and lovable rascal, Blackie Drago, whom our readers enjoyed so much in *Terms of Love* and *Terms of Surrender*.

The Comstock Lode comprised the richest mining boom in America's history. Its rapid rise and equally swift demise fitted the stark contrasts of Nevada itself, a place as beautiful as paradise—when there was water, but water was often scarce, leading one wag to scoff, "If hell had water, it would be paradise, too." The land and its people were as harsh and unyielding as Dorcas Sinclair's bigotry, and at the same time as strong and incorruptible as Ephraim Sinclair's faith. The descriptions of Virginia City and Carson City are as real as I could make them. Wellsville, however, is a fictional town, a composite drawn from descriptions of small agricultural communities along the rich river valleys of the Truckee, the Carson, and the Walker.

The incredible corruption of Nevada politics during the latter half of the nineteenth century is well documented, along with the unscrupulous stock manipulations of the mining and banking crowd, thus providing me with a cast of fascinating villains drawn from real life. These powerful men actually dynamited their own mine shafts, sealing the workers below in order to silence them. In making a killing on the stock market, they occasionally also made a killing, quite literally, in the mine shafts. Ryan Madigan's death is fiction, but many real miners met their deaths precisely that way.

Of the numerous excellent books on Nevada, the best general histories I found were *The Nevada Adventure* by James W. Hulse, *Desert Challenge* by Richard G. Lillard, and *History of Nevada* by Russell R. Elliott. For additional information regarding the evil chicanery of the silver barons and their banking cronies, I used *Nevada, The Great Rotten Borough 1859-1964* by Gilman M. Ostrander.

Nevada, because of early gold and silver strikes during the Civil War era, was one of the first Western territories to achieve statehood, in 1864. For details on the raw and colorful times in the capital and on the Comstock, I relied on Wells Drury's autobiography, *An Editor on the Comstock Lode.* The wonderful mix of characters who fill the pages of *Broken Vows* I owe to Wilbur S. Shepperson's *Restless Strangers*, a rich and fascinating account of Nevada's unique immigrant population.

Carol and I hope you enjoy this story of vows made, betrayed, and redeemed. Rory and Rebekah had a few surprises for me as I wrote their story, but no one amazed me more than old Ephraim Sinclair and his grandson. They have lived in our imagination. We hope they live in yours, too, long after you have read *Broken Vows.*

We love to hear from our readers. Please send a stamped, self-addressed business envelope and we will be delighted to answer your letters.

SHIRL HENKE
P. O. Box 72
Adrian, MI 49221

McCRORY'S LADY — SHIRL HENKE

"Historical romance at its best!"
—Romantic Times

Courageous and cunning, Maggie Worthington has survived alone in the rugged West, earning her keep in frontier cathouses. Once a proper, Boston-bred lady, she is more than a handful for any gunslinger with an eye for trouble. But the sharp-tongued madam finally meets her match in a rancher with the burr of a Scotsman and the body of a god.

To save his daughter's tattered reputation, Colin McCrory needs to take a wife. And even though women are scarce in the Arizona Territory, he is certain he could wed one whose past isn't as sordid as Maggie's. Yet the feisty and defiant beauty's scorching kisses fire his blood as never before, and one night in her silken embrace convinces him that he has to tame her, to possess her, to make her McCrory's lady.

_3773-4 $5.99 US/$6.99 CAN

SHIRL HENKE

WHITE APACHE'S WOMAN

By the bestselling author of *Terms of Surrender*

Running from his past, Red Eagle has no desire to become entangled with the haughty beauty who hires him to guide her across the treacherous Camino Real to Santa Fe. Although Elise Louvois's cool violet eyes betray nothing, her warm, willing body comes alive beneath his masterful touch. She will risk imprisonment and death, but not her vulnerable heart. Mystified, Red Eagle is certain of but one thing—the spirits have destined Elise to be his woman.

_3498-0 $4.99 US/$5.99 CAN

A FIRE IN THE BLOOD — SHIRL HENKE

Bestselling Author of *White Apache's Woman*

When half-breed Jess Robbins rides into Cheyenne to chase down a gang of cattle thieves, he is sure of three things. The townsfolk will openly scorn him, the women will secretly want him, and the rustlers will definitely fear him. What he doesn't count on is a flame-haired spitfire named Lissa Jacobsen, who has her own manhunt in mind.

Dark, dangerous, and deadly with his Colt revolver, Jess is absolutely forbidden to the spoiled, pampered daughter of Cheyenne's richest rancher. But from the moment Lissa stumbles upon him in his bath, she decides she has to have the virile gunman. Pitting her innocence against his vast experience, Lissa knows she is playing with fire...but she never guesses that the raging inferno of desire will consume them both.

_3601-0 $4.99 US/$5.99 CAN

An Angel's Touch

Heaven's Gift

JANELLE DENISON

The last thing J.T. Rafferty expects when he awakes from a concussion is to find a beautiful stranger tending to his wounds. She saved his life, but the lovely Caitlan Daniels has some serious explaining to do—like how she ended up on his isolated ranch lands, miles from civilization. Despite his wariness, J.T. finds himself increasingly drawn to Caitlan, whose gentle touch promises sweet satisfaction. She is passionate and independent and utterly enchanting—but Caitlan also has a secret. And when J.T. finally discovers the shocking truth, he'll have to defy heaven and earth to keep her close to his heart.

_52059-1 $5.99 US/$7.99 CAN

LAKOTA RENEGADE

MADELINE BAKER

"Madeline Baker's Indian romances should not be missed!"
                                        —*Romantic Times*

Handy with six-guns and fists, Creed Maddigan likes his women hot and ready. But the rugged half-breed isn't used to innocent girls like Jassy McCloud who curtsy and make ginger snaps. Then Creed is falsely jailed for a crime he didn't commit, and he can think of nothing besides escaping to savor Jassy's sweet love.

Alone on the Colorado frontier, Jassy can either work as a fancy lady or hope to find a husband. But what is she to do when the only man she hopes to marry is a wanted renegade? For Jassy, the decision is simple: She'll take Creed for better or worse, even if she has to spend the rest of her days dodging bounty hunters and bullets.

_3832-3 $5.99 US/$7.99 CAN

Touched By Moonlight

CAROLE HOWEY

Bestselling Author Of *Sweet Chance*

Terence Gavilan can turn a sleepy little turn-of-the-century village into a booming seaside resort overnight. But the real passion of his life is searching for Emma Hunt, the mysterious and elusive creator of the tantalizing romances he admires. When he finds her, he plans to prove that real life can be so much more exciting than fiction.

To the proper folk of Braedon's Beach, Philipa Braedon is the prim daughter of their community's founding father. Yet secretly, she enjoys swimming naked in the ocean and writing steamy novels. Philipa has no intention of revealing her double life to anyone, especially not to a man as arrogant and overbearing as Terence Gavilan. But she doesn't count on being touched by moonlight and ending up happier than any of her heroines.

_3824-2 $5.50 US/$7.50 CAN